THE BURNING LAND

Books by Bernard Cornwell

AGINCOURT

The Saxon Tales

THE LAST KINGDOM
THE PALE HORSEMAN
THE LORDS OF THE NORTH
SWORD SONG

The Sharpe Novels (in chronological order)

SHARPE'S TIGER
Richard Sharpe and the Siege of Seringapatam, 1799

SHARPE'S TRIUMPH
Richard Sharpe and the Battle of Assaye, September 1803

SHARPE'S FORTRESS
Richard Sharpe and the Siege of Gawilghur, December 1803

SHARPE'S TRAFALGAR
Richard Sharpe and the Battle of Trafalgar, 21 October 1805

SHARPE'S PREY
Richard Sharpe and the Expedition to Copenhagen, 1807

SHARPE'S RIFLES
Richard Sharpe and the French Invasion of Galicia, January 1809

SHARPE'S HAVOC
Richard Sharpe and the Campaign in Northern Portugal, Spring 1809

SHARPE'S EAGLE
Richard Sharpe and the Talavera Campaign, July 1809

SHARPE'S GOLD
Richard Sharpe and the Destruction of Almeida, August 1810

SHARPE'S ESCAPE
Richard Sharpe and the Bussaco Campaign, 1810

SHARPE'S FURY
Richard Sharpe and the Battle of Barrosa, March 1811

SHARPE'S BATTLE
Richard Sharpe and the Battle of Fuentes de Onoro, May 1811

SHARPE'S COMPANY
Richard Sharpe and the Siege of Badajoz, January to April 1812

SHARPE'S SWORD
Richard Sharpe and the Salamanca Campaign, June and July 1812

SHARPE'S ENEMY
Richard Sharpe and the Defense of Portugal, Christmas 1812

SHARPE'S HONOUR
Richard Sharpe and the Vitoria Campaign, February to June 1813

SHARPE'S REGIMENT
Richard Sharpe and the Invasion of France, June to November 1813

SHARPE'S SIEGE
Richard Sharpe and the Winter Campaign, 1814

SHARPE'S REVENGE
Richard Sharpe and the Peace of 1814

SHARPE'S WATERLOO
Richard Sharpe and the Waterloo Campaign, 15 June to 18 June 1815

SHARPE'S DEVIL
Richard Sharpe and the Emperor, 1820–1821

The Grail Quest Series

THE ARCHER'S TALE
VAGABOND
HERETIC

The Nathaniel Starbuck Chronicles

REBEL
COPPERHEAD
BATTLE FLAG
THE BLOODY GROUND

The Warlord Chronicles

THE WINTER KING
ENEMY OF GOD
EXCALIBUR

The Sailing Thrillers

STORMCHILD
SCOUNDREL
WILDTRACK
CRACKDOWN

THE BURNING LAND

A Novel

BERNARD CORNWELL

HARPER

An Imprint of HarperCollins*Publishers*
www.harpercollins.com

The Burning Land
is for
Alan and Jan Rust

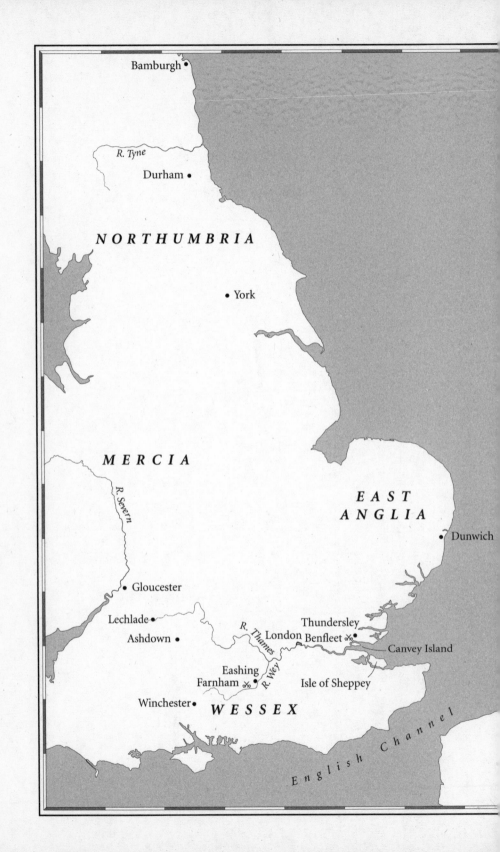

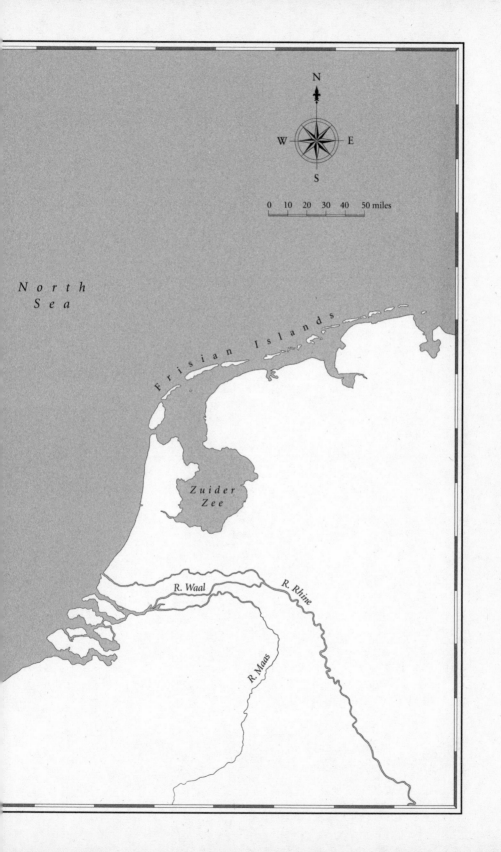

North
Sea

Frisian Islands

Zuider
Zee

R. Waal

R. Rhine

R. Maas

N

W   E

S

0   10   20   30   40   50 miles

CONTENTS

PLACE-NAMES

The spelling of place names in Anglo Saxon England was an uncertain business, with no consistency and no agreement even about the name itself. Thus London was variously rendered as Lundonia, Lundenberg, Lundenne, Lundene, Lundenwic, Lundenceaster and Lundres. Doubtless some readers will prefer other versions of the names listed below, but I have usually employed whichever spelling is cited in either the *Oxford Dictionary of English Place-Names* or the newer *Cambridge Dictionary of English Place-Names* for the years nearest or contained within Alfred's reign, 871–899 AD, but even that solution is not foolproof. Hayling Island, in 956, was written as both Heilincigae and Hæglingaiggæ. Nor have I been consistent myself; I have preferred the modern form Northumbria to Nor hymbralond to avoid the suggestion that the boundaries of the ancient kingdom coincide with those of the modern county. So this list, like the spellings themselves, is capricious.

Æsc's Hill	Ashdown, Berkshire
Æscengum	Eashing, Surrey
Æthelingæg	Athelney, Somerset
Beamfleot	Benfleet, Essex
Bebbanburg	Bamburgh Castle, Northumberland
Caninga	Canvey Island, Essex
Cent	Kent
Defnascir	Devonshire
Dumnoc	Dunwich, Suffolk (now mostly vanished beneath the sea)
Dunholm	Durham, County Durham
East Sexe	Essex
Eoferwic	York

Ethandun	Edington, Wiltshire
Exanceaster	Exeter, Devon
Farnea Islands	Farne Islands, Northumberland
Fearnhamme	Farnham, Surrey
Fughelness	Foulness Island, Essex
Grantaceaster	Cambridge, Cambridgeshire
Gleawecestre	Gloucester, Gloucestershire
Godelmingum	Godalming, Surrey
Hæthlegh	Hadleigh, Essex
Haithabu	Hedeby, southern Denmark
Hocheleia	Hockley, Essex
Hothlege	Hadleigh Ray, Essex
Humbre	River Humber
Hwealf	River Crouch, Essex
Lecelad	Lechlade, Gloucestershire
Liccelfeld	Lichfield, Staffordshire
Lindisfarena	Lindisfarne (Holy Island), Northumberland
Lundene	London
Sæfern	River Severn
Scaepege	Isle of Sheppey, Kent
Silcestre	Silchester, Hampshire
Sumorsæte	Somerset
Suthriganaweorc	Southwark, Greater London
Temes	River Thames
Thunresleam	Thundersley, Essex
Tinan	River Tyne
Torneie	Thorney Island, an island that has disappeared—it lay close to the West Drayton tube station near Heathrow Airport
Tuede	River Tweed
Uisc	River Exe, Devonshire
Wiltunscir	Wiltshire
Wintanceaster	Winchester, Hampshire
Yppe	Epping, Essex
Zegge	Fictional Frisian island

The Royal Family of Wessex

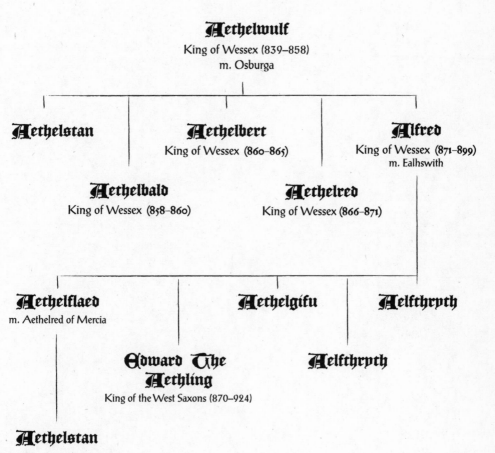

Aethelwulf
King of Wessex (839–858)
m. Osburga

Aethelstan

Aethelbert
King of Wessex (860–865)

Alfred
King of Wessex (871–899)
m. Ealhswith

Aethelbald
King of Wessex (858–860)

Aethelred
King of Wessex (866–871)

Aethelflaed
m. Aethelred of Mercia

Aethelgifu

Aelfthryth

Edward The Aethling
King of the West Saxons (870–924)

Aelfthryth

Aethelstan
King of the English (924–939)

PART ONE

THE WARLORD

ONE

Not long ago I was in some monastery. I forget where except that it was in the lands that were once Mercia. I was traveling home with a dozen men, it was a wet winter's day, and all we needed was shelter, food, and warmth, but the monks behaved as though a band of Norsemen had arrived at their gate. Uhtred of Bebbanburg was within their walls and such is my reputation that they expected me to start slaughtering them. "I just want bread," I finally made them understand, "cheese if you have it, and some ale." I threw money on the hall floor. "Bread, cheese, ale, and a warm bed. Nothing more!"

Next morning it was raining like the world was ending and so I waited until the wind and weather had done their worst. I roamed the monastery and eventually found myself in a dank corridor where three miserable-looking monks were copying manuscripts. An older monk, white-haired, sour-faced and resentful, supervised them. He wore a fur stole over his habit, and had a leather quirt with which he doubtless encouraged the industry of the three copyists. "They should not be disturbed, lord," he dared to chide me. He sat on a stool beside a brazier, the warmth of which did not reach the three scribblers.

"The latrines haven't been licked clean," I told him, "and you look idle."

So the older monk went quiet and I looked over the shoulders of the ink-stained copyists. One, a slack-faced youth with fat lips and a fatter goiter on his neck, was transcribing a life of Saint Ciaran, which told how a wolf, a badger, and a fox had helped build a church in Ireland, and if the young monk believed that nonsense then he was as big a fool as he looked. The second was doing something useful by copying a land grant, though in all probability it was a forgery. Monasteries are adept at inventing old land grants, proving that some ancient half-forgotten king has granted the church a rich estate, thus forcing the rightful owner to either yield the ground or pay a vast sum in compensation. They tried it on me once. A priest brought the documents and I pissed on them, and then I posted twenty sword-warriors on the disputed land and sent word to the bishop that he could come and take it whenever he wished. He never did. Folk tell their children that success lies in working hard and being thrifty, but that is as much nonsense as supposing that a badger, a fox, and a wolf could build a church. The way to wealth is to become a Christian bishop or a monastery's abbot and thus be imbued with heaven's permission to lie, cheat, and steal your way to luxury.

The third young man was copying a chronicle. I moved his quill aside so I could see what he had just written. "You can read, lord?" the old monk asked. He made it sound like an innocent inquiry, but the sarcasm was unmistakable.

" 'In this year,' " I read aloud, " 'the pagans again came to Wessex, in great force, a horde as had never been seen before, and they ravaged all the lands, causing mighty distress to God's people, who, by the grace of Our Lord Jesus Christ, were rescued by the Lord Æthelred of Mercia who came with his army to Fearnhamme, in which place he did utterly destroy the heathen.' " I prodded the text with a finger. "What year did this happen?" I asked the copyist.

"In the year of our Lord 892, lord," he said nervously.

"So what is this?" I asked, flicking the pages of the parchment from which he copied.

"They are annals," the elderly monk answered for the younger man, "the Annals of Mercia. That is the only copy, lord, and we are making another."

I looked back at the freshly written page. "Æthelred rescued Wessex?" I asked indignantly.

"It was so," the old monk said, "with God's help"

"God?" I snarled. "It was with my help! I fought that battle, not Æthelred!" None of the monks spoke. They just stared at me. One of my men came to the cloister end of the passageway and leaned there, a grin on his half-toothless face. "I was at Fearnhamme!" I added, then snatched up the only copy of the Annals of Mercia and turned its stiff pages. Æthelred, Æthelred, Æthelred, and not a mention of Uhtred, hardly a mention of Alfred, no Æthelflæd, just Æthelred. I turned to the page which told of the events after Fearnhamme. " 'And in this year,' " I read aloud, " 'by God's good grace, the lord Æthelred and the Ætheling Edward led the men of Mercia to Beamfleot where Æthelred took great plunder and made mighty slaughter of the pagans.' " I looked at the older monk. "Æthelred and Edward led that army?"

"So it is said, lord." He spoke nervously, his earlier defiance completely gone.

"I led them, you bastard," I said. I snatched up the copied pages and took both them and the original annals to the brazier.

"No!" the older man protested.

"They're lies," I said.

He held up a placatory hand. "For forty years, lord," he said humbly, "those records have been compiled and preserved. They are the tale of our people! That is the only copy!"

"They're lies," I said again. "I was there. I was on the hill at Fearnhamme and in the ditch at Beamfleot. Were you there?"

"I was just a child, lord," he said.

He gave an appalled shriek when I tossed the manuscripts onto the brazier. He tried to rescue the parchments, but I knocked his hand away. "I was there," I said again, staring at the blackening sheets that curled and crackled before the fire flared bright at their edges. "I was there."

"Forty years' work!" the old monk said in disbelief.

"If you want to know what happened," I said, "then come to me in Bebbanburg and I'll tell you the truth."

They never came. Of course they did not come.

But I was at Fearnhamme, and that was just the beginning of the tale.

5

TWO

Morning, and I was young, and the sea was a shimmer of silver and pink beneath wisps of mist that obscured the coasts. To my south was Cent, to my north lay East Anglia, and behind me was Lundene, while ahead the sun was rising to gild the few small clouds that stretched across the dawn's bright sky.

We were in the estuary of the Temes. My ship, the *Seolferwulf*, was newly built and she leaked, as new ships will. Frisian craftsmen had made her from oak timbers that were unusually pale, and thus her name, the *Silverwolf*. Behind me were the *Kenelm*, named by King Alfred for some murdered saint, and the *Dragon-Voyager*, a ship we had taken from the Danes. *Dragon-Voyager* was a beauty, built as only the Danes could build. A sleek killer of a ship, docile to handle yet lethal in battle.

Seolferwulf was also a beauty; long-keeled, wide-beamed, and high-prowed. I had paid for her myself, giving gold to Frisian shipwrights, and watching as her ribs grew and as her planking made a skin and as her proud bow reared above the slipway. On that prow was a wolf's head, carved from oak and painted white with a red lolling tongue and red eyes and yellow fangs. Bishop Erkenwald, who ruled Lundene, had chided me, saying I should have named the ship for some Christian milksop saint, and he had presented me with a crucifix that he wanted me to nail to *Seolferwulf*'s mast, but instead I burned the wooden god and his wooden cross and mixed their ashes with crushed apples, that I fed to my two sows. I worship Thor.

6

Now, on that distant morning when I was still young, we rowed eastward on that pink and silver sea. My wolf's-head prow was decorated with a thick-leaved bough of oak to show we intended no harm to our enemies, though my men were still dressed in mail and had shields and weapons close to their oars. Finan, my second in command, crouched near me on the steering platform and listened with amusement to Father Willibald, who was talking too much. "Other Danes have received Christ's mercy, Lord Uhtred," he said. He had been spouting this nonsense ever since we had left Lundene, but I endured it because I liked Willibald. He was an eager, hardworking, and cheerful man. "With God's good help," he went on, "we shall spread the light of Christ among these heathen!"

"Why don't the Danes send us missionaries?" I asked.

"God prevents it, lord," Willibald said. His companion, a priest whose name I have long forgotten, nodded earnest agreement.

"Maybe they've got better things to do?" I suggested.

"If the Danes have ears to hear, lord," Willibald assured me, "then they will receive Christ's message with joy and gladness!"

"You're a fool, father," I said fondly. "You know how many of Alfred's missionaries have been slaughtered?"

"We must all be prepared for martyrdom, lord," Willibald said, though anxiously.

"They have their priestly guts slit open," I said ruminatively, "they have their eyes gouged out, their balls sliced off, and their tongues ripped out. Remember that monk we found at Yppe?" I asked Finan. Finan was a fugitive from Ireland, where he had been raised a Christian, though his religion was so tangled with native myths that it was scarcely recognizable as the same faith that Willibald preached. "How did that poor man die?" I asked.

"They skinned the poor soul alive," Finan said.

"Started at his toes?"

"Just peeled it off slowly," Finan said, "and it must have taken hours."

"They didn't peel it," I said, "you can't skin a man like a lamb."

"True," Finan said. "You have to tug it off. Takes a lot of strength!"

"He was a missionary," I told Willibald.

"And a blessed martyr too," Finan added cheerfully. "But they must have got bored because they finished him off in the end. They used a tree-saw on his belly."

"It was probably an ax," I said.

"No, it was a saw, lord," Finan insisted, grinning, "and one with savage big teeth. Ripped him into two, it did." Father Willibald, who had always been a martyr to seasickness, staggered to the ship's side.

We turned the ship southward. The estuary of the Temes is a treacherous place of mudbanks and strong tides, but I had been patrolling these waters for five years now and I scarcely needed to look for my landmarks as we rowed toward the shore of Scaepege. And there, ahead of me, waiting between two beached ships, was the enemy. The Danes. There must have been a hundred or more men, all in chain mail, all helmeted, and all with bright weapons. "We could slaughter the whole crew," I suggested to Finan. "We've got enough men."

"We agreed to come in peace!" Father Willibald protested, wiping his mouth with a sleeve.

And so we had, and so we did.

I ordered *Kenelm* and *Dragon-Voyager* to stay close to the muddy shore, while we drove *Seolferwulf* onto the gently shelving mud between the two Danish boats. *Seolferwulf*'s bows made a hissing sound as she slowed and stopped. She was firmly grounded now, but the tide was rising, so she was safe for a while. I jumped off the prow, splashing into deep wet mud, then waded to firmer ground where our enemies waited.

"My Lord Uhtred," the leader of the Danes greeted me. He grinned and spread his arms wide. He was a stocky man, golden-haired and square-jawed. His beard was plaited into five thick ropes fastened with silver clasps. His forearms glittered with rings of gold and silver, and more gold studded the belt from which hung a thick-bladed sword. He looked prosperous, which he was, and something about the openness of his face made him appear trustworthy, which he was not. "I am so overjoyed to see you," he said, still smiling, "my old valued friend!"

"Jarl Haesten," I responded, giving him the title he liked to use, though in my mind Haesten was nothing but a pirate. I had known him for years. I had saved his life once, which was a bad day's work, and ever since that day I had been trying to kill him, yet he always managed to slither away. He had escaped me five years before and, since then, I had heard how he had been raiding deep inside Frankia. He had amassed silver there, had whelped another son on his wife, and had attracted followers. Now he had brought eighty ships to Wessex.

"I hoped Alfred would send you," Haesten said, holding out a hand.

"If Alfred hadn't ordered me to come in peace," I said, taking the hand, "I'd have cut that head off your shoulders by now."

"You bark a lot," he said, amused, "but the louder a cur barks, lord, the weaker its bite."

I let that pass. I had not come to fight, but to do Alfred's bidding, and the king had ordered me to bring missionaries to Haesten. Willibald and his companion were helped ashore by my men, then came to stand beside me, where they smiled nervously. Both priests spoke Danish, which is why they had been chosen. I had also brought Haesten a message gilded with treasure, but he feigned indifference, insisting I accompany him to his encampment before Alfred's gift was delivered.

Scaepege was not Haesten's main encampment, that was some distance to the east where his eighty ships were drawn up on a beach protected by a newly made fort. He had not wanted to invite me into that fastness, and so he had insisted Alfred's envoys meet him among the wastes of Scaepege which, even in summer, is a place of dank pools, sour grass, and dark marshes. He had arrived there two days before, and had made a crude fort by surrounding a patch of higher ground with a tangled wall of thorn bushes, inside which he had raised two sailcloth tents. "We shall eat, lord," he invited me grandly, gesturing to a trestle table surrounded by a dozen stools. Finan, two other warriors, and the pair of priests accompanied me, though Haesten insisted the priests should not sit at the table. "I don't trust Christian wizards," he explained, "so they can squat on the ground." The food was a fish stew and rock-hard bread, served by half-naked slave women, none more than fourteen or fifteen years old, and all of them Saxons.

Haesten was humiliating the girls as a provocation and he watched for my reaction. "Are they from Wessex?" I asked.

"Of course not," he said, pretending to be offended by the question. "I took them from East Anglia. You want one of them, lord? There, that little one has breasts firm as apples!"

I asked the apple-breasted girl where she had been captured, and she just shook her head dumbly, too frightened to answer me. She poured me ale that had been sweetened with berries. "Where are you from?" I asked her again.

Haesten looked at the girl, letting his eyes linger on her breasts. "Answer the lord," he said in English.

"I don't know, lord," she said.

"Wessex?" I demanded. "East Anglia? Where?"

"A village, lord," she said, and that was all she knew, and I waved her away.

"Your wife is well?" Haesten asked, watching the girl walk away.

"She is."

"I am glad," he said convincingly enough, then his shrewd eyes looked amused. "So what is your master's message to me?" he asked, spooning fish broth into his mouth and dripping it down his beard.

"You're to leave Wessex," I said.

"I'm to leave Wessex!" He pretended to be shocked and waved a hand at the desolate marshes. "Why would a man want to leave all this, lord?"

"You're to leave Wessex," I said doggedly, "agree not to invade Mercia, give my king two hostages, and accept his missionaries."

"Missionaries!" Haesten said, pointing his horn spoon at me. "Now you can't approve of that, Lord Uhtred! You, at least, worship the real gods." He twisted on the stool and stared at the two priests. "Maybe I'll kill them."

"Do that," I said, "and I'll suck your eyeballs out of their sockets."

He heard the venom in my voice and was surprised by it. I saw a flicker of resentment in his eyes, but he kept his voice calm. "You've become a Christian, lord?"

"Father Willibald is my friend," I said.

"You should have said," he reproved me, "and I would not have jested. Of course they will live and they can even preach to us, but they'll achieve nothing. So, Alfred instructs me to take my ships away?"

"Far away," I said.

"But where?" he asked in feigned innocence.

"Frankia?" I suggested.

"The Franks have paid me to leave them alone," Haesten said, "they even built us ships to hasten our departure! Will Alfred build us ships?"

"You're to leave Wessex," I said stubbornly, "you're to leave Mercia untroubled, you're to accept missionaries, and you are to give Alfred hostages."

"Ah." Haesten smiled. "The hostages." He stared at me for a few heartbeats, then appeared to forget the matter of hostages, waving seaward instead. "And where are we to go?"

"Alfred is paying you to leave Wessex," I said, "and where you go is not my concern, but make it very far from the reach of my sword."

Haesten laughed. "Your sword, lord," he said, "rusts in its scabbard." He jerked a thumb over his shoulder, toward the south. "Wessex burns," he said with relish, "and Alfred lets you sleep." He was right. Far to the south, hazed in the summer sky, were pyres of smoke from a dozen or more burning villages, and those plumes were only the ones I could see. I knew there were more. Eastern Wessex was being ravaged, and, rather than summon my help to repel the invaders, Alfred had ordered me to stay in Lundene to protect that city from attack. Haesten grinned. "Maybe Alfred thinks you're too old to fight, lord?"

I did not respond to the taunt. Looking back down the years I think of myself as young back then, though I must have been all of thirty-five or thirty-six years old that year. Most men never live that long, but I was fortunate. I had lost none of my sword-skill or strength, I had a slight limp from an old battle-wound, but I also had the most golden of all a warrior's attributes; reputation. But Haesten felt free to goad me, knowing that I came to him as a supplicant.

I came as a supplicant because two Danish fleets had landed in Cent, the easternmost part of Wessex. Haesten's was the smaller fleet, and so far he had been content to build his fortress and let his men raid only enough to provide themselves with sufficient food and a few slaves. He had even let the shipping in the Temes go unmolested. He did not want a fight with Wessex, not yet, because he was waiting to see what happened to the south, where another and much greater Viking fleet had come ashore.

Jarl Harald Bloodhair had brought more than two hundred ships filled with hungry men, and his army had stormed a half-built burh and slaughtered the men inside, and now his warriors were spreading across Cent, burning and killing, enslaving and robbing. It was Harald's men who had smeared the sky with smoke. Alfred had marched against both invaders. The king was old now, old and ever more sick, so his troops were supposedly commanded by his son-in-law, Lord Æthelred of Mercia, and by the Ætheling Edward, Alfred's eldest son.

And they had done nothing. They had put their men on the great wooded ridge at the center of Cent from where they could strike north against Haesten or south against Harald, and then they had stayed motionless, presumably frightened that if they attacked one Danish army the other would assault their rear. So Alfred, convinced that his enemies were too powerful, had sent me to persuade Haesten to leave Wessex. Alfred should have ordered me to lead my garrison against Haesten, allowed me to soak the marshes with Danish blood, but instead I was instructed to bribe Haesten. With Haesten gone, the king thought, his army might deal with Harald's wild warriors.

Haesten used a thorn to pick at his teeth. He finally scraped out a scrap of fish. "Why doesn't your king attack Harald?" he asked.

"You'd like that," I said.

He grinned. "With Harald gone," he admitted, "and that rancid whore of his gone as well, a lot of crews would join me."

"Rancid whore?"

He grinned, pleased that he knew something I did not. "Skade," he said flatly.

"Harald's wife?"

"His woman, his bitch, his lover, his sorceress."

"Never heard of her," I said.

"You will," he promised, "and if you see her, my friend, you'll want her. But she'll nail your skull to her hall gable if she can."

"You've seen her?" I asked, and he nodded. "You wanted her?"

"Harald's impulsive," he said, ignoring my question. "And Skade will goad him to stupidity. And when that happens a lot of his men will look for another lord." He smiled slyly. "Give me another hundred ships, and I could be King of Wessex inside a year."

"I'll tell Alfred," I said, "and maybe that will persuade him to attack you first."

"He won't," Haesten said confidently. "If he turns on me then he releases Harald's men to spread across all Wessex."

That was true. "So why doesn't he attack Harald?" I asked.

"You know why."

"Tell me."

He paused, wondering whether to reveal all he knew, but he could not resist showing off his knowledge. He used the thorn to scratch a line in the wood of the table, then made a circle that was bisected by the line. "The Temes," he said, tapping the line, "Lundene," he indicated the circle. "You're in Lundene with a thousand men, and behind you," he tapped higher up the Temes, "Lord Aldhelm has five hundred Mercians. If Alfred attacks Harald, he's going to want Aldhelm's men and your men to go south, and that will leave Mercia wide open to attack."

"Who would attack Mercia?" I asked innocently.

"The Danes of East Anglia?" Haesten suggested just as innocently. "All they need is a leader with courage."

"And our agreement," I said, "insists you will not invade Mercia."

"So it does," Haesten said with a smile, "except we have no agreement yet."

But we did. I had to yield *Dragon-Voyager* to Haesten, and in her

13

belly lay four iron-bound chests filled with silver. That was the price. In return for the ship and the silver, Haesten promised to leave Wessex and ignore Mercia. He also agreed to accept missionaries and gave me two boys as hostages. He claimed one was his nephew, and that might have been true. The other boy was younger and dressed in fine linen with a lavish gold brooch. He was a good-looking lad with bright blond hair and anxious blue eyes. Haesten stood behind the boy and placed his hands on the small shoulders. "This, lord," he said reverently, "is my eldest son, Horic. I yield him as a hostage." Haesten paused, and seemed to sniff away a tear. "I yield him as a hostage, lord, to show goodwill, but I beg you to look after the boy. I love him dearly."

I looked at Horic. "How old are you?" I asked.

"He is seven," Haesten said, patting Horic's shoulder.

"Let him answer for himself," I insisted. "How old are you?"

The boy made a guttural sound and Haesten crouched to embrace him. "He is a deaf-mute, Lord Uhtred," Haesten said. "The gods decreed my son should be deaf and mute."

"The gods decreed that you should be a lying bastard," I said to Haesten, but too softly for his followers to hear and take offense.

"And if I am?" he asked, amused. "What of it? And if I say this boy is my son, who is to prove otherwise?"

"You'll leave Wessex?" I asked.

"I'll keep this treaty," he promised.

I pretended to believe him. I had told Alfred that Haesten could not be trusted, but Alfred was desperate. He was old, he saw his grave not far ahead, and he wanted Wessex rid of the hated pagans. And so I paid the silver, took the hostages, and, under a darkening sky, rowed back to Lundene.

Lundene is built in a place where the ground rises in giant steps away from the river. There is terrace after terrace, rising to the topmost level where the Romans built their grandest buildings, some of which still stood, though they were sadly decayed,

14

patched with wattle and scabbed by the thatched huts we Saxons made.

In those days Lundene was part of Mercia, though Mercia was like the grand Roman buildings; half fallen, and Mercia was also scabbed with Danish jarls who had settled its fertile lands. My cousin Æthelred was the chief Ealdorman of Mercia, its supposed ruler, but he was kept on a tight lead by Alfred of Wessex, who had made certain his own men controlled Lundene. I commanded that garrison, while Bishop Erkenwald ruled everything else.

These days, of course, he is known as Saint Erkenwald, but I remember him as a sour weasel of a man. He was efficient, I grant him that, and the city was well governed in his time, but his unadulterated hatred of all pagans made him my enemy. I worshiped Thor, so to him I was evil, but I was also necessary. I was the warrior who protected his city, the pagan who had kept the heathen Danes at bay for over five years now, the man who kept the lands around Lundene safe so that Erkenwald could levy his taxes.

Now I stood on the topmost step of a Roman house built on the topmost of Lundene's terraces. Bishop Erkenwald was on my right. He was much shorter than I, but most men are, yet my height irked him. A straggle of priests, ink-stained, pale-faced, and nervous, were gathered on the steps beneath, while Finan, my Irish fighter, stood on my left. We all stared southward.

We saw the mix of thatch and tile that roof Lundene, all studded with the stubby towers of the churches Erkenwald had built. Red kites wheeled above them, riding the warm air, though higher still I could see the first geese flying southward above the wide Temes. The river was slashed by the remnants of the Roman bridge, a marvelous thing which was crudely broken in its center. I had made a roadway of timbers that spanned the gap, but even I was nervous every time I needed to cross that makeshift repair which led to Suthriganaweorc, the earth and timber fortress that protected the bridge's southern end. There were wide marshes there and a huddle of huts where a village had grown around the fort. Beyond the marshes the land rose to the hills of Wessex, low and green, and above those hills, far off, like ghostly pillars in the still, late-summer sky, were plumes of smoke. I counted fifteen, but the clouds hazed the horizon and there could have been more.

"They're raiding!" Bishop Erkenwald said, sounding both surprised and outraged. Wessex had been spared any large Viking raid for years now, protected by the burhs, which were the towns Alfred had walled and garrisoned, but Harald's men were spreading fire, rape, and theft in all the eastern parts of Wessex. They avoided the burhs, attacking only the smaller settlements. "They're well beyond Cent!" the bishop observed.

"And going deeper into Wessex," I said.

"How many of them?" Erkenwald demanded.

"We hear two hundred ships landed," I said, "so they must have at least five thousand fighting men. Maybe two thousand of those are with Harald."

"Only two thousand?" the bishop asked sharply.

"It depends how many horses they have," I explained. "Only mounted warriors will be raiding, the rest will be guarding his ships."

"It's still a pagan horde," the bishop said angrily. He touched the cross hanging about his neck. "Our lord king," he went on, "has decided to defeat them at Æscengum."

"Æscengum!"

"And why not?" the bishop bridled at my tone, then shuddered when I laughed. "There is nothing amusing in that," he said tartly. But there was. Alfred, or perhaps it had been Æthelred, had advanced the army of Wessex into Cent, placing it on high wooded ground between the forces of Haesten and Harald, and then they had done nothing. Now it seemed that Alfred, or perhaps his son-in-law, had decided to retreat to Æscengum, a burh in the center of Wessex, presumably hoping that Harald would attack them and be defeated by the burh's walls. It was a pathetic idea. Harald was a wolf, Wessex was a flock of sheep, and Alfred's army was the wolfhound that should protect the sheep, but Alfred was tethering the wolfhound in hope that the wolf would come and be bitten. Meanwhile the wolf was running free among the flock. "And our lord king," Erkenwald continued loftily, "has requested that you

16

and some of your troops join him, but only if I am satisfied that Haesten will not attack Lundene in your absence."

"He won't," I said, and felt a surge of elation. Alfred, at last, had called for my help, which meant the wolfhound was being given sharp teeth.

"Haesten fears we'll kill the hostages?" the bishop asked.

"Haesten doesn't care a cabbage-smelling fart for the hostages," I said. "The one he calls his son is some peasant boy tricked out in rich clothes."

"Then why did you accept him?" the bishop demanded indignantly.

"What was I supposed to do? Attack Haesten's main camp to find his pups?"

"So Haesten is cheating us?"

"Of course he's cheating us, but he won't attack Lundene unless Harald defeats Alfred."

"I wish we could be certain of that."

"Haesten is cautious," I said. "He fights when he's certain he can win, otherwise he waits."

Erkenwald nodded. "So take men south tomorrow," he ordered, then walked away, followed by his scurrying priests.

I look back now across the long years and realize Bishop Erkenwald and I ruled Lundene well. I did not like him, and he hated me, and we begrudged the time we needed to spend in each other's company, but he never interfered with my garrison and I did not intervene in his governance. Another man might have asked how many men I planned to take south, or how many would be left to guard the city, but Erkenwald trusted me to make the right decisions. I still think he was a weasel.

"How many men ride with you?" Gisela asked me that night.

We were in our house, a Roman merchant's house built on the northern bank of the Temes. The river stank often, but we were used to it and the house was happy. We had slaves, servants and guards, nurses and cooks, and our three children. There was Uhtred, our oldest, who must have been around ten that year, and Stiorra his sister, and Osbert, the youngest, just two and indomitably

17

curious. Uhtred was named after me, as I had been named after my father and he after his, but this newest Uhtred irritated me because he was a pale and nervous child who clung to his mother's skirts.

"Three hundred men," I answered.

"Only?"

"Alfred has sufficient," I said, "and I must leave a garrison here."

Gisela flinched. She was pregnant again, and the birth could not be far off. She saw my worried expression and smiled. "I spit babies like pips," she said reassuringly. "How long to kill Harald's men?"

"A month?" I guessed.

"I shall have given birth by then," she said, and I touched the carving of Thor's hammer which hung at my neck. Gisela smiled reassurance again. "I have been lucky with childbirth," she went on, which was true. Her births had been easy enough and all three children had lived. "You'll come back to find a new baby crying," she said, "and you'll get annoyed."

I answered that truth with a swift smile, then pushed through the leather curtain onto the terrace. It was dark. There were a few lights on the river's far bank where the fort guarded the bridge, and their flames shimmered on the water. In the west there was a streak of purple showing in a cloud rift. The river seethed through the bridge's narrow arches, but otherwise the city was quiet. Dogs barked occasionally, and there was sporadic laughter from the kitchens. *Seolferwulf*, moored in the dock beside the house, creaked in the small wind. I glanced downstream to where, at the city's edge, I had built a small tower of oak at the riverside. Men watched from that tower night and day, watching for the beaked ships that might come to attack Lundene's wharves, but no warning fire blazed from the tower's top. All was quiet. There were Danes in Wessex, but Lundene was resting.

"When this is over," Gisela said from the doorway, "maybe we should go north."

"Yes," I said, then turned to look at the beauty of her long face and dark eyes. She was a Dane and, like me, she was weary of Wessex's Christianity. A man should have gods, and perhaps there is

18

some sense in acknowledging only one god, but why choose one who loves the whip and spur so much? The Christian god was not ours, yet we were forced to live among folk who feared him and who condemned us because we worshiped a different god. Yet I was sworn to Alfred's service and so I remained where he demanded that I remain. "He can't live much longer," I said.

"And when he dies you're free?"

"I gave no oath to anyone else," I said, and I spoke honestly. In truth I had given another oath, and that oath would come back to find me, but it was so far from my mind that night that I believed I answered Gisela truthfully.

"And when he's dead?"

"We go north," I said. North, back to my ancestral home beside the Northumbrian sea, a home usurped by my uncle. North to Bebbanburg, north to the lands where pagans could live without the incessant nagging of the Christians' nailed god. We would go home. I had served Alfred long enough, and I had served him well, but I wanted to go home. "I promise," I told Gisela, "on my oath, we will go home."

The gods laughed.

We crossed the bridge at dawn, three hundred warriors with half as many boys who came to tend the horses and carry the spare weapons. The hooves clattered loud on the makeshift bridge as we rode toward the pyres of smoke that told of Wessex being ravaged. We crossed the wide marsh where, at high tide, the river puddles dark among lank grasses, and climbed the gentle hills beyond. I left most of the garrison to guard Lundene, taking only my own household troops, my warriors and oath-men, the fighters I trusted with my own life. I left just six of those men in Lundene to guard my house under the command of Cerdic, who had been my battle-companion for many years and who had almost wept as he had pleaded with me to take him. "You must guard Gisela and my family," I had told him, and so Cerdic stayed as we rode west, following tracks trampled by the sheep and cattle that were driven to slaughter in Lundene. We saw little panic. Folk were keeping their eyes on the distant smoke, and thegns had placed lookouts on rooftops and high among the trees. We were mistaken for Danes more than once, and there would be a flurry as people ran toward the woods, but once our identity was discovered they would come back. They were supposed to drive their livestock to the nearest burh if danger threatened, but folk are ever reluctant to leave their homes. I ordered whole villages to take their cattle, sheep, and goats to Suthriganaweorc, but I doubt they did. They would rather stay until the Danes were breathing down their throats.

Yet the Danes were staying well to the south, so perhaps those villagers had judged well. We swerved southward ourselves, climbing higher and expecting to see the raiders at any moment. I had scouts riding well ahead, and it was midmorning before one of them waved a red cloth to signal he had seen something to alarm him. I spurred to the hill crest, but saw nothing in the valley beneath.

"There were folk running, lord," the scout told me. "They saw me and hid in the trees."

"Maybe they were running from you?"

He shook his head. "They were already panicked, lord, when I saw them."

We were gazing out across a wide valley, green and lush beneath the summer sun. At its far side were wooded hills and the nearest smoke pyre was beyond that skyline. The valley looked peaceful. I could see small fields, the thatched roofs of a village, a track going west, and the glimmer of a stream twisting between meadows. I saw no enemy, but the heavy-leafed trees could have hidden Harald's whole horde. "What did you see exactly?" I asked.

"Women, lord. Women and children. Some goats. They were running that way." He pointed westward.

So the fugitives were fleeing the village. The scout had glimpsed them between the trees, but there was no sign of them now, nor of whatever had made them run. No smoke showed in this long wide valley, but that did not mean Harald's men were not there. I plucked the scout's reins, leading him beneath the skyline, and remembered the day, so many years before, when I had first gone to war. I had been with my father, who had been leading the fyrd, the host of men plucked from their farmlands who were mostly armed with hoes or scythes or axes. We had marched on foot and, as a result, we had been a slow, lumbering army. The Danes, our enemy, had ridden. Their ships landed and the first thing they did was find horses, and then they danced about us. We had learned from that. We had learned to fight like the Danes, except that Alfred was now trusting to his fortified towns to stop Harald's invasion, and that meant Harald was being given the freedom of the Wessex countryside. His men, I knew, would be mounted, except he led too many warriors, and so his raiding parties were doubtless still scouring the land for yet more horses. Our first job was to kill those raiders and take back any captured horses, and I suspected just such a band was at the eastern end of the valley. I found a man in my ranks who knew this part of the country. "Edwulf has an estate here, lord," he said.

"Edwulf?"

"A thegn, lord." He grinned and used a hand to sketch a bulge in front of his stomach. "He's a big fat man."

"So he's rich?"

"Very, lord."

All of which suggested some Danes had found a plump nest to plunder, and we had found an easy prey to slaughter. The only difficulty was getting three hundred men across the skyline without being seen from the valley's eastern end, but we discovered a route that was shrouded by trees, and by midday I had my men hidden in the woods to the west of Edwulf's estate. Then I baited the trap.

I sent Osferth and twenty men to follow a track that led south toward the smoke pyres. They led a half-dozen riderless horses and went slowly, as if they were tired and lost. I ordered them never to look directly at Edwulf's hall where, by now, I knew the Danes were busy. Finan, who could move among trees like a ghost, had crept close to the hall and brought back news of a village with a score of houses, a church, and two fine barns. "They're pulling down the thatch," Finan told me, meaning the Danes were searching the roofs of all the buildings, because some folk hid their treasures in the thatch before they fled. "And they're taking turns on some women."

"Horses?"

"Just women," Finan said, then caught my glance and stopped grinning. "They've a whole herd of horses in a paddock, lord."

So Osferth rode, and the Danes took the bait like a trout rising to a fly. They saw him, he pretended not to see them, and suddenly forty or more Danes were galloping to intercept Osferth, who pretended to wake to the danger, turned westward and galloped across the front of my hidden men.

And then it was as simple as stealing silver from a church. A hundred of my men crashed from the trees onto the flank of the Danes, who had no chance to escape. Two of the enemy turned their horses too fast and the beasts went down in a screaming chaos of hooves and turf. Others tried to turn back and were caught by spears in their spines. The experienced Danes swerved toward us, hoping to ride straight through our charge, but we were too many, and my men curled around the enemy horsemen so that a dozen were trapped in a circle. I was not there. I was leading the rest of my men to Edwulf's hall, where the remainder of the Danes were running to mount their horses. One man, bare below the waist, scrambled away from a screaming woman and twisted as he saw me coming. Smoka, my horse, slowed, the man dodged again, but Smoka needed no guidance from me, and Serpent-Breath, my sword, took the man in the skull. The blade lodged there, so that the dying Dane was dragged along as I rode. Blood sprayed up my arm, then at last his twitching body fell away.

I spurred on, taking most of the men east of the settlement, and so cutting off the retreat of the surviving Danes. Finan had already sent scouts to the southern hill crest. Why, I wondered, had the Danes not posted sentinels on the hilltop from which we had first seen the fugitives?

There were so many skirmishes in those days. The Danes of East Anglia would raid the farmlands about Lundene, and we would retaliate, taking men deep into Danish territory to burn, kill, and plunder. There was officially a peace treaty between Alfred's Wessex and East Anglia, but a hungry Dane took no notice of words on parchment. A man who wanted slaves, livestock, or simply wanted an adventure, would cross into Mercia and take what he wanted, and we would then ride east and do the same. I liked such raids. They gave me a chance to train my youngest men, to let them see the enemy and cross swords. You can drill a man for a year, practice sword craft and spear skills forever, but he will learn more in just five minutes of battle.

There were so many skirmishes that I have forgotten most, yet I recall that skirmish at Edwulf's hall. In reality it was nothing. The Danes had been careless and we took no casualties, yet I remember because, when it was over, and the swords were still, one of my men called me to the church.

It was a small church, hardly big enough for the fifty or sixty souls who lived or had lived around the hall. The building was made of oak and had a thatched roof on which a wooden cross stood tall. A crude bell hung at the western gable above the only door, while each side wall had two large timber-barred windows through which light streamed to illuminate a fat man who had been stripped naked and tied to a table that I assumed was the church's altar. He was moaning. "Untie him," I snarled, and Rypere, who had led the men who captured the Danes inside the church, started forward as if I had just woken him from a trance.

Rypere had seen much horror in his few years, but he, like the men he led, seemed numbed by the cruelty inflicted on the fat man. His eye sockets were a mess of blood and jelly, his cheeks laced red, his ears sliced off, his manhood cut, his fingers first broken and then chiseled from his palms. Two Danes stood beyond the table, guarded by my men, their reddened hands betraying they had been the torturers. Yet it was the leader of the Danish band who was chiefly responsible for the cruelty, and that is why I remember the skirmish.

Because that was how I met Skade, and if ever any woman ate the apples of Asgard that gave the gods their eternal beauty, it was Skade. She was tall, almost as tall as I was, with a wiry body disguised by the mail coat she wore. She was maybe twenty years old, her face was narrow, high-nosed, haughty, with eyes as blue as any I have ever seen. Her hair, dark as the feathers of Odin's ravens, hung long and straight to her slender waist, where a sword belt held an empty scabbard. I stared at her.

And she stared at me. And what did she see?

She saw Alfred's warlord. She saw Uhtred of Bebbanburg, the pagan in service to a Christian king. I was tall, and in those days I had broad shoulders. I was a sword-warrior, spear-warrior, and fighting had made me rich so that my mail shone and my helmet was inlaid with silver and my arm rings glittered above the mail sleeves. My sword belt was decorated with silver wolf-heads, Serpent-Breath's scabbard was cased with jet slivers, while my belt buckle and cloak clasp were made of heavy gold. Only the small image of Thor's hammer, hanging around my neck, was cheap, but I had owned that talisman since I was a child. I have it still. The glory of my youth has gone, eroded by time, but that was what Skade saw. She saw a warlord.

And so she spat at me. The spittle landed on my cheek and I left it there. "Who is the bitch?" I asked.

"Skade," Rypere gave me her name, then nodded at the two torturers, "they say she's their leader."

The fat man moaned. He had been cut free and now curled his body into a ball. "Find someone to tend him," I said irritably, and Skade spat again, this time striking my mouth. "Who is he?" I demanded, ignoring her.

"We think he's Edwulf," Rypere said.

"Get him out of here," I said, then turned to look at the beauty who spat at me. "And who," I asked, "is Skade?"

She was a Dane, born to a steading in the northern part of their bleak country, daughter to a man who had no great riches and so left his widow poor. But the widow had Skade, and her beauty was astonishing, and so she had been married to a man willing to pay for that long, lithe body in his bed. The husband was a Frisian chieftain, a pirate, but then Skade had met Harald Bloodhair, and Jarl Harald offered her more excitement than living behind a rotting palisade on some tide-besieged sandbank, and so she had run away with

24

him. All that I was to learn, but for now I just knew she was Harald's woman, and that Haesten had spoken the truth; to see her was to want her. "You will release me," she said with an astonishing confidence.

"I'll do what I choose," I told her, "and I don't take orders from a fool." She bridled at that, and I saw she was about to spit again, and so raised a hand as if to strike her and she went very still. "No lookouts," I said to her. "What leader doesn't post sentries? Only a fool." She hated that. She hated it because it was true.

"Jarl Harald will give you money for my freedom," she said.

"My price for your freedom," I said, "is Harald's liver."

"You are Uhtred?" she asked.

"I am the Lord Uhtred of Bebbanburg."

She gave a ghost of a smile. "Then Bebbanburg will need a new lord if you don't release me. I shall curse you. You will know agony, Uhtred of Bebbanburg, even greater agony than him." She nodded at Edwulf, who was being carried out of the church by four of my men.

"He's a fool too," I said, "because he set no sentries." Skade's raiding party had descended on the village in the morning sunlight and no one saw them coming. Some villagers, those we had seen from the skyline, escaped, but most had been captured, and of those only the young women and the children who might have been sold as slaves still lived.

We let one Dane live, one Dane and Skade. The rest we killed. We took their horses, their mail, and their weapons. I ordered the surviving villagers to drive their livestock north to Suthriganaweorc because Harald's men had to be denied food, though as the harvest was already in the barns and the orchards were heavy, that would be hard. We were still slaughtering the last of the Danes when Finan's scouts reported that horsemen were approaching the hill crest to the south.

I went to meet them, taking seventy men, the one Dane I would spare, Skade, and also the long piece of hemp rope that had been attached to the church's small bell. I joined Finan and we rode to where the hill's crest was gentle grassland and from where we could look far to the south. New smoke pyres thickened in the distant sky, but nearer, much nearer, was a band of horsemen who rode on the banks of a willow-shadowed stream. I estimated they numbered about the same as my men, who were now lined on the crest either side of my wolf's-head banner. "Get off the horse," I ordered Skade.

"Those men are searching for me," she said defiantly, nodding at the horsemen who had paused at the sight of my battle line.

"Then they've found you," I said, "so dismount."

She just stared at me proudly. She was a woman who hated being given orders.

"You can dismount," I said patiently, "or I can pull you out of the saddle. The choice is yours."

She dismounted and I gestured for Finan to dismount. He drew his sword and stood close to the girl. "Now undress," I told her.

A look of utter fury darkened her face. She did nothing, but I sensed an anger like a tensed adder inside her. She wanted to kill me, she wanted to scream, she wanted to call the gods down from the smoke-patterned sky, but there was nothing she could do. "Undress," I said, "or have my men strip you."

She turned as if looking for a way to escape, but there was none. There was a glint of tears in her eyes, but she had no choice but to obey me. Finan looked at me quizzically, because I was not known for being cruel to women, but I did not explain to him. I was remembering what Haesten had told me, how Harald was impulsive, and I wanted to provoke Harald Bloodhair. I would insult his woman and so hope to force Harald to anger instead of sober judgment.

Skade's face was an expressionless mask as she stripped herself of her mail coat, a leather jerkin, and linen breeches. One or two of my men cheered when her jerkin came off to reveal high, firm breasts, but they went silent when I snarled at them. I tossed the rope to Finan. "Tie it round her neck," I said.

She was beautiful. Even now I can close my eyes and see that long body standing in the buttercup-bright grass. The Danes in the valley were staring up, my men were gazing, and Skade stood there like a creature from Asgard come to the middle-earth. I did not doubt Harald would pay for her. Any man might have impoverished himself to possess Skade.

Finan gave me the rope's end and I kicked my stallion forward and led her a third of the way down the slope. "Is Harald there?" I asked her, nodding at the Danes who were two hundred paces away.

"No," she said. Her voice was bitter and tight. She was ashamed and angry. "He'll kill you for this," she said.

I smiled. "Harald Bloodhair," I said, "is a puking, shit-filled rat." I twisted in the saddle and waved to Osferth, who brought the surviving Danish prisoner down the slope. He was a young man and he looked up at me with fear in his pale blue eyes. "This is your chieftain's woman," I said to him, "look at her."

He hardly dared look at Skade's nakedness. He just gave her a glance then gazed back at me.

"Go," I told him, "and tell Harald Bloodhair that Uhtred of Bebbanburg has his whore. Tell Harald I have her naked, and that I'll use her for my amusement. Go, tell him. Go!"

The man ran down the slope. The Danes in the valley were not going to attack us. Our numbers were evenly matched, and we had the high ground, and the Danes are ever reluctant to take too many casualties. So they just watched us and, though one or two rode close enough to see Skade clearly, none tried to rescue her.

I had carried Skade's jerkin, breeches, and boots. I threw them at her feet, then leaned down and took the rope from her neck. "Dress," I said.

I saw her consider escape. She was thinking of running long-legged down the slope, hoping to reach the watching horsemen before I caught her, but I touched Smoka's flank and he moved in front of her. "You'd die with a sword in your skull," I told her, "long before you could reach them."

"And you'll die," she said, stooping for her clothes, "without a sword in your hand."

I touched the talisman about my neck. "Alfred," I said, "hangs captured pagans. You had better hope that I can keep you alive when we meet him."

"I shall curse you," she said, "and those you love."

"And you had better hope," I went on, "that my patience lasts, or else I'll give you to my men before Alfred hangs you."

"A curse and death," she said, and there was almost triumph in her voice.

"Hit her if she speaks again," I told Osferth.

Then we rode west to find Alfred.

THREE

The first thing I noticed was the cart.

It was enormous, big enough to carry the harvest from a dozen fields, but this wagon would never carry anything so mundane as sheaves of wheat. It had two thick axles and four solid wheels rimmed with iron. The wheels had been painted with a green cross on a white background. The sides of the cart were paneled, and each of the panels bore the image of a saint. There were Latin words carved into the top rails, but I never bothered to ask what they meant because I neither wanted to know nor needed to ask. They would be some Christian exhortation, and one of those is much like any other. The bed of the cart was mostly filled by woolsacks, presumably to protect the passengers from the jolting of the vehicle, while a well-cushioned chair stood with its high back against the driver's bench. A striped sailcloth awning supported by four serpentine-carved poles had been erected over the whole gaudy contraption, and a wooden cross, like those placed on church gables, reared from one of the poles. Saints' banners hung from the remaining three poles.

"A church on wheels?" I asked sourly.

"He can't ride anymore," Steapa told me gloomily.

Steapa was the commander of the royal bodyguard. He was a huge man, one of the few who were taller than me, and unremittingly fierce in battle. He was also unremittingly loyal to King Alfred. Steapa and I were friends, though we had started as enemies when I had been forced to fight him. It had been like attacking a mountain. Yet the two of us had survived that meeting, and there was no man I would rather have stood beside in a shield wall. "He can't ride at all?" I asked.

"He does sometimes," Steapa said, "but it hurts too much. He can hardly walk."

"How many oxen drag this thing?" I asked, gesturing at the wagon.

"Six. He doesn't like it, but he has to use it."

We were in Æscengum, the burh built to protect Wintanceaster from the east. It was a small burh, nothing like the size of Wintanceaster or Lundene, and it protected a ford which crossed the River Wey, though why the ford needed protection was a mystery because the river could be easily crossed both north and south of Æscengum. Indeed, the town guarded nothing of importance, which was why I had argued against its fortification. Yet Alfred had insisted on making Æscengum into a burh because, years before, some half-crazed Christian mystic had supposedly restored a raped girl's virginity at the place, and so it was a hallowed spot. Alfred had ordered a monastery built there, and Steapa told me the king was waiting in its church. "They're talking," he said bleakly, "but none of them knows what to do."

"I thought you were waiting for Harald to attack you here?"

"I told them he wouldn't," Steapa said, "but what happens if he doesn't?"

"We find Harald and kill the earsling, of course," I said, gazing east to where new smoke pyres betrayed where Harald's men were plundering new villages.

Steapa gestured at Skade. "Who's she?"

"Harald's whore," I said, loud enough for Skade to hear, though her face showed no change from her customary haughty expression. "She tortured a man called Edwulf," I explained, "trying to get him to reveal where he'd buried his gold."

"I know Edwulf," Steapa said, "he eats and drinks his gold."

"He did," I said, "but he's dead now." Edwulf had died before we left his estate.

Steapa held out a hand to take my swords. The monastery was

serving this day as Alfred's hall, and no one except the king, his relatives, and his guards could carry a weapon in the royal presence. I surrendered Serpent-Breath and Wasp-Sting, then dipped my hands in a bowl of water offered by a servant. "Welcome to the king's house, lord," the servant said in formal greeting, then watched as I looped the rope about Skade's neck.

She spat in my face and I grinned. "Time to meet the king, Skade," I said, "spit at him and he'll hang you."

"I will curse you both," she said.

Finan alone accompanied Steapa, Skade, and me into the monastery. The rest of my men took their horses through the western gate to water them in a stream while Steapa led us to the abbey church, a fine stone building with heavy oak roof beams. The high windows lit painted leather hides, and the one above the altar showed a white-robed girl being raised to her feet by a bearded and haloed man. The girl's apple-plump face bore a look of pure astonishment, and I assumed she was the newly restored virgin, while the man's expression suggested she might soon need the miracle repeated. Beneath her, seated on a rug-draped chair placed in front of the silver-piled altar, was Alfred.

A score of other men were in the church. They had been talking as we arrived, but the voices dropped to silence as I entered. On Alfred's left was a gaggle of churchmen, among whom were my old friend Father Beocca and my old enemy Bishop Asser, a Welshman who had become the king's most intimate adviser. In the nave of the church, seated on benches, were a half-dozen ealdormen, the leaders of those shires whose men had been summoned to join the army that faced Harald's invasion. To Alfred's right, seated on a slightly smaller chair, was his son-in-law, my cousin Æthelred, and behind him was his wife, Alfred's daughter, Æthelflæd.

Æthelred was the Lord of Mercia. Mercia, of course, was the country to the north of Wessex, and its northern and eastern parts were ruled by the Danes. It had no king, instead it had my cousin, who was the acknowledged ruler of the Saxon parts of Mercia, though in truth he was in thrall to Alfred. Alfred, though he never made the claim explicit, was the actual ruler of Mercia, and

Æthelred did his father-in-law's bidding. Though how long that bidding could continue was dubious, for Alfred looked sicker than I had ever seen him. His pale, clerkly face was thinner than ever and his eyes had a bruised look of pain, though they had lost none of their intelligence.

He looked at me in silence, waited till I had bowed, then nodded a curt greeting. "You bring men, Lord Uhtred?"

"Three hundred, lord."

"Is that all?" Alfred asked, flinching.

"Unless you wish to lose Lundene, lord, it's all."

"And you bring your woman?" Bishop Asser sneered.

Bishop Asser was an earsling, which is anything that drops out of an arse. He had dropped out of some Welsh arse, from where he had slimed his way into Alfred's favor. Alfred thought the world of Asser who, in turn, hated me. I smiled at him. "I bring you Harald's whore," I said.

No one answered that. They all just stared at Skade, and none stared harder than the young man standing just behind Alfred's throne. He had a thin face with prominent bones, pale skin, black hair that curled just above his embroidered collar, and eyes that were quick and bright. He seemed nervous, overawed perhaps by the presence of so many broad-shouldered warriors, while he himself was slender, almost fragile, in his build. I knew him well enough. His name was Edward, and he was the Ætheling, the king's eldest son, and he was being groomed to take his father's throne. Now he was gaping at Skade as though he had never seen a woman before, but when she met his gaze he blushed and pretended to take a keen interest in the rush-covered floor.

"You brought what?" Bishop Asser broke the surprised silence.

"Her name is Skade," I said, thrusting her forward. Edward raised his eyes and stared at Skade like a puppy seeing fresh meat.

"Bow to the king," I ordered Skade in Danish.

"I do what I wish," she said and, just as I supposed she would, she spat toward Alfred.

"Strike her!" Bishop Asser yapped.

"Do churchmen strike women?" I asked him.

"Be quiet, Lord Uhtred," Alfred said tiredly. I saw how his right hand was curled into a claw that clutched the arm of the chair. He gazed at Skade, who returned the stare defiantly. "A remarkable woman," the king said mildly, "does she speak English?"

"She pretends not to," I said, "but she understands it well enough."

Skade rewarded that truth with a sidelong look of pure spite. "I've cursed you," she said under her breath.

"The easiest way to be rid of a curse," I spoke just as softly, "is to cut out the tongue that made it. Now be silent, you rancid bitch."

"The curse of death," she said, just above a whisper.

"What is she saying?" Alfred asked.

"She is reputed to be a sorceress, lord," I said, "and claims to have cursed me."

Alfred and most of the churchmen touched the crosses hanging about their necks. It is a strange thing I have noticed about Christians, that they claim our gods have no power yet they fear the curses made in the names of those gods. "How did you capture her?" Alfred asked.

I gave a brief account of what had happened at Edwulf's hall and when I was done Alfred looked at her coldly. "Did she kill Edwulf's priest?" he asked.

"Did you kill Edwulf's priest, bitch?" I asked her in Danish.

She smiled at me. "Of course I did," she said, "I kill all priests."

"She killed the priest, lord," I told Alfred.

He shuddered. "Take her outside," he ordered Steapa, "and guard her well." He held up a hand. "She is not to be molested!" He waited till Skade was gone before looking at me. "You're welcome, Lord Uhtred," he said, "you and your men. But I had hoped you would bring more."

"I brought enough, lord King," I said.

"Enough for what?" Bishop Asser asked.

I looked at the runt. He was a bishop, but still wore his monkish robes cinched tight around his scrawny waist. He had a face like a starved stoat, with pale green eyes and thin lips. He spent half his time in the wastelands of his native Wales, and half whispering pious poison into Alfred's ears, and together the two men had made a law code for Wessex, and it was my amusement and ambition to break every one of those laws before either the king or the Welsh runt died. "Enough," I said, "to tear Harald and his men into bloody ruin."

Æthelflæd smiled at that. She alone of Alfred's family was my friend. I had not seen her in four years and she looked much thinner now. She was only a year or two above twenty, but appeared older and sadder, yet her hair was still lustrous gold and her eyes as blue as the summer sky. I winked at her, as much as anything to annoy her husband, my cousin, who immediately rose to the bait and snorted. "If Harald were that easy to destroy," Æthelred said, "we would have done it already."

"How?" I asked, "by watching him from the hills?" Æthelred grimaced. Normally he would have argued with me, because he was a belligerent and proud man, but he looked pale. He had an illness, no one knew what, and it left him tired and weak for long stretches. He was perhaps forty in that year, and his red hair had strands of white at his temples. This, I guessed, was one of his bad days. "Harald should have been killed weeks ago," I taunted him scornfully.

"Enough!" Alfred slapped the arm of his chair, startling a leatherhooded falcon that was perched on a lectern beside the altar. The bird flapped his wings, but the jesses held him firm. Alfred grimaced. His face told me what I well knew, that he needed me and did not want to need me. "We could not attack Harald," he explained patiently, "so long as Haesten threatened our northern flank."

"Haesten couldn't threaten a wet puppy," I said, "he's too frightened of defeat."

I was arrogant that day, arrogant and confident, because there are times when men need to see arrogance. These men had spent days arguing about what to do, and in the end they had done nothing, and all that time they had been multiplying Harald's forces in their minds until they were convinced he was invincible. Alfred, meanwhile, had deliberately refrained from seeking my help because he wanted to hand the reins of Wessex and Mercia to his son and to his son-in-law, which meant giving them reputations as leaders, but their leadership had failed, and so Alfred had sent for me. And now, because they needed it, I countered their fears with an arrogant assurance.

"Harald has five thousand men," Ealdorman Æthelhelm of Wiltunscir said softly. Æthelhelm was a good man, but he too seemed infected by the timidity that had overtaken Alfred's entourage. "He brought two hundred ships!" he added.

"If he has two thousand men, I'd be astonished," I said. "How many horses does he have?" No one knew, or at least no one answered. Harald might well have brought as many as five thousand men, but his army consisted only of those who had horses.

"However many men he has," Alfred said pointedly, "he must attack this burh to advance further into Wessex."

That was nonsense, of course. Harald could go north or south of Æscengum, but there was no future in arguing that with Alfred, who had a peculiar affection for the burh. "So you plan to defeat him here, lord?" I asked instead.

"I have nine hundred men here," he said, "and we have the burh's garrison, and now your three hundred. Harald will break himself on these walls." I saw Æthelred, Æthelhelm, and Ealdorman Æthelnoth of Sumorsæte all nod their agreement.

"And I have five hundred men at Silcestre," Æthelred said, as though that made all the difference.

"And what are they doing there?" I asked, "pissing in the Temes while we fight?"

Æthelflæd grinned, while her brother Edward looked affronted. Dear Father Beocca, who had been my childhood tutor, gave me a long-suffering look of reproof. Alfred just sighed. "Lord Æthelred's men can harry the enemy while they besiege us," he explained.

"So our victory, lord," I said, "depends on Harald attacking us here? On Harald allowing us to kill his men while they try to cross the wall?" Alfred did not answer. A pair of sparrows squabbled among the rafters. A thick beeswax candle on the altar behind

Alfred guttered and smoked and a monk hurried to trim the wick. The flame grew again, its light reflected from a high golden reliquary that seemed to contain a withered hand.

"Harald will want to defeat us." Edward made his first tentative contribution to the discussion.

"Why?" I asked, "when we're doing our best to defeat ourselves?" There was an aggrieved murmur from the courtiers, but I overrode it. "Let me tell you what Harald will do, lord," I said, speaking to Alfred. "He'll take his army north of us and advance on Wintanceaster. There's a lot of silver there, all conveniently piled in your new cathedral, and you've brought your army here so he won't have much trouble breaking through Wintanceaster's walls. And even if he does besiege us here," I spoke even louder to drown Bishop Asser's angry protest, "all he needs do is surround us and let us starve. How much food do we have here?"

The king gestured to Asser, requesting that he stop spluttering. "So what would you do, Lord Uhtred?" Alfred asked, and there was a plaintive note in his voice. He was old and he was tired and he was ill, and Harald's invasion seemed to threaten all that he had achieved.

"I would suggest, lord," I said, "that Lord Æthelred order his five hundred men to cross the Temes and march to Fearnhamme."

A hound whined in a corner of the church, but otherwise there was no sound. They all stared at me, but I saw some faces brighten. They had been wallowing with indecision and had needed the sword stroke of certainty.

Alfred broke the silence. "Fearnhamme?" he asked cautiously.

"Fearnhamme," I repeated, watching Æthelred, but his pale face displayed no reaction, and no one else in the church made any comment.

I had been thinking about the country to the north of Æscengum. War is not just about men, nor even about supplies, it is also about the hills and valleys, the rivers and marshes, the places where land and water will help defeat an enemy. I had traveled through Fearnhamme often enough on my journeys from Lundene to Wintanceaster, and wherever I traveled I noted how the land lay and how it might be used if an enemy was near. "There's a hill just north of the river at Fearnhamme," I said.

"There is! I know it well," one of the monks standing to Alfred's right said, "it has an earthwork."

I looked at him, seeing a red-faced, hook-nosed man. "And who are you?" I asked coldly.

"Oslac, lord," he said, "the abbot here."

"The earthwork," I asked him, "is it in good repair?"

"It was dug by the ancient folk," Abbot Oslac said, "and it's much overgrown with grass, but the ditch is deep and the bank is still firm."

There were many such earthworks in Britain, mute witnesses to the warfare that had rolled across the land before we Saxons came to bring still more. "The bank's high enough to make defense easy?" I asked the abbot.

"You could hold it forever, given enough men," Oslac said confidently. I gazed at him, noting the scar across the bridge of his nose. Abbot Oslac, I decided, had been a warrior before he became a monk.

"But why invite Harald to besiege us there?" Alfred asked, "when we have Æscengum and its walls and its storehouses?"

"And how long will those storehouses last, lord?" I asked him. "We have enough men inside these walls to hold the enemy till Judgment Day, but not enough food to reach Christmas." The burhs were not provisioned for a large army. The intent of the walled towns was to hold the enemy in check and allow the army of household warriors, the trained men, to attack the besiegers in the open country outside.

"But Fearnhamme?" Alfred asked.

"Is where we shall destroy Harald," I said unhelpfully. I looked at Æthelred. "Order your men to Fearnhamme, cousin, and we'll trap Harald there."

There was a time when Alfred would have questioned and tested my ideas, but that day he looked too tired and too sick to argue, and he plainly did not have the patience to listen to other men challenging my plans. Besides, he had learned to trust me when it came to warfare, and I expected his assent to my vague proposal, but then he surprised me. He turned to the churchmen and gestured that one of them should join him, and Bishop Asser took the elbow of a young, stocky monk and guided him to the king's chair. The monk had a hard, bony face and black tonsured hair as bristly and stiff as a badger's pelt. He might have been handsome except his eyes were milky, and I guessed he had been blind from birth. He groped for the king's chair, found it and knelt beside Alfred, who laid a fatherly hand on the monk's bowed head. "So, Brother Godwin?" he asked gently.

"I am here, lord, I am here," Godwin said in a voice scarce above a hoarse whisper.

"And you heard the Lord Uhtred?"

"I heard, lord, I heard." Brother Godwin raised his blind eyes to the king. He said nothing for a while, but his face was twisting all that time, twisting and grimacing like a man possessed by an evil spirit. He started to utter a choking noise, and what astonished me was that none of this alarmed Alfred, who waited patiently until, at last, the young monk regained a normal expression. "It will be well, lord King," Godwin said, "it will be well."

Alfred patted Brother Godwin's head again and smiled at me. "We shall do as you suggest, Lord Uhtred," he said decisively. "You will direct your men to Fearnhamme," he spoke to Æthelred, then looked back to me, "and my son," he went on, "will command the West Saxon forces."

"Yes, lord," I said dutifully. Edward, the youngest man in the church, looked embarrassed, and his eyes flicked nervously from me to his father.

"And you," Alfred turned to look at his son, "will obey the Lord Uhtred."

Æthelred could contain himself no longer. "What guarantees do we have," he asked petulantly, "that the heathens will go to Fearnhamme?"

"Mine," I said harshly.

"But you cannot be certain!" Æthelred protested.

"He will go to Fearnhamme," I said, "and he will die there."
I was wrong about that.

Messengers rode to Æthelred's men at Silcestre, ordering them to march on Fearnhamme at first light next morning. Once there they were to occupy the hill that stands just north of the river. Those five hundred men were the anvil, while the men at Æscengum were my hammer, but to lure Harald onto the anvil would mean dividing our forces, and it is a rule of war not to do that. We had, at my best estimate, about five hundred men fewer than the Danes, and by keeping our army in two parts I was inviting Harald to destroy them separately. "But I'm relying on Harald being an impulsive fool, lord," I told Alfred that night.

The king had joined me on Æscengum's eastern rampart. He had arrived with his usual entourage of priests, but had waved them away so he could talk with me privately. He stood for a moment just staring at the distant dull glow of fires where Harald's men had sacked villages and I knew he was lamenting all the burned churches. "Is he an impulsive fool?" he inquired mildly.

"You tell me, lord," I said.

"He's savage, unpredictable, and given to sudden rages," the king said. Alfred paid well for information about the northmen and kept meticulous notes on every leader. Harald had been pillaging in Frankia before its people bribed him to leave, and I did not doubt that Alfred's spies had told him everything they could discover about Harald Bloodhair. "You know why he's called Bloodhair?" Alfred asked.

"Because before every battle, lord, he sacrifices a horse to Thor and soaks his hair in the animal's blood."

"Yes," Alfred said. He leaned on the palisade. "How can you be sure he'll go to Fearnhamme?" he asked.

"Because I'll draw him there, lord. I'll make a snare and pull him onto our spears."

"The woman?" Alfred asked with a slight shudder.

"She is said to be special to him, lord."

"So I hear," he said. "But he will have other whores."

"She's not the only reason he'll go to Fearnhamme, lord," I said, "but she's reason enough."

"Women brought sin into this world," he said so quietly I almost did not hear him. He rested against the oak trunks of the parapet and gazed toward the small town of Godelmingum that lay just a few miles eastward. The people who lived there had been ordered to flee, and now the only inhabitants were fifty of my men who stood sentinel to warn us of the Danish approach. "I had hoped the Danes had ceased wanting this kingdom," he broke the silence plaintively.

"They'll always want Wessex," I said.

"All I ask of God," he went on, ignoring my truism, "is that Wessex should be safe and ruled by my son." I answered nothing to that. There was no law that decreed a son should succeed his father as king, and if there had been then Alfred would not be Wessex's ruler. He had succeeded his brother, and that brother had a son, Æthelwold, who wanted desperately to be king in Wessex. Æthelwold had been too young to assume the throne when his father died, but he was in his thirties now, a man in his ale-sozzled prime. Alfred sighed, then straightened. "Edward will need you as an adviser," he said.

"I should be honored, lord," I said.

Alfred heard the dutiful tone in my voice and did not like it. He stiffened, and I expected one of his customary reproofs, but instead he looked pained. "God has blessed me," he said quietly. "When I came to the throne, Lord Uhtred, it seemed impossible that we should resist the Danes. Yet by God's grace Wessex lives. We have churches, monasteries, schools, laws. We have made a country where God dwells, and I cannot believe it is God's will that it should vanish when I am called to judgment."

"May that be many years yet, lord," I said as dutifully as I had spoken before.

"Oh, don't be a fool," he snarled with sudden anger. He shuddered, closed his eyes momentarily, and when he spoke again his voice was low and wan. "I can feel death coming, Lord Uhtred. It's like an ambush. I know it's there and I can do nothing to avoid it. It will take me and it will destroy me, but I do not want it to destroy Wessex with me."

"If it's your God's will," I said harshly, "then nothing I can do nor anything Edward can do will stop it."

"We're not puppets in God's hands," he said testily. "We are his instruments. We earn our fate." He looked at me with some bitterness for he had never forgiven me for abandoning Christianity in favor of the older religion. "Don't your gods reward you for good behavior?"

"My gods are capricious, lord." I had learned that word from Bishop Erkenwald who had intended it as an insult, but once I had learned its meaning I liked it. My gods are capricious.

"How can you serve a capricious god?" Alfred asked.

"I don't."

"But you said . . ."

"They are capricious," I interrupted him, "but that's their pleasure. My task is not to serve them, but to amuse them, and if I do then they will reward me in the life to come."

"Amuse them?" He sounded shocked.

"Why not?" I demanded. "We have cats, dogs, and falcons for our pleasure, the gods made us for the same reason. Why did your god make you?"

"To be His servant," he said firmly. "If I'm God's cat then I must catch the devil's mice. That is duty, Lord Uhtred, duty."

"While my duty," I said, "is to catch Harald and slice his head off. That, I think, will amuse my gods."

"Your gods are cruel," he said, then shuddered.

"Men are cruel," I said, "and the gods made us like themselves, and some of the gods are kind, some are cruel. So are we. If it amuses the gods then Harald will slice my head off." I touched the hammer amulet.

Alfred grimaced. "God made you his instrument, and I do not know why he chose you, a pagan, but so he did and you have served me well."

He had spoken fervently, surprising me, and I bowed my head in acknowledgment. "Thank you, lord."

"And now I wish you to serve my son," he added.

I should have known that was coming, but somehow the request took me by surprise. I was silent a moment as I tried to think what to say. "I agreed to serve you, lord," I said finally, "and so I have, but I have my own battles to fight."

"Bebbanburg," he said sourly.

"Is mine," I said firmly, "and before I die I wish to see my banner flying over its gate and my son strong enough to defend it."

He gazed at the glow of the enemy fires. I was noticing how scattered those fires were, which told me Harald had not yet concentrated his army. It would take time to pull those men together from across the ravaged countryside, which meant, I thought, that the battle would not be fought tomorrow, but the next day. "Bebbanburg," Alfred said, "is an island of the English in a sea of Danes."

"True, lord," I said, noting how he used the word "English." It embraced all the tribes who had come across the sea, whether they were Saxon, Angle, or Jute, and it spoke of Alfred's ambition, that he now made explicit.

"The best way to keep Bebbanburg safe," he said, "is to surround it with more English land."

"Drive the Danes from Northumbria?" I asked.

"If it is God's will," he said, "then I will wish my son to do that great deed." He turned to me, and for a moment he was not a king, but a father. "Help him, Lord Uhtred," he said pleadingly. "You are my *dux bellorum*, my lord of battles, and men know they will win when you lead them. Scour the enemy from England, and so take your fortress back and make my son safe on his God-given throne."

He had not flattered me, he had spoken the truth. I was the warlord of Wessex and I was proud of that reputation. I went into battle glittering with gold, silver, and pride, and I should have known that the gods would resent that.

"I want you," Alfred spoke softly but firmly, "to give my son your oath."

I cursed inwardly, but spoke respectfully. "What oath, lord?"

"I wish you to serve Edward as you have served me."

And thus Alfred would tie me to Wessex, to Christian Wessex that lay so far from my northern home. I had spent my first ten years in Bebbanburg, that great rock-fastness on the northern sea, and when I had first ridden to war the fortress had been left in the care of my uncle, who had stolen it from me.

"I will swear an oath to you, lord," I said, "and to no one else."

"I already have your oath," he said harshly.

"And I will keep it," I said.

"And when I'm dead," he asked bitterly, "what then?"

"Then, lord, I shall go to Bebbanburg and take it, and keep it, and spend my days beside the sea."

"And if my son is threatened?"

"Then Wessex must defend him," I said, "as I defend you now."

"And what makes you think you can defend me?" He was angry now. "You would take my army to Fearnhamme? You have no certainty that Harald will go there!"

"He will," I said.

"You can't know that!"

"I shall force it on him," I said.

"How?" he demanded.

"The gods will do that for me," I said.

"You're a fool," he snapped.

"If you don't trust me," I spoke just as forcibly, "then your son-in-law wants to be your lord of battles. Or you can command the army yourself? Or give Edward his chance?"

He shuddered, I thought with anger, but when he spoke again his voice was patient. "I just wish to know," he said, "why you are so sure that the enemy will do what you want."

"Because the gods are capricious," I said arrogantly, "and I am about to amuse them."

"Tell me," he said tiredly.

"Harald is a fool," I said, "and he is a fool in love. We have his woman. I shall take her to Fearnhamme, and he will follow because he is besotted with her. And even if I did not have his woman," I went on, "he would still follow me."

I had thought he would scoff at that, but he considered my words quietly, then joined his hands prayerfully. "I am tempted to doubt you, but Brother Godwin assures me you will bring us victory."

"Brother Godwin?" I had wanted to ask about the strange blind monk.

"God speaks to him," Alfred said with a quiet assurance.

I almost laughed, but then thought that the gods do speak to us, though usually by signs and portents. "Does he take all your decisions, lord?" I asked sourly.

"God assists me in all things," Alfred said sharply, then turned away because the bell was summoning the Christians to prayer in Æscengum's new church.

The gods are capricious, and I was about to amuse them. And Alfred was right. I was a fool.

What did Harald want? Or, for that matter, Haesten? It was simpler to answer for Haesten, because he was the cleverer and more ambitious man, and he wanted land. He wanted to be a king.

The northmen had come to Britain in search of kingdoms, and the lucky ones had found their thrones. A northman reigned in Northumbria, and another in East Anglia, and Haesten wanted to be their equal. He wanted the crown, the treasures, the women, and the status, and there were two places those things could be found. One was Mercia and the other Wessex.

Mercia was the better prospect. It had no king and was riven by warfare. The north and east of the country was ruled by jarls, powerful Danes who kept strong troops of household warriors and barred their gates each night, while the south and east was Saxon land. The Saxons looked to my cousin, Æthelred, for protection and he gave it to them, but only because he had inherited great wealth and enjoyed the firm support of his father-in-law, Alfred. Mercia was not part of Wessex, but it did Wessex's bidding, and Alfred was the true power behind Æthelred. Haesten might attack Mercia and he would find allies in the north and east, but eventually he would find himself facing the armies of Saxon Mercia and Alfred's Wessex. And Haesten was cautious. He had made his camp on a desolate shore of Wessex, but he did nothing provocative. He waited, certain that Alfred would pay him to leave, which Alfred had done. He also waited to see what damage Harald might achieve.

Harald probably wanted a throne, but above all he wanted everything that glittered. He wanted silver, gold, and women. He was like a child that sees something pretty and screams until he possesses it. The throne of Wessex might fall into his hands as he greedily scooped up his baubles, but he did not aim for it. He had come to Wessex because it was full of treasures, and now he was ravaging the land, taking plunder, while Haesten just watched. Haesten hoped, I think, that Harald's wild troops would so weaken Alfred that he could come behind and take the whole land. If Wessex was a bull, then Harald's men were blood-maddened terriers who would attack in a pack and most would die in the attacking, but they would weaken the bull, and then Haesten, the mastiff, would come and finish the job. So to deter Haesten I needed to crush Harald's stronger forces. The bull could not be weakened, but the terriers had to be killed, and they were dangerous, they were vicious, but they were also ill-disciplined, and I would now tempt them with treasure. I would tempt them with Skade's sleek beauty.

The fifty men I had posted in Godelmingum fled from that town next morning, retreating from a larger group of Danes. My men splashed their horses through the river and streamed into Æscengum as the Danes lined the farther bank to stare at the banners hanging bright on the burh's eastern palisade. Those banners showed crosses and saints, the panoply of Alfred's state, and to make certain the enemy knew the king was in the burh I made Osferth walk slowly along the wall dressed in a bright cloak and with a circlet of shining bronze on his head.

Osferth, my man, was Alfred's bastard. Few people knew, even though Osferth's resemblance to his father was striking. He had been born to a servant girl whom Alfred had taken to his bed in the days before Christianity had captured his soul. Once, in an unguarded moment, Alfred had confided to me that Osferth was a continual reproof. "A reminder," he had told me, "of the sinner I once was."

"A sweet sin, lord," I had replied lightly.

"Most sins are sweet," the king said, "the devil makes them so."

What kind of perverted religion makes pleasures into sins? The old gods, even though they never deny us pleasure, fade these days. Folk abandon them, preferring the whip and bridle of the Christians' nailed god.

So Osferth, a reminder of Alfred's sweet sin, played the king that morning. I doubt he enjoyed it, for he resented Alfred, who had tried to turn him into a priest. Osferth had rebelled against that destiny, becoming one of my house-warriors instead. He was not a natural fighter, not like Finan, but he brought a keen intelligence to the business of war, and intelligence is a weapon that has a sharp edge and a long reach.

All war ends with the shield wall, where men hack in drink-sodden rage with axes and swords, but the art is to manipulate the enemy so that when that moment of screaming rage arrives it comes to your advantage. By parading Osferth on Æscengum's wall I was trying to tempt Harald. Where the king is, I was suggesting to our enemies, there is treasure. Come to Æscengum, I was saying, and to increase the temptation I displayed Skade to the Danish warriors who gathered on the river's far bank.

A few arrows had been shot at us, but those ended when the enemy recognized Skade. She unwittingly helped me by screaming at the men across the water. "Come and kill them all!" she shouted.

"I'll shut her mouth," Steapa volunteered.

"Let the bitch shout," I said.

She pretended to speak no English, yet she gave me a withering glance before looking back across the river. "They're cowards," she shouted at the Danes, "Saxon cowards! Tell Harald they will die like sheep." She stepped close to the palisade. She could not cross the wall because I had ordered her tied by a rope that was looped about her neck and held by one of Steapa's men.

"Tell Harald his whore is here!" I called over the river, "and that she's noisy! Maybe we'll cut out her tongue and send it to Harald for his supper!"

"Goat turd," she spat at me, then reached over the palisade's top and plucked out an arrow that had lodged in one of the oak trunks. Steapa immediately moved to disarm her, but I waved him back. Skade ignored us. She was gazing fixedly at the arrowhead which, with a sudden wrench, she freed from the feathered shaft, which she tossed over the wall. She gave me a glance, raised the arrowhead to her lips, closed her eyes, and kissed the steel. She muttered some words I could not hear, touched her lips to the steel again, then pushed it beneath her gown, hesitated, then jabbed the point into one of her breasts. She gave me a triumphant look as she brought the bloodstained steel into view, then she flung the arrowhead into the river and lifted her hands and face to the late summer sky. She screamed to get the attention of the gods, and when the scream faded she turned back to me. "You're cursed, Uhtred," she said with a tone she might have used to remark on unremarkable weather.

I resisted the impulse to touch the hammer hanging about my neck because to have done so would have shown that I feared her curse, which instead I pretended to dismiss with a sneer. "Waste your breath, whore," I said, yet I still moved my hand to my sword and rubbed a finger across the silver cross embedded in Serpent-Breath's hilt. The cross meant nothing to me, except it had been a gift from Hild, once my lover and now an abbess of extraordinary piety. Did I think that touching the cross was a substitute for the hammer? The gods would not think so.

"When I was a child," Skade said suddenly, and still using a conversational tone as though she and I were old friends, "my father beat my mother senseless."

"Because she was like you?" I asked.

She ignored that. "He broke her ribs, an arm, and her nose," she went on, "and later that day he took me to the high pastures to help bring back the herd. I was twelve years old. I remember there were snowflakes flying and I was frightened of him. I wanted to ask why he had hurt my mother, but I didn't like to speak in case he beat me, but then he told me anyway. He said he wanted to marry me to his closest friend, and my mother had opposed the idea. I hated it too, but he said I would marry the man anyway."

"Am I supposed to feel sorry for you?" I asked.

"So I pushed him over a bluff," she said, "and I remember him falling through the snowflakes and I watched him bounce on the rocks and I heard him scream. His back was broken." She smiled. "I left him there. He was still alive when I brought the herd down. I scrambled down the rocks and pissed on his face before he died." She looked calmly at me. "That was my first curse, Lord Uhtred, but not my last. I will lift the curse on you if you let me go."

"You think you can frighten me into giving you back to Harald?" I asked, amused.

"You will," she said confidently, "you will."

"Take her away," I ordered, tired of her.

Harald came at midday. One of Steapa's men brought me the news and I climbed again to the ramparts to discover that Harald Blood-hair was on the river's farther bank with fifty companions, all in mail. His banner showed an ax blade and its pole was surmounted by a wolf-skull that had been painted red.

He was a big man. His horse was big too, but even so Harald Bloodhair seemed to dwarf the stallion. He was too distant for me to see him clearly, but his yellow hair, long, thick, and unstained with any blood, was plainly visible, as was his broad beard. For a time he just stared at Æscengum's wall, then he unbuckled his sword belt, threw the weapon to one of his men, and spurred his horse into the river. It was a warm day, but his mail was still covered by a great cloak of black bear fur that made him appear monstrously huge. He wore gold on his wrists and about his neck, and more gold decorated his horse's bridle. He urged the stallion to the river's center where the water surged over his boot tops. Any of the archers on Æscengum's wall could have shot an arrow, but he had ostentatiously disarmed himself, which meant he wanted to talk, and I gave orders that no one was to loose a bow at him. He took off his helmet and searched the men crowding the rampart until he saw Osferth in his circlet. Harald had never seen Alfred and mistook the bastard for the father. "Alfred!" he shouted.

"The king doesn't talk with brigands," I called back.

Harald grinned. His face was broad as a barley-shovel, his nose hooked and crooked, his mouth wide, his eyes as feral as any wolf's. "Are you Uhtred Turdson?" he greeted me.

"I know you're Harald the Gutless," I responded with a dutiful insult.

He gazed at me. Now that he was closer I could see that his yellow hair and beard were dirt-flecked, ropy and greasy, like the hair from a corpse buried in dung. The river surged by his stallion. "Tell your king," Harald called to me, "that he can save himself much trouble by giving me his throne."

"He invites you to come and take it," I said.

"But first," he leaned forward and patted his horse's neck, "you will return my property."

"We have nothing of yours," I said.

"Skade," he said flatly.

"She's yours?" I asked, pretending surprise. "But surely a whore belongs to whoever can pay her?"

He gave me a look of instant hatred. "If you have touched her," he said, pointing a leather-gloved finger at me, "or if any of your men have touched her, then I swear on Thor's prick I'll make your deaths so slow that your screams will stir the dead in their caves of ice." He was a fool, I thought. A clever man would have pretended the woman meant little or nothing to him, but Harald was already revealing his price. "Show her to me!" he demanded.

I hesitated, as if making up my mind, but I wanted Harald to see the bait and so I ordered two of Steapa's men to fetch Skade. She arrived with the rope still around her neck, yet such was her beauty and her calm dignity that she dominated the rampart. I thought, at that moment, that she was the most queenlike of any woman I had ever seen. She moved to the palisade and smiled at Harald, who kicked his horse a few paces forward. "Have they touched you?" he shouted up to her.

She gave me a mocking look before answering. "They're not men enough, my lord," she called.

"Promise me!" he shouted, and the desperation was plain in his voice.

"I promise you," she answered, and her voice was a caress.

Harald wheeled his horse so it was sideways to me, then raised his gloved hand to point at me. "You showed her naked, Uhtred Turdson."

"Would you like me to show her that way again?"

"For that you will lose your eyes," he said, prompting Skade to laugh. "Let her go now," Harald went on, "and I won't kill you! Instead I'll keep you blind and naked, on a rope's end, and display you to all the world."

"You yelp like a puppy," I called.

"Take the rope from her neck," Harald ordered me, "and send her to me now!"

"Come and take her, puppy!" I shouted back. I was feeling elated. Harald, I thought, was proving to be a headstrong fool. He wanted Skade more than he wanted Wessex, indeed more than he wanted all the treasures of Alfred's kingdom. I remember thinking that I had him exactly where I wished him to be, on the end of my lead, but then he turned his horse and gestured toward the growing crowd of warriors on the river bank.

And from the trees that grew thick on that far bank emerged a line of women and children. They were our people, Saxons, and they were roped together because they had been taken for slavery. Harald's men, as they ravaged through eastern Wessex, had doubtless captured every child and young woman they could find, and, when they had finished amusing themselves, would ship them to the slave markets of Frankia. But these women and infants were brought to the river's edge where, on an order from Harald, they were made to kneel. The youngest child was about the age of my own Stiorra, and I can still see that child's eyes as she stared up at me. She saw a warlord in shining glory and I saw nothing but pitiable despair.

"Start," Harald called to his men.

One of his warriors, a grinning brute who looked as if he could out-wrestle an ox, stepped behind the woman at the southern end of the line. He was carrying a battle-ax that he swung high, then brought down so that the blade split her skull and buried itself in her trunk. I heard the crunch of the blade in bone over the noise of the river, and saw blood jetting higher than Harald on his horse. "One," Harald called, and gestured to the blood-spattered axman who stepped briskly to his left to stand behind a child who was screaming because she had just seen her mother murdered. The red-bladed ax rose.

"Wait," I called.

Harald held up his hand to check the ax, then gave me a mocking smile. "You said something, Lord Uhtred?" he asked. I did not answer. I was watching a swirl of blood vanish and fade downstream. A man severed the rope tying the dead woman to her child, then kicked the corpse into the river. "Speak, Lord Uhtred, please do speak," Harald said with exaggerated courtesy.

There were thirty-three women and children left. If I did nothing then all would die. "Cut her free," I said softly.

The rope round Skade's neck was cut. "Go," I told her.

I hoped she would break her legs as she jumped from the palisade, but she landed lithely, climbed the ditch's far slope, then walked to the river's edge. Harald spurred his horse to her, held out a hand, and she swung up behind his saddle. She looked at me, touched a finger to her mouth, and held the hand toward me. "You're cursed, Lord Uhtred," she said, smiling, then Harald kicked his horse back to the far bank where the women and children had been led back into the thick-leaved trees.

So Harald had what he wanted.

But Skade wanted to be queen, and Harald wanted me blind.

"What now?" Steapa asked in his deep growling voice.

"We kill the bastard," I said. And, like a faint shadow on a dull day, I sensed her curse.

That night I watched the glow of Harald's fires; not the nearer ones in Godelmingum, though they were thick enough, but the fainter glimmer of more distant blazes, and I noted that much of the sky was now dark. For the last few nights the fires had been scattered across eastern Wessex, but now they drew closer and that meant Harald's men were concentrating. He doubtless hoped that Alfred would stay in Æscengum and so he was gathering his army, not to besiege us, but probably to launch a sudden and fast attack on Alfred's capital, Wintanceaster.

A few Danes had crossed the river to ride round Æscengum's walls, but most were still on the far bank. They were doing what I wanted, yet my heart felt dour that night and I had to pretend confidence. "Tomorrow, lord," I told Edward, Alfred's son, "the enemy will cross the river. They will be pursuing me, and you will let them all get past the burh, wait one hour and then follow."

"I understand," he said nervously.

"Follow them," I said, "but don't get into a fight till you reach Fearnhamme."

Steapa, standing beside Edward, frowned. "Suppose they turn on us?"

"They won't," I said. "Just wait till his army has gone past, then follow it all the way to Fearnhamme."

That sounded an easy enough instruction, but I doubted it would be so easy. Most of the enemy would cross the river in a great rush, eager to pursue me, but the stragglers would follow all day. Edward had to judge when the largest part of Harald's army was an hour ahead and then, ignoring those stragglers, pursue Harald to Fearnhamme. It would be a difficult decision, but he had Steapa to advise him. Steapa might not have been clever, but he had a killer's instinct that I trusted.

"At Fearnhamme," Edward began, then hesitated. The half-moon, showing between clouds, lit his pale and anxious face. He looked like his father, but there was an uncertainty in him which was not surprising. He was only about seventeen years old, yet he was being given a grown man's responsibility. He would have Steapa with him, but if he was to be a king then he would have to learn the hard business of making choices.

"Fearnhamme will be simple," I said dismissively. "I shall be north of the river with the Mercians. We'll be on a hill protected by earthworks. Harald's men will cross the ford to attack us, and you will attack their rear. When you do that we attack their vanguard."

"Simple?" Steapa echoed with a trace of amusement.

"We crush them between us," I said.

"With God's help," Edward said firmly.

"Even without that," I snarled.

Edward questioned me for the better part of an hour, right until the bell summoned him to prayers. He was like his father. He wanted to understand everything and have everything arranged in neat lists, but this was war and war was never neat. I believed Harald would follow me, and I trusted Steapa to bring the greater part of Alfred's army behind Harald, but I could give Edward no promises. He wanted certainty, but I was planning battle, and I was relieved when he went to pray with his father.

Steapa left me and I stood alone on the rampart. Sentries gave me room, somehow aware of my baleful mood, and when I heard footsteps I ignored them, hoping that whoever it was would go away and leave me in peace.

"The Lord Uhtred," a gently mocking voice said when the steps paused behind me.

"The Lady Æthelflæd," I said, not turning to look at her.

She came and stood beside me, her cloak touching mine. "How is Gisela?"

I touched Thor's hammer at my neck. "About to give birth again."

"The fourth child?"

"Yes," I said, and shot a prayer toward the house of the gods that Gisela would survive the birth. "How is Ælfwynn?" I asked. Ælfwynn was Æthelflæd's daughter, still an infant.

"She thrives."

"An only child?"

"And going to stay that way," Æthelflæd said bitterly and I looked at her profile, so delicate in the moonlight. I had known her since she was a small child when she had been the happiest, most carefree of Alfred's children, but now her face was guarded, as though she shrank from bad dreams. "My father's angry with you," she said.

"When is he not?"

She gave a hint of a smile, quickly gone. "He wants you to give an oath to Edward."

"I know."

"Then why won't you?"

"Because I'm not a slave to be handed on to a new master."

"Oh!" she sounded sarcastic, "you're not a woman?"

"I'm taking my family north," I said.

"If my father dies," Æthelflæd said, then hesitated. "When my father dies, what happens to Wessex?"

"Edward rules."

"He needs you," she said. I shrugged. "As long as you live, Lord Uhtred," she went on, "the Danes hesitate to attack."

"Harald didn't hesitate."

"Because he's a fool," she said scornfully, "and tomorrow you'll kill him."

"Perhaps," I said cautiously.

A murmur of voices made Æthelflæd turn to see men spilling from the church. "My husband," she said, investing those two words with loathing, "sent a message to Lord Aldhelm."

"Aldhelm leads the Mercian troops?"

Æthelflæd nodded. I knew Aldhelm. He was my cousin's favorite and a man of unbounded ambition, sly and clever. "I hope your husband ordered Aldhelm to Fearnhamme," I said.

"He did," Æthelflæd said, then lowered and quickened her voice, "but he also sent word that Aldhelm was to withdraw north if he thought the enemy too strong."

I had half suspected that would happen. "So Aldhelm is to preserve Mercia's army?"

"How else can my husband take Wessex when my father dies?" Æthelflæd asked in a voice of silken innocence. I glanced down at her, but she just gazed at the fires of Godelmingum.

"Will Aldhelm fight?" I asked her.

"Not if it means weakening Mercia's army," she said.

"Then tomorrow I shall have to persuade Aldhelm to his duty."

"But you have no authority over him," Æthelflæd said.

I patted Serpent-Breath's hilt. "I have this."

"And he has five hundred men," Æthelflæd said. "But there is one person he will obey."

"You?"

"So tomorrow I ride with you," she said.

"Your husband will forbid it," I answered.

"Of course he will," she said calmly, "but my husband won't know. And you will do me a service, Lord Uhtred."

"I am ever at your service, my lady," I said, too lightly.

"Are you?" she asked, turning to look up into my eyes.

I looked at her sad lovely face, and knew her question was serious. "Yes, my lady," I said gently.

"Then tomorrow," she said bitterly, "kill them all. Kill all the Danes. Do that for me, Lord Uhtred," she touched my hand with the tips of her fingers, "kill them all."

She had loved a Dane and she had lost him to a blade, and now she would kill them all.

There are three spinners at the root of Yggdrasil, the Tree of Life, and they weave our threads, and those spinners had made a skein of purest gold for Æthelflæd's life, but in those years they wove that bright thread into a much darker cloth. The three spinners see our future. The gift of the gods to humankind is that we cannot see where the threads will go.

I heard songs from the Danes camped across the river.

And tomorrow I would draw them to the old hill by the river. And there kill them.

FOUR

Next day was a Thursday, Thor's Day, which I took as a good omen. Alfred had once proposed renaming the days of the week, suggesting the Thursday become Maryday, or perhaps it was Haligastday, but the idea had faded like dew under the summer sun. In Christian Wessex, whether its king liked it or not, Tyr, Odin, Thor, and Frigg were still remembered each week.

And on that Thor's Day I was taking two hundred warriors to Fearnhamme, though more than six hundred horsemen gathered in the burh's long street before the sun rose. There was the usual chaos. Stirrup leathers broke and men tried to find replacements, children darted between the big horses, swords were given a last sharpening, the smoke of cooking fires drifted between the houses like fog, the church bell clanged, monks chanted, and I stood on the ramparts and watched the river's far bank.

The Danes who had crossed to our bank the previous day had gone back before nightfall. I could see smoke from their fires rising among the trees, but the only visible enemy was a pair of sentries crouching at the river's edge. For a moment I was tempted to abandon everything I had planned and instead lead the six hundred men across the river and let them rampage through Harald's camp, but it was only a fleeting temptation. I assumed most of his men were in Godelmingum, and they would be well awake by the time we reached them. A swirling battle might result, but the Danes would inevitably realize their advantage in numbers and grind us to bloody shreds. I wanted to keep my promise to Æthelflæd. I wanted to kill them all.

56

I made my first move when the sun rose, and I made it loudly. Horns were sounded inside Æscengum, then the northern gate was dragged open, and four hundred horsemen streamed into the fields beyond. The first riders gathered at the river bank, in clear view of the Danes, and waited while the rest of the men filed through the gate. Once all four hundred were gathered they turned west and spurred away through the trees toward the road that would eventually lead to Wintanceaster. I was still on the ramparts from where I watched the Danes gather to stare at the commotion on our bank, and I did not doubt that messengers were galloping to find Harald and inform him that the Saxon army was retreating.

Except we were not retreating because, once among the trees, the four hundred men doubled back and reentered Æscengum by the western gate, which was out of the enemy's sight. It was then that I went down to the main street and hauled myself into Smoka's saddle. I was dressed for war in mail, gold, and steel. Alfred appeared at the church door, his eyes half closing against the sudden sunlight as he came from the holy gloom. He returned my greeting with a nod, but said nothing. Æthelred, my cousin, was noisier, demanding to know where his wife was. I heard a servant report that Æthelflæd was at prayer in the nunnery, and that seemed to satisfy Æthelred, who assured me loudly that his Mercian troops would be waiting at Fearnhamme. "Aldhelm's a good man," he said, "he likes a fight."

"I'm glad of it," I said, pretending friendship with my cousin, just as Æthelred was pretending that Aldhelm had not been given secret instructions to retreat northward if he took fright at the numbers opposing him. I even held my hand down from Smoka's high saddle. "We shall win a great victory, Lord Æthelred," I said loudly.

Æthelred seemed momentarily astonished by my apparent affability, but clasped my hand anyway. "With God's help, cousin," he said, "with God's help."

"I pray for that," I answered. The king gave me a suspicious look, but I just smiled cheerfully. "Bring the troops when you think best," I called to Alfred's son, Edward, "and always take Lord Æthelred's advice."

Edward looked to his father for some guidance on what he should reply, but received none. He nodded nervously. "I shall, Lord Uhtred," he said, "and God go with you!"

God might go with me, but Æthelred would not. He had chosen to ride with the West Saxon troops who would follow the Danes, and thus be part of the hammer that would shatter Harald's forces on the anvil of his Mercian warriors. I had half feared he would come with me, but it made sense for Æthelred to stay with his father-in-law. That way, if Aldhelm chose to retreat, Æthelred could not be blamed. I suspected there was another reason. When Alfred died, Edward would be named king unless the witan wanted an older and more experienced man, and Æthelred doubtless believed he would gain more renown by fighting with the West Saxons this day.

I pulled on my wolf-crested helmet and nudged Smoka toward Steapa who, grim in mail and hung with weapons, waited beside a smithy. Charcoal smoke sifted from the door. I leaned down and slapped my friend's helmet. "You know what to do?" I asked.

"Tell me one more time," he growled, "and I'll rip your liver out and cook it."

I grinned. "I'll see you tonight," I said. I was pretending that Edward commanded the West Saxons, and that Æthelred was his chief adviser, but in truth I trusted Steapa to make the day go as I had planned. I wanted Steapa to choose the moment when the seven hundred warriors left Æscengum to pursue Harald's men. If they left too soon Harald could turn and cut them to ribbons, while leaving too late would mean my seven hundred troops would be slaughtered at Fearnhamme. "We're going to make a famous victory this day," I told Steapa.

"If God wills it, lord," he said.

"If you and I will it," I said happily, then leaned down and took my heavy linden shield from a servant. I hung the shield on my back, then spurred Smoka to the northern gate where Alfred's gaudy wagon waited behind a team of six horses. We had harnessed horses to the cumbersome cart because they were faster than oxen. Osferth, looking miserable, was the wagon's only passenger. He was dressed in a bright blue cloak and wearing a circlet of bronze on his head. The Danes did not know that Alfred eschewed most symbols of kingship. They expected a king to wear a crown and so I had ordered Osferth to wear the polished bauble. I had also persuaded Abbot Oslac to give me two of his monastery's less valuable reliquaries. One, a silver box molded with pictures of saints and studded with stones of jet and amber, had held the toe bones of Saint Cedd, but now contained some pebbles which would puzzle the Danes if, as I hoped, they captured the wagon. The second reliquary, also of silver, had a pigeon feather inside, because Alfred famously traveled nowhere without the feather that had been plucked from the dove Noah had released from the ark. Besides the reliquaries we had also put an iron-bound wooden chest in the wagon. The chest was half filled with silver and we would probably lose it, but I expected to gain far more. Abbot Oslac, wearing a mail coat beneath his monkish robes, had insisted on accompanying my two hundred men. A shield hung at his left side and a monstrous war ax was strapped to his broad back. "That looks well used," I greeted him, noting the nicks in the ax's wide blade.

"It's sent many a pagan to hell, Lord Uhtred," he answered happily.

I grinned and spurred to the gate where Father Beocca, my old and stern friend, waited to bless us. "God go with you," he said as I reached him.

I smiled down at him. He was lame, white-haired, cross-eyed, and clubfooted. He was also one of the best men I knew, though he mightily disapproved of me. "Pray for me, father," I said.

"I never cease," Beocca said.

"And don't let Edward lead the men out too soon! Trust Steapa! He might be dumb as a parsnip, but he knows how to fight."

"I shall pray that God gives them both good judgment," my old friend said. He reached up his good hand to clutch my gloved hand. "How is Gisela?"

"Maybe a mother again. And Thyra?"

His face lit up like tinder catching flame. This ugly, crippled man who was mocked by children in the street had married a Dane of startling beauty. "God keeps her in his loving hand," he told me. "She is a pearl of great price!"

"So are you, father," I said, then ruffled his white hair to annoy him.

Finan spurred beside me. "We're ready, lord."

"Open the gate!" I shouted.

The wagon was first through the wide arch. Its holy banners swayed alarmingly as it lurched onto the rutted track, then my two hundred men, bright in mail, rode after it and turned westward. We flew standards, braying horns announced our departure, and the sun shone on the royal wagon. We were the lure, and the Danes had seen us. And so the hunt began.

The wagon led the way, lumbering along a farm track that would lead us to the Wintanceaster road. A shrewd Dane might well wonder why, if we wanted to retreat to the larger burh at Wintanceaster, we would use Æscengum's northern gate instead of the western, which led directly onto the road, but I somehow doubted those worries would reach Harald. Instead he would hear that the King of Wessex was running away, leaving Æscengum to be protected by its garrison that was drawn from the fyrd. The men of the fyrd were rarely trained warriors. They were farmers and laborers, carpenters and thatchers, and Harald would undoubtedly be tempted to assault their wall, but I did not believe he would yield to the temptation, not while a much greater prize, Alfred himself, was apparently vulnerable. The Danish scouts would be telling Harald that the King of Wessex was in the open country, traveling in a slow wagon protected by a mere couple of hundred horsemen, and Harald's army, I was certain, would be ordered to the pursuit.

Finan commanded my rearguard, his job to tell me when the enemy pursuit got too close. I stayed near the wagon and, just as we reached the Wintanceaster road a half-mile west of Æscengum, a slender rider spurred alongside me. It was Æthelflæd, clad in a long mail coat that appeared to be made from silver rings close-linked over a

deerskin tunic. The mail coat fitted her tightly, clinging to her thin
body, and I guessed that it was fastened at the back with loops and but-
tons because no one could pull such a tight coat over their head and
shoulders. Over the mail she wore a white cloak, lined with red, and
she had a white-scabbarded sword at her side. A battered old helmet
with face-plates hung from her saddle's pommel and she had doubtless
used the helmet to hide her face before we left Æscengum, though she
had also taken the precaution of covering her distinctive cloak and
armor with an old black cape that she tossed into the ditch as she
joined me. She grinned, looking as happy as she had once looked before her marriage, then nodded toward the lumbering wagon. "Is that
my half-brother?"

"Yes. You've seen him before."

"Not often. Doesn't he look like his father!"

"He does," I said, "and you don't, for which I'm grateful." That
made her laugh. "Where did you get the mail?" I asked.

"Æthelred likes me to wear it," she said. "He had it made for me
in Frankia."

"Silver links?" I asked. "I could pierce those with a twig!"

"I don't think my husband wants me to fight," she said drily, "he
just wants to display me." And that, I thought, was understandable.
Æthelflæd had grown to be a lovely woman, at least when her
beauty was not clouded by unhappiness. She was clear-eyed and
clear-skinned, with full lips and golden hair. She was clever, like her
father, and a good deal cleverer than her husband, but she had been
married for one reason only, to bind the Mercian lands to Alfred's
Wessex, and in that sense, if in no other, the marriage had been a
success.

"Tell me about Aldhelm," I said.

"You already know about him," she retorted.

"I know he doesn't like me," I said happily.

"Who does?" she asked, grinning. She slowed her horse, that was
getting too close to the crawling wagon. She wore gloves of soft kid
leather over which six bright rings glittered with gold and rare stones.
"Aldhelm," she said softly, "advises my husband, and he has persuaded
Æthelred of two things. The first is that Mercia needs a king."

"Your father won't allow it," I said. Alfred preferred Mercia look to Wessex for its kingly authority.

"My father will not live forever," she said, "and Aldhelm has also persuaded my husband that a king needs an heir." She saw my grimace and laughed. "Not me! Ælfwynn was enough!" She shuddered. "I have never known such pain. Besides, my dear husband resents Wessex. He resents his dependency. He hates the hand that feeds him. No, he would like an heir from some nice Mercian girl."

"You mean . . ."

"He won't kill me," she interrupted blithely, "but he would love to divorce me."

"Your father would never allow that!"

"He would if I was taken in adultery," she said in a remarkably flat tone. I stared at her, not quite believing what she told me. She saw my incredulity and mocked it with a smile. "Well," she said, "you did ask me about Aldhelm."

"Æthelred wants you to . . ."

"Yes," she said, "then he can condemn me to a nunnery and forget I ever existed."

"And Aldhelm encourages this idea?"

"Oh, he does, he does." She smiled as if my question was silly. "Luckily I have West Saxon attendants who protect me, but after my father dies?" She shrugged.

"Have you told your father?"

"He's been told," she said, "but I don't think he believes it. He does, of course, believe in faith and prayer, so he sent me a comb that once belonged to Saint Milburga and he says it will strengthen me."

"Why doesn't he believe you?"

"He thinks I am prone to bad dreams. He also finds Æthelred very loyal. And my mother, of course, adores Æthelred."

"She would," I said gloomily. Alfred's wife, Ælswith, was a sour creature and, like Æthelred, a Mercian. "You could try poison," I suggested. "I know a woman in Lundene who brews some vicious potions."

"Uhtred!" she chided me, but before she could say more, one of

62

Finan's men came galloping from the rearguard, his horse throwing up clods of earth torn from the meadow beside the road.

"Lord!" he shouted, "time to hurry!"

"Osferth!" I called, and our pretend king happily jumped from his father's wagon and hauled himself into the saddle of a horse. He threw the bronze circlet back into the wagon and pulled on a helmet.

"Dump it," I shouted to the wagon's driver. "Take it into the ditch!"

He managed to get two wheels in the ditch and we left the heavy vehicle there, canted over, the frightened horses still in their harness. Finan and our rearguard came pounding up the road and we spurred ahead of them into a stretch of woodland where I waited until Finan caught up, and just as he did so the first of the pursuing Danes came into sight. They were pushing their horses hard, but I reckoned the abandoned wagon with its tawdry treasures would delay them a few moments and, sure enough, the leading pursuers milled about the vehicle as we turned away.

"It's a horse race," Finan told me.

"And our horses are faster," I said, which was probably true. The Danes were mounted on whatever animals their raiding parties had succeeded in capturing, while we were riding some of Wessex's best stallions. I snatched a last glance as dismounted enemies swarmed over the wagon, then plunged deeper into the trees. "How many of them are there?" I shouted at Finan.

"Hundreds," he called back, grinning. Which meant, I guessed, that any man in Harald's army who could saddle a horse had joined the pursuit. Harald was feeling the ecstasy of victory. His men had plundered all eastern Wessex, now he believed he had turned Alfred's army out of Æscengum, which effectively opened the way for the Danes to maraud the whole center of the country. Before those pleasures, however, he wanted to capture Alfred himself and so his men were wildly following us, and Harald, unconcerned about their lack of discipline, believed his good fortune must hold. This was the wild hunt, and Harald had loosed his men and sent them to deliver him the King of Wessex.

We led them, we enticed them, and we tempted them. We did not ride as fast as we might; instead we kept the pursuing Danes in sight and only once did they catch us. Rypere, one of my valued men, was riding wide to our right and his horse thrust a hoof into a molehill. He was thirty paces away, but I heard the crack of breaking bone and saw Rypere tumbling and the horse flailing as it collapsed in screaming pain. I turned Smoka toward him and saw a small group of Danes coming fast. I shouted at another of my men, "Spear!"

I grabbed his heavy ash-shafted spear and headed straight toward the leading Danes who were spurring to kill Rypere. Finan had turned with me, as had a dozen others, and the Danes, seeing us, tried to swerve away, but Smoka was pounding the earth now, nostrils wide, and I lowered the spear and caught the nearest Dane in the side of his chest. The ash shaft jarred back, my gloved hand slid along the wood, but the spear-point pierced deep and blood was welling and spilling in the spaces between the links of the Dane's mail coat. I let the spear go. The dying man stayed in his saddle as a second Dane flailed at me with a sword, but I threw the stroke off with my shield and turned Smoka by the pressure of my knees as Finan ripped his long blade across another man's face. I snatched the reins from the man I had speared and dragged his horse to Rypere. "Throw the bastard off and get up," I called.

The surviving Danes had retreated. There had been fewer than a dozen and they were the forerunners, the men on the fastest horses, and it took time for reinforcements to reach them and by then we had spurred safely away. Rypere's legs were too short to reach his new stirrups, and he was cursing as he clung to the saddle's pommel. Finan was smiling. "That'll annoy them, lord," he said.

"I want them mad," I said.

I wanted them to be impetuous, careless, and confident. Already, on that summer's day, as we followed the road alongside a meandering stream where crowsfoot grew thick, Harald was doing all I could ask. And was I confident? It is a dangerous thing to assume that your enemy will do what you want, but on that Thor's Day I had a growing conviction that Harald was falling into a carefully laid trap.

Our road led to the ford where we could cross the river to reach Fearnhamme. If we had truly been fleeing to Wintanceaster we would have stayed south of the river and taken the Roman road which led west, and I wanted the Danes to believe that was our intention. So, when we reached the river, we stopped just south of the ford. I wanted our pursuers to see us, I wanted them to think we were indecisive, I wanted them, eventually, to think we panicked.

The land was open, a stretch of river meadow where folk grazed their goats and sheep. To the east, where the Danes were coming, was woodland, to the west was the road Harald would expect us to take, and to the north were the crumbling stone piers of the bridge the Romans had made across the Wey. Fearnhamme and its low hill were on the ruined bridge's farther side. I stared at the hill and could see no troops.

"That's where I wanted Aldhelm," I snarled, pointing to the hill.

"Lord!" Finan shouted in warning.

The pursuing Danes were gathering at the edge of a wood a half-mile eastward. They could see us clearly, and they understood that we were too many to attack until more pursuers arrived, but those reinforcements were appearing by the minute. I looked across the river again and saw no one. The hill, with its ancient earthwork, was supposed to be my anvil strengthened with five hundred Mercian warriors, yet it looked deserted. Would my two hundred men be enough?

"Lord!" Finan called again. The Danes, who now outnumbered us by two to one, were spurring their horses toward us.

"Through the ford!" I shouted. I would spring the trap anyway, and so we kicked our tired horses through the deep ford which lay just upstream of the bridge and, once across, I called for my men to gallop to the hill's top. I wanted the appearance of panic. I wanted it to look as though we had abandoned our ambitions to reach Wintanceaster and instead were taking refuge on the nearest hill.

We rode through Fearnhamme. It was a huddle of thatched huts around a stone church, though there was one fine-looking Roman building that had lost its tiled roof. There were no inhabitants, just a single cow bellowing pathetically because she needed to be milked. I assumed the folk had fled from the rumors of the approaching Danes. "I hope your damned men are on the hill!" I shouted to Æthelflæd, who was staying close to me.

"They'll be there!" she called back.

She sounded confident, but I was dubious. Aldhelm's first duty, at least according to her husband, was to keep the Mercian army intact. Had he simply refused to advance on Fearnhamme? If he had, then I would be forced to fight off an army of Danes with just two hundred men, and those Danes were approaching fast. They smelled victory and they pounded their horses through the river and up into Fearnhamme's street. I could hear their shouts, and then I reached the grassy bank that was the ancient earthwork and, as Smoka crested the bank's summit, I saw that Æthelflæd was right. Aldhelm had come, and he had brought five hundred men. They were all there, but Aldhelm had kept them at the northern side of the old fortress so they would be hidden from an enemy approaching from the south.

And so, just as I had planned, I had seven hundred men on the hill, and another seven hundred, I hoped, approaching from Æscengum, and between those two forces were some two thousand rampaging, careless, overconfident Danes who believed they were about to achieve the old Viking dream of conquering Wessex.

"Shield wall!" I shouted at my men. "Shield wall!"

The Danes had to be checked for a moment, and the easiest way to do that was to show them a shield wall at the hill's top. There was a moment of chaos as men slid from their saddles and ran to the bank's top, but these were good men, well trained, and their shields locked together fast. The Danes, coming from the houses onto the hill's lower slope, saw the wall of iron-bound willow, they saw the spears, the swords and the ax blades, and they saw the steepness of the slope, and their wild charge stopped. Scores of men were crossing the river and still more were coming from the trees on the southern bank, so in a few moments they would have more than enough warriors to overwhelm my short shield wall, but for now they paused.

"Banners!" I said. We had brought our banners, my wolf's-head flag and Wessex's dragon, and I wanted them flown as an invitation to Harald's men.

Aldhelm, tall and sallow, had come to greet me. He did not like me and his face showed that dislike, but it also showed astonishment at the number of Danes who converged on the ford.

"Divide your men into two," I told him peremptorily, "and line them either side of my men. Rypere!"

"Lord?"

"Take a dozen men and tether those horses!" Our abandoned horses were wandering the hilltop and I feared some would stray back over the bank.

"How many Danes are there?" Aldhelm asked.

"Enough to give us a day's good killing," I said. "Now bring your men here."

He bridled at my tone. He was a thin man, elegant in a superb long coat of mail that had bronze crescent moons sewn to the links. He had a cloak of blue linen, lined with red cloth, and he wore a chain of heavy gold looped twice about his neck. His boots and gloves were black leather, his sword belt was decorated with golden crosses, while his long black hair, scented and oiled, was held at the nape of his neck with a comb of ivory teeth clasped in a golden frame. "I have my orders," he said distantly.

"Yes, to bring your men here. We have Danes to kill."

He had always disliked me, ever since I had spoiled his handsome looks by breaking his jaw and his nose, though on that far day he had been armed and I had not. He could barely bring himself to look at me, instead he stared at the Danes gathering at the foot of the hill. "I am instructed," he said, "to preserve the Lord Æthelred's forces."

"Your instructions have changed, Lord Aldhelm." A cheerful voice spoke from behind us, and Aldhelm turned to gaze in astonishment at Æthelflæd, who smiled from her high saddle.

"My lady," he said, bowing, then glancing from her to me. "Is the Lord Æthelred here?"

"My husband sent me to countermand his last orders,"

Æthelflæd said sweetly. "He is now so confident of victory that he requires you to stay here despite the numbers opposing us."

Aldhelm began to reply, then assumed I did not know what his last orders from Æthelred had been. "Your husband sent you, my lady?" he asked instead, plainly confused by Æthelflæd's unexpected presence.

"Why else would I be here?" Æthelflaed asked beguilingly, "and if there were any real danger, my lord, would my husband have allowed me to come?"

"No, my lady," Aldhelm said, but without any conviction.

"So we are going to fight!" Æthelflæd called those words loudly, speaking to the Mercian troops. She turned her gray mare so they could see her face and hear her more clearly. "We are going to kill Danes! And my husband sent me to witness your bravery, so do not disappoint me! Kill them all!"

They cheered her. She rode her horse along their front rank and they cheered her wildly. I had always thought Mercia a miserable place, defeated and sullen, kingless and downtrodden, but in that moment I saw how Æthelflæd, radiant in silver mail, was capable of lifting the Mercians to enthusiasm. They loved her. I knew they had small fondness for Æthelred, Alfred was a distant figure and, besides, King of Wessex, but Æthelflæd inspired them. She gave them pride.

The Danes were still gathering at the foot of the hill. There must have been three hundred men who had dismounted and who now made their own shield wall. They could still only see my two hundred men, but it was time to sweeten the bait. "Osferth," I shouted, "get back on your horse, then come and be kingly."

"Must I, lord?"

"Yes, you must!"

We made Osferth stand his horse beneath the banners. He was cloaked, and he now wore a helmet that I draped with my own gold chain so that, from a distance, it looked like a crowned helmet. The Danes, seeing him, bellowed insults up the gentle slope. Osferth looked kingly enough, though anyone familiar with Alfred should have known the mounted figure was not Wessex's king simply because he was not surrounded by priests, but I decided Harald would never notice the lack. I was amused to see Æthelflæd, obviously curious about her half-brother, push her horse next to his stallion.

I turned to look back to the south where still more Danes were crossing the river and, so long as I live, I will never forget that landscape. All the country beyond the river was covered with Danish horsemen, their stallions' hooves kicking up dust as the riders spurred toward the ford, all eager to be present at the destruction of Alfred and his kingdom. So many men wanted to cross the river that they were forced to wait in a great milling herd at the ford's farther side.

Aldhelm was ordering his men forward. He probably did it unwillingly, but Æthelflæd had inspired them and he was caught between her disdain and their enthusiasm. The Danes at the foot of the hill saw my short line lengthen, they saw more shields and more blades, more banners. They would still outnumber us, but now they would need half their army to make an assault on the hill. A man in a black cloak and carrying a red-hafted war ax was marshaling Harald's men, thrusting them into line. I guessed there were five hundred men in the enemy shield wall now, and more were coming every moment. Some of the Danes had stayed on horseback, and I supposed they planned to ride about our rear to make an attack when the shield walls met. The enemy line was only a couple of hundred paces away, close enough for me to see the ravens and axes and eagles and serpents painted on their iron-bossed shields. Some began clashing their weapons against those shields, making the thunder of war. Others bellowed that we were milksop children, or goat-begotten bastards.

"Noisy, aren't they?" Finan remarked beside me. I just smiled. He raised his drawn sword to his helmet-framed face and kissed the blade. "Remember that Frisian girl we found in the marshes? She was noisy." It is strange what men think of before battle. The Frisian girl had escaped a Danish slaver and had been terrified. I wondered what had happened to her.

Aldhelm was nervous, so nervous that he overcame his hatred of me and stood close. "What if Alfred doesn't come?" he asked.

"Then we each have to kill two Danes before the rest lose heart," I said with false confidence. If Alfred's seven hundred men did not come then we would be surrounded, cut down, and slaughtered.

Only about half the Danes had crossed the river, such was the congestion at the narrow ford, and still more horsemen were streaming from the east to join the crowd waiting to cross the Wey. Fearnhamme was filled with men pulling down thatch in search of treasure. The unmilked cow lay dead in the street. "What," Aldhelm began, then hesitated. "What if Alfred's forces come late?"

"Then all the Danes will be across the river," I said.

"And attacking us," Finan said.

I knew Aldhelm was thinking of retreat. Behind us, to the north, were higher hills that offered greater protection, or perhaps, if we retreated fast enough, we could cross the Temes before the Danes caught and destroyed us. For unless Alfred's men came we would surely die, and at that moment I felt the death-serpent slither cold about my heart that was thumping like a war drum. Skade's curse, I thought, and I suddenly understood the magnitude of the risk I was running. I had assumed the Danes would do exactly what I wanted, and that the West Saxon army would appear at just the right moment, but instead we were stranded on a low hill and our enemy was getting ever stronger. There was still a great crowd on the river's far bank, but in less than an hour the whole of Harald's army would be across the river, and I felt the imminence of disaster and the fear of utter defeat. I remembered Harald's threat, that he would blind me, geld me, and then lead me about on a rope's end. I touched the hammer and stroked Serpent-Breath's hilt.

"If the West Saxon troops don't arrive," Aldhelm began, his voice grim with purpose.

"God be praised," Æthelflæd interrupted from behind us.

Because there was a glint of sun-reflecting steel from the far distant trees.

And more horsemen appeared. Hundreds of horsemen.

The army of Wessex had come.

And the Danes were trapped.

Poets exaggerate. They live by words and my household bards fear I will stop throwing them silver if they do not exaggerate. I remember skirmishes where a dozen men might have died, but in the poets' telling the slain are counted in the thousands. I am forever feeding the ravens in their endless recitations, but no poet could exaggerate the slaughter that occurred that Thor's Day on the banks of the River Wey.

It was a swift slaughter too. Most battles take time to start as the two sides summon their courage, hurl insults, and watch to see what the enemy will do, but Steapa, leading Alfred's seven hundred men, saw the confusion on the river's southern bank and, just as soon as he had sufficient men in hand, charged on horseback. Æthelred, Steapa told me later, had wanted to wait till all seven hundred had gathered, but Steapa ignored the advice. He began with three hundred men and allowed the others to catch up as they emerged from the trees into the open land.

The three hundred attacked the enemy's rear where, as might be expected, the least enthusiastic of Harald's army were waiting to cross the river. They were the laggards, the servants and boys, some women and children, and almost all of them were cumbered with pillage. None was ready to fight; there was no shield wall, some did not even possess shields. The Danes most eager for a battle had already crossed the river and were forming to attack the hill, and it took them some moments to understand that a vicious slaughter had begun on the river's farther bank.

"It was like killing piglets," Steapa told me later. "A lot of squealing and blood."

The horsemen slammed into the Danes. Steapa led Alfred's own household troops, the remainder of my men, and battle-hardened warriors from Wiltunscir and Sumorsæte. They were eager for a fight, well mounted, armed with the best weapons, and their attack caused chaos. The Danes, unable to form a shield wall, tried to run, except the only safety lay across the ford and that was blocked by the men waiting to cross, and so the panicked enemy clawed at their own men, stopping any chance of a shield wall forming, and Steapa's men, huge on their horses, hacked and slashed and stabbed their way into the crowd. More Saxons came from the woods to join the fight. Horses were fetlock-deep in blood, and still the swords and axes crushed and cut. Alfred had endured the ride despite the pain the saddle caused him, and he watched from the edge of the trees while the priests and monks sang praises to their god for the slaughter of the heathen that was reddening the water-meadows on the Wey's southern bank.

Edward fought with Steapa. He was a slight young man, but Steapa was full of praise afterward. "He has courage," he told me.

"Does he have sword craft?"

"He has a quick wrist," Steapa said approvingly.

Æthelred understood before Steapa that eventually the horsemen must be stopped by the sheer crush of bodies, and he persuaded Ealdorman Æthelnoth of Sumorsæte to dismount a hundred of his men and form a shield wall. That wall advanced steadily and, as horses were wounded or killed, more Saxons joined that wall, which went forward like a row of harvesters wielding sickles. Hundreds of Danes died. On that southern bank, under the high sun, there was a massacre, and the enemy never once managed to organize themselves and so fight back. They died or else they crossed the river or else they were taken captive.

Yet perhaps half of Harald's army had crossed the ford, and those men were ready for a fight and, even as the slaughter began behind them, they came to kill us. Harald himself had arrived, a servant bringing a packhorse behind, and Harald came a few steps forward of his swelling shield wall to make certain we saw the ritual with which he scared his enemies. He faced us, huge in cloak and mail, then spread his arms as though crucified, and in his right hand was a massive battle ax with which, after bellowing that we would all be fed to the slime worms of death, he killed the horse. He did it with one stroke of the ax and, while the beast was still twitching in its death throes, he slit open its belly and plunged his unhelmeted head deep into the bloody entrails. My men watched in silence. Harald, ignoring the spasms of the hooves, held his head deep in the horse's belly, then stood and turned to show a blood-masked face and blood-soaked hair and a thick beard dripping with blood. Harald Bloodhair was ready for battle. "Thor!" he shouted, lifting his face and ax to the sky, "Thor!" He pointed the ax toward us. "Now we kill you all!" he screamed. A servant brought him his great ax-painted shield.

I am not certain Harald knew what happened on the river's farther bank, that was hidden from him by the houses in Fearnhamme. He must have known that Saxons were attacking his rear, indeed he would have heard reports of fighting all morning because, as Steapa was to tell me, the pursuing Saxons were forever meeting Danish stragglers on the road from Æscengum, but Harald's attention was fixed on Fearnhamme's hill where, he believed, Alfred was trapped. He could lose the battle on the river's southern bank and still win a kingdom on the northern bank. And so he led his men forward.

I had planned to let the Danes attack us, and to rely on the ancient earthwork to give us added protection, but as Harald's line advanced with a great bellow of rage, I saw they were vulnerable. Harald might have been unaware of the disaster his men were suffering across the river, but many of his Danes were turning, trying to see what happened there, and men scared of an attack on their rear will not fight with full vigor. We had to attack them. I sheathed Serpent-Breath and drew Wasp-Sting, my short-sword. "Swine head!" I shouted, "swine head!"

My men knew what I wanted. They had rehearsed it hundreds of times until they were tired of practicing it, but now those hours of practice paid off as I led the way off the earthen bank and crossed the ditch.

A swine head was simply a wedge of men, a human spear-point, and it was the fastest way I knew to break a shield wall. I took the lead, though Finan tried to edge me aside. The Danes had slowed, perhaps surprised that we were abandoning the earthwork, or perhaps because at last they understood the trap that closed on them. There was only one way out of that trap, and that was to destroy us. Harald knew it and bellowed at his men to charge uphill. I was shouting at my men to charge downhill. That fight started so fast. I was taking the swine head down the shallow slope and he was urging his men up, but the Danes were confused, suddenly frightened, and his wall frayed before we even reached it. Some men obeyed Harald, others hung back, and so the line bent, though at the center, where Harald's banner of the wolf-skull and the ax flew, the shield wall remained firm. That was where Harald's own crewmen were concentrated, and where my swine head was aimed.

We were screaming a great shout of defiance. My shield, iron-rimmed, was heavy on my left arm, Wasp-Sting was drawn back. She was a short stabbing blade. Serpent-Breath was my magnificent sword, but a long sword, like a long-hafted ax, can be a hindrance in a battle of shield walls. I knew when we clashed, that I would be pressed close as a lover to my enemies and in that crush a short blade could be lethal.

I aimed for Harald himself. He wore no helmet, relying on the sun-glistening blood to terrify his enemies, and he was terrifying; a big man, snarling, eyes wild, ropy hair dripping red, his shield painted with an ax blade and a short-hafted, heavy-bladed war ax as his chosen weapon. He was shouting like a fiend, his eyes fixed on me, his mouth a snarl in a mask of blood. I remember thinking as we charged downhill that he would use the ax to chop down at me, which would make me raise my shield, and his neighbor, a dark-faced man with a short stabbing sword, would slide the blade beneath my shield to gut my belly. But Finan was on my right and that meant the dark-faced man was doomed. "Kill them all!" I shouted Æthelflæd's war cry, "Kill them all!" I did not even turn to see if Aldhelm had brought his men forward, though he had. I just felt the fear of the shield wall fight and the elation of the shield wall fight. "Kill them all!" I screamed.

And the shields crashed together.

The poets say six thousand Danes came to Fearnhamme, and

sometimes they reckon it was ten thousand and, doubtless, as the story gets older the number will become higher. In truth I think Harald brought around sixteen hundred men, because some of his army stayed close to Æscengum. He led many more men than those who were at Æscengum and Fearnhamme. He had crossed from Frankia with some two hundred ships, and maybe five or six thousand men came in all those ships, but fewer than half had found horses, and not all those mounted men rode to Fearnhamme. Some stayed in Cent where they laid claim to captured land, others stayed to plunder Godelmingum, so how many men did we face? Perhaps half of Harald's force had crossed the river, so my troops and Aldhelm's warriors were attacking no more than eight hundred, and some of those were not even in the shield wall, but were still seeking plunder in Fearnhamme's houses. The poets tell me we were outnumbered, but I think we probably had more men.

And we were more disciplined. And we had the advantage of the higher ground. And we hit the shield wall.

I struck with my shield. To make the swine head work the thrust must be hard and fast. I remember shouting Æthelflæd's war cry, "Kill them all!" then leaping the last pace, all my weight concentrated into my left arm with its heavy shield, and it slammed into Harald's shield and he was thrown back as I rammed Wasp-Sting beneath the lower rim of my round shield. The blade struck and pierced. That moment is vague, a confusion. I know Harald swung down with his ax because the blade mangled the mail on my back, though without touching my skin. My sudden leap must have carried me inside the swing. I later found my left shoulder was bruised a deep black, and I guess that was where his ax's haft struck, but I was unaware of the pain during the fight.

I call it a fight, but it was soon over. I do remember Wasp-Sting piercing and I felt the sensation of the blade in flesh, and I knew I had wounded Harald, but then he twisted away to my left, thrust aside by the weight and speed of our attack, and Wasp-Sting was wrenched free. Finan, on my right, covered me with his shield as I slammed into the second rank and I lunged Wasp-Sting again, and still I was moving forward. I slammed the shield's iron boss at a Dane and saw Rypere's spear take him in the eye. There was blood in the air, screaming, and a sword lunged from my right, going between the shield and my body, and I just kept going forward as Finan sliced his short-sword at the man's arm. The sword fell feebly away. I was moving slowly now, pushing against a crush of men and being pushed by my men behind. I was stabbing Wasp-Sting in short hard lunges, and in my memory that passage of the battle was quite silent. It cannot have been silent, of course, but so it seems when I remember Fearnhamme. I see men's mouths open, full of rotting teeth. I see grimaces. I see the flash of blades. I recall crouching as I shoved forward, I remember the ax swing that came from my left, and how Rypere caught it on his shield, which split open. I remember tripping on the corpse of the horse Harald had sacrificed to Thor, but I was pushed upright by a Dane who tried to gut me with a short blade that was stopped by the gold buckle of my sword belt, and I remember ripping Wasp-Sting up between his legs and sawing her backward and watching his eyes open in terrible pain, and then he was suddenly gone and, just as suddenly, so very suddenly, there were no shields in front of me, just a vegetable plot and a dungheap and a cottage with its mauled thatch heaped on the ground, and I remember all that, but I do not remember any noise.

Æthelflæd told me later that our swine head had gone straight through Harald's line. It must have seemed that way as she watched from the hilltop, though to me it had seemed slow and hard work, but we did get through, we split Harald's shield wall and now the real slaughter could begin.

The Danish shield wall was shattered. Now, instead of neighbor helping neighbor, each man was on his own, and our men, West Saxon and Mercian alike, were still ranked shield to shield and they slashed and cut and stabbed at frantic enemies. The panic spread fast, like fire in dry stubble, and the Danes fled and my only regret was that our horses were still on the hilltop, guarded by boys, or else we could have pursued and cut them down from behind.

Not all the Danes ran. Some horsemen who had been readying to circle the hill and attack us from behind charged our shield wall, but horses are reluctant to slam home into a well-made wall. The Danes rammed spears at shields and forced our line to bend, and more Danes came to help the horsemen. My swine head was no longer wedge-shaped, but my men were still staying together and I led them toward the sudden fury. A horse reared at me, hooves flailing, and I let my shield take the thumping blows. The stallion snapped its teeth at me and the rider hacked down with a sword that was stopped by the shield's iron rim. My men were encircling the attackers, who realized their danger and pulled away, and it was then I saw why they had attacked in the first place. They had come to rescue Harald. Two of my men had captured Harald's standard, the red-colored wolf-skull still fixed to its ax-banner staff, but Harald himself lay in blood among pea-plants. I shouted that we should capture him, but the horse was in my way and the rider was still slashing wildly with the sword. I rammed Wasp-Sting into the beast's belly and saw Harald being dragged backward by his ankles. A huge Dane threw Harald over a saddle and other men led the horse away. I tried to reach him, but Wasp-Sting was embedded in the shuddering horse and the rider was still ineptly trying to kill me, so I let go of the short-sword's hilt, grabbed his wrist, and hauled. I heard a shriek as the rider toppled from the saddle. "Kill him," I snarled at the man beside me, then pulled Wasp-Sting free, but it was too late, the Danes had managed to rescue the wounded Harald.

I sheathed Wasp-Sting and drew Serpent-Breath. There would be no more shield wall fighting this day, because now we would hunt the Danes through Fearnhamme's alleys and beyond. Most of Harald's men fled eastward, but not all. Our two attacks had pinched Harald's horde, splitting it, and some had to run westward, deeper into Wessex. The first Saxon horsemen were crossing the river now and they pursued the fugitives. The Danes that survived that pursuit would be hunted by peasants. The men who went eastward, the ones who carried their fallen leader, were more numerous and they checked to rally a half-mile away, though as soon as West Saxon horsemen appeared those Danes went on retreating. And still there were Danes in Fearnhamme, men who had taken refuge in the houses where we hunted them like rats. They shouted for mercy, but we showed none because we were still under the thrall of Æthelflæd's savage wish.

I killed a man on a dungheap, hacking him down with Serpent-Breath and slicing his throat with her point. Finan chased two into a house and I hurried after him, but both were dead when I crashed through the door. Finan tossed me a golden arm ring, then we both went into the sunlit chaos. Horsemen cantered up the street, looking for victims. I heard shouting from behind a hovel and Finan and I ran there to see a huge Dane, bright with silver and gold rings and with a golden chain about his neck, fighting off three Mercians. He was a shipmaster, I guessed, a man who had brought his crews to Harald's service in hope of finding West Saxon lands, but instead he was finding a West Saxon grave. He was good and fast, his sword and his battered shield holding off his attackers, and then he saw me and recognized the wealth in my war-gear and, at the same moment, the three Mercians stepped back as if to give me the privilege of killing the big man. "Hold your sword tight," I told him.

He nodded. He glanced at the hammer hanging at my neck. He was sweating, but not with fear. It was a warm day and we were all in leather and mail.

"Wait for me in the feast hall," I said.

"My name is Othar."

"Uhtred."

"Othar the Storm-Rider," he said.

"I have heard that name," I said politely, though I had not. Othar wanted me to know so that I could tell men that Othar the Storm-Rider had died well, and I had told him to keep a tight hold of his sword so that Othar the Storm-Rider would go to the feast hall in Valhalla where all warriors who die bravely go after death. These days, although I am old and feeble, I always wear a sword, so that when death comes I will go to that far hall where men like Othar wait for me. I look forward to meeting them.

"The sword," he said, lifting the weapon, "is called Brightfire." He kissed the blade. "She has served me well." He paused. "Uhtred of Bebbanburg?"

"Yes."

"I met Ælfric the Generous," Othar said.

It took me a heartbeat or two to realize he meant my uncle who had usurped my inheritance in Northumbria. "The generous?" I asked.

"How else does he keep his lands?" Othar asked in return, "except by paying Danes to stay away?"

"I hope to kill him too," I said.

"He has many warriors," Othar said, and with that he thrust Brightfire fast, hoping to surprise me, hoping that he could go to Valhalla with my death as a boast, but I was as quick as him and Serpent-Breath sliced the lunge aside and I hammered my shield boss into him, pushing him back, and brought my sword round fast and realized he was not even trying to parry as Serpent-Breath slid across his throat.

I took Brightfire from his dead hand. I had cut his throat to keep his mail from further damage. Mail is expensive, a trophy as valuable as the rings on Othar's arms.

Fearnhamme was filled with the dead and with the triumphant living. Almost the only Danes to survive were those who had taken refuge in the church, and they only lived because Alfred had crossed the river and insisted that the church was a refuge. He sat in the saddle, his face tight with pain, and the priests surrounded him as the Danes were led out of the church. Æthelred was there, his sword bloody. Aldhelm was grinning. We had won a famous victory, a great victory, and news of the slaughter would spread wherever the northmen took their boats, and shipmasters would know that going to Wessex was a short route to the grave. "Praise God," Alfred greeted me.

My mail was sheeted with blood. I knew I was grinning like Aldhelm. Father Beocca was almost crying with joy. Æthelflæd appeared then, still on horseback, and two of her Mercians were leading a prisoner. "She was trying to kill you, Lord Uhtred!" Æthelflæd said happily, and I realized the prisoner was the rider whose horse I had stabbed with Wasp-Sting.

It was Skade.

Æthelred was staring at his wife, no doubt wondering what she did in Fearnhamme dressed in mail, but he had no time to ask because Skade began howling. It was a terrible shrieking like the screams of a woman being eaten by the death-worm, and she tore at her hair and fell to the ground and started writhing. "I curse you all," she wailed. She grabbed handfuls of earth and rubbed them into her black hair, crammed them into her mouth, and all the time she writhed and screeched. One of her guards was carrying the mail coat she had been wearing in battle, leaving her in a linen shift that she suddenly ripped open to expose her breasts. She smeared earth on her breasts and I had to smile as Edward, beside his father, stared wide-eyed at Skade's nakedness. Alfred looked even more pained.

"Silence her," he ordered.

One of the Mercian guards cracked a spear pole across her skull and Skade fell sideways onto the street. There was blood mixed with the soil in her raven hair now, and I thought she was unconscious, but then she spat out the soil and looked up at me. "Cursed," she snarled.

And one of the spinners took my thread. I like to think she hesitated, but maybe she did not. Maybe she smiled. But whether she hesitated or not, she thrust her bone needle sideways into the darker weave.

Wyrd bið ful āræd.

FIVE

Sharp blades thrusting, spear-blades killing
As Æthelred, Lord of Slaughter, slaughtered thousands,
Swelling the river with blood, sword-fed river,
And Aldhelm, noble warrior, followed his lord
Into the battle, hard-fought, felling foemen

And so the poem goes on for many, many, many more lines. I have
the parchment in front of me, though I shall burn it in a moment.
My name is not mentioned, of course, and that is why I shall burn it.
Men die, women die, cattle die, but reputation lives on like the echo
of a song. Yet why should men sing of Æthelred? He fought well
enough that day, but Fearnhamme was not his battle, it was mine.

I should pay my own poets to write down their songs, but they
prefer lying in the sun and drinking my ale and, to be frank, poets
bore me. I endure them for the sake of the guests in my hall who
expect to hear the harp and the boasts. Curiosity drove me to buy
this about-to-be-burned parchment from a monk who sells such
things to noble halls. He had come from the lands that were Mercia, of course, and it is natural that Mercian poets should extol
their country or else no one would ever hear of it, and so they
write their lies, but even they cannot compete with the churchmen. The annals of our time are all written by monks and priests,
and a man might have run away from a hundred battles and
never once have killed a Dane, but so long as he gives money to
the church he will be written down as a hero.

The battle at Fearnhamme was won by two things. The first was that Steapa brought Alfred's men to the field just when they were needed and, looking back, that could so easily have gone wrong. The Ætheling Edward, of course, was notionally in charge of that half of the army, and both he and Æthelred possessed far more authority than Steapa, indeed they both insisted he gave the command to leave Æscengum too soon and countermanded his order, but Alfred overruled them. Alfred was too sick to command the army himself, but, like me, he had learned to trust Steapa's brute instinct. And so the horsemen arrived at the rear of Harald's army when it was disorganized and when half still waited to cross the river.

The second reason for success was the speed with which my swine head shattered Harald's shield wall. Such attacks did not always work, but we had the advantage of the slope, and the Danes, I think, were already dispirited by the slaughter beyond the ford. And so we won.

> The Lord God granted victory, blessings to Æthelred,
> Who, beside the river, broke the hedge of shields.
> And Edward was there, noble Edward, Alfred's son.
> Who, shielded by angels, watched as Æthelred
> Cut down the northmen's leader . . .

Burning is too good for it. Maybe I shall tear it to squares and leave it in the latrine.

We were too tired to organize a proper pursuit, and our men were dazed by the speed of their triumph. They had also found ale, mead, and Frankish wine in the Danes' saddlebags and many became drunk as they wandered the butcher's shop they had made. Some men began heaving Danish corpses into the river, but there were so many that the bodies jammed against the Roman bridge piers to make a dam that flooded the ford's banks. Mail coats were being heaped and captured weapons piled. The few prisoners were under guard in a barn, their sobbing women and children gathered outside, while Skade had been placed in an empty granary where two of my men now guarded her. Alfred, naturally, went to the church to give thanks to his god, and all the priests and monks went with him. Bishop Asser paused before going to his prayers. He stared at the dead and at the plunder, then turned his cold eyes on me. He just gazed at me, as if I were one of those two-headed calves that are shown at fairs, then he looked puzzled and gestured that Edward should go with him to the church.

Edward hesitated. He was a shy young man, but it was plain he felt he should say something to me and had no idea what words to use. I spoke instead. "I congratulate you, lord," I said.

He frowned and for a moment looked as puzzled as Asser, then he twitched and straightened. "I'm not a fool, Lord Uhtred."

"I never thought so," I said.

"You must teach me," he said.

"Teach you?"

He waved at the carnage and, for a heartbeat, looked horrified. "How you do this," he blurted out.

"You think like your enemy, lord," I said, "and then you think harder." I would have said more, but just then I saw Cerdic in an alley between two cottages. I half turned, then was distracted by Bishop Asser sternly calling Edward away, and when I looked back there was no Cerdic. Nor could there have been, I told myself. I had left Cerdic in Lundene to guard Gisela, and I decided it was just one of the tricks that tired thoughts can play.

"Here, lord." Sihtric, who had been my servant, but was now one of my household warriors, dumped a heavy coat of mail at my feet. "It's got gold links, lord," he said excitedly.

"You keep it," I said.

"Lord?" He stared up at me with astonishment.

"Your wife has expensive tastes, doesn't she?" I asked. Sihtric had married a whore, Ealhswith, much against my advice and without my permission, but I had forgiven him and then been surprised that the marriage was happy. They had two children now, both sturdy little boys. "Take it away," I said.

"Thank you, lord." Sihtric scooped up the mail coat.

Time slows.

It is strange how I have forgotten some things. I cannot truly remember the moment when I led the swine head into Harald's line. Was I looking into his face? Do I truly remember the horse's fresh blood flicking from his beard as his head turned? Or was I looking at the man to his left whose shield half protected Harald? I forget so much, but not that moment as Sihtric picked up the mail coat. I saw a man leading a dozen captured horses across the flooded ford. Two other men were tugging bodies free of the corpse-dam at the ruined bridge. One of the men had red curly hair and the other was doubled over in laughter at some jest. Three other men were tossing corpses into the river, adding to the blockage of bodies faster than the pair could relieve it. A thin dog was scratching itself on the street where Osferth, Alfred's bastard, was talking to the Lady Æthelflæd, and I was surprised that she was not in the church with her father, brother, and husband, and surprised that she and her half-brother appeared to have struck up a friendly relationship so soon. I remember Oswi, my new servant lad, leading Smoka into the street and pausing to talk to a woman, and I realized that Fearnhamme's townsfolk were returning already. I supposed they must have hidden in the nearby woods as soon as they saw armed men across the river. Another woman, wearing a dull yellow cloak, was using a paring knife to cut a ring-circled finger from a dead Dane's hand. I remember a raven, circling blue-black in the blood-smelling sky, and I felt a sharp elation as I stared at the bird. Was that one of Odin's two ravens? Would the gods themselves hear of this carnage? I laughed aloud, the sound incongruous because in my memory there was just silence at that moment.

Till Æthelflæd spoke. "Lord?" She had come close and was staring at me. "Uhtred?" she said gently. Finan was a couple of paces behind her, and with him was Cerdic, and that was when I knew. I knew, but I said nothing, and Æthelflæd walked to me and laid a hand on my arm. "Uhtred?" she said again. I think I just stared into her face. Her blue eyes were bright with tears. "Childbirth," she said gently.

"No," I said, quite quietly, "no."

"Yes," she said simply. Finan was looking at me, pain on his face.

"No," I said louder.

"Mother and child," Æthelflæd said very softly.

I closed my eyes. My world went dark, had gone dark, for my Gisela was dead.

Wyn eal gedreas. That is from another poem I sometimes hear chanted in my hall. It is a sad poem, and thus a true poem. Wyrd bið ful āræd, it says. Fate is inexorable. And wyn eal gedreas. All the joy has died.

All my joy had died and I had gone into the dark. Finan said I howled like a wolf, and perhaps I did, though I do not remember that. Grief must be hidden. The man who first chanted that fate is inexorable went on to say that we must bind our inmost thoughts in chains. A saddened mind does no good, he said, and its thoughts must be hidden, and maybe I did howl, but then I shook off Æthelflæd's hand and snarled at the men heaving corpses into the river, ordering that two of them should help the men trying to clear the bodies from between the ruined bridge piers. "Make sure all our horses are down from the hilltop," I told Finan.

I did not think of Skade at that moment, or else I might have let Serpent-Breath take her rotten soul. It was her curse, I realized later, that killed Gisela, because she had died on the same morning that Harald had forced me to free Skade. Cerdic had ridden to tell me, his heart heavy as he took his horse through Dane-infested country to Æscengum, only to find us gone.

Alfred, when he heard, came to me, took my arm and walked down Fearnhamme's street. He was limping and men stepped aside to give us room. He gripped my elbow, and seemed about to speak a dozen times, yet the words always died on his lips. Finally he checked me and looked into my eyes. "I have no answer why God inflicts such grief," he said, and I said nothing. "Your wife was a jewel," Alfred went on. He frowned, and his next words were as generous as they were difficult for him to say. "I pray your gods give you comfort, Lord Uhtred." He led me to the Roman house which had been sequestered as the royal hall, and there Æthelred looked uncomfortable, while Father Beocca, dear man, embarrassed me by clinging to my sword hand and praying aloud that his god should treat me with mercy. He was crying. Gisela might have been a pagan, but Beocca had loved her. Bishop Asser, who hated me, nevertheless spoke gentle words, while Brother Godwin, the blind monk who eavesdropped on God, made a plangent moaning sound until Asser led him away. Finan, later that day, brought me a jar of mead and sang his sad Irish songs until I was too drunk to care. He alone saw me weep that day, and he told no one.

"We're ordered back to Lundene," Finan told me next morning. I just nodded, too oblivious of the world to care what my orders were. "The king returns to Wintanceaster," Finan went on, "and the Lords Æthelred and Edward are to pursue Harald."

Harald, badly wounded, had been taken by the remnants of his army north across the Temes until, in too much agony to continue, he ordered them to find refuge, which they did on a thorn-covered island called, naturally enough, Torneie. The island was in the River Colaun, not far from where it joins the Temes, and Harald's men fortified Torneie, first making a great palisade with the plentiful thorn bushes, then throwing up earthworks. Lord Æthelred and the Ætheling Edward caught up with them there and laid siege. Alfred's household troops, under Steapa, swept eastward through Cent, driving out the last of Harald's men and recovering vast quantities of plunder. Fearnhamme was a magnificent victory, leaving Harald stranded on a fever-infested island, while the remainder of his men fled to their boats and abandoned Wessex, though many of the crews joined Haesten, who was still camped on Cent's northern shore.

And I was in Lundene. Tears still come to my eyes when I remember greeting Stiorra, my daughter, my little motherless daughter who clung to me and would not let go. And she was crying and I was crying, and I held her as though she was the only thing that could ever keep me alive. Osbert, the youngest, wept and clung to his nurse, while Uhtred, my eldest son, might have wept for all I know, but never in front of me, and that was not an admirable reticence, but rather because he feared me. He was a nervous, fussy child and I found him irritating. I insisted he learned sword craft, but he had no skill with a blade, and when I took him downriver in *Seolferwulf*, he showed no enthusiasm for ships or the sea.

He was with me aboard *Seolferwulf* on the day that I next saw Haesten. We had left Lundene in the dark, feeling our way downriver on the tide and beneath a paling moon. Alfred had passed a law, he loved making laws, which said that the sons of ealdormen and thegns must go to school, but I refused to allow Uhtred the Younger to attend the school which Bishop Erkenwald had established in Lundene. I did not care whether he learned to read and write, both skills are much overrated, but I did care that he should not be exposed to the bishop's preaching. Erkenwald tried to insist I send the boy, but I argued that Lundene was really part of Mercia, which in those days it was, and that Alfred's laws did not apply. The bishop glowered at me, but was helpless to force the boy's attendance. I preferred to train my son as a warrior and, that day on the *Seolferwulf*, I had dressed him in a leather coat and given him a boy's sword belt so he would become accustomed to wearing war-gear, but instead of showing pride he just looked abashed. "Put your shoulders back," I snarled, "stand straight. You're not a puppy!"

"Yes, Father," he whined. He was slouch-shouldered, just staring at the deck.

"When I die you'll be Lord of Bebbanburg," I said, and he said nothing.

"You must show him Bebbanburg, lord," Finan suggested.

"Maybe I will," I said.

"Take the ship north," Finan said enthusiastically, "a proper sea voyage!" He slapped my son's shoulder. "You'll like that, Uhtred! Maybe we'll see a whale!"

My son just stared at Finan and said nothing. "Bebbanburg is a fortress beside the sea," I told my son, "a great fortress. Windswept, sea-washed, invincible." And I felt the prick of tears, for I had so often dreamed of making Gisela the Lady of Bebbanburg.

"Not invincible, lord," Finan said, "because we'll take it."

"We will," I said, though I could feel no enthusiasm, not even for the prospect of storming my own stronghold and slaughtering my uncle and his men. I turned from my pale son and stood in the ship's prow, beneath the wolf's head, and gazed east to where the sun was rising, and there, in the haze beneath the rising sun, in the mist of sea and air, in the shimmer of light above the slow-swelling sea, I saw the ships. A fleet. "Slow!" I called.

Our oar-banks rose and fell gently, so it was mostly the ebbing tide that swept us toward that fleet, which rowed northward across our path. "Back oars!" I called, and we slowed, stopped, and slewed broadside to the current. "That must be Haesten," Finan said. He had come to stand beside me.

"He's leaving Wessex," I said. I was certain it was Haesten, and so it was, for a moment later a single ship turned from the fleet and I saw the flash of its oar-blades as the rowers pulled hard toward us. Beyond it the other ships went on northward and there were many more than the eighty that Haesten had brought to Cent, because his fleet had been swollen by the fugitives from Harald's army. The approaching ship was close now. "That's *Dragon-Voyager*," I said, recognizing the ship, the same one we had given to Haesten on the day he took Alfred's treasure and gave us the valueless hostages.

"Shields?" Finan asked.

"No," I said. If Haesten wanted to attack me he would have brought more than one ship, and so our shields stayed in *Seolferwulf*'s bilge.

Dragon-Voyager backed her oars a ship's half-length away. She lay close, heaving on the water's slow swell, and for a moment her crew stared at my crew, and then I saw Haesten climbing up to the steering platform. He waved. "Can I come aboard?" he shouted.

"You can come aboard," I called back, and watched as his aftermost oarsmen expertly turned *Dragon-Voyager* so her stern came close to ours. The long oars were shipped as the two vessels closed, then Haesten leaped. Another man was waving to me from *Dragon-Voyager*'s steering platform, and I saw it was Father Willibald. I waved back, then worked my way aft to greet Haesten.

He was bareheaded. He spread his hands as I approached, a gesture that spoke of helplessness, and he seemed to have difficulty speaking, but he finally found his voice. "I am sorry, lord," he said, and his tone was humble, convincing. "There are no words, Lord Uhtred," he said.

"She was a good woman," I said.

"Famously," he said, "and I do feel sorrow, lord."

"Thank you."

He glanced at my oarsmen, doubtless casting an eye on their weaponry, then looked back to me. "That sad news, lord," he said, "shadowed the reports of your victory. It was a great triumph, lord."

"It seems to have persuaded you to leave Wessex," I said drily.

"I always intended to leave, lord," he said, "once we had our agreement, but some of our ships needed repair." He noticed Uhtred then, and saw the silver plates sewn onto the boy's sword belt. "Your son, lord?" he asked.

"My son," I said, "Uhtred."

"An impressive boy," Haesten lied.

"Uhtred," I called, "come here!"

He approached nervously, his eyes darting left and right as if expecting an attack. He was about as impressive as a duckling. "This is the Jarl Haesten," I told him, "a Dane. One day I'll kill him, or he'll kill me." Haesten chuckled, but my son just looked at the deck. "If he kills me," I went on, "your duty is to kill him."

Haesten waited for some response from Uhtred the Younger, but the boy just looked embarrassed. Haesten grinned wickedly. "And my own son, Lord Uhtred?" he asked innocently, "he thrives, I trust, as a hostage?"

"I drowned the little bastard a month ago," I said.

Haesten laughed at the lie. "There was no need for hostages anyway," he said, "as I shall keep our agreement. Father Willibald will confirm that." He gestured toward *Dragon-Voyager*. "I was going to send Father Willibald to Lundene," he went on, "with a letter. You might take him there yourself, lord?"

"Just Father Willibald?" I asked. "Didn't I bring you two priests?"

"The other one died," Haesten said carelessly, "after eating too many eels. You'll take Willibald?"

"Of course," I said and glanced at the fleet that still rowed northward. "Where do you go?"

"North," Haesten said airily, "East Anglia. Somewhere. Not Wessex."

He did not want to tell me his destination, but it was plain that his ships were heading toward Beamfleot. We had fought there five years before and Haesten might have had bad memories of the place, yet Beamfleot, on the northern bank of the Temes estuary, offered two priceless assets. First was the creek called Hothlege, tucked behind the island of Caninga, and that creek could shelter three hundred ships, while above it, rearing high on a green hill, was the old fort. It was a place of great safety, much safer than the encampment Haesten had made on the shore of Cent, but he had only made that to entice Alfred to pay him to leave. Now he was leaving, but going to a place far more dangerous to Wessex. In Beamfleot he would have an almost unassailable fortress, yet still be within easy striking distance of Lundene and Wessex. He was a serpent.

That was not Father Willibald's opinion. We had to bring the two ships within touching distance so the priest could clamber from one to the other. He sprawled clumsily onto *Seolferwulf*'s deck, then bade a friendly farewell to Haesten, who gave me a parting grin before leaping back aboard his own ship.

Father Willibald looked at me with confusion. One moment his face was all concern, the next it was excitement, both expressions accompanied by an impatient fidgeting as he tried to find words for one mood or the other. Concern won. "Lord," he said, "tell me, tell me it isn't true."

"It's true, father."

"Dear God!" he shook his head and made the sign of the cross. "I shall pray for her soul, lord. I shall pray for her soul nightly, lord, and for the souls of your dear children." His voice trailed away under my baleful gaze, but then his excitement got the better of him. "Such news, lord," he said, "such news I have!" Then, despairing of my expression, he turned to pick up his pathetic sack of belongings that had been tossed from the *Dragon-Voyager*.

"What news?" I asked.

"The Jarl Haesten, lord," Willibald said eagerly. "He's requesting that his wife and two sons be baptized, lord!" He smiled as if expecting me to share his joy.

"He's what?" I asked in surprise.

"He seeks baptism for his family! I wrote the letter for him, addressed to our king! It seems our preaching bore fruit, lord. The jarl's wife, God bless her soul, has seen the light! She seeks our Lord's redemption! She has come to love our Savior, lord, and her husband has approved of her conversion."

I just looked at him, corroding his joy with my sour face, but Willibald was not to be so easily discouraged. He gathered his enthusiasm again. "Don't you see, lord?" he asked. "If she converts then he will follow! It's often thus, lord, that the wife first finds salvation, and when wives lead, husbands follow!"

"He's lulling us to sleep, father," I said. *Dragon-Voyager* had rejoined the fleet by now and was rowing steadily north.

"The jarl is a troubled soul," Willibald said, "he talked to me often." He raised his hands to the sky where a myriad waterfowl beat south on throbbing wings. "There is rejoicing in heaven, lord, when just one sinner repents. And he is so close to redemption! And when a chieftain converts, lord, then his people follow him to Christ."

"Chieftain?" I sneered. "Haesten's just an earsling. He's a turd. And he's not troubled, father, except by greed. We'll have to kill him yet."

Willibald despaired of my cynicism and went to sit beside my son. I watched the two of them talk and wondered why Uhtred never showed any enthusiasm for my conversation, though he seemed fascinated by Willibald's. "I hope you're not poisoning the boy's brain," I called.

"We're talking about birds, lord," Willibald explained brightly, "and where they go in winter."

"Where do they go?"

"Beneath the sea?" he suggested.

The tide slackened, stilled, and turned, and we rode the flood back up the river. I sat brooding on the steering platform while Finan tended the big steering oar. My men rowed gently, content to let the tide do the work, and they sang the song of Ægir, god of the sea, and of Rán, his wife, and of his nine daughters, all of whom must be flattered if a ship is to be safe on the wild waters. They sang the song because they knew I liked it, but the tune seemed empty and the words meaningless, and I did not join in. I just gazed at the smoke haze above Lundene, the darkness darkening a summer sky, and wished I were a bird, high in that nothingness, vanishing.

Haesten's letter stirred Alfred to a new liveliness. The letter, he said, was a sign of God's grace, and Bishop Erkenwald, of course, agreed. God, the bishop preached, had slaughtered the heathen at Fearnhamme and now had worked a miracle in the heart of Haesten. Willibald was sent to Beamfleot with an invitation for Haesten to bring his family to Lundene where both Alfred and Æthelred would stand as godfathers to Brunna, Haesten the Younger, and the real Horic. No one now bothered to pretend that the deaf and dumb hostage was Haesten's son, but the deception was forgiven in the ebullience that marked Wessex as that summer faded into autumn.

The deaf and dumb hostage, I gave him the name Harald, was sent to my household. He was a bright lad and I set him to work in the armory where he showed a skill with the sharpening stone and an eagerness to learn weapons. I also had custody of Skade, because no one else seemed to want her. For a time I displayed her in a cage beside my door, but that humiliation was small consolation for her curse. She was valueless as a hostage now, for her lover was mewed up on Torneie Island and one day I took her upriver in one of the smaller boats we kept above Lundene's broken bridge.

Torneie was close to Lundene and, with thirty men on the oars, we reached the River Colaun before midday. We rowed slowly up the smaller river, but there was little to be seen. Harald's men, they numbered fewer than three hundred, had made an earth wall topped by a thick thorn palisade. Spears showed above that spiny obstacle, but no roofs, because Torneie had no timber with which to make houses. The river flowed sluggish either side of the island, and was edged by marshland, beyond which I could see the twin camps of the Saxon forces that besieged the island. Two ships were moored in the river, both manned by Mercians, their job to prevent any supplies reaching the trapped Danes. "There's your lover," I told Skade, pointing to the thorns.

I ordered Ralla, who was steering the ship, to take us as close as he could to the island, and, when our bows were almost touching the reeds, I dragged Skade to the bows. "There's your one-legged, impotent lover," I told Skade. A handful of Danes had deserted, and they reported that Harald had been wounded in the left leg and groin. Wasp-Sting had evidently struck him beneath the skirt of his mail, and I remembered the blade striking bone and how I had forced it harder so that the steel had slid up his thigh, ripping muscles and opening blood vessels, and ended in his groin. The leg had turned rotten and had been cut off. He still lived, and perhaps it was his hatred and fervor that gave life to his men, who now faced the bleakest of futures.

Skade said nothing. She gazed at the thorn wall above which a few spear-points showed. She was dressed in a slave's tunic, belted tight around her thin waist.

"They've eaten their horses," I told her, "and they catch eels, frogs, and fish."

"They will live," she said dully.

"They're trapped," I said scornfully, "and this time Alfred won't pay bright gold for them to go away. When they starve this winter, they'll surrender, and Alfred will kill them all. One by one, woman."

"They will live," she insisted.

"You see the future?"

"Yes," she said, and I touched Thor's hammer.

I hated her, and I found it hard to take my eyes from her. She had been given the gift of beauty, yet it was the beauty of a weapon. She was sleek, hard and shining. Even as a degraded captive, unwashed and dressed in rags, she shone. Her face was bony, but softened by lips and by the thickness of her hair. My men gazed at her. They wanted me to give her to them as a plaything, and then kill her. She was reckoned to be a Danish sorceress, as dangerous as she was desirable, and I knew it was her curse that had killed my Gisela, and Alfred would not have objected had I executed her, yet I could not kill her. She fascinated me.

"You can go to them," I said.

She turned her big, dark eyes onto me, said nothing.

"Jump overboard," I said. We were not that far from Torneie's shelving bank. She might have to swim a couple of paces, but then she would be able to wade ashore. "Can you swim?"

"Yes."

"Then go to him," I said, and waited. "Don't you want to be Queen of Wessex?" I sneered.

She looked back to the bleak island. "I dream," she told me quietly, "and in my dreams Loki comes to me."

Loki was the trickster god, the nuisance in Asgard, the god who deserved death. The Christians talk of the serpent in paradise, and that was Loki. "He talks evil to you?" I asked.

"He is sad," she said, "and he talks. I comfort him."

"What has that to do with you jumping overboard?"

"It is not my fate," she said.

"Loki told you that?"

She nodded.

"Did he tell you that you would be Queen of Wessex?"

"Yes," she said simply.

"But Odin has more power," I said, and wished Odin had thought to protect Gisela instead of Wessex, and then I wondered why the gods had allowed the Christians to win at Fearnhamme instead of letting their worshippers capture Wessex, but the gods are capricious, full of mischief, and none more so than the cunning Loki. "And what does Loki tell you to do now?" I asked harshly.

"To submit."

"I have no need of you," I said, "so jump. Swim. Go. Starve."

"It is not my fate," she said again. Her voice was dull, as though there was no life in her soul.

"What if I push you?"

"You won't," she said confidently, and she was right. I left her in the bows as we turned the ship and let the swift current take us back to the Temes and Lundene. That night I released her from the storeroom that served as her prison. I told Finan she was not to be touched, she was not to be restrained, that she was free, and in the morning she was still in my courtyard, crouching, watching me, saying nothing.

She became a kitchen slave. The other slaves and servants feared her. She was silent, baleful, as if the life had been drained from her. Most of my household were Christian and they made the sign of the cross when Skade crossed their path, but my orders that she was to be unmolested were obeyed. She could have left any time, but she stayed. She could have poisoned us, but no one fell ill.

The autumn brought wet, cold winds. Envoys had been sent to the lands across the sea, and to the Welsh kingdoms, announcing that Haesten's family was to be baptized and inviting envoys to witness the ceremony. Alfred evidently regarded Haesten's willingness to sacrifice his wife and sons to Christianity as a victory to set alongside Fearnhamme, and he ordered that the streets of Lundene were to be hung with banners to welcome the Danes. Alfred came to the city late one afternoon in a seething rainstorm. He hurried to Bishop Erkenwald's palace that lay beside the rebuilt church at the top of the hill, and that evening there was a service of thanksgiving that I refused to attend.

Next morning I took my three children to the palace. Æthelred andÆthelflæd, who at least pretended to a happy marriage when ceremony demanded, had come to Lundene, and Æthelflæd had offered to let my three children play with her daughter. "Does that mean," I asked her, "that you're not going to the church?"

"Of course I'm going," she said, smiling, "if Haesten even arrives." Every church bell in the city was ringing in anticipation of the arrival of the Danes, and crowds were gathering in the streets, despite a spitting cold rain that blew from the east.

"He's coming," I said.

"You know that?"

"They left at dawn," I said. I kept watchers on the mudflats of the widening Temes and the beacons had been lit at first light, signaling that ships had left Beamfleot's creek and were heading upriver.

"He's only doing it," Æthelflæd said, "so my father doesn't attack him."

"He's a weasel's earsling," I said.

"He wants East Anglia," she said. "Eohric's a weak king and Haesten would like his crown."

"Maybe," I said dubiously, "but he'd prefer Wessex."

She shook her head. "My husband has an informer in his encampment and he's certain Haesten plans an attack on Grantaceaster."

Grantaceaster was where East Anglia's new Danish king had his capital, and a successful attack might well give Haesten the throne of East Anglia. He certainly wanted a throne, and all reports said that Eohric was a feeble ruler, but Alfred had made a treaty with Guthrum, the previous king, which agreed that Wessex would not interfere in East Anglia's affairs, so if Haesten's ambition was to take that throne, why should he need to placate Alfred? Haesten really wanted Wessex, of course, but Fearnhamme would have persuaded him that it was far too difficult an ambition. Then I remembered the one vacant throne, and it all made sense to me. "I think he's more interested in Mercia," I said.

Æthelflæd considered that idea, then shook her head. "He knows he'd have to fight both us and Wessex to conquer Mercia. And my husband's spy is certain it's East Anglia."

"We'll see."

She glanced into the next room where the children were playing with carved wooden toys. "Uhtred's old enough to attend church," she said.

"I'm not raising him as a Christian," I said firmly.

She smiled at me, her lovely face momentarily showing the mischief I remembered from her childhood. "Dear Lord Uhtred," she said, "still swimming against the current."

"And you, lady?" I asked, remembering how nearly she had fled with a pagan Dane.

"I drift in my husband's boat," she sighed, then servants came to summon her to Æthelred's side. Haesten, it seemed, was within sight of the city walls.

He arrived in *Dragon-Voyager*, which he berthed at one of the decaying quays downstream of my house. He was greeted by Alfred and by Æthelred, both men wearing fur-trimmed robes and bronze coronets. Horns sounded and drummers beat out a swift rhythm that was spoiled when the rain became harder and made the drum skins soggy. Haesten, presumably advised by Willibald, wore no armor or weapons, though his long leather coat looked thick enough to withstand a sword thrust. His beard plaits were tied with leather laces and I swore a hammer amulet was tucked inside one of the braids. His wife and two sons were in penitential white and they walked barefoot in the procession that climbed Lundene's hill. His wife was called Brunna, though on this day she would be given a new and Christian name. She was small and dumpy with nervous eyes that flickered left and right as though she expected an attack from the crowds that lined the narrow streets. I was surprised by her unattractive looks. Haesten was an ambitious man, eager to be recognized as one of the great warlords, and to such a man a wife's appearance was as important as the splendor of his armor or the wealth of his followers, but Haesten had not married Brunna for her looks. He had married her because she had brought a dowry that had started him on his upward journey. She was his wife, but I guessed she was not his companion in bed, hall, or anywhere else. He was willing to have her baptized simply because she was not important to him, though Alfred, with his high-minded view of marriage, would never have comprehended such cynicism. As to Haesten's sons, I doubt he took their baptism seriously and, just as soon as he got them away from Lundene, he would order them to forget the ceremony. Children are easily swayed by religion, which is why it is a good thing that most eventually grow into sense.

Chanting monks led the procession, then came children with

green boughs, more monks, a group of abbots and bishops, then Steapa and fifty men of the royal guard, who walked immediately in front of Alfred and his guests. Alfred walked slowly, clearly in discomfort, but he had refused the offer of a cart. His old wagon, which I had ditched outside Fearnhamme, had been recovered, but Alfred insisted on walking because he liked the humility of approaching his god on foot. He leaned on Æthelred sometimes, and so king and son-in-law limped painfully uphill together. Æthelflaed walked a pace behind her husband and, behind her and behind Haesten, were the emissaries from Wales and Frankia who had traveled to witness the miracle of this Danish conversion.

Haesten hesitated before entering the church. I suspect he half thought it was an ambush, but Alfred encouraged him, and the Danes stepped gingerly inside to find nothing more threatening than a black-robed gaggle of monks. There was precious little room in the church. I had not wanted to be there, but a messenger from Alfred had insisted on my presence, and so I stood at the very back and watched the smoke rise from tall candles and listened to the chanting of the monks that, at times, was drowned by the sheer beat of rain on the thatched roof. A crowd had gathered in the small square outside, and a bedraggled priest stood on a stool in the sanctuary door to repeat Bishop Erkenwald's words to the sopping people. The priest had to bellow to make himself heard above the wind and the rain.

Three silver-hooped barrels stood in front of the altar, each half filled with water from the Temes. Brunna, looking completely confused, was persuaded to climb into the center barrel. She gave a small cry of horror as she dropped into the cold water, then stood shivering with her arms crossed over her breasts. Her two sons were unceremoniously dumped into the barrels on either side, then Bishop Erkenwald and Bishop Asser used ladles to scoop water over the frightened boys' heads. "Behold the spirit descends!" Bishop Asser shouted as he drenched the lads. Both bishops then soaked Brunna's hair and pronounced her new Christian name, Æthelbrun. Alfred beamed with delight. The three Danes stood shivering as a choir of white-robed children sang an endless song. I remember Haesten turning slowly to catch my eye. He raised an eyebrow and had a hard time suppressing a grin and I suspected he had enjoyed the watery humiliation of his plain-looking wife.

Alfred talked with Haesten after the ceremony, and then the Danes left, laden down with gifts. Alfred gave them coins in a chest, a great silver crucifix, a gospel book, and a reliquary which held a finger bone of Saint Æthelburg, a saint who had apparently been drawn up to heaven by golden chains, but must have left at least one finger behind. The rain was pouring down even harder as *Dragon-Voyager* eased away from the quay. I heard Haesten snap an order at his oarsmen, the blades dug into the filthy Temes water, and the ship surged eastward.

That night there was a feast to celebrate the great day's events. Haesten, it seemed, had begged to be excused from the meal, which was discourteous of him as the food and ale were in his honor, but it was probably a wise decision. Men may not carry weapons in a royal hall, but the ale would doubtless have started fights between Haesten's men and the Saxons. Alfred, anyway, took no offense. He was simply too happy. He might have seen his own death approaching, but he reckoned his god had granted him great gifts. He had seen Harald utterly defeated and watched as Haesten brought his family for baptism. "I will leave Wessex safe," he told Bishop Erkenwald in my hearing.

"I trust you will not leave us for many years to come, lord," Erkenwald replied piously.

Alfred patted the bishop's shoulder. "That is in God's hands, bishop."

"And God listens to his people's prayers, lord."

"Then pray for my son," Alfred said, turning to look at Edward, who sat uneasily at the top table.

"I never cease to pray," the bishop said.

"Then pray now," Alfred said happily, "and ask God to bless our feast!"

Erkenwald waited for the king to seat himself at the high table, then he prayed loud and long, beseeching his god's blessing on the food that was getting cold, and then thanking his god for the peace that now ensured the future of Wessex.

But his god was not listening.

It was the feast that started the trouble. I suppose the gods were bored with us; they looked down and saw Alfred's happiness and decided, as the gods will, that it was time to roll the dice.

We were in the great Roman palace, a building of brick and marble patched with Saxon thatch and wattle. There was a dais on which a throne usually sat, but now had a long trestle table hung with green linen cloths. Alfred sat in the center of the table's long side, flanked by Ælswith, his wife, and Æthelflæd, his daughter. They were the only women present, other than servants. Æthelred sat beside Æthelflæd, while Edward sat beside his mother. The other six places at the high table were occupied by Bishop Erkenwald, Bishop Asser, and the most important envoys from other countries. A harpist sat to one side of the dais and chanted a long hymn of praise to Alfred's god.

Beneath the dais, between the hall's pillars, were four more trestle tables where the guests ate. Those guests were a mixture of churchmen and warriors. I sat between Finan and Steapa in the darkest corner of the hall, and I confess I was in a foul temper. It seemed plain to me that Haesten had fooled Alfred. The king was one of the wisest men I ever knew, yet he had a weakness for his god, and it never occurred to him that there might have been a political calculation behind Haesten's apparent concessions. To Alfred it simply seemed that his god had worked a miracle. He knew, of course, from his son-in-law and from his own spies, that Haesten had an ambition to take the throne of East Anglia, but that did not worry him because he had already conceded that country to Danish rule. He dreamed of recovering it, but he knew what was possible and what was just aspiration. In those last years of his life Alfred always referred to himself as the King of the An-

gelcynn, King of the English folk, and by that he meant all the
land in Britain where the Saxon languages were spoken, but he
knew that title was a hope, not a reality. It had fallen to Alfred to
make Wessex secure and to extend its authority over much of
Mercia, but the rest of the Angelcynn were under Danish rule, and
Alfred could do little about that. Yet he was proud that he had
made Wessex strong enough to destroy Harald's great army and to
force Haesten to seek baptism for his family.

I brooded on those things. Steapa growled conversation, which I
hardly heard, and Finan made sour jokes at which I dutifully
smiled, but all I wanted was to get out of that hall. Alfred's feasts
were never festive. The ale was in short supply and the entertainment was pious. Three monks chanted a long Latin prayer, then the
children's choir sang a ditty about being lambs of god, which made
Alfred beam with pleasure. "Beautiful!" he exclaimed when the
grubby-robed infants had finished their caterwauling. "Truly beautiful!" I thought he was about to demand another song from the
children, but Bishop Asser leaned behind Ælswith and evidently
suggested something that made Alfred's eyes light up. "Brother
Godwin," he called down to the blind monk, "you haven't sung for
us in many weeks!"

The young monk looked startled, but a table companion took him
by the elbow and led him to the open space as the children, shep-
herded by a nun, were taken away. Brother Godwin stood alone as
the harpist struck a series of chords on his horsehair strings. I
thought the blind monk was not going to sing at all, because he made
no sounds, but then he started to jerk his head backward and forward as the chords became swooping and eerie. Some men crossed
themselves, then Brother Godwin began to make small whimpering
noises. "He's moon mad," I muttered to Finan.

"No, lord," Finan whispered, "he's possessed." He fingered the
cross which always hung from his neck. "I've seen holy men in Ireland," he went on softly, "just like him."

"The spirit talks through him," Steapa said in awe. Alfred must
have heard our low voices because he turned an irritated face on us.
We went silent, and suddenly Godwin began to writhe and then he

let out a great shout that echoed in the hall. Smoke from the braziers wreathed around him before vanishing through the smokehole ripped in the Roman roof.

I learned much later that Brother Godwin had been discovered by Bishop Asser, who had found the young, blind monk locked in a cell at the monastery of Æthelingæg. He was kept locked away because the abbot believed Godwin to be mad as a bat, but Bishop Asser decided Godwin really did hear his god's voice and so had brought the monk to Alfred who, of course, believed that anything from Æthelingæg was auspicious because that was where he had survived the greatest crisis of his reign.

Godwin began to yelp. The sound was of a man in great pain and the harpist took his hands from the strings. Dogs responded to the sounds, howling in the dark back rooms of the palace. "The holy spirit comes," Finan whispered reverently, and Godwin let out a great scream as if his bowels were being torn from him.

"Praise God," Alfred said. He and his family were gazing at the monk who now stood as though crucified, then he relaxed his outspread arms and began speaking. He shivered as he spoke and his voice meandered up and down, now shrill, then almost too low to hear. If it was singing, then it was the strangest noise I ever heard. At first his words sounded like nonsense, or else were being chanted in an unknown language, but slowly, from the jabber, coherent sentences emerged. Alfred was the chosen of God. Wessex was the promised land. Milk and honey abounded. Women brought sin into the world. God's bright angels had spread their wings over us. The Lord most high is terrible. The waters of Israel were turned to blood. The whore of Babylon was among us.

He stopped after chanting that. The harpist had detected a rhythm in Godwin's words and was playing softly, but his hands checked on the strings again as the monk turned his blind face about the hall with a look of puzzlement. "The whore!" he suddenly started shouting over and over. "The whore! The whore! The whore! She is among us!" He made a mewing sound and twisted down to his knees and began sobbing.

No one spoke, no one moved. I heard the wind in the smoke-hole and I thought of my children somewhere in Æthelflæd's quarters and wondered if they were listening to this craziness.

"The whore," Godwin said, drawing the word "whore" into a long throbbing howl. Then he stood and looked quite sane. "The whore is among us, lord," he said toward Alfred, in a perfectly normal voice.

"The whore?" Alfred asked uncertainly.

"The whore!" Godwin screamed again, then once again reverted to sanity. "The whore, lord, is the maggot in the fruit, the rat in the granary, the locust in the wheatfield, the disease in the child of God. It saddens God, lord," he said, and began weeping.

I touched Thor's hammer. Godwin was mad beyond help, I thought, but all the Christians in that hall gazed at him as though he had been sent from heaven. "Where's Babylon?" I whispered to Finan.

"Somewhere a long way off, lord," he answered softly, "maybe beyond Rome even?"

Godwin was weeping silently, but saying nothing, so Alfred gestured that the harpist should touch his strings again. The chords sounded and Godwin responded by starting to chant again, though now his words lacked rhythm. "Babylon is the devil's home," he shouted, "the whore is the devil's child, the yeast in the bread will fail, the whore has come to us. The whore died and the devil raised her up, the whore will destroy us, stop!"

This last command was to the harpist who, in frightened obedience, flattened his hands on the strings to stop their quivering.

"God is on our side," Alfred said in a kindly voice, "so who can destroy us?"

"The whore can destroy us," Bishop Asser said, and I thought, I could not be sure, that he glanced toward me, though I doubt he could see me because I was deep in the shadows.

"The whore!" Godwin shouted at Alfred, "you fool! The whore!"

No one reproved him for calling the king a fool.

"God will surely protect us!" Bishop Erkenwald said.

"The whore was among us, and the whore died, and God sent her to the fires of hell and the devil raised her and she is here," Godwin said forcibly. "She is here! Her stench sours God's chosen people! She must be killed. She must be cut into pieces and her foul parts cast into the bottomless sea! God commands it! God weeps in his heaven because you do not obey his commandments, and he commands that the whore must die! God weeps! He hurts! God weeps! The tears of God fall on us like drops of fire, and it is the whore who makes those tears!"

"What whore?" Alfred asked, then Finan put a warning hand on my arm.

"She was called Gisela," Godwin had hissed.

At first I thought I had misheard. Men were looking at me, and Finan was holding my arm, and I was certain I had misheard, but then Godwin began to chant again. "Gisela, the great whore, is now Skade. She is a piece of filth in human guise, a whore of rottenness, a devil's turd with breasts, a whore, Gisela! God killed her because she was filth and now she is back!"

"No," Finan said to me, but without much urgency. I had stood.

"Lord Uhtred!" Alfred called sharply. Bishop Asser was watching me, half smiling, as his pet monk writhed and screamed. "Lord Uhtred!" Alfred called again, slapping the table.

I had strode to the hall's center where I took Godwin's shoulder and turned his blind face toward me.

"Lord Uhtred!" Alfred had stood.

"You lie, monk," I said.

"She was filth!" Godwin spat at me. He began striking my chest with his fists. "Your wife was the devil's whore, a whore hated by God, and you are the devil's instrument, you whore-husband, heathen, sinner!"

The hall was in uproar. I was aware of none of it, only of a red anger that consumed me and flared in me and filled my ears with its howling sound. I had no weapons. This was a royal hall and weapons were forbidden, but the mad monk was hitting me and howling at me and I drew back my right hand and hit him.

My hand half hit him. Maybe he sensed the blow was coming because he backed away fast, and my hand caught him on the jaw, dislocating it so that his chin was skewed sideways as blood poured from his lips. He spat out a tooth and took a wild swing at me.

"Enough!" Alfred shouted. Men were at last moving, but it seemed to me they moved with exaggerated slowness as Godwin spat blood at me.

"Whore-lover," he snarled, or I think that was what he said.

"Stop! I command it!" Alfred called.

"Whore-husband," the bloody mouth said distinctly.

So I hit him again, and with that second blow I broke his neck.

I had not meant to kill him, merely silence him, but I heard his neck crunch. I saw his head loll unnaturally to one side, and then he fell across one of the braziers and his short black hair blazed into bright flame. He collapsed on the floor's broken mosaics and the hall was filled with the stink of burning hair and scorched flesh.

"Arrest him!" I heard Bishop Asser's loud shout.

"He must die!" Bishop Erkenwald called.

Alfred was staring at me in horror. His wife, who had ever hated me, was screaming that I must pay for my sins.

Finan took my arm and pulled me toward the hall's door. "To the house, lord," he said.

"Steapa! Hold him!" Alfred called.

But Steapa liked me. He did move toward me, but slowly enough so that I reached the door where the royal guards made a half-hearted effort to bar my way, but a menacing growl from Finan drove their spears aside. He dragged me into the night. "Now come," he said, "fast!"

We ran down the hill to the dark river.

And behind us was a dead monk and uproar.

PART TWO

VIKING

ONE

I stayed furious, unrepentant, pacing the large room beside the river where servants, cowed to silence by my rage, revived the fire. It is strange how news spreads in a city. Within minutes a crowd had gathered outside the house to see how the night would end. The folk were silent, just watching. Finan had barred the outer doors and ordered torches lit in the courtyard. Rain hissed in the flames and slicked the paving stones. Most of my men lived close by and they came one by one, some of them drunk, and Finan or Cerdic met them at the outer door and sent them to fetch their mail and weapons. "Are you expecting a fight?" I asked Finan.

"They're warriors," he said simply.

He was right, so I put on my own mail. I dressed as a warlord. I dressed for battle, with gold on my arms and both swords at my waist, and it was just after I had buckled the belt that Alfred's emissary arrived.

The emissary was Father Beocca. My old friend came alone, his priest's robes muddy from the streets and wet from the rain. He was shivering and I put a stool beside the central hearth and draped a fur cloak about his shoulders. He sat, then held his good hand toward the flames. Finan had escorted him from the front gate and he stayed. I saw that Skade, too, had crept into a shadowed corner. I caught her eye and gave a curt nod that she could remain.

"You've looked under the floor?" Father Beocca said suddenly.

"Under the floor?"

"The Romans," he said, "would heat this house with a furnace that vented its heat into the space under the floor."

"I know."

"And we hack holes in their roofs and make hearths," he said sadly.

"You'll make yourself ill if you insist on walking about on cold, wet nights," I said.

"Of course a lot of those floors have collapsed," Beocca said as if it was a very important point he needed to make. He rapped the tiles with the stick he now used to help himself walk. "Yours seems in good repair, though."

"I like a hearth."

"A hearth is comforting," Beocca said. He turned his good eye to me and smiled. "The monastery at Æscengum cleverly managed to flood the space under their floor with sewage, and the only solution was to pull the whole house down and build anew! It was a blessing, really."

"A blessing?"

"They found some gold coins among the turds," he said, "so I suspect God directed their effluent, don't you?"

"My gods have better things to do than worry about shit."

"That's why you've never found gold among your turds!" Beocca said and started laughing. "There, Uhtred," he said triumphantly, "I have at last proved my God is mightier than your false idols!" He smiled at me, but the smile slowly faded so that he looked old and tired again. I loved Beocca. He had been my childhood tutor and he was always exasperating and pedantic, but he was a good man. "You have until dawn," he said.

"To do what?"

He spoke tiredly, as if he despaired of what he told me. "You will go to the king in penitence," he said, "without mail or weapons. You will abase yourself. You will hand the witch to the king. All the land you hold in Wessex is forfeited. You will pay a wergild to the church for the life of Brother Godwin, and your children will be held hostages against that payment."

Silence.

Sparks whirled upward. A couple of my wolfhounds came into the room. One smelled Beocca's robes, whined, and then both settled by the fire, their doleful eyes looking at me for a moment before closing.

"The wergild," Finan asked for me, "how much?"

"One thousand and five hundred shillings," Beocca said.

I sneered. "For a mad monk?"

"For a saint," Beocca said.

"A mad fool," I snarled.

"A holy fool," Beocca said mildly.

The wergild is the price we pay for death. If I am judged guilty of unjustly killing a man or woman I must pay their kin a price, that price depending on their rank, and that is fair, but Alfred had set Godwin's wergild at almost a royal level. "To pay that," I said, "I'd have to sell almost everything I own, and the king has just taken all my land."

"And you must also swear an oath of loyalty to the etheling," Beocca said. He usually became exasperated with me and would splutter as his exasperation grew, but that night he was very calm.

"So the king would impoverish me," I asked, "and tie me to his son?"

"And he will return the sorceress to her husband," Beocca said, looking at the black-cloaked Skade, whose eyes glittered from the room's darkest corner. "Skirnir has offered a reward for her return."

"Skirnir?" I asked. The name was unfamiliar to me.

"Skirnir is her husband," Beocca said. "A Frisian."

I looked at Skade who nodded abruptly.

"If you return her," I said, "she dies."

"Does that concern you?" Beocca asked.

"I don't like killing women."

"The law of Moses tells us we should not allow a witch to live," Beocca said. "Besides, she is an adulterer, so her husband has the God-given right to kill her if that is his wish."

"Is Skirnir a Christian?" I asked, but neither Skade nor Father Beocca answered. "Will he kill you?" I asked Skade and she just nodded. "So," I turned back to Beocca, "until I pay the wergild, make my oath to Edward, and send Skade to her death, my children are hostages?"

"The king has decreed that your children will be cared for in the Lady Æthelflæd's household," Beocca answered. He looked me up and down with his good eye. "Why are you dressed for war?" I made no answer and Beocca shrugged. "Did you think the king would send his guards?"

"I thought he might."

"And you would have fought them?" He sounded shocked.

"I would have them know who they came to arrest," I said.

"You killed a man!" Beocca at last found some energy. "The man offended you, I know, but it was the Holy Spirit who spoke in him! You hit him, Uhtred! The king forgave the first blow, but not the second, and you must pay for that!" He leaned back, looking tired again. "The wergild is well within your ability to pay. Bishop Asser wished it set much higher, but the king is merciful." A log in the hearth spat suddenly, startling the hounds, who twitched and whined. The fire found new life, brightening the room and casting shaky shadows.

I faced Beocca across the flames. "Bishop Asser," I spat angrily.

"What of him?"

"Godwin was his puppy."

"The bishop saw holiness in him, yes."

"He saw a way to his ambition," I snarled, "to rid Wessex of me." I had been thinking of the feast's events ever since my hand took Godwin's life, and I had decided that Asser was behind the mad monk's words. Bishop Asser believed Wessex safe. Harald's power was destroyed, and Haesten had sent his family to be baptized, so Wessex had no need of a pagan warlord, and Asser had used Godwin to poison Alfred's mind against me. "That twist of Welsh shit told Godwin what to say," I said. "It wasn't the holy spirit speaking in Godwin, father, it was Bishop Asser."

Beocca looked at me through the shimmer of fire. "Did you know," he asked, "that the flames in hell cast no light?"

"I didn't," I said.

"It is one of the mysteries of God," Beocca said, then grunted as he stood. He shrugged off the borrowed fur cloak and leaned heavily on his stick. "What shall I tell the king?"

"Is your god responsible for hell?" I asked.

He frowned, thinking. "A good question," he finally said, though he did not answer it. "As is mine. What shall I tell the king?"

"That he will have my answer at dawn."

Beocca half smiled. "And what will that answer be, Lord Uhtred?"

"He will discover that at dawn."

Beocca nodded. "You are to come to the palace alone, without weapons, without mail, and dressed simply. We shall send men to take the witch. Your children will be returned on payment of one hundred shillings, the remainder of the wergild is to be paid within six months." He limped toward the courtyard door, then turned and stared at me. "Let me die in peace, Lord Uhtred."

"By watching my humiliation?"

"By knowing that your sword will be at King Edward's command. That Wessex will be safe. That Alfred's work will not die with him."

That was the first time I heard Edward called king.

"You'll have my answer at sunrise," I said.

"God be with you," Beocca responded, and hobbled into the night. I listened to the heavy outer door bang shut and the locking bar drop into place, and I remembered Ravn, the blind skald who had been Ragnar the Elder's father, telling me that our lives are like a voyage across an unknown sea, and sometimes, he said, we get tired of calm waters and gentle winds, and we have no choice but to slam the steering oar's loom hard over and head for the gray clouds and the whitecaps and the tumult of danger. "That is our tribute to the gods," he had told me, and I still do not know quite what he meant, but in that sound of the door closing I heard the echo of the steering oar slamming hard to one side.

"What do we do?" Finan asked me.

"I tell you what I won't do," I snarled. "I will not give that damned child my oath."

"Edward's no child," Finan said mildly.

"He's a milksop little bastard," I said angrily. "He's addled by his god, just like his father. He was weaned on that bitch wife's vinegar tits, and I will not give him an oath."

"He'll be King of Wessex soon," Finan observed.

"And why? Because you and I kept their kingdom safe, you and I! If Wessex lives, my friend, it's because an Irish runt and a Northumbrian pagan kept it alive! And they forget that!"

"Runt?" Finan asked, smiling.

"Look at the size of you," I said. I liked teasing him because of his small stature, though that was deceptive because he had a speed with the sword that was astonishing. "I hope their god damns their damn kingdom," I spat, then went to a chest in the corner of the room. I opened it and felt inside, finding a bundle that I carried to Skade. I felt a pang as I touched the leather wrapping, for these things had belonged to Gisela. "Read those," I said, tossing her the package.

She unwrapped the alder sticks. There were two dozen, none longer than a man's forearm, and all polished with beeswax to a fine gleam. Finan made the sign of the cross as he saw this pagan magic, but I had learned to trust the runesticks. Skade held them in one hand, raised them slightly, closed her eyes, and let them fall. The sticks clattered on the floor and she leaned forward to deduce their message.

"She won't see her own death there," Finan warned me softly, implying I could not trust her interpretation.

"We all die," Skade said, "and the sticks don't talk of me."

"What do they say?" I asked.

She stared at the pattern. "I see a stronghold," she finally said, "and I see water. Gray water."

"Gray?" I asked.

"Gray, lord," she said, and that was the first time she called me "lord." "Gray like the frost giants," she added, and I knew she meant northward toward the ice-world where the frost giants stalk the world.

"And the fortress?" I asked.

"It burns, lord. It burns and it burns and it burns. The sand of the shore is black with its ashes."

I motioned her to sweep up the runesticks, then walked onto the terrace. It was still the middle of the night and the sky was black with cloud and spiteful with small rain. I listened to the rush of water squeezing through the piles of the old bridge and I thought of Stiorra, my daughter.

"Gray?" Finan asked, joining me.

"It means north," I said, "and Bebbanburg is in the north and a south wind will carry its ashes to the sands of Lindisfarena."

"North," Finan said quietly.

"Tell the men they have a choice," I said. "They can stay and serve Alfred, or they can come with me. You have the same choice."

"You know what I'll do."

"And I want *Seolferwulf* ready by dawn."

Forty-three men came with me, the rest stayed in Lundene. Forty-three warriors, twenty-six wives, five whores, a huddle of children, and sixteen hounds. I wanted to take my horses, especially Smoka, but the boat was not equipped with the wooden frames that hold stallions safe during a voyage, and so I patted his nose and felt sad to abandon him. Skade came aboard, because to stay in Lundene would mean her death. I had put my mail and weapons and helmets and shields and treasure chest into the small space beneath the steering platform, and I saw her place her own small bundle of clothes in the same place.

We did not have a full crew, but sufficient men took their places on the rowing benches. The dawn was breaking as I ordered the wolf's head mounted on the prow. That carving, with its snarling mouth, was stored beneath the platform in the bows and was only displayed when we were away from our home waters. It risks bad fortune to threaten the spirits of home with a defiant dragon or a snarling wolf or a carved raven, but now I had no home and so I let the wolf defy the spirits of Lundene. Alfred had sent men to guard my house, and though those mailed warriors could see us in the dock beside the terrace, none interfered as we cast off the lines and pushed *Seolferwulf* into the Temes's strong current. I turned and watched the city beneath its smear of smoke. "Raise!" Finan called, and twenty oar-blades were poised above the river's filth.

"And strike!" Finan called and the boat surged toward the dawn. I was without a lord. I was outcast. I was free. I was going Viking.

There is a joy at being afloat. I was still under the thrall of Gisela's death, but going to sea brought hope again. Not much, but some. To drive a boat into the gray waves, to watch the wolf's head dip into the crests and rear in an explosion of white water, to feel the wind hard and cold, to see the sail taut as a pregnant woman's belly, to hear the hiss of the sea against the hull, and to feel the steering oar tremble in the hand like the very heartbeat of the boat, all that brings joy.

For five years I had not taken a ship beyond the wide waters of the Temes estuary, but once we had cleared the treacherous shoals at the point of Fughelness we could turn north and there I had hoisted the sail, shipped the long oars, and let *Seolferwulf* run free. Now we went northward into the wider ocean, into the angry wind-whipped ship-killing sea, and the coast of East Anglia lay low and dull on our left and the gray sea ran into the gray sky to our right, while ahead of me was the unknown.

Cerdic was with me, and Sihtric, and Rypere, as were most of my best men. What surprised me was that Osferth, Alfred's bastard, came too. He had stepped silently aboard, almost the last man to make the choice, and I had raised an eyebrow and he had just given a half-smile and taken his place on a rower's bench. He had been beside me as we lashed the oars to the cradles that usually held the sail on its long yard and I had asked if he was certain about his decision.

"Why should I not be with you, lord?" he asked.

"You're Alfred's son," I said, "a West Saxon."

"Half these men are West Saxons, lord," he said, glancing at the crew, "probably more than half."

"Your father won't be pleased you've stayed with me."

"And what has he done for me?" Osferth asked bitterly. "Tried to make me a monk or priest so he could forget I existed? And if I stayed in Wessex what could I expect? Favor?" he laughed bitterly.

116

"You may never see Wessex again," I said.

"Then I'll thank God for that," he said and then, unexpectedly, he smiled. "There's no stench, lord," he added.

"Stench?"

"The stink of Lundene," he explained, "it's gone."

And so it had, because we were at sea and the sewage-soured streets were far behind us. We ran under sail all that day and saw no other ships except a handful of small craft that were fishing and those vessels, seeing our rampant wolf's head, scattered from our path, their men pulling desperately on oars to escape *Seolferwulf*'s threat. That evening we ran the ship close inshore, lowered the sail, and felt our way under oars into a shallow channel to make a camp. It was late in the year to be voyaging and so the cold dark came early. We had no horses so it was impossible to explore the country about our landing place, but I had no fears because I could see no settlements except for one reed-thatched hovel a long way north, and whoever lived there would fear us far more than we feared them. This was a place of mud and reed and grass and creeks beneath a vast wind-driven sky. I say camp, but all we did was carry cloaks above the thick tideline of weed and driftwood. I left sentries on the boat, and placed others at the small island's extremities, and then we lit fires and sang songs beneath the night clouds.

"We need men," Finan said, sitting next to me.

"We do," I agreed.

"Where do we find them?"

"In the north," I said. I was going to Northumbria, going far from Wessex and its priests, going to where my friend had a fortress in the bend of a river and my uncle had a fortress by the sea. I was going home.

"If we're attacked," Finan said, and did not finish the thought.

"We won't be," I said confidently. Any ship at sea was prey to pirates, but *Seolferwulf* was a warship, not a trader. She was longer than most merchant ships and, though her belly was wide, she had a sleekness that only fighting ships possessed. And from a distance she would appear fully manned because of the number of women aboard. A pair of ships might dare to attack us, but even that was unlikely while there was easier prey afloat. "But we do need men," I agreed, "and silver."

"Silver?" He grinned. "What's in that big treasure chest?" He jerked his head toward the grounded ship.

"Silver," I said, "but I need more. Much more." I saw the quizzical look on his face. "I am Lord of Bebbanburg," I explained, "and to take that stronghold I need men, Finan. Three crews at least. And even that might not be enough."

He nodded. "And where do we find silver?"

"We steal it, of course."

He watched the brilliant heart of the fire where the driftwood burned brightest. Some folk say that the future can be read from the shifting shapes inside that glowing inferno, and perhaps he was trying to scry what fate held for us, but then he frowned. "Folk have learned to guard their silver," he said softly. "There are too many wolves and the sheep have become canny."

"That's true," I said. In my childhood, when the northmen returned to Britain, the plundering was easy. Viking men landed, killed, and stole, but now almost anything of value was behind a palisade guarded by spears, though there were still a few monasteries and churches that trusted their defense to the nailed god.

"And you can't steal from the church," Finan said, thinking the same thoughts.

"I can't?"

"Most of your men are Christians," he said, "and they'll follow you, lord, but not into the gates of hell."

"Then we'll steal from the pagans," I said.

"The pagans, lord, are the thieves."

"Then they have the silver I want."

"And what of her?" Finan asked softly, looking at Skade, who crouched close to me, but slightly behind the ring of folk around the fire.

"What of her?"

"The women don't like her, lord. They fear her."

"Why?"

"You know why."

"Because she's a sorceress?" I twisted to look at her. "Skade," I asked, "do you see the future?"

She looked at me in silence for a while. A night-bird called in the marsh and perhaps its harsh voice prompted her because she gave a curt nod. "I glimpse it, lord," she said, "sometimes."

"Then say what you see," I ordered her, "stand up and tell us. Tell us what you see."

She hesitated, then stood. She was wearing a black woolen cloak and it shrouded her body so that, with her black hair that she wore unbound like an unmarried girl, she appeared a tall slim night-dark figure in which her pale face shone white. The singing faltered, then died away, and I saw some of my people make the sign of the cross. "Tell us what you see," I commanded her again.

She raised her pale face to the clouds, but said nothing for a long while. No one else spoke. Then she shuddered and I was irresistibly reminded of Godwin, the man I had murdered. Some men and women do hear the whisper of the gods, and other folk fear them, and I was convinced Skade saw and heard things hidden from the rest of us. Then, just as it seemed as though she would never speak, she laughed aloud.

"Tell us," I said irritably.

"You will lead armies," she said, "armies to shadow the land, lord, and behind you the crops will grow tall, fed by the blood of your enemies."

"And these people?" I asked, waving at the men and women who listened to her.

"You are their gold-giver, their lord. You will make them rich."

There were murmurs round the fire. They liked what they heard. Men follow a lord because the lord is a gift-giver.

"And how do we know you do not lie?" I asked her.

She spread her arms. "If I lie, lord," she said, "then I will die now." She waited, as if inviting a blow from Thor's hammer, but the only sounds were the sighing of wind in the reeds, the crackle of burning driftwood, and the slur of water creeping into the marsh on the night's tide.

"And you?" I asked, "what of you?"

119

"I am to be greater than you, lord," she said, and some of my people hissed, but the words gave me no offense.

"And what is that, Skade?" I asked.

"What the Fates decide, lord," she said, and I waved her to sit down. I was thinking back across the years to another woman who had eavesdropped on the murmurs of the gods, and she had also said I would lead armies. Yet now I was a man who was the most contemptible of men; a man who had broken an oath, a man running from his lord.

Our peoples are bound by oaths. When a man swears his loyalty to me he becomes closer than a brother. My life is his as his is mine, and I had sworn to serve Alfred. I thought of that as the singing began again and as Skade crouched behind me. As Alfred's oathman I owed him service, yet I had run away, and that stripped me of honor and left me despicable.

Yet we do not control our lives. The three spinners make our threads. Wyrd bið ful āræd, we say, and it is true. Fate is inexorable. Yet if fate decrees, and the spinners know what that fate will be, why do we make oaths? It is a question that has haunted me all my life, and the closest I have come to an answer is that oaths are made by men, while fate is decreed by the gods, and that oaths are men's attempts to dictate fate. Yet we cannot decree what we would wish. Making an oath is like steering a course, but if the winds and tides of fate are too strong, then the steering oar loses its power. So we make oaths, but we are helpless in the face of wyrd. I had lost honor by fleeing from Lundene, but the honor had been taken from me by fate, and that was some consolation in that dark night on the cold East Anglian shore.

There was another consolation. I woke in the dark and went to the ship. Her stern was rising gently on the incoming tide. "You can sleep," I told the sentries. Our fires ashore were still glowing, though their flames were low now. "Join your women," I told them, "I'll guard the ship."

Seolferwulf did not need guarding because there was no enemy, but it is a habit to set sentries, and so I sat in her stern and thought of fate and of Alfred, and of Gisela and of Iseult, of Brida and of Hild, and of all the women I had known and all the twists of life, and I ignored the slight lurch as someone climbed over *Seolferwulf*'s stillgrounded bow. I said nothing as the dark figure threaded the rowers' benches.

"I did not kill her, lord," Skade said.

"You cursed me, woman."

"You were my enemy then," she said, "what was I supposed to do?"

"And the curse killed Gisela," I said.

"That was not the curse," she said.

"Then what was it?"

"I asked the gods to yield you captive to Harald," she said.

I looked at her then for the first time since she had come aboard. "It didn't work," I said.

"No."

"So what kind of sorceress are you?"

"A frightened one," she said.

I would flog a man for not keeping alert when he is supposed to be standing watch, but a thousand enemies could have come that night, for I was not doing my duty. I took Skade beneath the steering platform, to the small space there, and I took off her cloak and I lay her down, and when we were done we were both in tears. We said nothing, but lay in each other's arms. I felt *Seolferwulf* lift from the mud and pull gently at her mooring line, yet I did not move. I held Skade close, not wanting the night to end.

I had persuaded myself that I had left Alfred because he would impose an oath on me, an oath I did not want, the oath to serve his son. Yet that had not been the whole truth. There was another of his conditions I could not accept, and now I held her close. "Time to go," I said at last because I could hear voices. I later learned that Finan had seen us and had held the crew ashore. I loosened my embrace, but Skade held onto me.

"I know where you can find all the gold in the world," she said.

I looked into her eyes. "All the gold?"

She half smiled. "Enough gold, lord," she whispered, "more than enough, a dragon-haunted hoard, lord, gold."

Wyrd bi∂ ful āræd.

I took a golden chain from my treasure chest and I hung it about Skade's neck, which was announcement enough, if any announcement were needed, of her new status. I thought that my people would resent her more, but the opposite happened. They seemed relieved. They had seen her as a threat, but now she was one of us, and so we sailed north.

North along East Anglia's low coast beneath gray skies and driven by a southerly wind that brought thick and constant fogs. We sheltered in marshy creeks when the fog blew dense above the sea or, if a fog took us by surprise and gave us no time to discover a safe inlet, we steered the ship offshore where there were no mudbanks to wreck us.

The fog slowed us, so that it took six long days to reach Dumnoc. We arrived at that port on a misted afternoon, rowing *Seolferwulf* into the river's mouth between glistening mounds of mud thick with waterfowl. The channel was well marked with withies, though I still had a man in the bows probing with an oar in case the withies betrayed us onto some shipwrecker's shoal. I had taken down the wolf's head to show that we came peacefully, but sentries keeping watch from a rickety wooden tower still sent a boy racing to the town to warn of our coming.

Dumnoc was a good and wealthy port. It was built on the river's southern bank and a palisade surrounded the town to deter a land attack, though the port was wide open from the water that was studded with piers and thick with fishing and trading boats. The tide was almost at the flood when we arrived and I saw how the sea spread from the muddy banks to drown the lower part of the palisade. Some of the houses nearest the sea were built on short stilts, and all the town's timbers had been weather-beaten to a silvery gray. It was an attractive place, smelling richly of salt and shellfish. A church tower crowned with a wooden cross was the highest building, a reminder that Guthrum, the Dane who had become King of East Anglia, had converted his realm to Christianity.

My father had never loved the East Anglians because, years in the past, their kingdom had combined with Mercia to attack Northumbria. Later, much later, during my own childhood, the East Anglians had provided food, horses, and shelter to the Danish army that had conquered Northumbria, though that treachery had rebounded on them when the Danes returned to take East Anglia that still remained a Danish kingdom, though now it was supposedly a Christian kingdom as the church tower attested. Mist blew past the high cross as I steered *Seolferwulf* to the river's center, just upstream of the piers. We turned her there, slewing her about by backing one bank of oars, and only when her wolfless bows faced the sea did I take her alongside a fat-bellied merchant ship that was tied to the largest of the piers. Finan grinned. "Ready to make a quick escape to sea, lord?" he asked.

"Always," I said. "Remember the *Sea-Raven*?"

He laughed. Shortly after we had captured Lundene, the *Sea-Raven*, a Danish ship, had come to the city and innocently tied to a wharf only to discover that a West Saxon army now occupied the place and was not friendly to Danes. The crew had fled back to their ship, but needed to turn her before they could escape downriver, and panic muddled them so that their oars clashed and she had drifted back to the wharf, where we captured her. She was a horrible boat, leaky and with a stinking bilge, and eventually I broke her up and used her ribs as roofbeams for some cottages we built at Lundene's eastern side.

A big-bellied, fat-bearded man in rusty mail clambered from the pier onto the trading boat, then, after receiving permission, hauled himself up and over *Seolferwulf*'s flank. "Guthlac," he introduced himself, "Reeve of Dumnoc. Who are you?" The question was peremptory, backed by a dozen men who waited on the pier with swords and axes. They looked nervous, and no wonder, for my crew outnumbered them.

"My name is Uhtred," I said.

"Uhtred of where?" Guthlac asked. He spoke Danish and was belligerent, pretending to be unworried by my crew's formidable appearance. He had long mustaches bound with black-tarred twine that hung well below his clean-shaven chin. He kept tugging on one mustache, a sign, I deduced, of nervousness.

"Uhtred of Bebbanburg," I said.

"And where's Bebbanburg?"

"Northumbria."

"You're a long way from home, Uhtred of Bebbanburg," Guthlac said. He was peering into our bilge to see what cargo we carried. "A long way from home," he repeated. "Are you trading?"

"Do we look like traders?" I asked. Other men were gathering on the low shore in front of the closest houses. They were mostly unarmed, so their presence was probably explained by curiosity.

"You look like vagabonds," Guthlac said. "Two weeks ago there was an attack a few miles south. A steading was burned, men killed, women taken. How do I know that wasn't you?"

"You don't know it," I said, returning a mild answer to his hostility.

"Maybe I should hold you here until we can prove it one way or the other?"

"And maybe you should clean your mail?" I suggested.

He challenged me with a glare, held my gaze a few heartbeats, then nodded abruptly. "So what's your business here?" he demanded.

"We need food, ale."

"That we have," he said, then waited as some gulls screamed above us, "but first you have to pay the king's wharfage fee." He held out a hand. "Two shillings."

"Two pence, perhaps."

We settled on four pence, of which no doubt two went into Guthlac's pouch, and after that we were free to go ashore, though Guthlac sensibly insisted we were to carry no weapons other than short knives. "The Goose is a good tavern," he said, pointing to a large building hung with the sign of a painted goose, "and it can sell you dried herring, dried oysters, flour, ale, and Saxon whores."

"The tavern is yours?" I asked.

"What of it?"

"I just hope its ale is better than its owner's welcome," I said.

He laughed at that. "Welcome to Dumnoc," he said, climbing back onto the trading ship, "and I give you leave to spend a night here in peace. But if any of you commit a crime I'll hold you all in custody!" He paused and looked toward *Seolferwulf*'s stern. "Who's that?"

He was staring at Skade, though he must have noticed her earlier. She was again cloaked in black so that her pale face seemed bright in the misted late afternoon. There was gold at her neck. "Her name is Edith," I said, "and she's a Saxon whore."

"Edith," he repeated, "maybe I'll buy her from you?"

"Maybe you will," I said, and we looked at each other and neither trusted the other, and then Guthlac gave a careless wave and turned away.

We drew lots to decide who could go ashore that evening. I needed men to stay and guard the boat, and Osferth volunteered to command that group. We put twenty-three dried peas in a bowl with twenty silver coins, then Finan took the bowl and stood with his back to me as I faced the assembled crew. One by one Finan drew either a coin or a pea from the bowl and held it aloft. "Who'll have this one?" he would ask and I would pick a man from the crew without knowing whether Finan held a pea or a coin. Those who drew peas had to stay with Osferth, the rest were allowed ashore. I could have just chosen which men should stay aboard, but a crew work better when they believe their lord is fair. The children all stayed, but the wives of the shore party accompanied their men. "You stay in the tavern," I told them. "This town isn't friendly! We stay together!"

The town might have been unfriendly, but the Goose was a good tavern. The ale was pungent, freshly brewed in the great vats in the inn's yard. The large main room was beamed with keels from broken-up ships, and warmed by a driftwood fire burning in a central hearth. There were tables and benches, but before I let my men loose on the ale I negotiated for smoked herring, flitches of bacon, barrels of ale, bread, and smoked eels, and had all those supplies carried to the *Seolferwulf*. Guthlac had placed guards on the landward end of the pier, and those men were supposed to make certain none of us carried weapons, but I had Wasp-Sting hanging in a scabbard at my back where she was hidden by a cloak, and I did not doubt that most of my crew were similarly armed. I went from table to table and told them they were to start no fights. "Not unless you want to fight me," I warned them, and they grinned.

The tavern was peaceable enough. A dozen local men drank there, all Saxons and none showing any interest in the *Seolferwulf*'s crew. Sihtric had drawn a silver shilling in the lottery and I ordered him to make frequent visits to the yard. "Look for men with weapons," I told him.

"What do you fear, lord?" he asked me.

"Treachery," I said. The *Seolferwulf* was worth a thegn's annual income from a substantial estate and Guthlac must have realized we carried coin on board. His men would find it hard to capture the ship while Osferth and his band defended the pier's end, but drunken men in a tavern were easier prey. I feared he could hold us hostage and demand a huge ransom, and so Sihtric slipped constantly through the back door, returning each time with a shake of his head. "Your bladder's too small," one of my men mocked him.

I sat with Skade, Finan, and his Scottish wife, Ethne, in a corner of the room where I ignored the laughter and songs that were loud at the other tables. I wondered how many men lived in Dumnoc, and why so few were in the Goose. I wondered if weapons were being sharpened. I wondered where all the gold in the world was hidden. "So," I asked Skade, "where is all the gold in the world?"

"Frisia," she said.

"A large place."

"My husband," she said, "has a stronghold on the sea."

"So tell us of your husband."

"Skirnir Thorson," she said.

"I know his name."

"He calls himself the Sea-Wolf," she said, looking at me, but aware that Finan and Ethne were listening.

"He can call himself what he likes," I said, "but that doesn't make it true."

"He has a reputation," she said, and she told us of Skirnir and what she said made sense. There were nests of pirates on the Frisian coast, where they were protected by treacherous shoal waters and shifting dunes. Finan and I, when we had been enslaved by Sverri, had rowed through those waters, sometimes feeling our oar-blades strike the sand or mud. Sverri, a clever shipmaster, had escaped the pursuing red ship because he knew the channels, and I did not doubt that Skirnir knew the waters intimately. He called himself a jarl, the equivalent of a lord, but in truth he was a savage pirate who preyed on ships. The Frisian Islands had always produced wreckers and pirates, most of them desperate men who died soon enough, but Skade insisted that Skirnir had flourished. He captured ships or else took payment for safe passage and by so doing he had made himself rich and notorious.

"How many crews does he have?" I asked Skade.

"When last I was there," she said, "sixteen small ships and two large."

"When were you last there?"

"Two summers ago."

"Why did you leave?" Ethne asked.

Skade gave the Scottish woman a speculative look, but Ethne held the gaze. She was a small, red-haired, and fiery woman whom we had freed from slavery, and she was fiercely loyal to Finan, by whom she now had a son and a daughter. She could see where this conversation was going, and before her husband went into battle she wanted to know all she could discover.

"I left," Skade said, "because Skirnir is a pig."

"He's a man," Ethne said, and got a reproving dig in her ribs from Finan.

I watched a servant girl carry logs to the tavern's hearth. The fire brightened and I wondered again why so few men were drinking in the Goose.

"Skirnir ruts like a pig," Skade said, "and he snorts like a pig, and he hits women."

"So how did you escape the pig?" Ethne persisted.

"Skirnir captured a ship which had a chest of gold coins," Skade said, "and he took some of the gold to Haithabu to buy new weapons, and he took me with him."

"Why?" I asked.

She looked at me levelly. "Because he could not bear to be without me," she said.

I smiled at that. "But Skirnir must have had men to guard you in Haithabu?"

"Three crews."

"And he let you meet Harald?"

She shook her head. "I never met him," she said, "I just took one look at him and he looked at me."

"So?"

"That night Skirnir was drunk," she said, "snoring, and his men were drunk, so I walked away. I walked to Harald's ship and we sailed. I had never even spoken to him."

"Stop that!" I shouted at two of my men who were squabbling over one of the Goose's whores. The whores earned their living in a loft that was reached by a ladder, and one of the men was trying to pull the other off the rungs. "You first," I pointed at the more drunken of the two, "and you after. Or both of you together, I don't care! But don't start a fight over her!" I watched till they subsided, then turned back to Skade. "Skirnir," I said simply.

"He has an island, Zegge, and lives on a *terpen*."

"*Terpen*?"

"A hill made by hand," she explained, "it is the only way men can live on most of the islands. They make a hill with timber and clay, build the houses, and wait for the tide to wash it away. Skirnir has a stronghold on Zegge."

"And a fleet of ships," I said.

"Some are very small," Skade said. Even so I reckoned Skirnir had at least three hundred fighting men, and maybe as many as five hundred. I had forty-three. "They don't all live on Zegge," Skade went on, "it is too small. Most have homes on nearby islands."

"He has a stronghold?"

"A hall," she said, "built on a *terpen*, and ringed with a palisade."

"But to reach the hall," I said, "we have to get past the other is-lands." Any ship going through what would doubtless be a shallow and tide-torn channel would find Skirnir's men following, and I could imagine landing on Zegge with two crews of enemies close be-hind me.

"But in the hall," Skade said, lowering her voice, "is a hole in the floor, and beneath the floor is a chamber lined with elm, and inside the chamber is gold."

"There was gold," Finan corrected her.

She shook her head. "He cannot bear parting with it. He is gener-ous with his men. He buys weapons, mail, ships, oars, food. He buys slaves. But he keeps what he can. He loves to open the trapdoor and stare at his hoard. He shudders when he watches it. He loves it. He once made a bed of gold coins."

"They dug into your back?" Ethne asked, amused.

Skade ignored that, looking at me. "There's gold and silver in that chamber, lord, enough to light your dreams."

"Other men must have tried to take it," I said.

"They have," she said, "but water, sand, and tide are as good a de-fense as stone walls, lord, and his guard is loyal. He has three broth-ers, six cousins, and they all serve him."

"Sons?" Ethne asked.

"No children by me. Many by his slaves."

"Why did you marry him?" Ethne asked.

"I was sold to him. I was twelve, my mother had no money, and Skirnir wanted me."

"He still does," I said speculatively, remembering that his offer of a reward for Skade's return had reached Alfred's ears.

"The bastard has a lot of men," Finan said dubiously.

"I can find men," I said softly, and then turned because Sihtric had come running from the tavern's back door.

"Men," he told me, "there's at least thirty out there, lord, and all with weapons."

So my suspicions were right. Guthlac wanted me, my treasure, my ship, and my woman.

And I wanted Skirnir's gold.

TWO

I snatched open the tavern's front door and saw more men waiting on the quay. They looked startled when I appeared, so startled that most took an involuntary step backward. There were at least fifty of them, a few armed with spears and swords, but most with axes, sickles, or staves, which suggested they were townsfolk roused by Guthlac for a night's treacherous work, but, far more worryingly, a handful of them carried bows. They had made no attempt to capture *Seolferwulf*, which was lit at the pier's end by the dull glow of the herring-driers' fires that burned above the narrow beach's high-water line. That small light reflected from the mail which Osferth and his men were wearing, and from the blades of their spears, swords, and axes. Osferth had made a shield wall across the pier, and it looked formidable.

I closed the door and dropped its locking bar into place. It seemed clear that Guthlac had no appetite for attacking Osferth's men, which suggested he wanted to capture us first, then use us as hostages to take the ship.

"We have a fight on our hands," I told our men. I slid Wasp-Sting from her hiding place and watched, amused, as other weapons appeared. They were mostly short-swords like Wasp-Sting, but Rorik, a Dane I had captured in one of the punitive raids on East Anglia and who had sworn an oath to me rather than go back to his old lord, had somehow managed to bring a war ax. "There are men that way," I told them, pointing to the front door, "and that way," I pointed toward the brewing house.

130

"How many, lord?" Cerdic asked.

"Too many," I said. I had no doubt that we could fight our way to *Seolferwulf* because townsfolk armed with sickles and staves would prove easy foes for my trained warriors, but the archers outside the door could give my crew grievous casualties, and I was already shorthanded. The bows I had seen were short hunting bows, but their arrows were still lethal against men not wearing mail.

"If they're too many, lord," Finan suggested, "then best to attack them now rather than wait till there are more of them?"

"Or wait till they get tired," I said, and just then a timid knock sounded on the tavern's back door. I nodded to Sihtric, who unbarred the door and pulled it inward to reveal a sorry-looking creature, scrawny and frightened, dressed in a threadbare black robe over which hung a wooden cross that he clutched nervously. He bobbed his head at us. I had a glimpse of the armed men in the yard before the man edged into the tavern and Sihtric closed and barred the door behind him. "Are you a priest?" I demanded, and he nodded his head. "So Guthlac sends a priest," I went on, "because he's too frightened to show his face in here?"

"The reeve means you no harm, lord," the priest said. He was a Dane, and that surprised me. I knew the Danes of East Anglia had converted to Christianity, but I had thought it a cynical conversion, done to appease the threat of Alfred's Wessex, but some Danes, it seemed, truly had become Christians.

"What's your name, priest?"

"Cuthbert, lord."

I sneered. "You took a Christian name?"

"We do, lord, upon conversion," he said nervously, "and Cuthbert, lord, was a most holy man."

"I know who he is," I said, "I've even seen his corpse. So if Guthlac means us no harm then we can go back to our ship?"

"Your men may, lord," Father Cuthbert said very timidly, "so long as you and the woman stay, lord."

"The woman?" I asked, pretending not to understand him, "you mean Guthlac wants me to stay with one of his whores?"

"His whores?" Cuthbert asked, confused by my question, then shook his head vigorously. "No, he means the woman, lord. Skade, lord."

So Guthlac knew who Skade was. He had probably known ever since we had landed at Dumnoc, and I cursed the fog that had made our voyage so slow. Alfred must have guessed we would put in to an East Anglian port to resupply, and he had doubtless offered a reward to King Eohric for our capture, and Guthlac had seen a swift, if not easy, way to riches. "You want me and Skade?" I asked the priest.

"Just the two of you, lord," Father Cuthbert said, "and if you yield yourselves, lord, then your men may leave on the morning tide."

"Let's start with the woman," I said, and held Wasp-Sting out to Skade. She stood as she took the sword, and I stepped aside. "You can have her," I told the priest.

Father Cuthbert watched as Skade ran a long slow finger up the short-sword's blade. She smiled at the priest, who shuddered. "Lord?" he asked plaintively.

"So take her!" I told him.

Skade held the sword low, its blade pointing upward, and Father Cuthbert did not need much imagination to envisage that shining steel ripping through his belly. He frowned, embarrassed by the grins on my men's faces, then he summoned his courage and beckoned to Skade. "Put the blade down, woman," he said, "and come with me."

"Lord Uhtred told you to take me, priest," she said.

Cuthbert licked his lips. "She'll kill me, lord," he complained to me.

I pretended to think about that statement, then nodded. "Very likely," I said.

"I shall consult the reeve," he said with what little dignity he could muster, and almost ran back to the door. I nodded to Sihtric to let the priest go, then took my sword back from Skade.

"We could make a dash for the ship, lord?" Finan suggested. He was peering through a knothole in the tavern's front door and evidently did not have a great opinion of the men waiting in ambush.

"You see they've got bows?" I asked.

"Ah, so they do," he said, "and that puts a big fat turd in the ale barrel, doesn't it?" He straightened from the peephole. "So we wait for them to get tired, lord?"

"Or for me to have a better idea," I suggested, and just then there was another rap on the back door, louder this time, and again I nodded to Sihtric to unbar.

Guthlac now stood in the doorway. He still wore his mail, but had donned a helmet and carried a shield as added protection. "A truce while we talk?" he suggested.

"You mean we're at war?" I asked.

"I mean you let me talk, then let me go," he said truculently, tugging at one of his long black mustaches.

"We shall talk," I agreed, "then you can go."

He took a cautious step into the room, where he looked somewhat surprised to see how well armed my men were. "I've sent for my lord's household troops," he said.

"That was probably wise," I said, "because your men can't beat mine."

He frowned at that. "We don't want a fight!"

"We do," I said enthusiastically, "we were hoping for a fight. Nothing finishes an evening in a tavern so well as a fight, don't you agree?"

"Maybe a woman?" Finan suggested, grinning at Ethne.

"True," I agreed. "Ale first, next a fight, then a woman. Just like Valhalla. So tell us when you're ready, Guthlac, and we'll have the fight."

"Yield yourself, lord," he said. "We were told you might be coming, and it seems Alfred of Wessex wants you. He doesn't want your life, lord, just your body. Yours and the woman's."

"I don't want Alfred to have my body," I said.

Guthlac sighed. "We're going to stop you leaving, lord," he said patiently. "I've got fourteen hunters with bows waiting for you.

You'll doubtless kill some men, lord, and that will be another crime to add to your offenses, but my archers will kill some of your men, and we don't want to. Your men and your ship are free to leave, but you're not. Nor is the woman," he looked at Skade, "Edith."

I smiled at him. "So take me! But remember I'm the man who killed Ubba Lothbrokson beside the sea."

Guthlac looked at my sword, tugged on his mustache again, and took a step backward. "I won't die on that blade, lord," he said, "I'll wait for my lord's troops. They'll take you, and kill the rest of you. So I advise that you yield, lord, before they arrive."

"You want me to yield now so you get the reward?"

"And what's wrong with that?" he asked belligerently.

"How much is it?"

"Enough," he said. "So do you yield?"

"Wait outside," I told him, "and you'll find out."

"What of them?" he asked, nodding toward the local men who had been trapped inside the Goose with us. None held any value as a hostage and so I sent them away with Guthlac. They ran into the back yard, doubtless relieved they were not to be part of the slaughter they expected to redden the tavern's floor.

Guthlac was a fool. What he should have done was charge into the tavern and overwhelm us, or, if he merely wanted to trap us until trained troops arrived, he should have barricaded both doors with some of the giant ale barrels from the yard. As it was he had split his troops into two bands. I estimated there were fifty waiting between us and *Seolferwulf*, and as many again in the back yard. I was thinking that my score of men could fight their way through those fifty on the quay, but I knew we would take casualties reaching the ship. The bows would kill a handful of men and women before we got among the enemy, and none of us wore mail. I wanted to escape without any of my people being killed or wounded.

I ordered Sihtric to keep a watch on the back yard, which was easily done through a gap in the wattle wall. Another man watched the quay. "Tell me when they leave," I said.

"Leave?" Finan asked, grinning, "why would they leave, lord?"

"Always make the enemy do what you want them to do," I said, and I climbed the ladder to the whore-loft where three girls clung to each other on one of the straw mattresses. I grinned at them. "How are you, ladies?" I asked. None of the three answered, but just watched as I attacked the underside of the low thatched roof with Wasp-Sting. "We're leaving soon," I said to them, speaking English, "and you're welcome to come with us. A lot of my men don't have a woman. Better to be married to a warrior than whoring for that fat Dane. Is he a good master?"

"No," one of them said in a very low voice.

"He likes to whip you?" I guessed. I had ripped out a great bundle of reeds and the smoke from the tavern fire began to drift through the new smoke-hole I had made. Guthlac would doubtless see the fresh hole I had made in his roof, but it was unlikely he would send men to block it. He would need ladders.

"Finan!" I called down, "bring me fire!"

An arrow thumped into the roof, confirming that Guthlac had indeed seen the hole. He must have thought I was trying to lead my men out of the torn thatch and his archers now shot up at the roof, but they were in the wrong place to send their arrows through the new gap. They could only shoot across the ragged hole, which meant that any man trying to escape would have been hit as soon as he clambered through the thatch, but that was not why I had torn down the moldering reed. I looked back to the girls. "We'll be leaving very soon," I said. "If you want to come with us then get dressed, go down the ladder, and wait by the front door."

After that it was simple. I hurled burning scraps of driftwood from the tavern fire as far as I could and watched them fall onto the thatched roofs of the nearby cottages. I burned my hand, but that was a small price to pay as the flames caught the reeds and flared bright. A dozen of my men were passing the fiery brands up the ladder, and I threw each flaming timber as far as I could, trying to set fire to as many houses as I could reach.

No man could watch his town burning. Fire is a huge fear, for thatch and timber burn easily, and a fire in one house will quickly spread to others, and Guthlac's men, hearing the screams of their women and children, deserted him. They used rakes to pull the burning thatch off the rafters and they carried pails of water from the river, and all we had to do was open the tavern's front door and go to the ship.

Most of my men and two of the whores did just that, running down the pier and reaching the safety of the ship, where Osferth's men were armored and armed, but Finan and I dodged into the alley beside the Goose. The town was lurid with flames now. Men shouted, dogs barked, and woken gulls screamed. The fire was noisy, and panicking folk screamed contrary orders as they desperately tried to save their property. Heaps of burning thatch filled the streets while the sky was red with sparks. Guthlac, intent on saving the Goose, was shouting at men to pull down the house nearest to the tavern, but in the confusion no one was taking any notice of him. Nor did they notice Finan and me as we emerged into the street behind the tavern.

I had armed myself with a log from the tavern, one of those waiting to be put on the fire, and I just swung it hard so that it smashed into the side of Guthlac's helmet, and he went down like an ox that had been spiked between the eyes. I took hold of his mail coat and used it to haul him back into the alley, then down the pier. He was heavy, so it took three of my men to carry him across the trading ship and throw him onto *Seolferwulf*, and then, satisfied that all my crew was safe, we loosed the mooring lines. The ship drifted upstream on the incoming tide, and we countered it with oar strokes, backing water as we waited for the ebb to start.

We watched Dumnoc burn. Six or seven houses were alight now, their flames roaring like a furnace and spewing sparks high into the night sky. The fires lit the scene, throwing a raw shaky light across the river. We saw men pull down houses to make a gap over which they hoped the flames would not jump and we saw a chain of folk passing water from the river, and we just watched, amused. Guthlac recovered his senses to find himself sitting on the small prow platform, stripped of his mail and bound hand and foot. I had put the wolf's head back on the bows. "Enjoy the view, Guthlac," I said.

He groaned, then remembered the purse at his waist into which he had put the silver I had paid him for our supplies. He felt inside, and found no coins left. He groaned again and looked up at me and this time saw the warrior who had killed Ubba Lothbrokson beside the sea. I was in full war-gear, mailed and helmeted, with Serpent-Breath hanging from my silver-studded belt.

"I was doing my duty, lord," Guthlac said.

I could see mailed men ashore and guessed the household troops of whoever was Guthlac's lord had arrived, but they could do nothing to hurt us unless they decided to crew one of the moored ships, but they made no attempt to do that. They just watched the town burning, and sometimes turned to gaze at us. "They could at least piss on the flames," Finan said reprovingly, "do something useful!" He frowned down at Guthlac. "What do we do with this one, lord?

"I was thinking of giving him to Skade," I said. Guthlac looked at her, she smiled, and he shuddered. "When I first met her," I told Guthlac, "she'd just tortured a thegn. She killed him and it wasn't pretty."

"I wanted to know where his gold was," she explained.

"It wasn't pretty at all," I said. Guthlac flinched.

Seolferwulf hung in the slack tide. It was high-water now and the river looked wide, but that was deceptive because beneath the shivering red-reflecting surface were shoals of mud and sand. The current would help us soon, but I wanted to wait until there was sufficient daylight to see the channel markers, and so my men stirred their oars to keep us lingering off the burning town. "What you should have done," I told Guthlac, "is brought your men right into the tavern while we were drinking. You'd have lost a few, but you'd at least have stood a chance."

"You're going to put me ashore?" he asked plaintively.

"Of course I am," I said pleasantly, "but not yet. Look at that!" A house had just collapsed into its own flames and the great beams and rafters exploded gouts of flame, smoke, and sparks toward the clouds. The roof of the Goose had caught the fire now and, as it flared bright in the sky, my men cheered.

We left unmolested, sliding down the river in the day's first wan light. We rowed to the channel's end where the water fretted white and wide on the long shoals, and it was there that I untied Guthlac's bonds and pushed him to *Seolferwulf*'s stern. I stood beside him on the steering platform. The tide was taking us farther out to sea, and the ship was shuddering and bucking to the wind-driven waves. "Last night," I said to Guthlac, "you told us we were welcome in Dumnoc. You gave us leave to spend the night in peace, remember?"

He just looked at me.

"You broke your word," I said. He still said nothing. "You broke your word," I said again, and all he could do was shake his head in terror. "So you want to go ashore?"

"Yes, lord," he said.

"Then make your own way," I said, and pushed him overboard. He gave a cry, there was a splash as he fell, then Finan rapped the order for the oars to bite.

Later, many days later, Osferth asked me why I had killed Guthlac. "He was harmless, surely, lord?" he asked, "just a fool?"

"Reputation," I answered, and saw Osferth's puzzlement. "He challenged me," I explained, "and if I had let him live then he would have boasted that he challenged Uhtred of Bebbanburg and lived."

"So he had to die, lord?"

"Yes," I said, and Guthlac did die. We rowed offshore and I watched the reeve struggle in our wake. For a moment or two he managed to keep his head above water, then he vanished. We hoisted the sail, felt the ship lean to the long wind, and headed north.

We had more fog, more days and nights in empty creeks, but then the winds swung to the east and the air cleared and *Seolferwulf* leaped northward. Winter had touched the air.

The last day of the voyage was bright and cold. We had spent the night offshore, and so reached our destination in the morning. The wolf's head was on the prow, and the sight of it sent small fishing boats scurrying for shelter among the scatter of rocky islands where seals glistened and stubby puffins whirred into the sky. I had taken down the sail and, in the long gray swells, rowed *Seolferwulf* closer to the sandy beach. "Hold her here," I ordered Finan. The oars rested and the ship heaved slow. I stood in the prow with Skade and gazed westward. I was dressed in my war-glory. Mail and helmet and sword and arm rings.

I was remembering a far-off day when I had been on this same beach and had watched, amazed, as three ships came southward to ride the waves as *Seolferwulf* now rode them. I had been a child, and that had been my first glimpse of the Danes. I had marveled at their ships, so lean and beautiful, and at the symmetry of their oar-banks that had risen and fallen like magic wings. I had watched, astonished, as the Danish leader had run the oars in full armor, stepping from shaft to shaft, risking death with every step, and I had listened to my father and my uncle curse the newcomers. Within hours my brother had been killed, and within weeks my father followed him to the grave, and my uncle had stolen Bebbanburg and I had joined the family of the oar-runner, Ragnar the Fearless. I learned Danish, fought for the Danes, forgot Christ and welcomed Odin, and it had all begun here, at Bebbanburg.

"Your home?" Skade asked.

"My home," I said, for I am Uhtred of Bebbanburg and I was gazing at that great fortress on its rearing rock above the sea. Men lined the wooden ramparts and stared back. Above them, flying from a staff erected on the seaward gable of the great hall, was the flag of my family, the wolf's head, and I ordered the same flag hoisted on our mast, though there was hardly enough wind to display it. "I'm letting them know that I live," I told her, "and that so long as I live they should be frightened." And then fate put a thought into my head and I knew I would never retake Bebbanburg, would never scale the rock and climb the walls unless I did what Ragnar had done so many years before. The prospect frightened me, but fate is inexorable. The spinners were watching me, waiting, needles poised, and unless I did their bidding then my fate would be failure. I had to run the oars.

"Hold the oars steady!" I ordered the twenty rowers on the landward flank. "Hold them level and hold them hard!"

"Lord," Skade said warningly, but I saw the excitement in her eyes too.

I had worn my full armor to appear as a warlord to my uncle's men in Bebbanburg, and now they might watch me die because one slip on the long shafts would send me to the sea's bed, dragged down by the mail I wore. But the conviction was too strong on me. To gain everything a man must risk everything.

I drew Serpent-Breath. I held her high in the air so that the garrison of the stronghold would see the sun glint on the long steel, then I stepped off the ship's side.

The trick of walking the oar-bank is to do it fast, but not so fast that it looks like a panicked run. It was twenty steps that had to be taken with a straight back to make it look easy, and I remember the ship rolling and the fear twitching in me, and each oar dipping beneath my tread, yet I made those twenty steps and leaped off the last oar to scramble onto the stern where Sihtric steadied me as my men cheered.

"You damned fool, lord," Finan said fondly.

"I'm coming!" I shouted at the fortress, but I doubt the words carried. The waves broke white and sucked back from the beach. The rocks above the beach were white with frost. It was a gray-white fortress. It was home. "One day," I said to my men, "we shall all live there." Then we turned the ship, hoisted the sail again, and went south. I watched the ramparts till they vanished.

And that same day we slid into the river mouth I knew so well. I had taken the wolf's head off the prow because this was friendly land, and I saw the beacon on the hill and the ruined monastery and the beach where the red ship had rescued me, and then, on the height of the tide, I ran *Seolferwulf* onto the shingle where over thirty other ships were already beached, all guarded by a small fort beside the ruined monastery on the hill. I jumped ashore, stamped my feet in the shingle, and watched the horsemen riding from the fort. They came to discover our business and one lowered a spear toward me. "Who are you?" he demanded.

"Uhtred of Bebbanburg."

The spear-point lowered and the man smiled. "We were told to expect you sooner, lord."

"There was fog."

"And you are welcome, lord. Whatever you need is yours. Whatever!"

And there was warmth, food, ale, welcome, and next morning horses for Finan, Skade, and myself, and we rode southwest, not far, and my crew came with me. An ox-drawn cart carried the treasure chest, our armor, and our weapons. *Seolferwulf* was safe in the river, guarded by the garrison there, but we went to the greater fortress, the place I had known we would be welcomed, and the lord of that greater fortress rode to greet us. He was roaring incoherently, shouting and laughing, and he leaped from his horse, as I did, and we met on the track where we embraced.

Ragnar. Jarl Ragnar, friend and brother. Ragnar of Dunholm, Dane and Viking, lord of the north, and he clasped me, then punched a fist into my shoulder. "You look older," he said, "older and much uglier."

"Then I get more like you," I said.

He laughed at that. He stepped back and I saw how big his belly had grown in the years since we had last met. He was not fat, just bigger, but he seemed as happy as ever. "You're all welcome," he bellowed at my crew. "Why didn't you come sooner?"

"We were slowed by fog," I explained.

"I thought you might be dead," he said, "then I thought that the gods don't want your miserable company yet." He paused, remembering suddenly, and his face straightened. He frowned, and could not look into my eyes. "I wept when I heard about Gisela."

"Thank you."

He nodded abruptly, then put an arm round my shoulder and

walked with me. The shield hand draped round my neck was mangled from the battle at Ethandun, where Alfred had destroyed
Guthrum's great army. I had fought for Alfred that day, and Ragnar,
my closest friend, had fought for Guthrum.

Ragnar looked so like his father. He had a broad generous face,
bright eyes, and the fastest smile of anyone I knew. His hair was fair,
like mine, and we had often been taken as brothers. His father had
treated me as a son and, if I had a brother, it was Ragnar. "You heard
what happened in Mercia?" he asked me.

"No."

"Alfred's forces assaulted Harald," he said.

"On Torneie?"

"Wherever he was. What I hear is that Harald was bedridden, his
men were starving, they were trapped, they were outnumbered, so
the Mercians and West Saxons decided to finish them off."

"So Harald's dead?"

"Of course he's not dead!" Ragnar said happily. "Harald's a Dane!
He fought the bastards off, sent them running away." He laughed.
"Alfred, I hear, is not a happy man."

"He never was," I said. "He's god-haunted."

Ragnar turned and stole a look at Skade, who was still in her saddle. "Is that Harald's woman?"

"Yes."

"She looks like trouble," he said. "So do we sell her back to
Skirnir?"

"No."

He grinned. "So she isn't Harald's woman now?"

"No."

"Poor woman," he said, and laughed.

"What do you know about Skirnir?"

"I know he's offering gold for her return."

"And Alfred's offering gold for my return?"

"He is indeed!" Ragnar said cheerfully. "I was thinking I could
truss you up like a goat and make myself even wealthier." He
paused because we had come within sight of Dunholm that stood

atop its great rock in the loop of the river. His standard of the eagle's wing flew above the fortress. "Welcome home," he said warmly.

I had come north and, for the first time in years, felt free.

Brida waited in the fortress. She was an East Anglian and Ragnar's woman, and she took me in her arms, said nothing, and I just felt her sorrow for Gisela. "Fate," I said.

She stepped back and ran a finger down my face, looking at me as if wondering what the years had done. "Her brother is dying too," she said.

"But he's still king?"

"Ragnar rules here," she said, "and lets Guthred call himself king." Guthred, Gisela's brother, ruled Northumbria from his capital at Eoferwic. He was a good-natured man, but weak, and he held the throne only because Ragnar and the other great northern jarls permitted it. "He's gone mad," Brida said bleakly, "mad and happy."

"Better than mad and sad."

"The priests look after him, but he won't eat. He throws the food at the walls and claims he's Solomon."

"He's still a Christian then?"

"He worships every god," she said tartly, "as a precaution."

"Will Ragnar call himself king?" I asked.

"He hasn't said," Brida spoke softly.

"Would you want that?"

"I want Ragnar to find his fate," she said, and there was something ominous in her words.

There was a feast in the hall that night. I sat next to Brida and the roaring fire lit her strong, dark face. She looked something like Skade, only older, and the two women had recognized their similarity and had immediately bridled with hostility. A harpist played at the hall's side, chanting a song about a raid Ragnar had made on Scotland, but the words were drowned by the sound of voices. One of Ragnar's men staggered to the door, but threw up before he could reach the open air. Dogs ran to eat the vomit, and the man went back to his table and shouted for more ale. "We are too comfortable here," Brida said.

"Is that bad?"

"Ragnar is happy," she said, too softly for her lover to hear. He sat to her right, and Skade was beyond him. "He drinks too much," Brida said, then sighed. "Who would have thought it?"

"That Ragnar likes ale?"

"That you would be so feared." She inspected me as though she had never seen me before. "Ragnar the Elder would be proud of you," she said. Brida, like me, had been raised in Ragnar's house. We had been children together, then lovers, and now were friends. She was wise, unlike Ragnar the Younger, who was impulsive and hot-headed, but sensible enough to trust Brida's wisdom. Her one great regret was that she was childless, though Ragnar himself had fathered enough bastards.

One of those bastards was helping to serve the feast, and Ragnar took hold of the girl's elbow. "Are you mine?" he asked.

"Yours, lord?"

"Are you my daughter?"

"Oh yes, lord!" she said happily.

"I thought you were," he said and slapped her rump. "I make pretty daughters, Uhtred!"

"You do!"

"And fine sons!" He smiled happily, then let go a huge belch.

"He doesn't see the danger," Brida said to me. She alone in the hall was unsmiling, but life had always been a serious business for Brida.

"What are you telling Uhtred?" Ragnar demanded.

"That our barley was diseased this year," she said.

"Then we buy some barley in Eoferwic," he said carelessly, and turned back to Skade.

"What danger?" I asked.

Brida lowered her voice again. "Alfred has made Wessex powerful."

"He has."

"And he's ambitious."

"He doesn't have long to live," I said, "so his ambition doesn't matter."

"Then he's ambitious for his son," she said impatiently. "He wants to extend Saxon rule northward."

"True," I said.

"And that threatens us," she said fiercely. "What does he call himself? King of the Angelcynn?" I nodded, and she put an urgent hand on my arm. "Northumbria has more than enough English speakers. He wants his priests and scholars to rule here."

"True," I said again.

"So they must be stopped," she said simply. She stared at me, her eyes flicking between mine. "He didn't send you to spy?"

"No," I said.

"No," she agreed. She toyed with a lump of bread, her gaze looking down the long benches of roaring warriors. "It's simple, Uhtred," she said bleakly, "if we don't destroy Wessex, then Wessex will destroy us."

"It would take years for the West Saxons to reach Northumbria," I said dismissively.

"Does that make the result any better?" Brida asked bitterly. "And no, it won't take years. Mercia is divided and weak and Wessex will swallow it in the next few years. Then they'll march on East Anglia, and after that all three kingdoms will be turned on us. And where the West Saxons go, Uhtred," her voice was very bitter now, "they destroy our gods. They bring their own god with his rules and his anger and his fear." Like me, Brida had been raised as a Christian, but had turned pagan. "We have to stop them before they begin, which means striking first. And striking soon."

"Soon?"

"Haesten plans to invade Mercia," she said, dropping her voice so it was almost a whisper. "That will draw Alfred's forces north of the Temes. What we should do is take a fleet and land on Wessex's south coast." Her hand tightened on my arm. "And next year," she said, "there'll be no Uhtred of Bebbanburg to protect Alfred's land."

"Are you two still talking of barley?" Ragnar roared. "How's my sister? Still married to that crippled old priest?"

"He makes her happy," I said.

"Poor Thyra," Ragnar said, and I thought how strange fate was, how weird its threads. Thyra, Ragnar's sister, had married Beocca, a match so unlikely as to be unimaginable, yet she had found pure happiness. And my thread? That night I felt as though my whole world had been turned upside down. For so many years my oath-sworn duty had been to protect Wessex, and I had done that duty, nowhere better than at Fearnhamme. Now, suddenly, I was hearing Brida's dreams of destroying Wessex. The Lothbroks had tried and failed to do that, Guthrum had come close before being defeated, and Harald had met disaster. Now Brida would try to persuade Ragnar to conquer Alfred's kingdom? I looked at my friend, who was singing loudly and thumping the table with an ale horn in time to the song.

"To conquer Wessex," I told Brida, "you'll need five thousand men and five thousand horses, and one thing more. Discipline."

"The Danes fight better than the Saxons," she said dismissively.

"But Danes fight only when they want to," I said harshly. Danish armies were coalitions of convenience, with jarls lending their crews to an ambitious man, but melting away as soon as easier plunder offered itself. They were like packs of wolves that would attack a flock, but sheer away if enough dogs defended the sheep. Danes and Norsemen were constantly listening for news of some country that offered easy plunder, and a rumor of an undefended monastery might send a score of ships on a scavenging voyage, but in my own lifetime I had seen how easily the Danes were repulsed. Kings had built burhs all across Christendom and the Danes had no appetite for long sieges. They wanted quick plunder, or else they wanted to settle rich land. Yet the days of easy conquest, of facing undefended towns and rabbles of half-trained warriors, were long gone. If Ragnar or any other northman wanted to take Wessex, then he must lead an army of disciplined men prepared to undertake siege warfare. I looked at my friend, lost in the joy of feast and ale, and could not imagine him with the patience to defeat Alfred's organized defenses.

"But you could," Brida said very quietly.

"Are you reading my thoughts?"

She leaned closer to me, her voice a whisper. "Christianity is a disease that spreads like a plague. We have to stop it."

"If the gods want it stopped," I suggested, "they'll do it themselves."

"Our gods prefer feasting. They live, Uhtred. They live and laugh and enjoy, and what does their god do? He broods, he's vengeful, he scowls, he plots. He's a dark and lonely god, Uhtred, and our gods ignore him. They're wrong."

I half smiled. Brida, alone of all the men or women I knew, would see nothing strange in chiding the gods for their faults, and even try to do their work for them. But she was right, I thought, the Christian god was dark and threatening. He had no appetite for feasting, for laughter in the hall, for ale and mead. He set rules and demanded discipline, but rules and discipline were just what we needed if we were to defeat him.

"Help me," Brida said.

I watched two jugglers toss flaming brands into the smoky air. Gusts of laughter echoed in the great hall and I felt a sudden surge of hatred for Alfred's pack of black-robed priests, for the whole tribe of life-denying churchmen whose only joy was to disapprove of joy. "I need men," I told Brida.

"Ragnar has men."

"I need my own," I insisted. "I have forty-three. I need at least ten times that number."

"If men know you're leading an army against Wessex," she said, "they'll follow."

"Not without gold," I said, glancing at Skade who was watching me suspiciously, curious what secrets Brida whispered in my ear. "Gold," I went on, "gold and silver. I need gold."

I needed more. I needed to know whether Brida's dreams of defeating Wessex were known beyond Dunholm. Brida claimed she had told no one except Ragnar, but Ragnar was famously loose-tongued.

Give Ragnar a horn of ale and he would share every secret known to man, and if Ragnar had told just one man, then Alfred would learn of the ambition soon enough, which was why I was glad when Offa, his women, and his dogs arrived at Dunholm.

Offa was a Saxon, a Mercian who had once been a priest. He was tall, thin, with a lugubrious face that suggested he had seen every folly the world offered. He was old now, old and gray-haired, but he still traveled all across Britain with his two squabbling women and his troupe of performing terriers. He showed the dogs at fairs and at feasts, where the dogs walked on their hind legs, danced together, leaped through hoops, and one even rode a small pony while the others carried leather buckets to collect coins from the spectators. It was not the most spectacular entertainment, but children loved the terriers and Ragnar, of course, was entranced by them.

Offa had left the priesthood, thus incurring the enmity of the bishops, but he had the protection of every ruler in Britain because his real livelihood was not his terriers, but his extraordinary capacity for information. He talked to everyone, he drew conclusions, and he sold what he deduced. Alfred had used him for years. The dogs gave Offa an entry into almost every noble hall in Britain, and Offa listened to gossip and carried what he learned from ruler to ruler, eking out his facts coin by coin. "You must be rich," I told Offa the day he arrived.

"You are pleased to jest, lord," he said. He sat at a table outside Ragnar's hall, his eight dogs sitting obediently in a semicircle behind his bench. A servant had brought him ale and bread. Ragnar had been delighted at Offa's unexpected arrival, anticipating the laughter which always accompanied the dogs' performance.

"Where do you keep all that money?" I asked.

"You really wish me to answer that, lord?" Offa asked. Offa would answer questions, but his answers always had to be paid for.

"It's late for you to be traveling north," I said.

"Yet so far the winter is surprisingly mild. And business brought me north, lord," he said, "your business." He groped in a large leather bag and took out a sealed and folded parchment that he pushed across the table. "That is for you, lord."

I picked up the letter. The seal was a blob of wax which bore no imprint and seemed undisturbed. "What does the letter say?" I asked Offa.

"Are you suggesting I've read it?" he asked, offended.

"Of course you did," I said, "so save me the trouble of reading it."

He gave a hint of a smile. "I suspect you will find it of little importance, lord," he said. "The writer is your friend, Father Beocca. He says your children are safe in the Lady Æthelflæd's household and that Alfred is still angry with you, but will not order your death if you return south as, he reminds you, your sworn oath demands. Father Beocca finishes by saying that he prays for your soul daily, and demands that you return to your oath-given duties."

"Demands?"

"Most sternly, lord," Offa said with another ghost of a smile.

"Nothing else?"

"Nothing, lord."

"So I can burn the letter?"

"A waste of parchment, lord. My women can scrape the skin clean and reuse it."

I pushed the letter back to him. "Let them scrape," I said. "What happened at Torneie?"

Offa considered the question for a few heartbeats, then decided that the answer would be common knowledge soon enough and so he could tell me without any payment. "King Alfred ordered an assault, lord, to end Jarl Harald's occupation of the island. The Lord Steapa was to bring men upstream in ships while Lord Æthelred and the Ætheling Edward attacked across the shallower branch of the river. Both attacks failed."

"Why?"

"Harald, lord, had placed sharpened stakes in the river bed, and the West Saxon ships struck those stakes and most never reached the island. Lord Æthelred's assault simply became bogged down. They floundered in the mud and Harald's warriors shot arrows and threw spears, and no Saxon even reached the thorn palisade. It was a massacre, lord."

"Massacre?"

"The Danes made a sally, lord, and slaughtered many of Lord Æthelred's men in the river."

"Cheer me up," I said, "and tell me that Lord Æthelred was killed."

"He lives, lord," Offa said.

"And Steapa?"

"He lives too, lord."

"So what happens now?"

"Now that is a question," Offa said distantly. He waited until I had placed a coin on the table. "There is argument among the king's counselors, lord," he said, slipping the silver into his pouch, "but the cautious advice of Bishop Asser will prevail, I'm sure."

"And that advice is?"

"Oh, to pay Harald silver, of course."

"Bribe him to leave?" I asked, shocked. Why would any man have to bribe a fugitive band of defeated Danes to leave their territory?

"Silver often achieves what steel cannot," Offa said.

"Ten men and a boy could capture Torneie," I said angrily.

"If you led them, maybe," Offa said, "but you're here, lord."

"So I am."

It cost me more silver to learn what Brida had already told me, that Haesten, safe in the high fort at Beamfleot, planned an assault on Mercia. "Did you tell that to Alfred?" I asked Offa.

"I did," he said, "but his other spies contradict me, and he believes me wrong."

"Are you wrong?"

"Rarely, lord," he said.

"Is Haesten strong enough to take Mercia?"

"Not at present. He has been joined by many of Harald's crews who fled your victory at Fearnhamme, but I don't doubt he needs more men."

"He'll seek them from Northumbria?" I asked.

"It's a possibility, I suppose," Offa said, and that answer told me what I wanted to know, that even Offa, with his uncanny ability to sniff out secrets, was ignorant of Brida's ambition for Ragnar to lead an army against Wessex. If Offa had known of that ambition he would have hinted that the Northumbrian Danes might have better things to do than assault Mercia, but he had slid past my question without sensing any opportunity to take my silver. "But ships still join the Jarl Haesten," Offa went on, "and he may be strong enough by the spring. I'm sure he'll seek your help too, lord."

"I imagine so," I said.

Offa stretched his long thin legs under the table. One of the terriers whined and he snapped his fingers and the dog went instantly still. "The Jarl Haesten," he said cautiously, "will offer you gold to join him."

I smiled. "You didn't come here as a messenger, Offa. If Alfred wanted a letter sent to me he had cheaper ways of sending it than by satisfying your greed." Offa looked offended at the word greed, but made no protest. "And it was Alfred who ordered Father Beocca to write, wasn't it?" I asked, and Offa nodded slightly. "So," I said, "Alfred sent you to find out what I'm going to do."

"There is curiosity in Wessex about that," he said distantly.

I laid two silver coins on the table. "So tell me," I said.

"Tell you what, lord?" he asked, gazing at the coins.

"Tell me what I'm going to do," I said.

He smiled at being paid for an answer I surely knew already. "Generous, lord," he said as his long fingers closed round the coins. "Alfred believes you will attack your uncle."

"I might."

"But for that, lord, you need men, and men need silver."

"I have silver."

"Not enough, lord," Offa said confidently.

"So perhaps I will join Haesten?"

"Never, lord, you despise him."

"So where will I find the silver?" I asked.

"From Skirnir, of course," Offa said, his eyes steady on mine.

I tried to betray nothing. "Is Skirnir one of the men who pays you?" I asked.

"I cannot bear journeying in ships, lord, so avoid them. I have never met Skirnir."

"So Skirnir doesn't know what I plan?"

"From what I hear, lord, Skirnir believes every man plans to rob him, so, being ready for all, he will be ready for you."

I shook my head. "He's ready for thieves, Offa, not for a warlord."

The Mercian just raised an eyebrow, a signal more silver was needed. I put one coin on the table and watched it vanish into that capacious purse. "He will be ready for you, lord," he said, "because your uncle will warn him."

"Because you will tell my uncle?"

"If he pays me, yes."

"I should kill you now, Offa."

"Yes, lord," he said, "you should. But you won't." He smiled.

So Skirnir would learn I was coming, and Skirnir had ships and men, but fate is inexorable. I would go to Frisia.

THREE

I tried to persuade Ragnar to come with me to Frisia, but he laughed it away. "You think I want to get a wet arse at this time of year?" It was a cold day, the countryside sodden from two days of heavy rain that had crashed in from the sea. The rain had ended, but the land was heavy, the winter colors dark, and the air damp.

We rode across the hills. Thirty of my men and forty of Ragnar's. We were all in mail, all helmeted, all armed. Shields hung at our sides or on our backs, and there were long scabbarded swords at our waists. "I'm going in winter," I explained, "because Skirnir won't expect me till spring."

"You hope," he said, "but maybe he's heard you're an idiot?"

"So come," I said, "and let's fight together again."

He smiled, but did not meet my gaze. "I'll give you Rollo," he said, naming one of his best fighters, "and whoever volunteers to go with him. You remember Rollo?"

"Of course."

"I have duties," he said vaguely. "I should stay here." It was not cowardice that made him refuse my invitation. No one could ever accuse Ragnar of timidity. Instead, I think, it was laziness. He was happy and did not need to disturb that happiness. He curbed his horse on the crest of a rise and gestured at the wide strip of coastland that lay beneath us. "There it is," he said, "the English kingdom."

"The what?" I asked indignantly. I was gazing at the rain-darkened land with its small hills and smaller fields with their familiar stone walls.

"That's what everyone calls it," Ragnar said. "The English king-dom."

"It isn't a kingdom," I said sourly.

"That's what they call it," he said patiently. "Your uncle has done well." I made a vomiting noise which made Ragnar laugh. "Think of it," he said, "the whole of the north is Danish, all except Bebban-burg's land."

"Because none of you could take the fort," I retorted.

"It probably can't be taken. My father always said it was too hard."

"I shall take it," I said.

We rode down from the hills. Trees were losing their last leaves in the sea wind. The pastures were dark, the thatch of the cottages al-most black, and the rich smell of the year's decay thick in our nos-trils. I stopped at one farmstead, deserted because the folk had seen us coming and fled to the woods, and I looked inside the granary to find the harvest had been good. "He gets richer," I said of my uncle. "Why don't you tear his land apart?"

"We do when we're bored," Ragnar said, "and then he tears ours apart."

"Why don't you just capture his land?" I asked, "and let him starve in the fortress."

"Men have tried that. He either fights or pays them to leave."

My uncle, who called himself Ælfric of Bernicia, was said to keep over a hundred household warriors in his fortress, and could raise four times that many from the villages scattered across his realm. It was, indeed, a small kingdom. To the north its boundary ran along the Tuede, beyond which lay the land of the Scots who were forever raiding for cattle and crops. To the south of Bebbanburg's land was the Tinan, where *Seolferwulf* now lay, and to the west were hills, and all the land beyond the hills and all to the south of the Tinan was in Danish hands. Ragnar ruled south of the river. "We sometimes raid your uncle's land," he said, "but if we take twenty cows he'll come back and take twenty of ours. And when the Scots are trouble-some?" he shrugged, leaving the thought unfinished.

"The Scots are always troublesome," I said.

"His warriors are useful when they raid," Ragnar admitted.

So Ælfric of Bernicia could be a good neighbor, cooperating with the Danes to repel and punish the Scots, and in return he asked only to be left in peace. That was how Bebbanburg had survived as a Christian enclave in a country of Danes. Ælfric was my father's younger brother, and he had always been the clever one in the family. If I had not hated him so much I might have admired him. He knew one thing well, that his survival depended on the great fortress where I had been born and which, all my life, I have thought of as home. There had once been a real kingdom ruled from Bebbanburg. My ancestors had been the kings of Bernicia, ruling deep into what the Scots impudently claim as their land, and south toward Eoferwic, but Bernicia had been swallowed into Northumbria, and Northumbria had fallen to the Danes, yet still the old fortress stood and around it was the remnant of that old English kingdom. "Have you met Ælfric?" I asked Ragnar.

"Many times."

"You didn't kill him for me?"

"We meet under a truce."

"Tell me about him."

"Old, gray, sly, watchful."

"His sons?"

"Young, cautious, sly, watchful."

"I heard Ælfric was ill."

Ragnar shrugged. "He's close to fifty years old, what man isn't ill who lives that long? But he recovers."

My uncle's eldest son was called Uhtred. That name was an affront. For generations the oldest son in our family has been named Uhtred, and if that heir dies then, as had happened to me, the next youngest son takes the name. My uncle, by naming his eldest Uhtred, was proclaiming that his descendants would be the rulers of Bebbanburg, and their greatest enemy was not the Danes, not even the Scots, but me. Ælfric had tried to kill me, and as long as he lived he would go on trying. He had put a reward on my head, but I was a hard man to kill and it had been years since any warrior dared the attempt. Now I rode toward him, my borrowed horse stepping high through the muck of the cattle-track we followed down from the hills. I could smell the sea and, though the waves were not yet visible, the sky to the east had the empty look of air above water. "He'll know we're coming?" I suggested to Ragnar.

"He knows. He never stops watching."

Horsemen would have sped to Bebbanburg and told of Danes crossing the hills. Even now, I knew, we were being watched. My uncle would not realize I was among the horsemen. His sentinels would have reported Ragnar's eagle's-wing banner, but I was not flying my own flag. Not yet.

We had our own scouts riding ahead and to our flanks. For so many years this had been my life. Whenever some restless East Anglian Dane had thought fit to steal a couple of sheep or snatch a cow from some pasture close to Lundene, we would ride in vengeance. This was very different country, though. Near Lundene the ground was flat, while here the small hills hid much of the landscape and so our scouts kept close to us. They saw nothing to alarm them, and they finally stopped on a wooded crest and that was where we joined them.

And beneath me was home.

The fortress was vast. It lay between us and the sea on its great lump of rock, connected to the land by a thin strip of sandy ground. To north and south were the high dunes, but the fortress broke the coast, its crag sheltering a wide shallow pool where a few fishing boats were moored. The village had grown, I saw, but so had the fortress. When I had been a child, a man crossed the sandy spit to reach a wooden palisade with a large gate surmounted by a fighting platform. That entrance, the Low Gate, was still there, and if any enemy fought through that archway he would still have had to climb to a second gate in another wooden palisade that was built on the rock itself, but that second palisade was gone entirely, and in its place was a high stone wall without any gate. So the old main entrance, the High Gate, was gone, and an attacker, if he breached the outer palisade to reach the smithy and the stables, would then have to scale that new stone wall. It was thick, high, and equipped with its own fighting platform, so arrows, spears, boiling water, rocks, and anything else the defenders could find would rain down on an attacking force.

The old gate had been at the fortress's southern end, but my uncle had made a path along the beach on the seaward side of Bebbanburg, and now a visitor had to follow the path to a new gate at the fort's northern extremity. The path began in the outer enclosure, so even to reach it, the old wall and its Low Gate had to be taken, then the attackers would have to advance along the new path beneath Bebbanburg's seaward ramparts, assailed by missiles, and then somehow fight through the new gate, which was also protected by a stone rampart. Even if the attackers somehow got through that new gate, a second wall waited with more defenders, and the attackers would need to capture that inner rampart before they broke through to Bebbanburg's heart, where two great halls and a church crowned the crag. Tendrils of smoke drifted above the fortress's roofs.

I swore softly.

"What are you thinking?" Ragnar asked.

I was thinking that Bebbanburg was impregnable. "I'm wondering who has Smoka now." I said.

"Smoka?"

"Best horse I ever owned."

Ragnar chuckled and nodded at the fort. "It's a brute, isn't it?" he said.

"Land ships at the northern end," I suggested. If ships came ashore where the new gate was built then the attackers would have no need to fight through the Low Gate.

"The beach is narrow there," Ragnar warned, though I probably knew the waters about Bebbanburg better than he did, "and you can't get ships into the harbor," he added, pointing to where the fishing boats were moored. "Little ships, yes, but anything bigger than a wash tub? Maybe at a spring high tide, but only for an hour or so, and that channel is a bitch when tide and wind are running. Waves build there. You'd be lucky to make it in one piece."

And even if I could land a dozen crews close to the new gate, what was to stop the defenders sending a force along the new path to trap the attackers? That would only happen if my uncle had warning of an attack and could assemble enough men to spare a force to make that counterattack. So the answer, I thought, was a surprise attack. But a surprise attack would be difficult. The sentries would see the ships approaching and call the garrison to arms, and the attacking crews would have to clamber ashore in the surf, then carry ladders and weapons over a hundred rocky paces to where the new stone wall barred them. It would hardly be a surprise by then, and the defenders would have plenty of time to assemble at the new gate. So two attacks? That meant starting a formal siege, using three or four hundred men to seal off the strip of land leading to the Low Gate. That would prevent reinforcements reaching the garrison and those besiegers could assault the Low Gate while the ships approached the new. That would split the defenders, but I would need at least as many men to attack the new gate, which meant I was looking for a thousand men, say twenty crews, and they would bring wives, servants, slaves, and children, so I would be feeding at least three thousand. "It has to be done," I said quietly.

"No one has ever captured Bebbanburg," Ragnar said.

"Ida did."

"Ida?"

"My ancestor. Ida the Flamebearer. One of the first Saxons in Britain."

"What kind of fort did he capture?"

I shrugged. "Probably a small one."

"Maybe nothing but a thorn fence guarded by half-naked savages," Ragnar said. "The best way to capture that place is to starve the bastards."

That was a possibility. A small army could seal off the landward approach, and ships could patrol the waters to stop supplies reaching my uncle, but bad weather would drive those ships away, leaving an opportunity for small local vessels to reach the fortress. It would take at least six months to starve Bebbanburg into surrender. Six months of feeding an army and persuading restless Danes to stay and fight. I stared at the Farnea Islands where the sea fretted white on rocks. Gytha, my stepmother, used to tell me tales of how Saint Cuthbert preached to the seals and the puffins on those rocks. He had lived on the islands as a hermit, eating barnacles and fern fronds, scratching his lice, and so the islands were sacred to Christians, but they were of little practical use. I could not shelter a blockading fleet there, for the scatter of islets offered no shelter, nor did Lindisfarena, that lay to the north. That island was much larger. I could see the remnants of the monastery there, but Lindisfarena offered no decent harbor.

I was still gazing at Lindisfarena, remembering how Ragnar the Elder had slaughtered the monks there. I had been a child, and that same day Ragnar the Elder had let me kill Weland, a man sent by my uncle to murder me, and I had hacked at him with my sword, cutting and slicing him, bleeding him to death in writhing agony. I stared at the island, remembering the death of enemies, when Ragnar touched my elbow. "They're curious about us," he said.

Horsemen were riding from the Low Gate. I counted them, reckoning there to be around seventy, which suggested my uncle was not looking for a fight. A man with a hundred household warriors does not want to lose ten in some meaningless skirmish, so he was matching our force with just enough men to deter either side from attacking the other. I watched the horsemen climb the hill toward us. They were in mail and helmeted, with shields and weapons, but they stopped a good four hundred paces away, all except three men who kept riding, though they ostentatiously laid aside their swords and shields before leaving their companions. They flew no banner.

"They want to talk," Ragnar said.

"Is that my uncle?"

"Yes."

The three men had curbed their horses halfway between the two armed bands. "I could kill the bastard now," I said.

"And his son inherits," Ragnar said, "and everyone knows you killed an unarmed man who had offered a truce."

"Bastard," I said of Ælfric. I unbuckled my two swords and tossed them to Finan, then spurred my borrowed horse. Ragnar came with me. I had half hoped my uncle was accompanied by his two sons, and if he had been I might have been tempted to try and kill all three, but instead his companions were two hard-looking warriors, doubtless his best men.

The three waited close to the rotting carcass of a sheep. I assume a wolf had killed the beast, then been driven off by dogs, and the corpse lay there, crawling with maggots, torn by ravens, and buzzing with flies. The wind blew the stench toward us, which was probably why Ælfric had chosen to stop there.

My uncle looked distinguished. He was slender and narrow-faced with a high hooked nose and dark, guarded eyes. His hair, the little that showed beneath his helmet's rim, was white. He watched me calmly, showing no fear as I stopped close. "I assume you are Uhtred?" he greeted me.

"Uhtred of Bebbanburg," I said.

"Then I should congratulate you," he said.

"Why?"

"For your victory over Harald. The news of it caused much rejoicing among good Christians."

"So you didn't rejoice?" I retorted.

"Jarl Ragnar," Ælfric ignored my small insult and nodded gravely to my companion, "you do me honor with this visit, lord, but you should have given me warning of your arrival. I would have made a feast for you."

"We're just exercising the horses," Ragnar said cheerfully.

"A long way from your home," Ælfric observed.

"Not from mine," I said.

The dark eyes brooded on me. "You are always welcome here, Uhtred," my uncle said, "any time you wish to come home, then just come. Believe me, I shall be glad to see you."

"I'll come," I promised him.

There was silence for a moment. My horse stamped a mud-clodded foot. The two lines of mail-clad warriors watched us. I could just hear the gulls at the distant shore. Their sound had been my childhood noise, never-ending like the sea. "As a child," my uncle broke the awkward silence, "you were disobedient, headstrong, and foolish. It seems you haven't changed."

"Ask Alfred of Wessex," I said, "he wouldn't be king now without my headstrong foolishness."

"Alfred knew how to use you," my uncle observed. "You were his dog. He fed you and held you. But like a fool you've slipped his lead. Who will feed you now?"

"I will," Ragnar said happily.

"But you, lord," Ælfric said respectfully, "don't have enough men to watch them die against my walls. Uhtred will have to find his own men."

"There are many Danes in Northumbria," I said.

"And Danes seek gold," Ælfric said, "do you really think there's enough inside my walls to draw the Danes of Northumbria to Beb-banburg?" He half smiled. "You will have to find your own gold, Uhtred." He paused, expecting me to say something, but I kept quiet. A raven, driven away from the sheep's carcass by our presence, protested from a bare tree. "Do you think your aglæcwif will lead you to the gold?" Ælfric asked.

An aglæcwif was a fiendish woman, a sorceress, and he meant Skade. "I have no aglæcwif," I said.

"She tempts you with her husband's riches," Ælfric said.

"Does she?"

"What else?" he asked. "But Skirnir knows she does that."

"Because you told him?"

My uncle nodded. "I saw fit to send him news of his wife. A courtesy, I think, to a neighbor across the sea. Skirnir, no doubt, will greet you in the spring as I would greet you, Uhtred, should you decide to come home." He stressed the last word, curdling it on his tongue, then gathered his reins. "I have nothing more to say to you." He nodded at Ragnar, then at his men, and the three turned away.

"I'll kill you!" I shouted after him, "and your cabbage-shitting sons!"

He just waved negligently and kept riding.

I remember thinking he had won that encounter. Ælfric had come from his fastness and he had treated me like a child, and now he rode back to that beautiful place beside the sea where I could not reach him. I did not move.

"What now?" Ragnar asked.

"I'll hang him with his son's intestines," I said, "and piss on his corpse."

"And how do you do that?"

"I need gold."

"Skirnir?"

"Where else?"

Ragnar turned his horse. "There's silver in Scotland," he said, "and in Ireland."

"And hordes of savages protect both," I said.

"Then Wessex?" he suggested.

I had not moved my horse and Ragnar was forced to turn back to me. "Wessex?" I echoed him.

"They say Alfred's churches are rich."

"Oh, they are," I said. "They're so rich they can afford to send silver to the Pope. They drip with silver. There's gold on the altars. There's money in Wessex, my friend, so much money."

Ragnar beckoned to his men and two of them rode forward with our swords. We buckled the belts around our waists and no longer felt naked. The two men walked their horses away, leaving us alone again. The sea wind brought the smell of home to lessen the smell of the carcass. "So will you attack next year?" I asked my friend.

He thought for a moment, then shrugged. "Brida thinks I've grown fat and happy," he said.

"You have."

He smiled briefly. "Why do we fight?" he asked.

"Because we were born," I answered savagely.

"To find a place we call home," Ragnar suggested. "A place where we don't need to fight anymore."

"Dunholm?"

"It's as safe a fortress as Bebbanburg," he said, "and I love it."

"And Brida wants you to leave it?"

He nodded. "She's right," he admitted wanly. "If we do nothing then Wessex will spread like a plague. There'll be priests everywhere."

We seek the future. We stare into its fog and hope to see a landmark that will make sense of fate. All my life I have tried to understand the past because that past was so glorious and we see remnants of that glory all across Britain. We see the great marble halls the Romans made, and we travel the roads they laid and cross the bridges they built, and it is all fading. The marble cracks in the frost and the walls collapse. Alfred and his like believed they were bringing civilization to a wicked, fallen world, but all he did was make rules. So many rules, but the laws were only ever an expression of hope, because the reality was the burhs, the walls, the spears on the ramparts, the glint of helmets in the dawn, the fear of mailed riders, the thump of hoofbeats, and the screams of victims. Alfred was proud of his schools and his monasteries and his silver-rich churches, but those things were protected by blades. And what was Wessex compared to Rome?

It is hard to bring thoughts into order, but I sense, I have always sensed, that we slide from light to darkness, from glory to chaos, and perhaps that is good. My gods tell us that the world will end in chaos, so perhaps we are living the last days and even I might survive long enough to see the hills crack and the sea boil and the heavens burn as the great gods fight. And in the face of that great doom, Alfred built schools. His priests scurried like mice in rotting thatch, imposing their rules as if mere obedience could stop the doom. Thou shalt not kill, they preached, then screamed at us warriors to slaughter the pagans. Thou shalt not steal, they preached, and forged charters to take men's lands. Thou shalt not commit adultery, they preached, and rutted other men's wives like besotted hares in springtime.

There is no sense. The past is a ship's wake etched on a gray sea, but the future has no mark. "What are you thinking?" Ragnar asked, amused.

"That Brida is right."

"I must go to Wessex?"

I nodded, yet I knew he did not want to go where so many had failed. All my life till that moment had been spent, one way or another, in attacking or defending Wessex. Why Wessex? What was Wessex to me? It was the bastion of a dark religion in Britain, it was a place of rules, a Saxon place, and I worshiped the older gods, the gods the Saxons themselves had worshiped before the missionaries came from Rome and gave them their new nonsense. Yet I had fought for Wessex. Time and again the Danes tried to capture Wessex, and time and again Uhtred of Bebbanburg had helped the West Saxons. I had killed Ubba Lothbrokson beside the sea, I had screamed in the shield wall that broke Guthrum's great army, and I had destroyed Harald. So many Danes had tried, and so many had failed, and I had helped them fail because fate had made me fight for the side with the priests. "Do you want to be King of Wessex?" I asked Ragnar.

He laughed. "No! Do you?"

"I want to be Lord of Bebbanburg."

"And I want to be Lord of Dunholm." He paused. "But."

"But if we don't stop them," I finished for him, "they'll come here."

"That's worth fighting for," Ragnar said reluctantly, "or else our children will be Christians."

I grimaced, thinking of my own children in Æthelflæd's household. They would be learning about Christianity. Maybe, by now, they had already been baptized, and that thought gave me a surge of anger and guilt. Should I have stayed in Lundene and meekly accepted the fate Alfred wanted for me? But Alfred had humiliated me once before, forcing me to crawl on my knees to one of his damned altars, and I would not do it again. "We'll go to Wessex," I said, "and make you king, and I'll defend you like I defended Alfred."

"Next year," Ragnar said.

"But I won't go naked," I said harshly. "I need gold, I need men."

"You can lead my men," Ragnar suggested.

"They're sworn to you. I want my own. I need gold."

He nodded. He understood what I was saying. A man is judged by his deeds, by his reputation, by the number of his oath-men. I was reckoned a warlord, but so long as I only led a handful of men, so long could people like my uncle afford to insult me. I needed men. I needed gold. "So you really will make a winter voyage to Frisia?" Ragnar asked.

"Why else did the gods send me Skade?" I retorted, and at that moment it was as if the fog had cleared and I could at last see the way ahead. Fate had sent me Skade, and Skade would lead me to Skirnir, and Skirnir's gold would let me raise the men who would fight with me through the burhs of Wessex, then I would take the silver of the Christian god and employ it to forge the army that would capture Bebbanburg.

It was all so clear. It even seemed easy.

We turned our horses and rode toward Dunholm.

Seolferwulf's prow slammed into a wave and the water exploded into white shards that whipped down the deck like ice missiles. Green sea surged over the bows and swilled cold into the bilge. "Bail!" I shouted, and the men not working the oars frantically scooped water over the side as our wolf's-head prow reared into the sky. "Row!" I bellowed, and the oars bit the water and *Seolferwulf* fell into a trough of the ocean with a crash that made her timbers tremble. I love the sea.

My forty-three men were on board, though I had allowed none of their women or children to accompany us, and Skade was only on board because she knew Zegge, the sandy island where Skirnir had his treasure hoard. I also had thirty-four of Ragnar's men, all of them volunteers, and together we sailed eastward into the teeth of a winter wind. This was no time to be at sea. Winter was when ships were laid up and men stayed in fire-bright halls, but Skirnir would expect me in the spring so I had risked this winter voyage.

"Wind's rising!" Finan shouted at me.

"It does that!" I shouted back, and was rewarded with a skeptical look. Finan was never as happy as I was at sea. For months we had shared a rowing bench, and he had endured the discomfort, but he had never reveled in the sea's threat.

"Shouldn't we turn and run?" he asked.

"In this little blow? Never!" I yelled at him over the wind's howl, then flinched as a slap of cold water hit my face. "Row, you bastards," I shouted, "if you want to live, row!"

We rowed and we lived, reaching the Frisian coast on a morning of cold air, dying winds, and sullen seas. The improving weather had released ships from the local harbors and I followed one into the intricate channels that led to the inner sea, a stretch of shallow water that lies between the islands and the mainland. The ship we followed had eight oarsmen and a cargo hidden beneath a great leather cloth, which suggested she carried salt, flour, or some other commodity that needed to be protected from the rain. The steersman was terrified by our close approach. He saw a wolf-headed ship crammed with fighting men and he feared he was about to be attacked, but I shouted that we merely needed guidance through the channels. The tide was rising, so even if we had gone aground, we would be safe enough, but the cargo ship led us safely into the deeper water, and it was there we first encountered Skirnir's reach.

A ship, much smaller than *Seolferwulf,* lay waiting a half-mile beyond the place where the channel emptied into the inner sea. I reckoned she had a crew of around twenty men and she was plainly watching the channels, ready to pounce on any shipping, though the sight of *Seolferwulf* made her cautious. I guessed she would normally have intercepted the incoming cargo ship, but instead she stayed motionless, watching us. The cargo ship's steersman pointed at the waiting boat. "I have to pay him, lord."

"Skirnir?" I asked.

"That's one of his ships, lord."

"So pay him!" I said. I spoke in English because the language of the Frisian people is so close to our own.

"He'll ask me about you, lord," he called back, and I understood his terror. The waiting ship would be curious about us, and they would demand answers from the trading ship's master, and if he had no satisfactory explanation they might well attempt to beat it out of him.

"Tell him we're Danes on our way home," I said. "My name is Lief Thorrson and if he wants money he must come and ask me."

"He won't ask you, lord," the man said. "A rat doesn't demand supper from a wolf."

I smiled at that. "You can tell the rat we mean no harm, we're just going home, and we merely followed you through the channel, nothing more." I tossed him a coin, making sure it bore the legend *Christiano Religio*, which meant it came from Frankia. I did not want to betray that we had come from Britain.

I watched the cargo ship row to Skirnir's vessel. Skade had been in the small space beneath the steering platform, but now joined me. "That's the *Sea-Raven*," she said, nodding at Skirnir's ship. "Her master is called Haakon. He's a cousin to my husband."

"So he'll recognize you?"

"Of course."

"Then don't let him see you," I said.

She bridled at that direct order, but did not argue. "He won't come near us," she said.

"No?"

"Skirnir leaves fighting ships alone, unless he outnumbers them by four or five to one."

I gazed at the *Sea-Raven*. "You said he had sixteen ships like that?"

"Two years ago," she said, "he had sixteen about that size, and two larger boats."

"That was two years ago," I said grimly. We had come into Skirnir's lair where we would be grossly outnumbered, but I reckoned he would still be wary of us. He would learn that a Viking ship was in his waters, and he would fear that an attack on us might bring other Vikings to take revenge. Would it cross his mind that Uhtred of Bebbanburg might have risked a winter voyage? Even if not, he would surely be curious about Lief Thorrson, and would not relax till that curiosity had been satisfied.

I ordered the wolf's head taken from the prow, then turned *Seolferwulf* toward the mainland shore. The *Sea-Raven* made no move to intercept us, but she did start to follow us, though when I checked the oars, as if waiting for her to catch up, she veered away. We rowed on and she fell out of sight behind us.

I wanted a place to hide, but there was too much shipping for that to be possible. Wherever we took shelter some local boat would see us, and the report would be passed from ship to ship until it reached Skirnir. If we were indeed a Danish ship on passage, going home for the dark winter nights, he would expect us to be gone from his waters in two or three days, so the longer we lingered, the greater his suspicion. And here, in the treacherous shoal waters of the inner sea, we were the rat and Skirnir the wolf.

We rowed north and east all day. We went slowly. Skirnir would hear that we were doing what he anticipated, making passage, and he would expect us to seek shelter for the night. We found that shelter in a creek on the mainland shore, though the tangle of marsh, sand, and inlets hardly deserved to be called a shore. It was a place of waterfowl, reeds, and hovels. A small village lay on the creek's southern bank, merely a dozen cottages and a small wooden church. It was a fishing community, and the folk watched *Seolferwulf* nervously, fearing we might come ashore to steal what little they possessed. Instead we purchased eel and herring from them, paying with Frankish silver, and we carried a barrel of Dunholm's ale to the village.

I took six men with me, leaving the remainder on *Seolferwulf*. All the men I took were Ragnar's Danes and we boasted of a successful summer cruise in the lands far to the south. "Our ship has a belly of gold and silver," I crowed, and the villagers just stared at us, trying to imagine the life of men who sailed to steal treasure from far shores. I let the ale-loosened conversation turn to Skirnir, though I learned little enough. He had men, he had ships, he had family, and he ruled the inner sea. He was evidently no fool. He would let fighting ships like *Seolferwulf* pass unmolested, but any other vessel had to pay to use the safe channels inside the islands where he had his lair. If a shipmaster could not pay, then he forfeited his cargo, his ship, and probably his life. "So they all pay," a man said glumly.

"Who does Skirnir pay?" I demanded.

"Lord?" he asked, not understanding the question.

"Who allows him to be here?" I asked, but they did not know the answer. "There must be a lord of this land," I explained, gesturing at the darkness beyond the fire, but if there was such a lord who permitted Skirnir to rule the sea then these villagers did not know of him. Even the village priest, a fellow as hairy and dirt-matted as his parishioners, did not know if there was a lord of the marshes. "So what does Skirnir want of you?" I asked him.

"We have to give him food, lord," the priest said.

"And men," one of the villagers added.

"Men?"

"The young men go to him, lord. They serve on his ships."

"They go willingly?"

"He pays silver," a villager said grudgingly.

"He takes girls too," the priest said.

"So he pays his men with silver and women?"

"Yes, lord."

They did not know how many ships Skirnir possessed, though the priest was certain he only had two the size of *Seolferwulf*. We heard the same things the next night when we stopped at another village in another creek on that treeless shore. We had rowed all day, the mainland to our right and the islands to our north and west. Skade had pointed to Zegge, but from our distance it looked little different from any other island. Many of them had mounds, the *terpen*, but we were so far off that we could see no detail. Sometimes only the shimmering dark shape of a *terpen* showing at the sea's edge betrayed that there was an island just beyond the horizon.

"So what do we do?" Finan asked me that night.

"I don't know," I admitted.

He grinned. The water lapped at *Seolferwulf*'s hull. We slept aboard her and most of the crew had already swathed themselves in cloaks and had lain down between the benches while Skade, Finan, Osferth, and Rollo, who was the leader of Ragnar's men, talked with me on the steering platform.

"Skirnir has around four hundred men," I said.

"Maybe four hundred and fifty," Skade said.

"So we kill six men apiece," Rollo said. He was an easygoing man like Ragnar, with a round and guileless face, though that was deceiving for, though he was young, he had already earned a reputation as a formidable fighter. He was called Rollo the Hairy, not just

169

because he wore his fair hair down to his waist, but because he had woven the locks of hair cut from his dead enemies into a thick sword belt. "I wish Saxons would grow their hair longer," he had grumbled to me as we crossed the sea.

"If they did," I had said, "you'd have ten sword belts."

"I already have seven," he said, and grinned.

"How many men on Zegge?" I now asked Skade.

"No more than a hundred."

Osferth spat out a fish bone. "You're thinking of attacking Zegge directly, lord?"

"It won't work," I said, "we won't find our way through the shoals." One thing I had learned from the villagers was that Zegge was surrounded by shallow waters, that the channels shifted with the sand and tide, and that none of the passages was marked.

"What then?" Osferth asked.

A star fell. It scratched a flicker of light across the darkness and was gone, and with its fall the answer came to me. I had been thinking that I would attack Skirnir's ships one by one, destroying the small ships and so weakening him, but within a day or two he would realize what was happening and he would use his larger ships to destroy us. There was no safe way to attack Skirnir. He had found a perfect refuge in the islands, and I would need ten ships like *Seolferwulf* to challenge him there.

So I had to lure him out of his perfect refuge. I smiled. "You're going to betray me," I told Osferth.

"I am?"

"Who's your father?"

"You know who my father is," he said resentfully. He never liked being reminded that he was Alfred's bastard.

"And your father is old," I said, "and his chosen heir is scarcely weaned, and you are a warrior. You want gold."

"I do?"

"You want gold to raise men, because you want to be King of Wessex."

Osferth snorted at that. "I don't," he said.

170

"You do now," I said, "because you're the bastard son of a king and you have a warrior's reputation. And tomorrow you betray me."

I told him how.

Nothing great is done without risk, but there are times I look back on those days and am amazed at the risk we ran in Frisia. It was, in its small way, like luring Harald to Fearnhamme, because again I divided my forces, and again I risked everything on the assumption that my enemy would do exactly what I wished him to do. And once again the lure was Skade.

She was so beautiful. It was a sinuous dark beauty. To look at her was to want her, to know her was to distrust her, but the distrust was ever conquered by that extraordinary beauty. Her face was high-boned, smooth-skinned, large-eyed, and full-mouthed. Her black hair was lustrous, her body was languorous. Of course many girls are beautiful, but life is hard on a woman. Childbirth racks her body like storms, and the never-ending work of pounding grains and spinning yarn takes its toll on that early loveliness, yet Skade, even though she had lived longer than twenty years, had kept her fresh beauty. She knew it too, and it mattered to her, for it had carried her from a widow's poor house to the high tables of long-beamed mead halls. She liked to say that she had been sold to Skirnir, but in truth she had welcomed him, then been disappointed by him because, for all the treasure he amassed, he had no ambitions beyond the Frisian Islands. He had found a plump patch for piracy, and it made no sense to Skirnir to sail far away to seek a plumper patch, and so Skade had found Harald, who promised her Wessex, and now she had found me.

"She's using you," Brida had told me in Dunholm.

"I'm using her," I had answered.

"There are a dozen whores here who'll prove cheaper," Brida had retorted scornfully.

So Skade was using me, but for what? She was demanding half

her husband's hoard, but what would she do with it? When I asked her, she shrugged as if the question was unimportant, but late that night, before Osferth's feigned betrayal, she spoke with me. Why did I want her husband's money?

"You know why."

"To take your fortress back?"

"Yes."

She lay silent for a while. The water made its small noise along *Seolferwulf*'s strakes. I could hear the snores of my men, the shifting feet of the sentries in the prow and above our heads on the steering platform. "And what then?" she asked.

"I will be the Lord of Bebbanburg," I said.

"As Skirnir is Lord of Zegge?"

"There was a time," I said, "when the Lord of Bebbanburg ruled far into the north and all the way down to the Humbre."

"They ruled Northumbria?"

"Yes."

I was bewitched by her. My ancestors had never ruled Northumbria, merely the northern part of that kingdom when it was divided between two thrones, but I was laying imaginary tribute at her feet. I was holding out the prospect of her being a queen, for that was what Skade wanted. She wanted to rule, and for that she needed a man who could lead warriors, and for the moment she believed I was that man.

"Guthred rules Northumbria now?" she asked.

"And he's mad," I said, "and he's sick."

"And when he dies?"

"Another man will be king," I said.

She slid a long thigh up mine, caressed a hand across my chest and kissed my shoulder. "Who?" she asked.

"Whoever is strongest," I said.

She kissed me again, then she lay still, dreaming. And I dreamed of Bebbanburg, of its windswept halls, its small fields and its tough, dour people. And I thought of the risk we must run in the dawn.

Earlier that night, under the cover of darkness, we had loaded a small boat with mail coats, weapons, helmets, and my iron-bound chest. We had carried that precious cargo to the uninhabited northern side of the creek and hidden it among reeds. Two men stayed to guard it, and their orders were to stay concealed.

In the morning, as the fishermen waded to their moored ships, we began the argument. We shouted, we bellowed insults, and then, as the villagers paused in their tasks to watch *Seolferwulf*, we began to fight. Swords clashed, there was the thump of steel on shield-wood, the screams of injured men, though none was really hurt. Some of my men were laughing at the pretense, but from the creek's shore it would have all looked real, and slowly a part of the crew was driven to *Seolferwulf*'s stern where they began to leap to safety. I was one of them. I wore no mail and the only weapon I had was Wasp-Sting and I held onto her as I leaped. Skade jumped with me. Our ship was anchored on the creek's southern side, away from the deeper water in the channel's center, and none of us needed to swim. I floundered for a moment, then my feet found the muddy bottom and I grabbed hold of Skade and dragged her toward the village. The men remaining on *Seolferwulf* jeered at us, and Osferth hurled a spear that came perilously close to me. "Go and die!" Osferth shouted.

"And take your whore with you!" Finan added. Another spear splashed into the creek, and I seized it as we struggled up the shelving beach.

There were thirty-two of us, just under half the crew, while the rest had stayed aboard *Seolferwulf*. We came ashore soaking wet, none of us in mail and some without even a weapon. The villagers gaped at us. The fishermen had paused to watch the fight, but now some headed out to sea, but not before I made certain they had a good view of Skade. She wore a thin linen shift that clung wetly to her shivering body, and she had gold at her neck and on her wrists. The villagers might not have recognized her, but they would remember her.

A pair of fishing boats still lay at their moorings and I waded out

to one and hauled myself aboard. Back on the beach my small band
was gathering round a herring-smoking fire to dry themselves. I had
Rollo and ten of his men, the rest were my warriors.

We watched as Osferth's men hauled up the stone anchor, then
took *Seolferwulf* out of the creek. She used ten oars on each side, and
she went slowly. I felt a moment of alarm as she turned northeast
and her pale hull was hidden from me by the intervening dunes. A
ship is a kind of fortress, and I had abandoned her, and I touched
Thor's hammer in a silent plea that the gods would preserve us.

Skirnir, I knew, would hear of the fight. He would learn that
Seolferwulf was half-crewed, and he would hear of the tall, black-
haired, gold-draped girl. He would know that we had been abandoned without mail and with few weapons. Thus I baited him. I had
thrown down the raw meat and now waited for the wolf to come to
the trap.

We used the fishing boat to cross the creek and made a driftwood
fire on the beach. We stayed all day, like men who had no plan. It
began to rain in the late morning, and after a while the rain became
harder, crashing down from a low gray sky. We piled wood on the
fire, the flames fighting the downpour that hid us as we brought
back the weapons and mail we had hidden the night before. I now
had thirty-four men, and I sent two of them to explore the creek's
higher reaches. Both men had been raised on the banks of the
Temes where it widens into the sea, and the coast there is not unlike
the shore where we were stranded. They could both swim, both
were at ease in the marshes, and I told them what I wanted and they
set off to find it. They came back in the late afternoon, just as the
rain was easing.

In the early evening, when the fishing boats returned on an incoming tide, I took six men over the creek and used a handful of silver scraps to buy fish. We all had swords, and the villagers treated us
with a cautious respect. "What lies that way?" I asked them, pointing up the creek.

They knew there was a monastery inland, but it was far off, and
only three of the men had ever seen the place. "It's a whole day's
journey," they said with awe.

"Well I can't go to sea," I said, "or Skirnir will catch us."

They said nothing to that. The very name of Skirnir was frightening.

"I hear he's a rich man," I remarked.

One of the old men made the sign of the cross. I had seen wooden idols in the village, but the folk knew of Christianity too, and his quick gesture told me that I had frightened him. "His treasure, lord," he told me quietly, "is in a great mound, and a huge dragon guards it."

"A dragon?"

"A fire dragon, lord, with black wings to shadow the moon." He made the sign of the cross again, then, to make certain, tugged a hammer amulet from beneath his filthy shirt and kissed it.

We took the food back to our side of the creek and then, on the last of the flood, we rowed the fishing boat inland. It was crowded and our small boat floated low. The villagers watched until we vanished, and still we rowed, gliding between reed beds and mudbanks until we reached the place that my two scouts had chosen. They had done well. The place was exactly what I wanted, an island of dunes isolated in a tangle of water, and accessible only in two places. We grounded the boat and lit another driftwood fire. The day was ending. The dark clouds had blown westward so that Skirnir's sea was in deep shadow, while to the east the land glowed beneath the dying sun. I could see the smoke of three settlements and, far on the horizon, some low hills where the tangle of marsh and sand ended and the higher land began. I assumed the monastery was in those hills, but it was too far away to be seen. Then the sun slid below the rain clouds and everything was in shadow, but a call from Rollo made me turn to see ships approaching the coast in the last of the daylight. Two large ships came first. They came from the direction of the islands, and then a third ship, paler than the first two and travelling much slower because she had fewer oarsmen.

Seolferwulf was the last of the three ships, while the darker pair belonged to Skirnir.

The wolf had come for his bitch.

FOUR

I had told Finan to play the madman, a thing he could do well. Not mad as in moon-touched, but dangerously mad as though one wrong word could send him into a welter of killing. Finan, if you did not know him well, was frightening. He was small and wiry, his strength tensed in a thin frame, while his face was all bone and scar. To look at Finan was to see a man who had endured battle and slavery and extreme hardship, a man who might have nothing to lose, and I counted on that to persuade Skirnir to treat *Seolferwulf*'s crew with caution. There was very little to stop Skirnir simply taking *Seolferwulf* and slaughtering its men, except the possibility that he might lose his own men in the capture. True, he would not lose many, but even twenty or thirty casualties would hurt him. Besides, Osferth and Finan brought him a gift and, as far as Skirnir knew, they were ready to help deliver that gift. I did not doubt that Skirnir would want to take *Seolferwulf* for his own, but guessed he would wait until he had gained Skade and my death before he made that attempt. So I told Finan to frighten him.

Osferth and Finan, once they left the creek, took *Seolferwulf* up the coast and then, as if they did not know what to do, rowed to the center of the inner sea and there let the ship roll on the small waves. "We saw the fishing boats racing over the water," Finan told me later, "and knew they were going to Zegge."

Skirnir, of course, heard about the fight in the creek and how the Viking ship was now wallowing aimlessly, and curiosity made him send one of his two large ships to investigate, though he did not go himself. His youngest brother talked with Finan and Osferth, and heard how they had mutinied against Uhtred of Bebbanburg, and heard too that Uhtred had Skade, and that now Uhtred, Skade, and a small group of men were stranded among the tangle of islands and creeks. "I let the brother come aboard," Finan told me later, "and I showed him the heap of mail and weapons. I said they were all yours."

"So he thought we were weaponless?"

"I told him you had a wee sword," Finan said, "but just a wee one." Grageld, Skirnir's brother, did not count the heaped coats, nor even the tangle of swords, spears, and axes. If he had, he might have suspected Finan's lies, because there were only enough mail coats and weapons to equip Finan's shrunken crew. Instead he simply believed what the Irishman told him. "So then," Finan went on, "we spun him our tale."

That tale began with truth. Finan told Grageld that we had sailed to the Frisian Islands in an attempt to rob Skirnir, but then he decorated the truth with fantasy. "I said we learned the gold was too well guarded, so we insisted you sold Skade back to her husband. But you wouldn't agree to that. I said we all hated the bitch, and he said we were right to hate her."

"Grageld didn't like her?"

"None of them liked her, lord, but Skirnir was stricken by her. The brother thought she'd cast a spell on Skirnir."

Finan told me this tale in Skirnir's hall, and I remember looking across at Skade in the light of the great fire that burned in the central hearth. She was an aglæcwif, I thought, a sorceress. Years ago Father Beocca told me a story from the olden days, from the far-off days when men built in shining marble, the days before the world turned dark and dirty. For once it was not a tale about God or his prophets, but about a queen who ran away from her husband because she fell in love with another man, and the husband took a great fleet of ships to get her back, and in the end a whole city was burned and all its men were killed, and all because of that long-dead aglæcwif. The poets say we fight for glory, for gold, for reputation, and for our homes, but in my life I have just as often fought for a

177

woman. They have the power. I frequently heard Ælswith, Alfred's sour wife who resented that Wessex never granted the title of queen, complain that it was a man's world. So it may be, but women have power over men. It is for women that the long fleets cross the salt seas, and for women that the proud halls burn, and for women that the sword-warriors are buried.

"Well, of course, Grageld wanted us to go to Skirnir," Finan said, "but we said no. He asked what we wanted, and we said we'd come for the reward because we wanted to make Osferth king and needed silver to do that."

"He believed that?"

"Do you need a reason to want silver?" Finan asked, then shrugged. "He believed us, lord, and Osferth was persuasive."

"When I told the story," Osferth put in wryly, "I found myself believing it."

I laughed at that. "You want to be king, Osferth?"

He smiled, and when he smiled he resembled his father so much that it was uncanny. "No, lord," he said gently.

"And I'm not really sure Grageld knew who Alfred was," Finan went on. "He knew the name well enough, and he knew his coins, of course, but he seemed to think Wessex was a way off. So I said it was a country where the silver grew on the ash trees, and that its king was old and tired, and that Osferth would be the new king and he would be a friend to Skirnir."

"He believed all this?"

"He must have done! The brother wanted us to go to Zegge, but I said no. I was not taking *Seolferwulf* through those channels, lord, for her to be trapped inside, and so we waited outside and Skirnir came out with the second ship and they put the boats either side of us and I could see they were thinking of capturing us."

Which is what I had feared. I imagined *Seolferwulf* with her shrunken crew flanked by Skirnir's two long ships packed with men.

"But we'd thought about that," Finan said happily, "and we'd hoisted the anchor stone on the sail yard." Our anchor stones are huge round wheels, the size of millstones, with a hole carved in their center, and Finan had hoisted *Seolferwulf*'s anchor by using the sail yard as a crane, and the message of that poised boulder was plain enough. If either of Skirnir's ships attacked, then the stone would be swung over that ship, the line holding it would be cut by an ax, and the stone would fall to crash through the attacking ship's bilge. Skirnir would gain one ship and lose another, and so, sensibly, he had pulled his ships away and pretended he had never even thought about capturing *Seolferwulf*.

"The anchor stone was a good idea," I said.

"Oh it was Osferth who thought of it, lord," Finan admitted, "and we had the thing ready before they even came out to us."

"And Skirnir believed your tale?"

"He wanted to believe it, lord, so he did! He wanted Skade, lord. He saw nothing but Skade, sir, you could see it in his eyes."

"And so you sailed to capture her."

"And so we did, lord," Finan said with a smile.

The three ships reached the creek as both the day and the tide ebbed. I knew Skirnir would not come till the morning flood had deepened the water in the creek, but I still posted sentries. Nothing disturbed them. We slept, though it seemed we did not. I remember lying awake, thinking I would never sleep, but dreams came all the same. I saw Gisela smiling, then had a waking dream of men with shields and of spears flying from their hands. I lay for a moment in the sand, watching the stars, then I stood, stretching the stiffness from my arms and legs. "How many men does he have, lord?" Cerdic asked me. He was reviving the fire, and the driftwood flamed bright. Cerdic did not lack bravery, but in the night he had been haunted by the memory of those large ships coming to the coast.

"He has two crews," I said. I saw that I had been the last to wake and men now drew toward the fire to listen to me. "Two crews," I said, "so he has at least one hundred men, maybe a hundred and fifty?"

"Jesus," Cerdic said quietly, touching the cross he wore.

"But they're pirates," Rollo said loudly.

"Tell them," I ordered, pleased that Ragnar's man understood what we faced.

Rollo stood in the flamelight. "Skirnir's men are like wild dogs," he said, "and they hunt what is weak, never what is strong. They don't fight on land and they don't know the shield wall. We do."

"He calls himself the Sea-Wolf," I said, "but Rollo is right. He's a dog, not a wolf. We're the wolves! We've faced the best warriors of Denmark and Britain and we've sent them to their graves! We are men of the shield wall, and before the sun climbs to its highest Skirnir will be in his grave!"

Not that we saw any sun because the day clouded over with the gray dawn. The clouds ran swift and low toward the sea, shrouding the marshes. The water rose with the tide, flooding the margins of the land where we had our refuge. I climbed to the top of the dune from where I watched the three ships come slowly up the creek. Skirnir was riding the flooding tide, rowing till his beast-headed ship grounded, then waiting for more water to carry him a few oar strokes farther. His two ships led and *Seolferwulf* followed, and I laughed at that. Skirnir, confident in his numbers and blinded by the prospect of regaining Skade, did not think for a moment that he had enemies behind him.

And what did Skirnir see? He was in the prow of the leading ship and he saw only five men standing on the dune, and none of the five was in mail. He thought he came to capture a bedraggled band of fugitives and so he was confident, and, as he drew closer, I called for Skade to stand beside me. "If he captured you," I asked her, "what would he do?"

"Humiliate me," she said, "shame me, then kill me."

"And that's worth silver to him?" I asked, thinking of the reward he had offered for Skade's return.

"Pride is expensive," she said.

"Why wouldn't he just keep you as a slave?"

"Because of that pride," she said. "He once had a slave girl killed because she betrayed him. He gave her to his men first, let them enjoy her, then he tied her to a stake and skinned her alive. He made her mother listen to her screams as she died."

I remembered Edwulf, skinned alive in his church, but I said nothing of that as I watched Skirnir's ship come still closer. The creek became too narrow to allow his oar-banks to dip in the water, so now his ship was being poled forward. The tide was rising slowly. As it neared its height it would rise more swiftly, and then Skirnir would know he had run out of water, but the creek, though narrow, was proving to have more than enough depth for his ships. "It's time to dress," I said.

I went down the dune's far side, hidden now from Skirnir, and Oswi, my servant, helped me into my mail. The leather lining stank in my nostrils as I pulled it over my head, but it felt good to have that familiar weight on my shoulders. Oswi put the sword belt around my waist and buckled it. "You stand behind me," I told him.

"Yes, lord."

"If it all goes wrong, boy," I said, "you run like a hare. You go inland, find the monastery and ask for shelter."

"Yes, lord."

"But it won't go wrong," I told him.

"I know it won't, lord," he said stoutly. He was eleven years old, an orphan who had been found scavenging in the mud beneath the terrace of my Lundene house. One of my men had accused him of theft and brought him to me so I could order a whipping, but I had liked the fire in the boy's eyes and so I had made him my servant and was now teaching him sword-craft. One day, like my previous servant, Sihtric, Oswi would become a warrior.

I went to the dune's edge and saw that Skirnir's ship was passing our beached and abandoned fishing craft. He was near enough to shout insults and he was bellowing at Skade, who now stood alone at the dune's summit. He was calling her a whore, a turd of the devil, and promising that she would scream her way into hell.

"Time to show ourselves," I said to Rollo, and picked up my linden shield, which had Bebbanburg's wolf's head painted around its iron boss.

Rollo carried a war ax and he kissed the wide blade. "I'll feed you soon, my darling," he promised the ax.

"They're close!" Skade called from the dune.

The island we had chosen was shaped like a crescent moon with the dune making the moon's high belly. The horns of the crescent touched the creek, and cradled in its belly was marshland. So the

181

dune could be approached from either horn, while the marsh, about a hundred paces wide and fifty paces at its deepest, was an obstacle. Men could cross that marshland, but it would have been slow work. The horn nearest to the sea was the wider of the two, a natural causeway leading to the sandy island, but ten men could bar that causeway easily, and I led twenty, leaving the remainder under Rollo's command. Their task was to protect the farther horn, but they were not to show themselves until Skirnir sent men to use that second causeway.

And what did Skirnir see? He saw a shield wall. He saw men in helmets and mail, men with bright weapons, men who were not the desperate fugitives he expected, but warriors dressed for battle, and he must have known that Finan and Osferth had lied to him, but he must have thought it was a small lie, a lie about weapons and mail, and his desperate hopes to regain Skade still persuaded him to believe the larger lie. Maybe he thought they had simply been mistaken? And still he was confident, because we were so few and he had so many, though the sight of a shield wall gave him pause.

Skirnir's helmsman was nosing the foremost ship into the bank when we appeared, and Skirnir immediately held up his hand to stop the men poling with the long oars. Skirnir had thought he would have little to do on that overcast morning, merely storm ashore and capture a small band of dispirited men, but our shields, weapons, and close-linked wall made him reconsider. I saw him turn and shout at the men poling his ship. He pointed up the creek and it was obvious he wanted the ship taken to the farther horn so that he could surround us. But then, to my surprise, he leaped off the bows. He and fifteen men splashed into the creek and waded ashore as the ship poled on. Skirnir and his small band were now about fifty paces away, but they would be swiftly reinforced by the crew of his second ship that was approaching fast. I stayed where I was.

Skirnir did not look back to see *Seolferwulf*, and would he have been alarmed if he had? She was the last of the three ships and her bows were filled with mailed and helmeted men. I could see Finan's black shield.

"Uhtred?" Skirnir shouted.

"I am Uhtred!"

"Give me the whore!" he bellowed. He was a heavy man with a face as flat as a flounder, small eyes, and a long black beard that half covered his mail. "Give her to me and I'll go away! You can live out your miserable life. Just give me the whore!"

"I haven't finished with her!" I called. I glanced left and saw that Skirnir's own ship had almost reached the second causeway. That crew would start landing in a moment. Meanwhile his second ship had grounded just behind Skirnir and the crew were tumbling over the side. There was not sufficient room on the small beach for more than thirty of them, so the rest, maybe another thirty men, waited on the ship. *Seolferwulf* crept closer.

"Oswi?" I said softly.

"Lord?"

"Fetch Rollo now."

I felt the exultation of victory. I had seventy men, including those on *Seolferwulf*, and Skirnir had done what I wanted, he had divided his forces. Sixty or seventy of his men were facing us at the first causeway, some still aboard their ship, while the rest had gone to the other landing place and though, once they were ashore, they would be able to attack us from behind, I expected to be master of the island by then. I heard *Seolferwulf* thump her bows on the grounded boat, then I gave the command. "Forward!"

We went as warriors, confident and disciplined. We could have charged as we had at Fearnhamme, but I wanted fear to work its wicked decay on Skirnir's men, and so we went slowly, the shields of our front rank overlapping, while the men behind beat blades against their shields in time to our steps. "Kill the scum!" I shouted and my men took up the shout. "Kill the scum, kill the scum!" We went step by step, slow and inexorable, and the blades between our shields promised death.

We were just eight men broad, but, as the causeway widened, Rollo brought his men onto our right. Most of the front rank carried spears, while I had Serpent-Breath. She was not the best blade for the close work of shield wall fighting, but I reckoned Skirnir's men would not stand long because they were not used to this kind of warfare. Their skill was the sudden rush onto a half-defended boat, the wild killing of frightened men, but now they faced sword-warriors and spearmen and behind them was Finan. And Finan now attacked.

He left just two boys on *Seolferwulf*. The tide was still flooding, so the current was holding *Seolferwulf* against the second of Skirnir's skull-prowed ships and Finan led his men over her bows and up between the rowing benches, and they were yelling a high-pitched scream of killing, and maybe for a moment, just for a moment, Skirnir believed they had come to help him. But then Finan began the slaughter.

And we struck at the same moment. "Now!" I shouted, and my shield wall lunged forward, spears seeking foemen, blades driving into flesh, and I slammed Serpent-Breath under a Frisian shield and twisted her long blade in the man's soft belly. "Kill them!" I bellowed, and Finan echoed the cry.

Spear-blades buried themselves in Frisian flesh. Men then dropped the spears' long ash shafts and drew swords or took axes from the men behind. Skirnir's men had not broken because they could not break. They were confined in a small space and my attack pushed them back against their dark ship's bows, while Finan's assault on the ship drove the remaining crew toward the prow platform. We pushed forward, giving them no room to fight, and we did the grim work of shield fighting. Cerdic was on my right and he used the blade of his ax like a hook to pull down the rim of the man to his front and, as soon as the shield was down, I lunged Serpent-Breath into the enemy's throat, and Cerdic drove the ax blade against the man's face, crushing it, then reached to hook down another shield. Rollo was screaming in Danish. He had dropped his shield and wielded his ax two-handed as he chanted a hymn to Thor. Rorik, one of the Danes who served me, was on his knees behind me, using a spear to rip open the legs of the Frisian pirates, and when they fell we killed them.

It was slaughter in a small space. We had given hours, days, weeks, and months to practicing this kind of fight. It does not matter how often a man stands in a shield wall, he will only live if he has rehearsed it, drilled it, and practiced it, and Skirnir's men had never trained as we did. They were seamen, and some did not even have shields because a great round slab of iron-bossed wood is a cumbersome thing to carry in a fight aboard a ship where the footing is uncertain and the rowing benches are obstacles. They were untrained and ill-equipped and so we killed them. They were in terror. They did not see our faces. Most of our helmets have cheek-pieces and so the enemy saw men of metal, metal-masked, metal-clad, and the steel of our weapons lanced at them, and we went relentlessly forward, metal-clad warriors behind overlapping shields, our blades remorseless until, on that gray morning, blood spread bright in the salt tide creek.

Finan had the harder job, but Finan was a warrior of renown who took joy in hard fighting, and he led his men up the dark boat and screamed as he killed. He sang the song of the sword, keening as he fed his blade, and Rollo, standing thigh-deep in the creek, ax swinging in murderous blows, blocked the enemy's escape. The Frisians, transported from confidence to bowel-loosening fear, began to drop their weapons. They knelt, they shouted for mercy, and I shouted at my rear rank to turn and be ready to face the men who had taken Skirnir's own ship higher up the creek to come around our rear.

Those men appeared about the dune just in time to see that the fighting was over. A few had sensibly jumped over the ship's farther side and struggled into the swamp beyond, but most of Skirnir's force were dead or prisoners. One of those prisoners was Skirnir himself, who was backed against the grounded strakes of his second ship with a spear-blade held at his beard. Cerdic was pressing the blade just enough to keep the big man still. "Shall I kill him, lord?"

"Not yet," I said, distracted. I was watching the newly arrived enemy. "Rollo? Keep them at a distance."

Rollo formed his men into a shield wall. He shouted at the uncertain Frisians, inviting them to come and taste the blood already on his blades, but they did not move.

A man screamed. He was a Frisian lying at the sand's edge and his legs were thrashing in the shallow, blood-tinged water. He had been wounded, and Skade now knelt beside him and was driving a dagger slowly into one eye and so through to his brain. "Stop that!" I shouted. The man was mewing in a high, pitiable voice, the ooze of his punctured eye spilling down his blood-laced cheek.

She turned to look at me and there was a wildness in her face like the savagery of a cornered beast. "I hate them," she said, and edged the dagger in again so that the man screamed and lost control of his bowels.

"Sihtric!" I snarled, and Sihtric stepped to the man and drove his sword hard into his throat to end his misery.

"I want to kill them all," Skade hissed at me. She was shuddering. "And him!" She pointed to Skirnir. "Especially him!"

"She's crazed," Finan said softly. He had jumped down to the beach beside me and now dipped his blade in the water to wash the blood away. "Sweet Jesus Christ," he said, "she's as crazy as a bitch in heat."

My men were staring at Skade in horror. It is one thing to kill in battle, but an enemy is a warrior too, and in defeat he deserves respect. I have killed often, and the killing can go on long after the fighting has finished, but that is the blood lust and battle fear that frenzies men who endure the shield wall, and when the lust dies then mercy takes its place. "You're not going to let them live!" Skade spat at me.

"Cerdic," I said, not turning around to look at him, "make it quick!"

I heard, but did not see, Skirnir die. The spear-blade was thrust so hard that it pierced his throat and then drove into the planks of the ship. "I wanted to kill him!" Skade shrieked.

I ignored her. Instead I walked past Rollo to approach the undefeated Frisians. These men were Skirnir's own crew, maybe sixty in all, who watched me come in silence. I had dropped my shield so they could see the blood spattered on my mail and see the blood streaked across my helmet's mask and see the blood congealing on Serpent-Breath's blade. My helmet was surmounted by a silver wolf, my belt had plates of gold, and my arm rings shone through their gloss of blood. They saw a warlord and I walked to within ten paces of them to show that I had no fear of pirates.

"I am Uhtred of Bebbanburg," I said, "and I give you a choice. You can live or you can die."

Rollo, behind me, had started the shield music. His men were beating blades against linden wood in the dark rhythm of death's promise.

"We are Danes," I told the Frisians, "and we are Saxons, and we are warriors who love to fight. In our halls at night we chant the tales of the men we have killed, of the women we have widowed, and of the children we have orphaned. So make your choice! Either give me a new song to sing or else lay down your weapons."

They laid down their weapons. I made them take off their mail, those that possessed it, or else their leather tunics. I took their boots, their belts, their armor, and their weapons and we piled that plunder in *Seolferwulf*, and then we burned both of Skirnir's long ships. They burned well, great plumes of flame climbing the masts beneath churning black smoke that drifted up into the low clouds.

Skirnir had come with one hundred and thirty-one men. We had killed twenty-three of those, while another sixteen were grievously wounded. One of Rollo's men had lost an eye to a spear thrust, and Ælric, a Saxon in my service, lay dying. He had fought beside Finan and had tripped on a rower's bench and had taken an ax blow in the back, and I knelt beside him on the sand and held his hand firm around his sword's hilt and promised I would give his widow gold and raise his children as though they were my own. He heard me, though he could not speak back, and I held his hand until the noise rattled in his throat and his body quivered as his soul went to the long darkness. We took his corpse away with us and buried him at sea. He was a Christian, and Osferth said a prayer over the dead Ælric before we tipped him into eternity. We took another corpse with us, Skirnir's, that we stripped naked and hung from our wolf's-head prow to show that we had conquered.

We poled *Seolferwulf* back down the creek on the ebbing tide. When the creek widened we turned and rowed her, towing the small fishing craft that I abandoned beside the village. Then we went out to sea and *Seolferwulf* shuddered to the first small waves. The gray clouds that had covered the place of slaughter were at last shredding, letting a watery sunlight beat down on the choppy sea. "You shouldn't have let them live," Skade told me.

"Skirnir's men?" I asked. "Why kill them? They were beaten."

"They should all be dead," she said vengefully, then turned a gaze of utter fury on me. "You left two of his brothers alive! They should be dead!"

"I let them live," I said. Without Skirnir and his large boats they were harmless, though Skade did not see it that way.

"Milksop!" she spat at me.

I stared at her. "Careful, woman," I said, and she went sulkily silent.

We had brought just one prisoner with us, the shipmaster from Skirnir's own vessel. He was an old man, over forty, and years of squinting at the sun-reflecting sea had made his eyes mere crinkled slits in a face beaten dark by salt and weather. He would be our guide. "If my ship so much as touches a sandbank," I told him, "I'll let Skade kill you in her own way."

Seolferwulf touched no sandbank as we rowed to Zegge. The channel was intricate, and misleading marks had been planted to lure attackers onto shoals, but the prisoner's pure terror of Skade made him careful. We arrived in the early evening, feeling our way gently, and led by the corpse hanging at the bows. Spray had washed Skirnir's carcass clean and gulls, smelling him, screamed as they wheeled in hungry frustration around our prow.

Men and women watched us pass through the crooked channel that twisted between two of the inner islands, and then we glided across sheltered water that reflected the settling sun in shivering gold. The watchers were Skirnir's followers, but these men had not sailed with their lord in the dawn, and now they saw our proud shields that we had hung from *Seolferwulf*'s topmost strakes, and they saw the corpse dangling white from the rope, and none wanted to challenge us.

There were fewer people on Zegge than on the outer islands, because it was from Zegge that the two defeated crews had sailed, and where most of the dead, wounded, or stranded men had lived. A crowd of women came to the gray wooden pier that jutted out beneath the mound which supported Skirnir's hall. The women watched our boat approach, then some recognized the body that was our trophy and they all fled, dragging their children by the hands. Eight men, dressed in mail and carrying weapons, came from the hall, but when they saw my crew disembarking they ostentatiously put their weapons down. They knew now their lord was dead, and not one of them was minded to fight for his reputation.

And so, in the twilight of that day, we came to the hall on the mound of Zegge, and I stared up at its black bulk and thought of the dragon sleeping on his hoard of silver and gold. The high-roofed hall had great wooden horns at its eaves, horns that reared into the darkening sky where the first stars pricked the dusk.

I left fifteen men to guard the ship, then climbed the hill, seeing how the mound was made from great baulks of timber planted in a long rectangle that had been filled with sand, and on that first layer another smaller rectangle had been built, and then a third, and at the summit a final layer where a palisade stood, though it offered no defiance now, for its heavy wooden gate stood wide open. There was no fight left in Skirnir's men. Their lord was dead.

The hall's door was framed by a pair of vast curved bones that had come from some sea monster. I passed beneath them with a drawn sword with Rollo and Finan flanking me. A fire burned in the central hearth, spitting like a cat as salt-caked driftwood does. Skade came behind us and the waiting servants shivered at the sight of her. Skirnir's steward, a plump man, bowed low to me. "Where's the treasure?" I asked harshly.

The steward was too frightened to answer and Skade thrust him aside. "Lanterns!" she called to the servants, and small rushlamps were brought and in their paltry light she led me to a door at the back of the hall which opened onto a small square chamber heaped with sealskins. "He slept here," she said.

"Above the dragon?"

"He was the dragon," she said scornfully, "he was a pig and a dragon," and then she dropped to her knees and scrabbled the stinking skins aside. I called for Skirnir's plump steward to help her.

Finan looked at me, an eyebrow raised in expectation, and I could not resist a smile.

To take Bebbanburg I needed men. To storm that great stone wall and slaughter my uncle's warriors, I needed men, and to buy men I needed gold. I needed silver. I needed a treasure guarded by a dragon to make that long dream come true, and so I smiled as Skade and the steward pulled away the high pile of pelts that covered the hiding place.

And then, in the light of the smoking lamps, the door was revealed.

It was a trapdoor of dark heavy wood into which an iron ring was set. I remember Father Beocca, years ago, telling me how he had visited a monastery in Sumorsæte and how the abbot had reverently showed him a crystal vial in which was kept milk from the Virgin Mary's breasts. "I shivered, Uhtred," Beocca had told me earnestly, "I shook like a leaf in the wind. I dared not hold the flask for fear of dropping it! I shook!"

I do not think I shook at that moment, but I felt the same awe, the same sense of being close to something inexplicable. My future lay beneath that trapdoor. My hopes, my sons' futures, my dreams of freedom beneath a northern sky, all lay so close. "Open it," I ordered, and my voice was hoarse, "open it."

Rollo and the steward took hold of the ring. The trapdoor was stiff, jammed in its frame, and they needed to tug it hard to move it at all. Then, abruptly, the heavy door came free and the two men staggered as they dragged it aside.

I stepped forward and looked down.

And started laughing.

There was no dragon. I have never seen a dragon, though I am assured they exist and I have heard men describe those awful beasts with their malevolent scarlet eyes, flame-shooting mouths, questing necks, and crackling wings the size of ship sails. They are the beasts of nightmare, and though I have sailed into the distant north, sailed to where the ice blanches the sky with its reflections, I have never been far enough north to the frost lands where dragons are said to roost.

There was no dragon in Skirnir's pit, but there was a skeleton and some rats. The rats looked up startled, their tiny eyes winking back the flames of our inadequate lanterns, then they scuttled into cracks between the elm planks that lined the pit. Two rats were inside the ribcage of the dead man and they were the last to leave, first wriggling between the bones then slithering fast into their hiding place.

And as my eyes adjusted to the gloom I saw the coins and the silver shards. I heard them first, chinking under the feet of the rats, then I saw them, dully gleaming, spilling from the leather sacks that had held them. The rotting sacks had been gnawed by rats. "What's the corpse?" I asked.

"A man who tried to steal Lord Skirnir's treasure, lord," the steward answered in a whisper.

"He was left here to die?"

"Yes, lord. He was blinded first, then his sinews were cut, and he was put in the pit to die slowly."

Skade smiled.

"Bring it all out," I ordered Finan, then pushed the steward toward the hall. "You feed us tonight," I ordered him, "all of us."

I went back into the hall. It had only one table, so that most men would have eaten on the rush-covered floor. It was dark now, the only light coming from the big fire that we fed with logs my men tore from the palisade. I sat at the table and watched as Skirnir's treasure was laid before me. I had laughed when the pit was first opened, and that laughter had been scornful because, in the feeble light, the treasure had appeared so paltry. What had I expected? A glittering heap of gold, studded with precious stones?

The laughter was sour because Skirnir's treasure was indeed paltry. He had boasted of his wealth, but the truth was hidden behind those boasts and beneath his stinking bed-skins. He was not poor, true, but his hoard was just what I should have expected from a man who did little except steal scraps of silver from small traders.

My men watched the table. It was important that they saw what they had won so they would know I did not cheat them when I divided the hoard. They mostly saw silver, but there were two pieces of gold, both thin torques made of twisted strands, and I put one in the pile for Rollo and his men, and kept the other for my followers. Then there were coins, mostly Frankish silver, but there were a few Saxon shillings and a handful of those mysterious coins that have curly writing no one can read and which are rumored to come from some great empire to the east. There were four silver ingots, but the greatest part of the treasure was in silver shards. The northmen have no coinage, other than what they steal, and so they pay for their goods, when they pay at all, with silver scraps. A Viking will steal a silver bracelet, and when he needs to buy something he will hack the bracelet into shards that a merchant will weigh on scales. The steward brought us a scale and we weighed the silver and the coins. There was just over thirty pounds.

That was not to be despised. We would all go home richer. Yet my share of the treasure would hardly raise one crew of men for one season's fighting. I stared at the divided treasure, the last silver shards still resting in the bowl of the scales, and knew that it would not bring me Bebbanburg. It would not give me an army. It would not buy the fulfillment of my dreams. I felt my spirits sink and thought of Ælfric's laughter. My uncle would soon enough learn that I had voyaged, captured, and been disappointed, and it was while I was thinking of his enjoyment that Skade chose to speak. "You said you would give me half," she demanded.

My fist crashed on the table so hard that the small piles of silver shuddered. "I said no such thing," I snarled.

"You said . . ."

I pointed at her, silencing her. "You want to go in the hole?" I asked. "You want to live with the rats in the silver vault?"

My men smiled. Since coming to Frisia they had learned to dislike Skade and at that moment she began to hate me. I had begun to hate her earlier, when I saw the cruelty beneath her beauty. She was like a sword haunted by a spirit of greed, like a blade of shining beauty, but with a heart as dark as blood. Later that night she demanded her share again and I reminded her that though she had asked for half her husband's treasure, I had never promised it. "And don't think to curse me again," I told her, "because if you do, woman, I shall sell you into slavery, but not before I disfigure you. You want a scarred face? You want me to make you ugly? Then keep your curses to yourself."

I do not know where she slept that night, nor did I care.

We left Zegge in the dawn. I burned the six smaller ships Skirnir had left in the harbor, but I did not burn the hall. Wind and tide would take care of it. The islands come and go, the channels change from year to year, and the sand shifts to make new islands. Folk live on those islands for a few years, and then the surging tides dissolve the land again. When I next saw the islands, many years later, Zegge was quite gone, as though it had never existed at all.

We went home, and we had fair weather for the crossing. The sun glinted off the sea, the sky was clear and the air cold. It was only as we approached the coast of Britain that the clouds came and the wind rose. It took me some time to find a landmark I knew, and then we had to row hard into a north wind to find the Tinan's mouth and it was almost dark as we rowed *Seolferwulf* into the river beneath the ruined monastery. We beached her and next day we went to Dunholm.

I did not know it, but I was never to see *Seolferwulf* again.

She was a noble ship.

PART THREE

BATTLE'S EDGE

ONE

The deep winter came and with it a fever. I have been lucky, rarely being ill, but a week after we reached Dunholm I began to shiver, then sweat, then feel as though a bear were clawing the insides of my skull. Brida made a bed for me in a small house where a fire burned day and night. That winter was cold, but there were moments when I thought my body was on fire, and then there were times when I shivered as if I were bedded in ice even though the fire roared in its stone hearth so fiercely that it scorched the roof beams. I could not eat. I grew weak. I woke in the night, and sometimes I thought of Gisela and of my lost children, and I wept. Ragnar told me I raved in my sleep, but I do not remember that madness, only that I was convinced I would die and so I made Brida tie my hand to Wasp-Sting's hilt.

Brida brought me infusions of herbs in mead, she spooned honey into my mouth, and she made certain that the small house was guarded against Skade's malevolence. "She hates you," she told me one cold night when the wind pulled at the thatch and bellied the leather curtain which served as a door.

"Because I didn't give her any silver?"

"Because of that."

"There was no hoard," I said, "not as she described it."

"But she denies cursing you."

"What else can have caused this?"

"We tied her to a post," Brida said, "and showed her the whip. She swore she had not cursed you."

197

"She would," I said bitterly.

"And she still denied it when her back was bloody."

I looked at Brida, dark-eyed, her face shadowed by her wild black hair. "Who used the whip?"

"I did," she said calmly, "and then I took her to the stone."

"The stone?"

She nodded eastward. "Across the river, Uhtred, is a hill, and on the hill is a stone. A big one, planted upright. It was put there by the ancient people and it has power. The stone has breasts."

"Breasts?"

"It's shaped that way," she said, momentarily cupping her hands over her own small breasts. "It's tall," she went on, "even taller than you, and I took her there at night and lit fires to the gods, and put skulls in a ring, and I told her I would summon the demons to turn her skin yellow and her hair white and to make her face wrinkled and her breasts sag and her back humped. She cried."

"Could you have done all that?"

"She believed so," Brida said with a sly smile, "and she promised me on her life she had not cursed you. She spoke true, I'm sure."

"So it's just a fever?"

"More than a fever, a sickness. Others have it. Two men died last week."

A priest came each week and bled me. He was a morose Saxon who preached his gospel in the small town that had appeared just to the south of Ragnar's fortress. Ragnar had brought prosperity to the local countryside and the town was growing quickly, the smell of newly sawn wood as constant as the stink of sewage flowing down-hill to the river. Brida, of course, had objected to the church being constructed, but Ragnar had allowed it. "They'll worship any god they choose," he had told me, "whatever I might wish. And the Saxons here were Christians before I arrived. A few have gone back to the real gods. The first priest wanted to pull down Brida's stone and called me an evil heathen bastard when I stopped him, so I drowned him and this new one is a lot more polite." The new priest was also reckoned to be a skilled healer, though Brida, who had her own knowledge of herbs, would not let him prescribe any potions for me. He would just open a vein in one of my arms and watch the blood pulse thick and slow into a horn cup. When it was done he was instructed to pour the blood onto the fire, then scour out the cup, which he always did with a scowl because it was a pagan precaution. Brida wanted the blood destroyed so no one could use it to cast a spell on me.

"I'm surprised Brida permits you to come into the fortress," I told the priest one day as my drawn blood hissed and bubbled on the logs.

"Because she hates Christians, lord?"

"Yes."

"She was sick three winters ago," the priest said, "and Jarl Ragnar sent for me when all else failed. I cured her, or else God Almighty worked the cure through me. Since then she has endured my presence."

Brida also endured Skade's presence. She would have killed her given an excuse, but Skade pleaded with Ragnar that she meant no harm and Ragnar, my friend, had no stomach for slaughtering women, especially good-looking women. He put Skade to work in the hall kitchen. "She worked in my kitchen in Lundene," I told Brida.

"From where she slithered her way into your bed," Brida said tartly, "though I don't suppose that took much effort on her part."

"She's beautiful."

"And you're still the fool you always were. And now another fool will find her and she'll make trouble again. I told Ragnar he should have split her from the crotch to the gullet, but he's as stupid as you."

I was on my feet by Yule, though I could take no part in the games that so delighted Ragnar. There were races, tests of strength and, his favorite, wrestling. He took part himself, winning his first six bouts, then losing to a giant Saxon slave who was rewarded with a handful of silver. On the afternoon of the great feast the fortress dogs were allowed to attack a bull, an entertainment that reduced Ragnar to tears of laughter. The bull, a wiry and savage creature, dashed around the hilltop between the buildings, attacking when he had a chance and tossing careless dogs into gut-spilled ruin, but eventually he lost too much blood and the hounds converged on him. "What happened to Nihtgenga?" I asked Brida as the roaring bull collapsed in a frantic heap of scrabbling dogs.

"He died," Brida said, "long, long ago."

"He was a good dog," I said.

"He was," she said, watching the hounds tear at the thrashing bull's belly. Skade was on the far side of the killing ground, but she avoided my gaze.

The Yule feast was lavish because Ragnar, like his father, had always adored the winter celebrations. A great fir tree had been cut and dragged to the hall where it was hung with silver coins and jewelry. Skade was among the servants who brought the beef, pork, venison, bacon, blood sausages, bread, and ale. She still avoided my eye. Men noticed her, how could they not? One drunken man tried to seize her and pull her onto his lap, but Ragnar slapped the table so hard that the blow upset a horn of wine and the sound was enough to persuade the man to let Skade go.

There were harpists and skalds. The skalds chanted verses in praise of Ragnar and his family, and Ragnar beamed with delight when his father's exploits were described. "Say that again," he would roar when some treasured exploit was recounted. He knew many of the words and chanted along, but then startled the skald by slapping the table again. "What did you just sing?" he demanded.

"That your father, lord, served the great Ubba."

"And who killed Ubba?"

The skald frowned. "A Saxon dog, lord."

"This Saxon dog," Ragnar shouted, lifting my arm. It was while men were still laughing that the messenger arrived. He came from the dark and for a moment no one noticed the tall Dane who, it turned out, had just ridden from Eoferwic. He was clad in mail because there were brigands on the roads, and the skirts of his armor, his boots, and the richly decorated scabbard of his sword were spattered with mud. He must have been tired, but there was a broad smile on his face.

Ragnar noticed the man first. "Grimbald!" he bellowed the name in welcome. "You should arrive before a feast, not after! But worry not, there's food and ale!"

Grimbald bowed to Ragnar. "I bring you news, lord."

"News that couldn't wait?" Ragnar asked good-naturedly. The hall had gone quiet because men wondered what could have brought Grimbald in such haste through the cold, wet darkness.

"News that will please you, lord," Grimbald said, still smiling.

"The price of virgins has dropped?"

"Alfred of Wessex, lord," Grimbald paused, "is dead."

There was a moment's silence, then the hall burst into cheers. Men beat the table with their hands and whooped with delight. Ragnar was half drunk, but had enough sense to hold up his hands for silence. "How do you know this?"

"The news was brought to Eoferwic yesterday," Grimbald said.

"By whom?" I demanded.

"By a West Saxon priest, lord," Grimbald said. The tall messenger was one of mad King Guthred's household warriors and, though he did not know me, my place of honor beside Ragnar persuaded him to call me lord.

"So his whelp is the new king?" Ragnar asked.

"So it is said, lord."

"King Edmund?" Ragnar inquired, "that'll take some getting used to."

"Edward," I said.

"Edmund or Edward, who cares? He's not long for this life," Ragnar said happily. "What kind of boy is he?" he asked me.

"Nervous."

"Not a warrior?"

"His father was no warrior either," I said, "yet he defeated every Dane who came to take his throne."

"You did that for him," Ragnar said cheerfully and slapped my back. The hall was suddenly full of talk as men glimpsed a new future. There was so much excitement, though I remember looking down at one of the tables and saw Osferth frowning in lonely silence. Then Ragnar leaned close to me. "You don't look happy, Uhtred."

How did I feel at that moment? I was not happy. I had never liked

Alfred. He was too pious, too humorless, and too stern. His delight was order. He wanted to reduce the whole world to lists, to organization, to obedience. He loved to collect books and write laws. He believed that if only every man, woman, and child were to obey the law, then we would have a heavenly kingdom on earth, but he forgot the earthly pleasures. He had known them as a young man, Osferth was proof of that, but then he had allowed the nailed Christian god to persuade him that pleasure was sin and so he tried to make laws that would outlaw sin. A man might as well try to shape water into a ball.

So I did not like Alfred, but I had always been aware that I was in the presence of an extraordinary man. He was thoughtful, and he was no fool. His mind had been fast and open to ideas, so long as those ideas did not contradict his religious convictions. He was a king who did not believe that kingship implied omniscience and he was, in his way, a humble man. Above everything, he had been a good man, though never a comfortable one. He had also believed in fate, a thing all religions seem to share, though the difference between Alfred and me had been his conviction that fate was progress. He wanted to improve the world, while I did not believe and never have believed that we can improve the world, just merely survive as it slides into chaos.

"I respected Alfred," I told Ragnar. I was still not certain I believed the news. Rumors fly around like summer gossamer, and so I beckoned Grimbald closer. "What exactly did the priest tell you?"

"That Alfred was in the church at Wintanceaster," he said, "and that he collapsed during the rituals and was taken to his bed."

That sounded convincing. "And his son is king now?"

"The priest said so."

"Is Harald still trapped in Wessex?" Ragnar asked.

"No, lord," Grimbald said, "Alfred paid him silver to depart."

Ragnar bellowed for silence and made Grimbald repeat his last words about Harald, and the news that the wounded jarl had been paid to leave Torneie prompted another cheer in the hall. Danes love to hear of Saxons paying silver to rid themselves of Danes. It encourages them to attack Saxon lands in hope of similar bribes.

"Where did Harald go?" Ragnar asked, and I saw Skade listening.

"He joined Haesten, lord."

"In Beamfleot?" I asked, but Grimbald did not know.

The news of Alfred's death and of the wounded Harald's enrichment gave the feast an added happiness. For once there were not even any fights as the mead, ale, and wine took hold of the tables. Every man in that hall, except perhaps a handful of my Saxon followers, saw a new opportunity to capture and plunder the rich fields, villages and towns of Wessex.

And they were right. Wessex was vulnerable, except for one thing.

The news was a rumor after all.

Alfred lived.

Yet, in the dark of the year, every man in northern Britain believed the rumor, and it energized Brida. "It's a sign from the gods," she declared, and persuaded Ragnar to summon the northern jarls. The meeting was set for the early spring, when the winter rains would have ended and the fords made passable again. The prospect of war stirred Dunholm from its winter torpor. In town and fortress the smiths were set to forging spear-blades, and Ragnar let every shipmaster know that he would welcome crews in the spring. Word of that generosity would eventually reach Frisia and far Denmark, and hungry men would come to Northumbria, though for the moment Ragnar spread the rumor that he merely raised troops to invade the land of the Scots. Offa, the Mercian with his trained dogs, heard the rumors and came north despite the weather. He pretended he always struggled through the wet cold rains of Northumbria in the dead days of the year, but it was clear he wanted to learn what Ragnar planned. Ragnar, for once, was reticent, and refused to allow Offa into the high fortress on its river-bound rock. Brida, I think, threatened him with her displeasure, and Brida could always control Ragnar.

I went to meet Offa in a tavern beneath the fortress. I took Finan and Osferth, and I pretended to get drunk. "I heard you were sick, lord," Offa said, "and I'm glad you are recovered."

"I hear Alfred of Wessex was also sick?" Osferth put in.

Offa, as ever, considered his answer, wondering whether he was about to give away information that was better sold, then realized that whatever news he possessed would soon be known anyway. Besides, he was here to dig information from us. "He collapsed in church," he said, "and the physicians were sure he would die. He was very ill! He was given the last rites twice, to my certain knowledge, but God relented."

"God loves him," I said, slurring my words and thumping the table for more ale.

"Not enough to give him a full recovery," Offa said guardedly. "He is still weak."

"He was always weak," I said. That was true about Alfred's health, if not his resolve, but I had spoken sourly, as a deliberate insult, and Offa gazed at me, doubtless wondering just how drunk I truly was.

I have often scorned Christian priests because they are forever telling us that the proof of their religion is the magic that Christ performed, but then they claim that such magic disappeared with him. If a priest could cure a cripple or make the blind see, then I would believe in their god, but at that moment, in the smoke-filled tavern beneath Dunholm's high fortress walls, a miracle did occur. Offa paid for the ale and even ordered more.

I have always been able to drink more than most men, yet even so I could feel the room swirling like the smoke billowing from the tavern hearth. I kept my wits, though. I dropped Offa some gossip about Skade, admitted my disappointment about Skirnir's hoard, and then complained bitterly that I had neither money nor sufficient men. That last drunken complaint opened the door for Offa. "And why, lord, would you need men?" he asked.

"We all need men," I said.

"True," Finan put in.

"More men," Osferth said.

"Always more men," Finan was also pretending to be drunker than he was.

"I hear the northern jarls are gathering here?" Offa asked innocently. He was desperate to know what was being planned. All Britain knew that the Northumbrian lords were invited to Dunholm, but no one was certain why, and Offa could become wealthy on that knowledge.

"That's why I want men!" I said to him in a very earnest voice.

Offa poured me more ale. I noticed he was hardly touching his own horn. "The northern jarls have men enough," he said, "and I hear Jarl Ragnar is offering silver for crews."

I leaned forward confidingly. "How can I talk to them as an equal if all I lead is one crew?" I paused to belch. "And a small crew at that?"

"You have reputation, lord," he said, somehow managing not to recoil from my ale-staled breath.

"I need men," I said, "men, men, men."

"Good men," Osferth said.

"Spear-Danes, sword-Danes," Finan added dreamily.

"The jarls will have enough men to crush the Scots," Offa suggested, dangling the words like a baited hook.

"The Scots!" I said scornfully. "Why waste a single crew on the Scots?" Finan touched my elbow warningly, but I pretended to be oblivious of his gesture. "What is Scotland?" I asked belligerently. "Wild men in a bare country with scarce a scrap of cloth to cover their cocks. The kingdom of Alba," I spat the name of Scotland's largest kingdom, "isn't worth the produce of one decent Saxon estate. They're nothing but hairy bastards with frozen cocks. Who wants them?"

"Yet Jarl Ragnar would conquer them?" Offa asked.

"He would," Finan said firmly.

"He would end their nuisance," Osferth added, but Offa ignored both of them. He gazed at me, and I looked back into his eyes.

"Bebbanburg," I said confidingly.

"Bebbanburg, lord?" he asked innocently.

"I am Lord of Bebbanburg, am I not?" I demanded.

"You are, lord," he said.

"The Scots!" I said derisively, then let my head fall onto my arms as if I was sleepy.

Within a month all Britain knew why Jarl Ragnar was asking for men. Alfred, lying on his sickbed, knew, as did Æthelred, Lord of Mercia. They probably knew in Frankia, while Offa, I heard, had become wealthy enough to buy a fair house and a pasture in Liccelfeld and was contemplating taking a young girl as a wife. The money for such extravagances, of course, came from my uncle, Ælfric, to whom Offa had hurried as soon as the weather allowed. The news he carried was that Jarl Ragnar was helping his friend, the Lord Uhtred, to regain Bebbanburg and there would be a summer war in Northumbria.

And meanwhile Ragnar sent spies to Wessex.

It might not have been a bad idea to assemble an army to invade the Scots. They were trouble back then, they are trouble now, and I daresay they will still be trouble when the world dies. As that winter ended a party of Scots raided Ragnar's northern lands and killed at least fifteen men. They stole cattle, women, and children. Ragnar made a retaliatory raid and I took twenty of my men with his hundred, but it was a frustrating errand. We were not even sure when we crossed into Scottish land because the frontier was an uncertain thing, forever shifting with the power of the lords on either side, but after two days' riding we came across a poor and deserted village. The folk, warned of our approach, had fled, taking their livestock with them. Their low houses had rough stone walls topped by sod roofs that almost touched the ground, while their dunghills were taller than the hovels. We collapsed the roofs by breaking the rafters, and shoveled horse dung into the small rough-stone church, but there was little other damage we could do. We were being watched by four horsemen on a hill to the north. "Bastards," Ragnar shouted, though they were much too far away to hear him.

The Scots, like us, used horsemen as scouts, but their riders never wore heavy mail and usually carried no weapon except a spear. They were mounted on nimble, quick horses, and though we might chase them, we could never catch them. "I wonder who they serve?" I said.

"Domnal, probably," Ragnar said, "King of Alba." He spat the last word. Domnal ruled the greater part of the land north of Northumbria. All that land is called Scotland because it had been largely conquered by the Scots, a wild tribe of Irish, though, like England, the name Scotland meant little. Domnal ruled the largest kingdom, though there were others like Dalriada and Strathclota, and then there were the stormbound islands of the western coast where savage Norse jarls made their own petty kingdoms. Dealing with the Scots, my father had always said, was like trying to geld wildcats with your teeth, but luckily the wildcats spent much of their time fighting each other.

Once the village was ruined we withdrew to higher ground, fearing that the presence of the four scouts might mean the arrival of a larger force, but none appeared. We went west next day, seeking something alive on which we could take revenge, but four days of riding produced nothing except a sick goat and a lame bullock. The scouts never left us. Even when a thick mist draped the hills and we used its concealment to change direction, they found us as soon as the mist lifted. They never came close, just watched us.

We turned for home, following the spine of the great hills that divide Britain. It was still cold and there was snow in the creases of the high land. We had failed to retaliate for the Scottish raid, but our spirits were high because it felt good to be riding in open country with swords by our sides. "I'll beat the bastards bloody when we've finished with Wessex," Ragnar promised me cheerfully, "I'll give them a raid they won't forget."

"You really want to fight Wessex?" I asked him. The two of us were alone, riding a hundred paces ahead of our men.

"Fight Wessex?" He shrugged. "In truth? No. I'm happy up here."

"Then why do it?"

"Because Brida's right. If we don't take Wessex then Wessex will take us."

"Not in your lifetime," I said.

"But I have sons," he said. All his sons were bastards, but Ragnar did not care about their legitimacy. He loved them all and wanted one of them to hold Dunholm after him. "I don't want my sons bowing to some West Saxon king," he said. "I want them to be free."

"So you'll become King of Wessex?"

He gave a great neigh of a laugh. "I don't want that! I want to be Jarl of Dunholm, my friend. Maybe you should be King of Wessex?"

"I want to be Jarl of Bebbanburg."

"We'll find someone who wants to be king," he said carelessly. "Maybe Sigurd or Cnut?" Sigurd Thorrson and Cnut Ranulfson were, after Ragnar himself, the mightiest lords in Northumbria and, unless they joined their men to ours, we would have no chance of conquering Wessex. "We'll take Wessex," Ragnar said confidently, "and divide its treasures. You need men to take Bebbanburg? The silver in the Wessex churches will buy you enough to take a dozen fortresses like Bebbanburg."

"True."

"So be happy! Fate is smiling."

We were following the crest of a hill. Beneath us scrabbling streams glinted white in deep valleys. I could see for miles, and in all that wide view there was neither a house nor a tree. This was bare land where men scratched a living tending sheep, though our presence meant that the flocks had all been driven away. The Scottish outriders with their long spears were on the hill to our east, while to the south the crest ended suddenly in a long hill that dropped steeply into a deep-walled valley where two streams met. And there, where the streams churned about rocks in their shadowed meeting place, were fourteen horsemen. None was moving. They waited where the two streams became one, and it was obvious that they waited for us, and equally obvious that it had to be a trap. The fourteen men were bait, and that meant other men must be nearby. We stared back the way we had come, but there was no enemy in sight on the long crest, nor were any visible on the nearer hills. The four scouts who had shadowed us were kicking their horses down the heather-covered slope to join the larger group.

Ragnar watched the fourteen men. "What do they want us to do?" he asked.

"Go down there?"

"Which we have to do anyway," he said slowly, "and they must have known that, so why bother to entice us down there?" He frowned, then looked quickly about the surrounding hills, but still no enemy showed on the slopes. "Are they Scots?" he asked.

Finan had joined us and he had eyes like a hunting hawk. "They're Scots," he said.

"How can you tell?" I asked.

"There's a fellow wearing the symbol of a dove, lord," Finan said.

"A dove?" Ragnar asked, sounding disgusted. In his view, indeed in mine, a man's symbol should be warlike; an eagle or a wolf.

"It's the sign of Colum Cille, lord," Finan explained.

"Who is he?"

"Saint Columba, lord. An Irish saint. He came to the land of the Picts and drove away a great monster that lives in a lake here. The Scots revere him, lord."

"Useful people, saints," Ragnar said distractedly. He looked behind again, still expecting to see an enemy appear on the crest, but the skyline stayed empty.

"Two of them are prisoners," Finan said, gazing down at the men in the valley, "and one's just a wee boy."

"Is it a trap?" Ragnar asked of no one, then decided that only a fool would cede the high ground, and that therefore the fourteen men, who were now eighteen because the scouts had joined them, were not seeking a fight. "We'll go down," he decided.

Eighteen of us rode down the steep slope. When we reached the flatter land of the valley's bed two of the Scots rode to meet us, and Ragnar, copying their example, held up a hand to check his men so that only he and I rode to meet the pair. They were a man and a boy. The man, who was wearing the dove-embroidered jerkin beneath a long blue cloak, was a few years younger than I. He rode straight-backed and had a fine gold chain with a thick gold cross hanging about his neck. He had a handsome, clean-shaven face with bright blue eyes. He was hatless and his brown hair was cut short in Saxon style. The boy, riding a small colt, was only five or six years old and wore the same clothes as the man I assumed was his father. The pair curbed their horses a few paces from us and the man, who wore a jewel-hilted sword, looked from me to Ragnar and then back to me. "I am Constantin," he said, "son of Aed, Prince of Alba, and this is my son, Cellach mac Constantin, and also, despite his size, a Prince of Alba." He spoke in Danish, though it was obvious he was not comfortable with the language. He smiled at his son. It is strange how we know immediately whether we like people or not, and though he was a Scot, I liked Constantin at once. "I assume one of you is Jarl Ragnar," he said, "and the other is Jarl Uhtred, but forgive me for not knowing which is which."

"I am Ragnar Ragnarson," Ragnar said.

"Greetings," Constantin said pleasantly. "I hope you've enjoyed your travels in our country?"

"So much," Ragnar said, "that I intend to come again, only next time I shall bring more men to share the pleasures."

Constantin laughed at that, then spoke to his son in their own language, making the boy stare at us wide-eyed. "I was telling him that you are both great warriors," Constantin said, "and that one day he must learn how to beat such warriors."

"Constantin," I said. "That isn't a Scottish name."

"It is mine, though," he said, "and a reminder that I must emulate the great Roman emperor who converted his people to Christianity."

"He did them a disservice, then," I said.

"He did it by defeating the pagans," Constantin said smiling, though beneath that pleasant expression was a hint of steel.

"You're nephew to the King of Alba?" Ragnar asked.

"Domnal, yes. He's old, he won't live long."

"And you will be king?" Ragnar asked.

"If God wills it, yes." He spoke mildly, but I got the impression that his god's will would coincide with Constantin's own wishes.

My borrowed horse snorted and took some nervous sideways steps. I calmed him. Our sixteen men were not far behind, all of them with hands on sword hilts, but the Scots were showing no sign of hostility. I looked up at the hills and saw no enemy.

"This isn't a trap, Lord Uhtred," Constantin said, "but I could not resist this chance to meet you. Your uncle sent envoys to us."

"Looking for help?" I asked scornfully.

"He will pay us one thousand silver shillings," Constantin said, "if this summer we bring men to attack you."

"And why would you attack me?"

"Because you will be besieging Bebbanburg," he said.

I nodded. "So I must kill you as well as Ælfric?"

"That will certainly add to your renown," he said, "but I would propose a different arrangement."

"Which is?" Ragnar asked.

"Your uncle," Constantin still spoke to me, "is not the most generous of men. A thousand silver shillings would be welcome, of course, but it still seems to me a small payment for a large war."

I understood then why Constantin had taken such trouble to make this meeting a secret, for if he had sent envoys to Dunholm my uncle would hear of it and suspect treachery. "So what is your price?" I asked.

"Three thousand shillings," Constantin said, "will keep Alba's warriors safe in their homes all summer."

I did not have nearly that amount, but Ragnar nodded. Constantin plainly believed that we were planning to attack Bebbanburg, and of course we were not, but Ragnar still feared an invasion of his land by the Scots while he was away in Wessex. Such an invasion was always a possibility because Alfred took care to keep the Scottish kings friendly as a threat against the Danes in northern England. "Let me suggest," Ragnar said carefully, "that I pay you three thousand silver shillings and that you vow to keep your warriors out of all Northumbria for one full year."

Constantin considered that. Ragnar's suggestion differed hardly at all from what Constantin himself had proposed, but the small difference was important. Constantin glanced at me and I saw the shrewdness in his mind. He understood that maybe Bebbanburg was not our ambition. He nodded. "I could accept that," he said.

"And King Domnal?" I asked, "will he accept that?"

"He will do what I say," Constantin said confidently.

"But how do we know you will keep your word?" Ragnar demanded.

"I bring you a gift," Constantin said, and beckoned toward his men. The two prisoners were ordered out of their saddles and, with bound hands, fetched across the stream to stand beside Constantin. "These two men are brothers," Constantin said to Ragnar, "and they led the raid on your land. I shall return the women and children they captured, but for the moment I give you these two."

Ragnar glanced at the two bearded men. "Two lives as surety?" he asked, "and when they are dead, what's to stop you breaking your word?"

"I give you three lives," Constantin said. He touched his son's shoulder. "Cellach is my eldest and he is dear to me. I give him to you as a hostage. If one of my men crosses into Northumbria with a sword then you may kill Cellach."

I remembered Haesten's joy at foisting a false son on us as a hostage, but there was no doubt that Cellach was Constantin's boy. The resemblance was striking. I looked at the boy and felt an instant regret that my eldest son did not have his bold demeanor and firm gaze.

Ragnar thought for a moment, but saw no disadvantage. He kicked his horse forward and held out his hand, and Constantin took it. "I shall send the silver," Ragnar promised.

"And it will be exchanged for Cellach," Constantin promised. "You will permit me to send servants and a tutor with the boy?"

"They will all be welcome," Ragnar said.

Constantin looked pleased. "Our business is concluded, I think."

And so it was. The Scots rode away and we stripped the two prisoners naked, then Ragnar killed both men with his sword. He did it quickly. Mist was flowing soft and silent down the hills and we were in a hurry to leave. The two men were decapitated and their corpses left beside the junction of the streams. Then we mounted and rode on south.

Ragnar rode with the pledge that his northern frontier would be peaceful while he was fighting in Wessex. It was, indeed, a good agreement, but it left me uncomfortable. I had liked Constantin, but there was an intelligence and a calculation in him that promised he would be a difficult and formidable enemy. How had he arranged the secret meeting with Ragnar? By instigating the raid that had prompted our retaliatory attack, of course, and then Constantin had betrayed the men who had done his bidding in the first place. He was clever and he was young. I would have to live with Constantin a long time, and if I had known then what I know now I would have slit both his and his son's throats.

But, at least for the next twelve months, he kept his word.

Spring came late, but when at last it arrived the land greened swiftly. Lambs were born, the days grew long and warm, and men's minds turned to war.

The two powerful Northumbrian jarls, Sigurd Thorrson and Cnut Ranulfson, came to Dunholm together, and after them a slew of lesser lords, all of them Danes and even the least of them capable of leading more than a hundred trained warriors into battle. They came with just a handful of warriors, servants, and slaves each, but Ragnar's capacious halls were still insufficient and so some of the lesser jarls were accommodated in the town south of the fortress.

There was feasting and gift-giving and, during the day, talking. The jarls had arrived believing the tale that we gathered men for an assault on Bebbanburg, but Ragnar disabused them on the first day. "And Alfred will hear we plan to attack Wessex," he warned them, "because some of you will tell your men, and they will tell others, and this news will reach Alfred within days."

"So keep silent," Sigurd Thorrson growled.

Jarl Sigurd was a tall, hard-looking man with a beard plaited into two great ropes which he twisted about his thick neck. He owned land that stretched from southern Northumbria into northern Mercia and had learned his trade by fighting Æthelred's warriors. His friend, Cnut Ranulfson, was slighter, but had the same wiry strength that Finan possessed. Cnut was reputed to be the finest swordsman in all Britain, and his blade, together with the horde of household warriors his wealth commanded, had given him lands bordering Sigurd's estates. His hair was bone white, though he was only thirty years old, and he had the palest eyes I have ever seen, which, with his hair, gave him a spectral appearance. He had a quick smile, though, and an infinite store of jests. "I had a Saxon slave girl just as pretty as that one," he had told me when we first met. He was gazing at one of Ragnar's slaves who was carrying wooden platters to the great hall. "But she died," he went on gloomily, "died from drinking milk."

"The milk was bad?"

"The cow collapsed on top of her," Cnut said and burst into laughter.

Cnut was in a serious mood when Ragnar announced that he wanted to lead an assault on Wessex. Ragnar gave a good speech, explaining that West Saxon power was growing and that West Saxon ambitions were to capture Mercia, then East Anglia and finally to invade Northumbria. "King Alfred," Ragnar said, "calls himself King of the Angelcynn, and English is spoken in my land as it is in all your lands. If we do nothing then the English will take us one by one."

"Alfred is dying," Cnut objected.

"But his ambitions will live on," Ragnar said. "And Wessex knows its best defense is attack, and Wessex has a dream of pushing its boundary to touch the land of the Scots."

"Wish the bastards would conquer the Scots," a man interjected glumly.

"If we do nothing," Ragnar said, "then one day Northumbria will be ruled by Wessex."

There was an argument about the real power of Wessex. I kept silent, though I knew more than any man there. I let them talk their way to sense and, under Ragnar's guidance, they at last understood that Wessex was a country that had organized itself for war. Its defense was the burhs, garrisoned by the fyrd, but its offense was the growing number of household warriors who could gather under the king's banner. The Danes were more feared, man for man, but they had never organized themselves as Alfred had organized Wessex. Every Danish jarl protected his own land, and was reluctant to follow the orders of another jarl. It was possible to unite them, as Harald had done, but at the first setback the crews would scatter to find easier plunder.

"So," Sigurd growled dubiously, "we have to capture the burhs?"

"Harald captured one," Ragnar pointed out.

"I hear it was only half built," Sigurd said, looking at me for confirmation. I nodded.

"If you want Wessex," Ragnar said, "we must take the burhs." He forced a confident smile. "We sail to his south coast," he went on, "in a great fleet! We'll capture Exanceaster and then march on Wintanceaster. Alfred will be expecting an attack from the north, so we'll assault from the south."

"And his ships will see our fleet," Cnut objected, "and his warriors will be waiting for us."

"His warriors," a new voice intervened from the back of the hall, "will be fighting against my crews. So you will only have Alfred's fyrd to fight." The speaker stood in the open hall doorway and the sun was so bright that none of us could see him properly. "I shall assault Mercia," the man said in a loud and confident voice, "and Alfred's forces will march to defend it, and with them gone, Wessex will be ripe for your plucking." The man came a few paces forward, followed by a dozen mailed warriors. "Greetings, Jarl Ragnar," he said, "and to you all," he swept an expansive hand around the company, "greetings!"

It was Haesten. He had not been invited to this council, yet there he was, smiling and glittering with gold chains. It was a mild day, yet he had chosen to wear an otterskin cloak lined with rare yellow silk to show his wealth. There was a moment's embarrassment following his arrival as though no one was certain whether to treat him as a friend or an interloper, but then Ragnar leaped to his feet and embraced the newcomer.

I will not describe the tedium that followed over the next two days. The men assembled in Dunholm were capable of raising the greatest Danish army ever seen in Britain, yet they were still apprehensive because all knew that Wessex had defeated every assault. Ragnar now had to persuade them that the circumstances were changed. Alfred was sick and could not be expected to behave as a young and energetic leader, his son was inexperienced and, he flattered me, Uhtred of Bebbanburg had deserted Wessex. So it was at last agreed that Wessex was vulnerable, but who would be king? I had expected that argument to last forever, but Sigurd and Cnut had discussed it privately and agreed that Sigurd would rule Wessex while Cnut would take the throne of Northumbria when the sick, mad, and sad Guthred died. Ragnar had no ambition to live in the south, nor did I, and though Haesten doubtless hoped to be offered Wessex's crown, he accepted that he would be named King of Mercia.

Haesten's arrival made the whole idea of attacking Wessex appear more feasible. No one really trusted him, but few doubted that he planned an assault on Mercia. He really wanted our troops to join his, and in truth that would have made sense because, united, we would have made a mighty army, but no one could ever have agreed on who commanded that army. And so it was decided that Haesten would lead at least two thousand men westward from his stronghold at Beamfleot and, once the West Saxon troops marched to oppose him, the Northumbrian fleet would assault the south coast. Every man present swore to keep the plans secret, though I doubted that solemn oath was worth a whisker. Alfred would hear soon enough.

"So I'll be King of Mercia," Haesten told me on the last night, when again the great hall was lit by fire and filled with feasting.

"Only if you hold off the West Saxons long enough," I warned him. He waved a hand as though that task were trivial. "Capture a Mercian burh," I advised him, "and force them to besiege you."

He bit into a goose leg and the fat ran down into his beard. "Who'll command them?"

"Edward, probably, but he'll be advised by Æthelred and Steapa."

"They're not you, my friend," he said, jabbing my forearm with the goose bone.

"My children are in Mercia," I told him. "Make sure they live."

Haesten heard the grimness in my voice. "I promise you," he said earnestly, "I swear it on my life. Your children will be safe." He touched my arm as if to assure me, then pointed the goose bone at Cellach. "Who's that child?"

"A hostage from Scotland," I said. Cellach had arrived a week before with a small entourage. He had two warriors to guard him, two servants to dress and feed him, and a hunchbacked priest to educate him. I liked him. He was a sturdy little boy who had accepted his exile bravely. He had already made friends among the fortress's children and was forever escaping the hunchback's lessons to scamper wildly along the ramparts or scramble down the steep slope of Dunholm's rocks.

"So no trouble from the Scots?" Haesten asked.

"The boy dies if they so much as piss across the border," I said.

Haesten grinned. "So I'll be King of Mercia, Sigurd of Wessex, Cnut of Northumbria, but what of you?"

I poured him mead and paused a moment to watch a man juggle with flaming sticks. "I shall take West Saxon silver," I said, "and reclaim Bebbanburg."

"You don't want to be king of somewhere?" he asked disbelievingly.

"I want Bebbanburg," I said, "it's all I've ever wanted. I'll take my children there, raise them, and never leave."

Haesten said nothing. I did not think he had even heard me. He was staring in awe, and he stared at Skade. She was in drab servant's dress, yet even so her beauty shone like a beacon in the dark. I think, at that moment, I could have stolen the chains of gold from around Haesten's neck and he would have been unaware. He just stared and Skade, sensing his gaze, turned to face him. They locked eyes.

"Bebbanburg," I said again, "it's all I've ever wanted."

"Yes," he said distractedly, "I heard you." He still stared at Skade. No other folk existed for them in that roaring hall. Brida, sitting further along the high table, had seen their locked gazes and she turned to me and raised an eyebrow. I shrugged.

Brida was happy that night. She had arranged Britain's future, though her influence had been wielded through Ragnar. Yet it was her ambition that had spurred him, and that ambition was to destroy Wessex and, eventually, the power of the priests who spread their gospel so insidiously. In a year, we all believed, the only Christian king in England would be Eohric of East Anglia, and he would change allegiance when he saw how the wind had turned. Indeed, there would be no England at all, just Daneland. It all seemed so simple, so easy, so straightforward and, on that night of harp music and laughter, of ale and comradeship, none of us could anticipate failure. Mercia was weak, Wessex was vulnerable, and we were the Danes, the feared spear-warriors of the north.

Then, next day, Father Pyrlig came to Dunholm.

TWO

A storm came that night. It hurtled sudden from the north, its first
signs a violent gust of wind that shuddered across the fortress.
Within moments clouds drowned the stars and lightning shivered
the sky. The storm woke me in the house where I had sweated and
frozen through the sickness, and I heard the first few heavy drops of
rain fall plump and hard on the thatch, then it seemed as though a
river was emptying itself on Dunholm's fort. The sky seethed and
the rain's noise was louder than any thunder. I got out of bed
and wrapped a blanket of sheepskins around my naked shoulders
and went to stand in the doorway where I pulled aside the leather
curtain. The girl in my bed whimpered and I told her to join me.
She was a Saxon slave, and I lifted the blanket to enfold her and she
stood pressed against me, wide-eyed in the lightning flashes as she
watched the roaring darkness. She said something, but what it was I
could not tell because the wind and the rain drowned her words.

The storm came fast and it went fast. I watched the lightning
travel southward and heard the rain diminish, and then it seemed as
though the night held its breath in the silence that followed the
thunder. The rain stopped, though water still dripped from the
eaves, and some trickled through the thatch to hiss on the remnants
of the fire. I threw new wood onto the smoldering embers, added
kindling, and let the flames leap upward. The leather curtain was
still hooked open and I saw the firelight brighten in other houses
and in the two big halls. It was a restless night at Dunholm.
The girl lay on the bed again, swathing herself in fleeces and furs,

219

and her fire-bright eyes watched as I drew Serpent-Breath from her scabbard and slid the blade slowly through the newly revived flames. I did it twice, slowly bathing each side of her long blade, then wiping the steel with the sheepskin. "Why do you do that, lord?" she asked.

"I don't know," I said, nor did I, except that Serpent-Breath, like all swords, had been born in flames and sometimes I liked to bathe her in fire to preserve whatever sorcery had been enchanted into her at the moment of her creation. I kissed the warm steel reverently and slid it back into her scabbard. "We can be certain of nothing," I said, "except our weapons and death."

"We can be certain of God, lord," she insisted in a small voice.

I smiled, but said nothing. I wondered if my gods cared about us. Perhaps that was the advantage of the Christian god, that he had somehow convinced his followers that he did care, that he watched over them and protected them, yet I did not see that Christian children died any less often than pagan children, or that Christians were spared disease and floods and fire. Yet Christians forever declared their god's love.

Footsteps sounded wet outside. Someone was running toward my hut and, though I was safe inside Ragnar's fortress, I instinctively reached for Serpent-Breath, and was still holding the hilt as a burly man ducked inside the open doorway. "Dear sweet Jesus," he said, "but it's cold out there."

I let go of the sword as Father Pyrlig crouched on the fire's far side. "You couldn't sleep?" I asked.

"Now who in God's name could sleep through that storm?" he demanded. "You'd have to be deaf, blind, drunk, and stupid to sleep through that. Good morning, lord," he grinned at me, "naked like a newborn as you are." He twisted his head and smiled at the slave. "Blessings on you, child," he said.

She was nervous of the newcomer and glanced anxiously at me. "He's a kind man," I reassured her, "and a priest." Father Pyrlig was dressed in breeches and jerkin with no sign of any priestly robes. He had arrived the previous evening, earning a chill reception from Brida, but enchanting Ragnar with his exaggerated tales of battle.

He had been drunk by the time Ragnar went to bed, so I had found very little chance to talk with my old friend.

I took a cloak from a peg and clasped it around my throat. The wool was damp. "Does your god love you?" I asked Pyrlig.

He laughed at that. "My God, what a question, lord! Well, he keeps me miles away from my wife, so he does, and what greater blessing can a man ask? And he fills my belly and he keeps me amused! Did I tell you about the slave girl that died of drinking milk?"

"The cow collapsed on her," I said flatly.

"He's a funny man, that Cnut," Pyrlig said, "I'll regret it when you kill him."

"I kill him?" I asked. The girl stared at me.

"You'll probably have to," Pyrlig said.

"Don't listen to him," I told the girl, "he's raving."

"I'm Welsh, my darling," he explained to her, then turned back to me, "and can you tell me, lord, why a good Welshman should be doing Saxon business?"

"Because you're an interfering earsling," I said, "and god knows what arse you dropped out of, but here you are."

"God uses strange instruments for his wondrous purposes," Pyrlig said. "Why don't you dress and watch the dawn with me?"

Father Pyrlig, like Bishop Asser, was a Welshman who had found employment in Alfred's service, though he told me he had not come to Dunholm from Wessex, but rather from Mercia. "I was last in Wintanceaster at Christmas," he told me, "and my God, poor Alfred is sick! He looks like a warmed-up corpse, he does, and not very well warmed-up either."

"What were you doing in Mercia?"

"Smelling the place," he said mysteriously, then, just as mysteriously, added, "it's that wife of his."

"Whose wife?"

"Ælswith. Why did Alfred marry her? She should feed the poor man some butter and cream, make him eat some good beef."

Father Pyrlig had eaten his share of butter and cream. He was big-bellied, broad-shouldered, and eternally cheerful. His hair was a tangled mess, his grin was infectious, and his religion was carried lightly, though never shallowly. He stood beside me above Dunholm's south gate and I told him how Ragnar and I had captured the fortress. Pyrlig, before he became a priest, had been a warrior and he appreciated the tale of how I had sneaked inside Dunholm by a water-gate on the west side, and how we had survived long enough to open the gate above which we now stood, and how Ragnar had led his flame-bearing sword-Danes through the gate and into the fortress where we had fought Kjartan's men to defeat and death. "Ah," he said when the tale was finished, "I should have been here. It sounds like a rare fight!"

"So what brings you here now?"

He grinned at me. "A man can't just visit an old friend?"

"Alfred sent you," I said sourly.

"I told you, I came here from Mercia, not Wessex." He leaned on the palisade's top. "Do you remember," he asked me, "the night before you captured Lundene?"

"I do remember," I said, "that you told me you were dressed for prayer that night. You were in mail and carried two swords."

"What better time to pray than before a battle?" he asked. "And that was another rare fight, my friend."

"It was."

"And before it, lord," he said, "you made an oath."

My anger rose as swiftly as the river had been swollen by the storm's sudden rain. "Damn Alfred and his oaths," I said, "damn him to his hell. I gave that bastard the best years of my life! He wouldn't even sit on the throne of Wessex if I hadn't fought for him! Harald Bloodhair would be king now, and Alfred would be rotting in his tomb, and does he thank me? Once in a while he'd pat me on the head like a damned dog, but then he lets that turd-brained monk insult Gisela and he expects me to crawl to him for forgiveness after I kill the bastard. Yes," I said, turning to look into Pyrlig's broad face, "I took an oath. Then let me tell you I am breaking it. It is broken. The gods can punish me for that and Alfred can rot in hell's depth for all I care."

"I doubt it will be him in hell," Pyrlig said mildly.

"You think I'd want to be in your heaven?" I demanded. "All those priests and monks and dried-up nuns? I'd rather risk hell. No, father, I am not keeping my oath to Alfred. You can ride back and you can tell him that I have no oath to him, no allegiance, no duty, no loyalty, nothing! He's a scabby, ungrateful, cabbage-farting, squint-eyed bastard!"

"You know him better than I do," Pyrlig said lightly.

"He can take his oath and shit on it," I snarled. "Go back to Wessex and give him that answer." A shout made me turn, but it was only a servant bellowing at a protesting horse. One of the lords was leaving and evidently making an early start. A group of warriors, helmeted and in mail, were already mounted, while two horses waited with empty saddles. A pair of Ragnar's men ran to the gate beneath us and I heard the bar being lifted.

"Alfred didn't send me," Pyrlig said.

"You mean this is all your idea? To come and remind me of my oath? I don't need reminding."

"To break an oath is a . . ."

"I know!" I shouted.

"Yet men break oaths all the time," Pyrlig went on calmly, gazing south to where the first gray light of dawn was touching the crests of the hills. "Maybe that's why we hedge oaths with harsh law and strict custom, because we know they will be broken. I think Alfred knows you will not return. He is sad about that. If Wessex is attacked then he will lack his sharpest sword, but even so he didn't send me. He thinks Wessex is better without you. He wants a godly country and you were a thorn in that ambition."

"He might need some thorns if the Danes return to Wessex," I snarled.

"He trusts in God, Lord Uhtred, he trusts in God."

I laughed at that. Let the Christian god defend Wessex against the Northumbrian Danes when they stormed ashore in the summer. "If Alfred doesn't want me back," I said, "then why are you wasting my time?"

223

"Because of the oath you made on the eve of the battle for Lundene," Pyrlig said, "and it was the person to whom you made that promise who asked me to come here."

I stared at him and fancied I heard the laughter of the Norns. The three spinners. The busy-fingered Norns who weave our fate. "No," I said, but without anger or force.

"She sent me."

"No," I said again.

"She wants your help."

"No!" I protested.

"And she asked me to remind you that you once swore to serve her."

I closed my eyes. It was true, all true. Had I forgotten that oath I made in the night before we attacked Lundene? I had not forgotten it, but nor had I ever thought that oath would harness me. "No," I said again, this time a mere whisper of denial.

"We are all sinners, lord," Pyrlig said gently, "but even the church recognizes that some sins are worse than others. The oath you made to Alfred was duty and it should have been rewarded with gratitude, land, and silver. It is wrong of you to break that oath and I cannot approve, but I understand that Alfred was careless in his duty toward you. But the oath you made to the lady was sworn in love, and that oath you cannot break without destroying your soul."

"Love?" I made the query sound like a challenge.

"You loved Gisela, I know, and you did not break the oaths you gave to her, but you love the lady who sent me. You always have. I see it in your face, and I see it in hers. You are blind to it, but it dazzles the rest of us."

"No," I said.

"She is in trouble," Pyrlig said.

"Trouble?" I asked dully.

"Her husband is sick in the mind."

"Is he mad?"

"Not so you'd know."

Beneath me the hinges squealed as the two great gates were pushed outward. Ragnar, bare-legged beneath swathing cloaks, was shouting farewell to the horsemen who passed beneath us through Dunholm's High Gate, the hooves clattering on the stones of the road that led down through the town. One of the riders turned and I saw it was Haesten who raised a hand to salute me, and I raised a hand in return, then froze because the rider next to him also twisted in her saddle. She smiled, but savagely. It was Skade. She must have seen the astonishment on my face because she laughed, then kicked her heels so her horse rode free and fast downhill. "Trouble," I said, watching her, "more trouble than you know."

"Because Haesten will attack Mercia?" Pyrlig asked.

I did not confirm that, though I doubted Haesten would have kept his intentions secret. "Because that woman is with him," I said.

"Women brought sin into this world," Pyrlig said, "and by God they do keep it bubbling. But I can't imagine a world without them, can you?"

"She wants me to go to her?"

"Yes," Pyrlig said, "and she sent me to fetch you. She also told me to tell you something else. That if you cannot keep the oath then she releases you from it."

"So I don't have to go," I said.

"No."

"But I made the oath."

"Yes."

To Æthelflæd. I had escaped Alfred and felt nothing but relief at the freedom I had found, and now his daughter summoned me. And Pyrlig was right. Some oaths are made with love, and those we cannot break.

All winter I had felt like a steersman in a fog, tideswept to nowhere, windblown to no harbor, lost, but now it was as though the fog lifted. The Fates had shown me the landmark I had sought, and if it was not the landmark I had wished for, it still gave my ship direction.

I had indeed sworn an oath to Æthelflæd. Almost every promise I had ever made to her father had been wrung from me, sometimes forced from me, but so was the oath I swore to Æthelflæd. The promise to serve her had been her price for giving me men to help in the desperate assault on Lundene, and I remembered resenting that price, but I had still knelt to her and given her the vow.

I had known Æthelflæd since she was a child, the one child of Alfred's who had mischief and life and laughter, and I had seen those qualities curdled by the marriage to my cousin. And in the months and years after the oath I had come to love her, not as I loved Gisela who was a friend to Æthelflæd, but as a sparkling girl whose light was being doused by the cruelty of men. And I had served her. I had protected her. And now she asked me to protect her again, and the request filled me with indecision. I busied the next few days with activity, hunting and practicing weapons, and Finan, who often sparred sword-to-sword with me, stepped back one day and asked if I was trying to kill him. "I'm sorry," I said.

"It's the Welsh priest, isn't it?" he asked.

"It's fate," I said.

"And where's fate taking us, lord?" he asked.

"South," I said, "south," and I hated that word. I was a northerner, Northumbria was my country, yet the spinners were taking me south.

"To Alfred?" Finan asked in disbelief.

"No," I said, "to Æthelflæd," and as I said her name I knew I could delay no longer.

So, a week after Haesten left, I went to Ragnar and I lied to him because I did not want him to see my betrayal. "I'm going to protect my children," I told him.

"Haesten surely won't kill them," he tried to reassure me.

"But Skade will."

He thought about that, then nodded. "True."

"Or she'll sell them into slavery," I said bleakly. "She hates me."

"Then you must go," he said. And so I rode from Dunholm, and my men came with me because they were oath-sworn, and their families came too and because of that Ragnar knew I was riding away for good. He had watched my men load packhorses with mail and weapons, and he had gazed at me, hurt and puzzled. "Are you going to Wessex?" he asked.

"No," I promised him, and I spoke truthfully.

Brida knew it. "Then where?" she demanded angrily.

"To my children."

"You'll bring them back here?" Ragnar had asked eagerly.

"There is a friend," I avoided answering his question, "who has the care of my children, and she is in trouble."

Brida cut through my evasions. "Alfred's daughter?" she asked scornfully.

"Yes."

"Who hates the Danes," Brida said.

"She has pleaded for my help," I spoke to Ragnar, "and I cannot refuse her."

"Women weaken you," Brida snarled at me. "What of your promise to sail with Ragnar?"

"I made no such promise," I snapped back at her.

"We need you!" Ragnar pleaded.

"Me and my half-crew?"

"If you don't help destroy Wessex," Brida said, "you will get no share in Wessex's wealth, and without that, Uhtred, you have no hopes of Bebbanburg."

"I am riding to find my children," I said obstinately, and both Ragnar and Brida knew that was a half-truth at best.

"You were always a Saxon before you were a Dane," Brida said derisively. "You want to be a Dane, but you don't have the courage."

"You may be right," I admitted.

"We should kill you now," Brida said, and she meant it.

Ragnar laid a hand on Brida's arm to silence her, then embraced me. "You are my brother," he said. He held me close for an instant. He knew, and I knew, that I was going back to the Saxons, that we would forever be on opposing sides, and all I could do was promise that I would never fight against him.

"And will you betray our plans to Alfred?" Brida demanded. Ragnar might make his peace with my departure, but Brida was ever unforgiving.

"I hate Alfred," I said, "and wish you joy in toppling his kingdom."

There, I have written it, and it hurt me to write it because the memory of that parting is so painful. Brida hated me at that moment, and Ragnar was saddened, and I was a coward. I hid behind the fate of my children and betrayed my friendship. All winter Ragnar had sheltered me and fed my men, and now I deserted him. He had been happy with me at his side, and he was unhappy at the prospect of fighting Wessex, but he had thought he and I would wage that war together. Now I left him. He allowed me to leave him. Brida truly would have killed me that day, but Ragnar forgave me. It was a clear spring day. It was the day my life changed. Wyrd bið ful āræd.

So we rode south and for a long time I could not speak. Father Pyrlig sensed my mood and said nothing till at last I broke the morose silence. "You say my cousin's sick in the mind?" I asked.

"Yes," he said, "and no."

"Thank you for making it so plain," I said.

He half smiled. He rode beside me, eyes narrowed against the day's sun. "He's not mad as poor Guthred is mad," he said after a while, "he doesn't have visions or talk to the angels or chew the rushes. He's angry that he's not a king. Æthelred knows that when he dies Mercia will fall to Wessex. That's what Alfred wants, and what Alfred wants he usually gets."

"So why does Æthelflæd send for me?"

"Your cousin hates his wife," Pyrlig said, his voice low so it would not carry to Finan and Sihtric who rode close behind. A dog harried sheep out of our path, obeying the shrill whistle of a shepherd on a farther hill. Pyrlig sighed. "Every time he sees Æthelflæd," he went on, "he feels the chains that Alfred has hung on him. He would be king, and he cannot be king because Alfred will not allow it."

"Because Alfred wants to be King of Mercia?"

"Alfred wants to be King of England," Pyrlig said, "and if he cannot boast that title, then he would have his son wear that crown. And so there cannot be another Saxon king. A king is God's anointed, a king is sacred, so there must be no other anointed king to obstruct the path."

"And Æthelred resents that," I said.

"He does, and he would punish his wife."

"How?"

"By divorcing her."

"Alfred wouldn't stand for it," I said dismissively.

"Alfred is a sick man. He could die at any moment."

"Divorcing her," I said, "which means . . ." I paused. Æthelflæd, of course, had told me of her husband's ambitions before, but I still found them scarcely credible. "No, he wouldn't do that!"

"He tried when we all thought Alfred lay dying," Pyrlig said, "and Æthelflæd got word of what was to happen and took refuge in a nunnery at Lecelad."

"On the border of Wessex?"

Pyrlig nodded. "So she can flee to her father if they try again, which they will."

I swore softly. "Aldhelm?" I asked.

"The Lord Aldhelm," Pyrlig agreed.

"Æthelred will force her to Aldhelm's bed?" I asked, my voice rising with incredulity.

"That would be the Lord Æthelred's pleasure," Pyrlig said drily, "and doubtless Lord Aldhelm's greater pleasure. And when it is done Æthelred can offer the church proof of adultery, confine her to a nunnery and the marriage is over. Then he's free to marry again, beget an heir, and as soon as Alfred dies he can call himself king."

"So who protects her?" I asked, "and who protects my children?"

"Nuns."

"No man protects her?"

"Her husband is the giver of gold, not she," Pyrlig said. "Men love her, but she has no wealth to give them."

"She does now," I said savagely, and dug my spurs into the horse I had purchased in Dunholm. I did not have much wealth left. I had purchased more than seventy horses to make this journey

possible, and the little silver that remained was packed into two saddlebags, but I had Serpent-Breath and I had Wasp-Sting and now,
because the three spinners had twisted my life yet again, I had a
purpose. I would go to Æthelflæd.

Lecelad was a straggle of hovels built along the northern bank of
the Temes where the Lec, a boggy stream, flowed into the river. A wa-
termill stood where the stream emptied itself, and next to it was a
wharf where a handful of small, leaking boats was tied. At the eastern
end of the village street, which was a collection of mud-colored puddles, was the convent. It was surrounded by a palisade built, I suspected, to keep the nuns in rather than their enemies out, and over
that rain-darkened wall reared a gaunt and ugly church made of timber and wattle. The bell-tower scraped the low clouds as rain seethed
from the west. On the far side of the Temes was a wooden landing
stage and above it, on the bank, a group of men who sheltered beneath
a makeshift awning propped on poles. They were all in mail, their
spears stacked against a willow. I stepped onto the wharf, cupped my
hands, and shouted at them. "Who do you serve?"

"Lord Æthelnoth!" one of the men shouted back. He did not recognize me. I was swathed in a dark cloak and had a hood over my
fair hair.

"Why are you there?" I shouted, but the only reply was a shrug of
incomprehension.

That southern bank was West Saxon territory, which was doubtless why Æthelflæd had chosen Lecelad. She could flee into her father's kingdom at a moment's notice, though Alfred, who held the
bonds of marriage to be sacred, would doubtless be reluctant to offer
her refuge for fear of the resultant scandal. Nevertheless I guessed
he had ordered Ealdorman Æthelnoth of Sumorsæte to watch the
convent, if for no other reason than to report any strange happenings on the river's Mercian bank. They would have something to report now, I thought.

"Who are you, lord?" the man called back across the river. He might not have recognized me, but he saw I led a band of horsemen and perhaps the gold of my lavish cloak-brooch glinted in the dull rainy air.

I ignored his question, turning instead to Finan who grinned at me from horseback. "Just thirty men, lord," he told me. I had sent him to explore the village and find how many men guarded the convent.

"Is that all?"

"There are more in a village to the north," he said.

"Who commands the thirty?"

"Some poor bastard who almost shit himself when he saw us."

The thirty men were posted in Lecelad itself, presumably on my cousin's orders and presumably to make sure Æthelflæd stayed immured in the ugly convent. I hauled myself into the wet, slippery saddle and fiddled my right foot into the stirrup. "Let's kick this wasp's nest," I said.

I led my men eastward past cottages, dunghills, and rooting pigs. Some folk watched us from doorways, while at the street's end, in front of the convent itself, a straggle of men in leather jerkins and rusted helmets waited, but if they had orders to prevent anyone entering the convent they were in no mood to enforce them. They moved sullenly aside as we approached. I ignored them and they neither demanded my name nor tried to stop us.

I kicked the convent's gate, spattering rain from its upper edge. My horse whinnied, and I kicked the gate a second time. The Mercian troops watched. One ran into an alley and I suspected he was going to fetch help. "We'll be fighting someone before this day's through," I told Finan.

"I hope so, lord," he said gloomily, "it's been much too long."

A small hatch in the big gate slid open and a woman's face appeared in the hole. "What do you want?" the face demanded.

"To get out of this rain," I said.

"The villagers will offer you shelter," the woman said and began to slide the hatch shut, but I managed to get my toe into the space.

"You can open the gate," I said, "or you can watch us chop it to splinters."

"They are friends of the Lady Æthelflæd," Father Pyrlig intervened helpfully.

The hatch slid fully open again. "Is that you, father?"

"It is, sister."

"Have manners vanished from the surface of God's earth?" she asked.

"He can't help it, sister," Pyrlig said, "he's just a brute." He grinned at me.

"Remove your foot," the woman demanded crossly, and when I obeyed she closed the hatch and I heard the locking bar being lifted. Then the gate creaked wide.

I climbed out of the saddle. "Wait," I told my men, and walked into the nunnery's courtyard. The gaunt church comprised the whole of the southern part, while the other three sides were edged with low timber buildings, thatched with straw, in which I assumed the nuns slept, ate, and spun wool. The nun, who introduced herself as the Abbess Werburgh, bowed to me. "You're truly a friend of the Lady Æthelflæd?" she asked. She was an elderly woman, so small that she scarcely reached my waist, but she had a fierce face.

"I am."

Werburgh twitched with disapproval when she noticed the hammer of Thor hanging at my neck. "And your name?" she demanded, but just then a shriek sounded and a child hurtled out of a doorway and pelted across the puddled courtyard.

It was Stiorra, my daughter, and she threw herself at me, wrapping her arms around my neck and her legs around my waist. I was glad it was raining, or else the nun might have thought the drops on my face were tears. They were. "I knew you'd come," Stiorra said fiercely, "I knew, I knew, I knew."

"You're Lord Uhtred?" the abbess asked.

"Yes."

"Thank God," she said.

Stiorra was telling me of her adventures, and Osbert, my youngest, had run to me and was trying to climb my leg. Uhtred, my eldest son, was nowhere to be seen. I picked up Osbert and shouted for Finan to bring the other men inside. "I don't know how long we're staying," I told the Abbess Werburgh, "but the horses need stabling and food."

"You think we're a tavern?" she demanded.

"You won't leave again, will you?" Stiorra was asking insistently.

"No," I said, "no, no, no," and then I stopped talking because Æthelflæd had appeared in a doorway, framed there by the darkness behind and even on that drab gray day it seemed to me that, though she was dressed in a cloak and hood of coarse brown weave, she glowed.

And I remembered Iseult's prophecy made so many years ago, made when Æthelflæd was no older than Stiorra, a prophecy made when Wessex was at its weakest, when the Danes had overrun the country and Alfred was a fugitive in the marshes. Iseult, that strange and lovely woman, dark as shadows, had promised me that Alfred would give me power and that my woman would be a creature of gold.

And I stared at Æthelflæd and she stared back, and I knew the promise I had made to my daughter was one I would keep. I would not leave.

I put my children down, warning them to stay away from the horses' hooves, and I walked across the puddled courtyard, oblivious of the nuns who had crept out to watch our arrival. I planned to bow to Æthelflæd. She was, after all, a king's daughter and the wife of Mercia's ruler, but her face was at once tearful and happy and I did not bow. I held out my arms and she came to me, and I felt her body trembling as I held her close. Maybe she could feel my heart beating, for it seemed to me as loud as a great drumbeat. "You've come," she said.

"Yes."

"I knew you would."

I pushed back her hood to see her hair, as golden as mine. I smiled. "A creature of gold," I said.

"Foolish man," she said, smiling.

"What happens now?" I asked her.

"I imagine," she said, stepping gently away from me and pulling the hood back over her hair, "that my husband will try to kill you."

"And he can summon?" I asked, then paused to think, "fifteen hundred trained warriors?"

"At least that many."

"Then I see no difficulty," I said lightly. "I have at least forty men."

And that afternoon the first of the Mercian warriors came.

They arrived in groups, ten or twenty at a time, riding from the north and making a loose cordon about the nunnery. I watched them from the bell-tower, counting over a hundred warriors, and still more came. "The thirty men in the village," I asked Æthelflæd, "they were here to keep you from leaving?"

"They were supposed to stop food reaching the nunnery," she said, "though they weren't very effective. Supplies came across the river by boat."

"They wanted to starve you?"

"My husband thought that would make me leave. Then I'd have to go back to him."

"Not to your father?"

She grimaced. "He would have sent me back to my husband, wouldn't he?"

"Would he?"

"Marriage is a sacrament, Uhtred," she said almost wearily, "it is sanctified by God, and you know my father won't offend God."

"So why didn't Æthelred just drag you back?"

"Invade a nunnery? My father would disapprove of that!"

"He would," I said, watching a larger group of horsemen appear to the north.

"They thought my father would die at any moment," she said, and I knew she spoke of my cousin and his friend, Aldhelm, "and they were waiting for that."

"But your father lives."

"He recovers," Æthelflæd said, "God be thanked."

"And here comes trouble," I said, because the new band of horsemen, at least fifty in number, rode beneath a banner, suggesting that whoever commanded the troops guarding the nunnery was coming himself. As the horsemen drew nearer, I saw the banner displayed a cross made of two big-bladed war axes. "Whose badge is that?"

"Aldhelm's," Æthelflæd said flatly.

Two hundred men ringed the monastery now, and Aldhelm, riding a tall black stallion, placed himself fifty paces from the nunnery gates. He had a bodyguard of two priests and a dozen warriors. The warriors carried shields that bore their lord's crossed-ax badge, and those grim men gathered just behind him and, like their lord, gazed in silence at the closed gates. Did Aldhelm know I was inside? He might have suspected, but I doubt he had any certainty. We had ridden fast through Mercia, keeping to the eastern half where the Danes were strongest, so few men in Saxon Mercia would realize I had come south. Yet perhaps Aldhelm suspected I was there, for he made no attempt to enter the nunnery, or else he was under orders not to offend his god by committing sacrilege. Alfred might forgive Æthelred for making Æthelflæd unhappy, but he would never forgive an insult to his god.

I went down to the courtyard. "What's he waiting for?" Finan asked me.

"Me," I said.

I dressed for war. I dressed in shining mail, sword-belted, booted, with my wolf-crested helmet and my shield with the wolf badge, and I chose to carry a war ax as well as my two scabbarded swords. I ordered one leaf of the convent gate to be opened, then walked out alone. I did not ride because I had not been able to buy a battle-trained stallion.

I walked in silence and Aldhelm's men watched me. If Aldhelm had possessed a scrap of courage he should have ridden at me and chopped me down with the long sword hanging at his waist, and even without courage he could have ordered his personal guard to cut me down, but instead he just stared at me.

I stopped a dozen paces from him, then leaned the battle-ax on my shoulder. I had pushed open the hinged cheek-plates of my helmet so Aldhelm's men could see my face. "Men of Mercia!" I shouted so that not only Aldhelm's men could hear me, but the

West Saxon troops across the river. "Any day now Jarl Haesten will lead an attack on your country! He comes with thousands of men, hungry men, spear-Danes, sword-Danes, Danes who would rape your wives, enslave your children, and steal your lands. They will make a greater army than the horde of warriors you defeated at Fearnhamme! How many of you were at Fearnhamme?"

Men glanced at each other, but none raised a hand or shouted that they had been present at that great victory.

"You're ashamed of your triumph?" I asked them. "You made a slaughter that will be remembered so long as men live in Mercia! And you are ashamed of it? How many of you were at Fearn-hamme?"

Some found their courage then and lifted their arms, and one man cheered, and suddenly most of them were cheering. They cheered themselves. Aldhelm, confused, raised a hand to call for silence, but they ignored him.

"And who," I bellowed louder, "do you want to lead you against the Jarl Haesten who comes here with Vikings and pirates, with killers and slavers, with spears and axes, with murder and fire? It was the Lady Æthelflæd who encouraged you to victory at Fearn-hamme, and you want her locked in a nunnery? She begged me to come and fight with you again, and here I am, and you greet me with swords? With spears? So who do you want to lead you against Jarl Haesten and his killers?" I let that question hang for a few heartbeats, then I leveled the ax so it pointed at Aldhelm. "Do you want him?" I shouted, "or me?"

What a fool that man was. At that moment, in the remnants of rain that spat out of the west, he should have killed me fast, or else he should have embraced me. He could have leaped from his saddle and offered me friendship, and so pretended an alliance that would buy him the time during which he could arrange my death by stealth, but instead he showed fear. He was a coward, he had always been a coward, brave only when faced by the weak, and the fear was on his face, it was in his hesitation, and it was not till one of his followers leaned and whispered in his ear that he found his voice. "This man," he called, pointing at me, "is outlawed from Wessex."

That was news to me, but it was not surprising. I had broken my oath to Alfred, so Alfred would have little choice but to declare me outlaw and thus prey to anyone with the courage to capture me. "So I'm an outlaw!" I shouted, "so come and kill me! And who will protect you from Jarl Haesten then?"

Aldhelm came to his senses then and muttered something to the man who had whispered to him, and that man, a big broad-shouldered warrior, spurred his horse forward. His sword was drawn. He knew what he was doing. He did not ride at me franti-cally, but deliberately. He came to kill me, and I could see his eyes judging me from deep in the shadow of his helmet. His sword was already drawn back, his arm tensed for the sweeping stroke that would crash into my shield with the weight of man and horse be-hind the blade to throw me off balance. Then the horse would turn into me and the sword would come again from behind me, and he knew that I knew all that, but he was reassured when I raised my shield, for that meant I would do what he expected me to do. I saw his mouth tighten and his heels nudge back and his stallion, a big gray beast, lunged ahead and the sword flashed in the dull air.

All the man's great strength was in that stroke. It came from my right. My shield was in my left hand, the ax in my right. I did two things.

I dropped onto one knee and lifted the shield over my head so it was almost flat above my helmet, and at the same moment I lunged the ax into the horse's legs and let go of the haft.

The sword slammed onto my shield, skidded across the wood, clanged against the boss, and just then the horse, the ax tangled in its rear legs, whinnied and stumbled. I saw blood bright on a fetlock, and I was already standing as the horseman slashed again, but he and his horse were off balance and the stroke screeched harmlessly off the iron rim of my shield. Aldhelm shouted at men to help his champion, but Finan, Sihtric, and Osferth were already out of the convent's gate, mounted and armed, and Aldhelm's men hesitated as I took a pace toward the horseman. He slashed again, still ham-pered by his horse's skittishness, and this time I let my shield glance the blow downward and simply reached out and grasped the horseman's wrist. He shouted in alarm, and I pulled hard. He fell from the saddle, crashed onto the damp street and, for a heartbeat, looked dazed. His stallion, whinnying, twisted away as the man stood. His shield, looped onto his left arm, was streaked with mud.

I had stepped back. I drew Serpent-Breath, the blade hissing in the scabbard's tight throat. "What's your name?" I asked. More of my men were coming from the nunnery, though Finan held them back.

The man rushed at me, hoping to throw me off balance with his shield, but I stepped aside and let him go past me. "What's your name?" I asked again.

"Beornoth," he told me.

"Were you at Fearnhamme?" I asked, and he gave a curt nod. "I didn't come here to kill you, Beornoth," I said.

"I'm sworn to my lord," he said.

"An unworthy lord," I told him.

"You should know," he said, "you breaker of oaths," and with that he attacked again, and I raised my shield to take the stroke and he dropped his arm fast, taking the sword beneath my shield and the blade slammed into my calf, but I have always worn strips of iron sewn into my boots because the stroke beneath the shield is such a danger. Some men wear leg armor, but that display will deter an enemy from the stroke beneath the shield, while hidden strips of iron make the legs look vulnerable and invite the stroke, which opens the enemy to destruction. My strips stopped Beornoth's sword dead and he looked surprised as I rammed Serpent-Breath's hilt to hit him in the face with my gloved fist that was closed about the sword's handle. He staggered back. My left leg was aching from his blow, but he was bleeding from a broken nose and I slammed the shield into him, forcing him back again, then I bullied him again with the shield and this time he fell backward and I kicked his sword arm aside, put a foot on his belly, and placed Serpent-Breath's tip at his mouth. He stared up at me with hatred. He was wondering if he had time to sweep the sword up at me, but he knew there was no time left. I had but to move my hand and he would be choking on his own blood.

"Stay still, Beornoth," I said softly, then looked at Aldhelm's men.

"I didn't come here to kill Mercians!" I shouted. "I came here to fight Jarl Haesten!" I stepped away and took my sword from Beornoth's face. "Get up," I told him. He stood uncertainly, not sure whether the fight was over or not. The hatred was gone from his eyes, now he was just staring at me with puzzlement. "Go," I said.

"I am sworn to kill you," he said.

"Don't be a fool, Beornoth," I said wearily, "I just gave you your life. That makes you mine." I turned my back on him. "The Lord Aldhelm," I shouted, "sends a brave man to do what he dares not do! Would you be led by a coward?"

There were men here who remembered me, not just from Fearnhamme, but from the attack on Lundene. These were warriors, and all warriors want to be led by a man who brings them success. Aldhelm was no warrior. They knew that, but they were still confused and uncertain. All of these Mercians were sworn to Aldhelm and some had become wealthy from his gifts. Those men kicked their horses close to their lord and I saw their hands reaching for sword hilts.

"At Fearnhamme," a voice called from behind me, "the Lord Aldhelm wished to run away. Is he the man to protect us?" It was Æthelflæd, mounted on my horse and still wearing her drab convent clothes, though with her bright hair uncovered. "Who was it that led you to the slaughter?" she demanded, "who protected your homes? Who protected your wives and your children? Who would you rather serve?"

Someone from among the Mercian warriors shouted my name, and a cheer followed. Aldhelm had lost and he knew it. He shouted at Beornoth to kill me, but Beornoth stayed still and so Aldhelm, his voice desperate, ordered his supporters to cut me down.

"You don't want to fight each other!" I shouted, "you'll have real enemies enough soon!"

"God damn you," one of Aldhelm's men snarled. He drew his sword and spurred his horse, and his action broke the uncertainty. More swords were drawn and it was suddenly chaos.

Men made their decisions, either for or against Aldhelm, and the vast majority were against him. They turned on his guards just as the man attacking me slashed with his sword. I deflected the blow with my shield as the horsemen swirled around me in a clash of blades. Finan took care of my attacker. Osferth, I noted, had put his horse in front of Æthelflæd so he could protect his half-sister, but she was in no danger. It was Aldhelm's men who were being hacked down, though Aldhelm himself, in pure panic, managed to kick his horse free of the sudden and savage fight. His sword was drawn, but all he wanted was to escape, but there were men all around him and then, seeing me, he realized his advantage, that he was on horseback and I was not, and he drove his spurs back and came to kill me.

He attacked with the despair of a man who did not believe he could win. He did not gauge me, as Beornoth had, but just came as fast as he could and hacked with his sword as strongly as he was able, and I met the massive blow by holding Serpent-Breath upright. I knew that sword, I knew her strength, I had watched as Ealdwulf the Smith had forged the four rods of iron and three of steel into one long blade. I had fought with her, I had killed with her, and I had matched her against the blades of Saxons, Danes, Norsemen, and Frisians. I knew her and I trusted her, and when Aldhelm's sword met her with a clang that must have been heard far across the river, I knew what would happen.

His sword broke. It shattered. The broken end, two thirds of the blade, struck my helmet and fell to the mud, then I was pursuing Aldhelm who, holding a stump of sword, tried to flee, but there was no escape. The fight was over. The men who had supported him were either dead or disarmed, and the warriors who had sided with me formed a circle that ringed the two of us. Aldhelm curbed his stallion and stared at me. He opened his mouth, but could find no words. "Down," I told him, and when he hesitated, I shouted it again, "down!" I looked at Beornoth who had recovered his horse. "Give him your sword," I ordered.

Aldhelm was unsteady on his feet. He had a shield and now he had Beornoth's sword, but there was no fight in him. He was whim-pering. There was no pleasure in killing such a man and so I made it quick. One thrust above his crossed-ax shield, which made him lift it and I dropped Serpent-Breath before the blade struck and cut instead into his left ankle with enough force to topple him. He fell to one knee and Serpent-Breath took him on the side of his neck. He wore a mail hood beneath his helmet, and the links did not split, but the blow drove him into a puddle and I struck again, this time breaking the neck-mail so that his blood misted and splashed across the nearest horsemen. He was shaking and crying, and I sawed the blade toward me until the blade's point was in the ragged wound of blood and mangled mail, then I thrust her down hard into his gullet where I twisted her. He was quivering, bleeding like a pig, and then he was dead.

I threw his banner into the Temes, then cupped my hands and shouted at the men across the river. "Tell Alfred that Uhtred of Bebbanburg has returned!"

Only now I was fighting for Mercia.

Æthelflæd insisted that Aldhelm receive a Christian burial. There was a small church in the village, little more than a cattle byre with a cross nailed to its gable, and around it was a graveyard where we dug six graves for the six dead men. The existing graves were badly marked and one of the spades sliced into a corpse, tearing the woolen shroud and spilling stinking fat and ribs. We lay Aldhelm into that grave and, because so many of the Mercians had been his men and I did not want to strain their loyalty any further, I let him be buried in his fine clothes and mail coat. I kept his helmet, a gold chain, and his horse. Father Pyrlig prayed above the fresh burials, and then we could leave. My cousin was evidently at his estate near Gleawecestre, and so we rode there. I now led over two hundred men, mostly Mercians and, doubtless, in my cousin's eyes, rebels. "You want me to kill Æthelred?" I asked Æthelflæd.

"No!" She sounded shocked.

"Why not?"

"Do you want to be Lord of Mercia?" she retorted.

"No."

"He is the chief Ealdorman of Mercia," Æthelflæd said, "and my husband." She shrugged. "I may not like him, but I am wedded to him."

"You can't be wedded to a dead man," I said.

"Murder is still a sin," Æthelflæd said gently.

"Sin," I said scornfully.

"Some sins are so bad," she said, "that a lifetime's penance isn't enough to redeem them."

"Then let me do the sinning," I suggested.

"I know what's in your heart," she said, "and if I don't stop you then I am as guilty as you."

I growled some retort, then nodded curtly to folk who knelt as we passed through their village that was all thatch, dung, and pigs. The villagers had no idea who we were, but they recognized mail and weapons and shields. They would be holding their breath till we had gone, but soon, I thought, the Danes might come this way and the thatch would be burned and the children taken for slaves.

"When you die," Æthelflæd said, "you'll want a sword in your hand."

"Of course."

"Why?"

"You know why."

"So you'll go to Valhalla. When I die, Uhtred, I want to go to heaven. Would you deny me that?"

"Of course not."

"Then I cannot commit the awful sin of murder. Æthelred must live. Besides," she gave me a smile, "my father would never forgive me if I were to murder Æthelred. Or allow you to murder him. And I don't want to disappoint my father. He's a dear man."

I laughed at that. "Your father," I said, "will be angry anyway."

"Why?"

"Because you asked for my help, of course."

Æthelflæd gave me a curious look. "Who do you think suggested that I ask for your help?"

"What?" I gaped at her and she laughed. "Your father wanted me to come to you?" I asked in disbelief.

"Of course!" she said.

I felt like a fool. I thought I had escaped Alfred, only to discover that he had drawn me south. Pyrlig must have known, but had been very careful not to tell me. "But your father hates me!" I told Æthelflæd.

"Of course he doesn't. He just thinks of you as a very wayward hound, one that needs a whipping now and then." She gave me a deprecatory smile, then shrugged. "He knows Mercia will be attacked, Uhtred, and fears that Wessex won't be able to help."

"Wessex always helps Mercia."

"Not if Danes are landing on Wessex's coast," she said, and I almost laughed aloud. We had gone to such trouble in Dunholm to keep our plans secret, yet Alfred was already preparing for those plans. To which end he had used his daughter to draw me south, and I thought first how clever he was, then wondered just what sins that clever man was prepared to tolerate to keep the Danes from destroying Christianity in England.

We left the village to ride through sunlit country. The grass had greened and was growing fast. Cattle, released from their winter imprisonment, were gorging themselves. A hare stood on its hind legs to watch us, then skittered away before standing and staring at us again. The road climbed gently into the soft hills. This was good country, well watered and fertile, the kind of land the Danes craved. I had been to their homeland and seen how men scratched a bare living from small fields, from sand and from rock. No wonder they wanted England.

The sun was sinking as we passed through another village. A girl carrying two yoked pails of milk was so scared by the sight of armed men that she stumbled as she tried to kneel and the precious milk ran into the road's ruts. She began to cry. I tossed her a silver coin, enough to dry her tears, and asked her if there was a lord living nearby. She pointed us northward to where, behind a great stand of elm trees, we discovered a fine hall surrounded by a decaying palisade.

The thegn who owned the village was named Ealdhith. He was a stout, red-haired man who looked aghast at the number of horses and riders who came seeking shelter for the night. "I can't feed you all," he grumbled, "and who are you?"

"My name is Uhtred," I said, "and that is the Lady Æthelflæd."

"My lady," he said, and went onto one knee.

Ealdhith fed us well enough, though he complained next morning that we had emptied all his ale barrels. I consoled him with a gold link I chopped from Aldhelm's chain. Ealdhith had little news to tell us. He had heard, of course, that Æthelflæd had been a prisoner in the convent at Lecelad. "We sent eggs and flour to her, lord," he told me.

"Why?"

"Because I live a stone's throw from Wessex," he said, "and I like West Saxons to be friendly to my folk."

"Have you seen any Danes this spring?"

"Danes, lord? Those bastards don't come near here!" Ealdhith was sure of that, which explained why he had allowed his palisade to deteriorate. "We just till our land and raise our cattle," he said guardedly.

"And if Lord Æthelred summons you?" I asked, "you go to war?"

"I pray it doesn't happen, but yes, lord. I can take six good warriors to serve."

"You were at Fearnhamme?"

"I couldn't go, lord, I had a broken leg." He lifted his smock to show me a twisted calf. "I was lucky to live."

"Be ready for a summons now," I warned him.

He made the sign of the cross. "There's trouble coming?"

"There's always trouble coming," I said, and hauled myself into the saddle of Aldhelm's fine stallion. The horse, unused to me, trembled and I patted his neck.

We rode westward in the cool morning air. My children rode with me. A beggar was coming the other way and he knelt by the ditch to let us pass, holding out one mangled hand. "I was wounded in the fight at Lundene," he called. There were many such men reduced by war's injury to beggary. I gave my son Uhtred a silver coin and told him to toss it to the man, which he did, but then added some words. "May Christ bless you!"

"What did you say?" I demanded.

"You heard him." Æthelflæd, riding on my left, was amused.

"I offered him a blessing, Father," Uhtred said.

"Don't tell me you've become a Christian!" I snarled.

He reddened, but before he could say anything in reply Osferth spurred from among the horsemen behind. "Lord! Lord!"

"What is it?"

He did not answer, but just pointed back the way we had come.

I turned to see a thickening plume of smoke on the eastern horizon. How often I have seen those great smoke columns! I have caused many myself, the marks of war.

"What is it?" Æthelflæd asked.

"Haesten," I said, my son's idiocy forgotten. "It has to be Haesten." I could think of no other explanation.

The war had started.

THREE

Seventy of us rode toward the pyre of smoke that now appeared as a dark slow-moving smudge on the hazed horizon. Half the seventy were my men and half were Mercians. I had left my children in the village where Osferth and Beornoth were under orders to wait for our return.

Æthelflæd insisted on riding with us. I tried to stop her, but she would take no orders from me. "This is my country," she said firmly, "and my people, and I need to see what is being done to them."

"Probably nothing," I said. Fires were frequent. Houses had thatched roofs and open hearths, and sparks and straw go ill together, but I still had a sense of foreboding that had made me dress in mail before we started this return journey. My first response on seeing the smoke had been to suspect Haesten and, though reflection made that explanation seem ever more unlikely, I could not lose the suspicion.

"There's no other smoke," Finan noted when we had retraced half our steps. Usually, if an army scavenges through a land, it fires every village, yet only the one dark smoke plume drifted skyward. "And Lecelad's a far way from East Anglia," he went on, "if that fire is in Lecelad."

"True enough," I grunted. Lecelad was a long way from Haesten's camp in Beamfleot, indeed so deep in Saxon country that any Danish army marching straight on Lecelad was putting itself in danger. None of it made sense, unless, as both Finan and I wanted to believe, it was simply an errant spark and dry thatch.

The fire was indeed at Lecelad. It took some time to be certain of that for the land was flat and our view was obscured by trees, but we had no doubts once we were close enough to see the heat shimmering amidst the smoke. We were following the river, but now I turned away so that we could approach the village from the north. That, I believed, would be the direction in which any Danes retreated and we might have a chance to intercept them. Reason still said this had to be a simple house fire, but my instincts were also prickling uncomfortably.

We reached the northward road to see it had been churned by hooves. The weather had been dry, so the hoofprints were not distinct, but even at a glance I could tell they had not been left by Aldhelm's men who, just the day before, had used this same track to approach Lecelad. There were too many prints, and those that pointed northward had mostly obliterated the ones going south. That meant whoever had ridden to Lecelad had already ridden away.

"Been and gone," Father Pyrlig said. He was in his priestly robes, but had a big sword strapped at his waist.

"At least a hundred of them," Finan said, looking at the hoofprints that spread either side of the track.

I gazed northward, but could see nothing. If the raiding horsemen had still been close I would have seen dust hanging in the air, but the country was calm and green. "Let's see what the bastards did," I said, and turned southward.

Whoever had come and gone, and I was certain it was Haesten's men, they had been swift. I guessed they had arrived at Lecelad at dusk, had done whatever damage they wanted and then left in the dawn. They knew they were dangerously deep in Saxon Mercia and so they had not lingered. They had struck fast, and even now they were hurrying back to safer ground while we rode into the ever thickening smell of wood smoke. Of wood smoke and of burning flesh.

The convent was gone, or rather it had been reduced to a blazing framework of oak beams that, as we approached, finally collapsed with a great crash that made my stallion rear in fright. Embers whirled upward in a great gout of wind-billowed smoke. "Oh, dear God," Æthelflaed said, making the sign of the cross. She was gazing in horror at one section of the convent's palisade that had been spared the fire, and there, on the timbers, pinioned with widespread arms, was a small naked body. "No!" Æthelflæd said and spurred her horse through the hot ash that had spread from the fire.

"Come back!" I shouted, but Æthelflæd had thrown herself from her saddle to kneel at the foot of the corpse, a woman. It was Werburgh, the abbess, and she had been crucified on the palisade. Her hands and feet were pierced by great dark nails. Her small weight had torn the flesh, sinews, and bones about the great nails so that the wounds were stretched and rivulets of drying blood laced her pitifully thin arms. Æthelflæd was kissing the abbess's nailed feet and resisted when I tried to pull her away. "She was a good woman, Uhtred," Æthelflæd protested, and just then Werburgh's torn right hand ripped itself free of the nail and the corpse lurched and its arm swung down to strike Æthelflæd's head. Æthelflæd gave a small scream, then seized the ragged bloody hand and kissed it. "She blessed me, Uhtred. She was dead, but she blessed me! Did you see?"

"Come away," I said gently.

"She touched me!"

"Come away," I said again, and this time she let me draw her from the corpse and away from the heat of the fire just beyond.

"She must be buried properly," Æthelflæd insisted and tried to pull from me to return to the corpse.

"She will be," I said, holding her.

"Don't let her burn!" Æthelflæd said through tears, "she mustn't taste the fires of hell, Uhtred! Let me spare her the fire!"

Werburgh was very close to the furnace heat that was scorching the farther side of the palisade that I knew would ignite at any moment. I pushed Æthelflæd away, stepped back to Werburgh, and dragged her small body free of the remaining two nails. I draped her over my shoulder just as a gust of wind dipped a thick cloud of dark smoke to envelop me. I felt sudden heat on my back and knew the palisade had burst into flames, but Werburgh's body was safe. I laid her facedown on the river bank and Æthelflæd covered the corpse with a cloak. The West Saxon troops, reinforced now to around forty men, gaped at us from the southern bank.

"Jesus, Patrick, and Joseph," Finan said as he approached me. He glanced at Æthelflæd who was kneeling by the abbess's body and I sensed Finan did not want Æthelflæd to hear whatever he had to say, so I led him down the river toward the mill that was also burning. "The bastards dug up Aldhelm's grave," Finan said.

"I put him there," I said, "so I should worry what they did?"

"They mutilated him," Finan said angrily. "Took all his clothes, his mail, and cut up his corpse. There were pigs eating him when we found him." He made the sign of the cross.

I stared at the village. The church, convent, and mill had all been fired, but only two of the cottages had been burned, though doubtless all had been ransacked. The raiders had been in a hurry and had fired what was most valuable, but had not had the time to destroy the whole of Lecelad. "Haesten's a nasty creature," I said, "but mutilating a corpse and crucifying a woman? That isn't like him."

"It was Skade, lord," Finan said. He beckoned to a man dressed in a short mail coat and wearing a helmet that had rust on its riveted joints. "You! Come here!" he called.

The man knelt to me and clawed off his helmet. "My name's Cealworth, lord," he said, "and I serve Ealdorman Æthelnoth."

"You're one of the sentries across the river?" I asked.

"Yes, lord."

"We brought him across the river in a boat," Finan explained. "Now tell the Lord Uhtred what you saw."

"It was a woman, lord," Cealworth said nervously, "a tall woman with long black hair. The same woman, lord," he stopped, then decided he had nothing more to say.

"Go on," I said.

"The same woman I saw at Fearnhamme, lord. After the battle."

"Stand up," I told him. "Are any villagers alive?" I asked Finan.

"Some," he said bleakly.

"A few swam the river, lord," Cealworth said.

"And the ones that live," Finan said, "all tell the same tale."

"Skade?" I asked.

The Irishman nodded. "It seems she led them, lord."

"Haesten wasn't here?"

"If he was, lord, then no one noticed him."

"The woman gave all the orders, lord," Cealworth said.

I stared northward and wondered what happened in the rest of Mercia. I was looking for the telltale plumes of smoke, but saw none. Æthelflæd came to stand beside me and, without thinking, I put an arm about her shoulder. She did not move.

"Why did they come here?" Finan asked.

"For me," Æthelflæd said bitterly.

"That would make sense, my lady," Finan said.

In a way it made sense. I did not doubt that Haesten would have sent spies into Mercia. Those spies would have been merchants or vagabonds, anyone with a reason to travel, and they would have told him Æthelflæd was a prisoner in Lecelad, and Æthelflæd would certainly make a powerful and useful hostage, but why send Skade to capture her? I thought, though I did not speak the thought aloud, that it was much more likely that Skade had come for my children. Haesten's spies would have learned that the three were with Æthelflæd, and Skade hated me now. And when Skade hated there was no cruelty sufficient to slake her appetite. I knew my suspicion was right and I shuddered. If Skade had come just two days earlier she would have taken my children and had me in her power. I touched Thor's hammer. "We bury the dead," I said, "then we ride." Just then a bee landed on my right hand that was still resting on Æthelflæd's shoulder. I did not try to brush it off, for I did not want to take my arm away. I felt it first, then saw it crawling dozily toward my thumb. It would fly away, I thought, but then, for no reason, it stung me. I swore at the sudden pain and slapped the insect dead, startling Æthelflæd.

"Rub an onion on the sting," she told me, but I could not be bothered to hunt for an onion, so I left it alone. I knew the sting was an omen, a message from the gods, but I did not want to think about it, for it could surely be no good sign.

We buried the dead. Most of the nuns had been shrunken to

small burned corpses scarce bigger than children, and now they shared a grave with their crucified abbess. Father Pyrlig spoke words over their bodies, and then we rode westward again. By the time we discovered Osferth and Beornoth, their men, and my family, my hand was so swollen that I could scarcely fold the puffy fingers around the stallion's reins. I could certainly not hold a sword with any skill. "It'll be gone in a week," Finan said.

"If we have a week," I said gloomily. He looked at me quizzically, and I shrugged. "The Danes are on the move," I said, "and we don't know what's happening."

We were still traveling with my men's wives and families. They slowed us down, and so I left a score of men to guard them as they followed us, and hurried on toward Gleawecestre. We spent the night in the hills to the west of that city and, in the dawn, saw smears in the sky far to the east and north. There were too many to count and in places they joined together to make darker patches that might have been clouds, though I doubted it. Æthelflæd saw them too and frowned. "My poor country," she said.

"Haesten," I said.

"My husband should have marched against them already," she said.

"You think he has?"

She shook her head. "He'll wait for Aldhelm to tell him what to do."

I laughed at that. We had reached the hills above the valley of the Sæfern and I checked my horse to gaze down at my cousin's holdings that lay just south of Gleawecestre. Æthelred's father had been content with a hall half the size that his son had built, and beside that new and magnificent hall were stables, a church, barns, and a massive granary raised on stone mushrooms to keep the rats at bay. All the buildings, new and old, were surrounded by a palisade. We cantered down the hill. Guards stood on a timber platform above the gate, but they must have recognized Æthelflæd because they made no attempt to challenge us, but just ordered that the great gates be pushed open.

Æthelred's steward met us in the wide courtyard. If he was astonished to see Æthelflæd he showed no sign of it, but just bowed deeply and welcomed her graciously. Slaves brought us bowls of water so we could wash our hands, while stable boys took our horses. "My lord is in the hall, lady," the steward told Æthelflæd, and for the first time sounded nervous.

"Is he well?" Æthelflæd asked.

"God be praised, yes," he answered, and his eyes flicked to me and back to her. "You've come for the council, perhaps?"

"What council?" Æthelflæd asked, taking a woolen cloth from a slave to dry her hands.

"There is trouble from the heathens, lady," the steward said cautiously, then glanced at me again.

"This is the Lord Uhtred of Bebbanburg," Æthelflæd said with apparent carelessness, "and yes, we've come for the council."

"I shall tell your husband you are here," the steward said. He had looked startled when he heard my name and taken a hasty backward step.

"No need for an announcement," Æthelflæd said sharply.

"Your swords?" the steward asked. "If you please, my lords, your swords?"

"Is anyone else armed in the hall?" I asked.

"The ealdorman's own guards, lord, no one else."

I hesitated, then gave the steward my two swords. It was usual to wear no weapon in a king's hall, and Æthelred evidently saw himself as near enough to a king to demand the same courtesy. It was more than a courtesy, it was a precaution against the slaughter that could follow a drunken feast. I half wondered if I should keep Serpent-Breath, but reckoned the long blade would be a provocation.

I took Osferth, Finan, Father Pyrlig, and Beornoth. My hand was throbbing and red, the flesh so swollen that I thought the simple touch of a knife's edge would split it open like bursting fruit. I kept it hidden beneath my cloak as we went from the sunlight into the shadowed darkness of Æthelred's great hall.

If the steward's first response to seeing Æthelflæd had been restrained, her husband's was the very opposite. He looked irritated when we first walked into the hall, plainly offended at the interruption, then hopeful, because he must have thought Aldhelm had arrived, and then he recognized us and, for a gratifying instant, he appeared terrified. He was sitting in a chair, more of a throne than a chair, that was set on the dais where, normally, the high table would be set for feasting. He wore a thin bronze circlet on his red hair, a circlet that fell just short of a crown. He had a thick gold chain over his embroidered jerkin and a fur-trimmed cloak that had been dyed a deep scarlet. Two men with swords and shields stood at the back of the dais, while Æthelred was flanked by a pair of priests who sat facing four benches set on the rush-strewn floor. Eighteen men occupied the benches and they all turned to stare at us. The priest on Æthelred's right was my old enemy, Bishop Asser, and he was looking at me with wide-open eyes and unconcealed surprise. If Alfred had manipulated me into returning, then he had plainly not told Asser.

It was Asser who broke the silence, and that by itself was interesting. This hall belonged to Æthelred who was the Ealdorman of Mercia, yet the Welsh bishop thought nothing of assuming authority. It was a sign of Alfred's dominance over Saxon Mercia, a dominance that Æthelred secretly detested. He could not wait for Alfred to die so he could turn the circlet into a proper crown, yet he also needed the assistance that Wessex gave. Bishop Asser, shrewd and waspish, was undoubtedly here to pass on Alfred's commands, but now he stood and pointed a bony finger at me. "You!" he said. A pair of hounds had rushed to greet Æthelflæd. She soothed them. There was a babble of voices that Bishop Asser overrode. "You were declared outlaw," he yapped.

I told him to be silent, but of course he went on protesting, becoming ever more indignant until Father Pyrlig spoke to him in Welsh. I had no idea what Pyrlig said, but it silenced Asser who just spluttered and kept pointing at me. I assume Father Pyrlig revealed that Alfred had conspired at my return, but that was small consolation to the bishop, who regarded me as a creature sent by his religion's demon, the creature they call Satan. Whatever, he stayed silent as Æthelflaed went to the dais and snapped her fingers to a servant who hurried to fetch her a chair. She leaned down to

Æthelred and gave him a very public kiss on the cheek, but she also whispered something in his ear and I saw him redden. Then she sat next to him and reached for his hand. "Do sit down, bishop," she told Asser, then looked gravely at the assembled lords. "I bring bad news," she said. "The Danes have destroyed the convent at Lecelad. Every dear sister there is dead, as is my dear Lord Aldhelm. I pray for their souls."

"Amen," Father Pyrlig roared.

"How did the Lord Aldhelm die?" Bishop Asser asked.

"There will be a time for sad tales when our more urgent business is decided," Æthelflæd said without looking at Asser, "for the moment I wish to know how we are to defeat the Jarl Haesten."

The next few moments were confusing. The truth was that none of the assembled lords knew the extent of Haesten's invasion. At least a dozen messengers had come overnight to Gleawecestre and they had all brought dire tidings of savage and sudden attacks by Danish horsemen, and as I listened to the various reports I realized that Haesten had set out to confuse the Mercians. He must have led two or three thousand men and he had divided them into smaller groups and sent them to harry, plunder, and destroy all across northern Mercia. It was impossible to say where the Danes were because they appeared to be everywhere.

"What do they want?" Æthelred asked plaintively.

"He wants to sit where you're sitting," I answered.

"You have no authority here," Bishop Asser snarled.

"Bishop," Æthelflæd spoke crisply, "if you have something useful to say, then please feel free to say it. But if you simply wish to make a nuisance of yourself then go to the church and take your complaints to God." That caused an astonished silence. The real authority in the hall belonged to Bishop Asser because he was Alfred's envoy, yet Æthelflaed had publicly slapped him down. She met his indignant gaze calmly, and kept her eyes on his until he gave way. Then she turned to the lords. "The questions we need answered are simple," she said. "How many Danes are there? What is their aim? How many men can we assemble to oppose them? And where do we take those men?"

Æthelred still seemed stunned by his wife's return. Every lord in the hall must have known of their estrangement, yet here Æthelflæd was, calmly holding her husband's hand and no one dared challenge her presence. Æthelred himself was so shaken that he allowed her to dominate the council, and she did it well. There was a soft sweetness in Æthelflæd's look, but that sweetness disguised a mind as thoughtful as her father's and a will as strong as her mother's. "Don't all speak at once," she commanded, raising her voice over the confusion. "Lord Ælfwold," she smiled at a grim-looking man sitting on the bench closest to the dais, "your lands have suffered most, it seems, so what is your estimation of the enemy's numbers?"

"Between two and three thousand," he answered. He shrugged. "It could be many more, it's hard to tell."

"Because they ride in small groups?"

"At least a dozen bands," Ælfwold said, "maybe as many as twenty."

"And how many men can we lead against them?" she asked the question of her husband, her voice respectful.

"Fifteen hundred," he said surlily.

"We must have more warriors than that!" Æthelflæd said.

"Your father," Æthelred said, and he could not resist saying those two words with derision, "insists we leave five hundred to protect Lundene."

"I thought the Lundene garrison was West Saxon," I put in, and I should have known because I had commanded that garrison for five years.

"Alfred has left three hundred men in Lundene," Bishop Asser said, forcing cordiality into his voice, "and the rest have gone to Wintanceaster."

"Why?"

"Because Haesten sent us a warning," the bishop said bitterly. He paused, and his weasel face twitched uncontrollably, "that you and the northern jarls planned an attack on Wessex." The hatred in his voice was unmistakable. "Is that true?"

I hesitated. I had not betrayed Ragnar's plans because he was my friend, which meant I had left the discovery of the Northumbrian attack to fate, but Haesten, it seemed, had already sent a warning. He had done it, clearly, to keep West Saxon troops out of Mercia, and it seemed the warning had been successful.

"Well?" Æthelred, aware of my discomfort, pressed the attack.

"The Northumbrian jarls have discussed an attack on Wessex," I said weakly.

"Will it happen?" Asser wanted to know.

"Probably," I said.

"Probably," Bishop Asser sneered the word, "and what is your role, Lord Uhtred?" The derision with which he spoke my name had an edge as sharp as Serpent-Breath. "To mislead us? To betray us? To slaughter more Christians?" He stood again, sensing his advantage. "In Christ's name," he shouted, "I demand this man's arrest!"

No one moved to take hold of me. Æthelred gestured at his two household warriors, but the gesture lacked conviction and neither man moved.

"The Lord Uhtred is here to protect me," Æthelflæd broke the silence.

"You have a nation's warriors to protect you," Asser said, sweeping his arm to encompass the men sitting on the benches.

"What need I of a nation's warriors," Æthelflæd asked, "when I have Lord Uhtred?"

"The Lord Uhtred," Asser said in his sharp voice, "cannot be trusted."

"You'd listen to that Welsh piece of gristle," I addressed the men on the benches. "A Welshman saying a Saxon can't be trusted? How many men here have lost friends, sons, or brothers to Welsh treachery? If the Danes are Mercia's worst enemy, then the Welsh are the next worst. We're going to take lessons in loyalty from a Welshman?"

I heard Father Pyrlig mutter behind me, but again he spoke in Welsh. I suspect he was insulting me, but he knew well enough why I had spoken as I did. I was appealing to the deep-seated mistrust that all Mercians felt for the Welsh. Since the beginning of Mercia, deep in the lost times of our ancestors, the Welsh had raided Saxon lands to steal cattle, women, and treasure. They called our land their "lost land," and ever in Welsh hearts is a wish to drive the Saxons back across the sea, and so few men in Æthelred's hall had any love for their ancestral enemies.

"The Welsh," Asser shouted, "are Christians! And now is the time for all Christians to unite against the pagan filth that threatens our faith. Look!" His finger was pointing again. "The Lord Uhtred wears the symbol of Thor. He is an idolater, a heathen, an enemy of our dear Lord Jesus Christ!"

"He is my friend," Æthelflæd said, "and I trust him with my life."

"He is an idolater," Asser repeated, evidently thinking that was the worst he could say of me. "He betrayed his sworn oath! He killed a saint! He is an enemy of all that we hold most dear, he is the . . ." His voice died away.

He had gone silent because I had climbed the dais and pushed him hard in the chest so that he was forced to sit down. Now I leaned on the chair's arms and looked into his eyes. "You want martyrdom?" I asked. He took a deep breath to reply, then thought better of saying anything. I smiled into his furious face and patted his sallow cheek before turning back to the benches. "I am here to fight for the Lady Æthelflæd, and she is here to fight for Mercia. If any of you believe Mercia will suffer because of my help then I am sure she will relieve me of my oath and I will depart."

No one seemed to want my departure. The men in the hall were embarrassed, but Ælfwold, who had already suffered from Haesten's invasion, returned the discussion to its proper place. "We don't have the men to face Haesten," he said unhappily, "not without West Saxon help."

"And that help is not coming," I said, "isn't that true, bishop?" Asser nodded. He was too angry to speak. "There will be an attack on Wessex," I said, "and Alfred will need his army to meet that attack, so we must cope with Haesten on our own."

"How?" Ælfwold asked. "Haesten's men are everywhere and nowhere! We send an army to find them and they'll just ride around us."

"You retreat into your burhs," I said. "Haesten isn't equipped

257

to besiege fortified towns. The fyrd protects the burhs, and you take your cattle and silver behind those walls. Let Haesten burn as many villages as he likes, he can't capture a properly defended burh."

"So we just let him ravage Mercia while we cower behind walls?" Ælfwold asked.

"Of course not," I said.

"Then what?" Æthelred asked.

I hesitated again. Haesten, by all reports, had chosen a new strategy. When Harald had invaded Wessex the year before he had brought a great army and with it he had brought an army's baggage: the women and children and animals and slaves. But Haesten, if the urgent messages spoke true, had brought nothing but horsemen. He had brought his own men, the survivors of Harald's army, and the Danish warriors of East Anglia to plunder Mercia and they were moving fast, covering miles of ground, burning and stealing as they went. If we marched against them they could slide out of our path or, if we found ourselves in treacherous ground, assemble to attack us. Yet if we did nothing then inevitably Mercia would be weakened so much that men would rather seek Danish protection. So we had to strike a blow that would weaken the Danes before they weakened us. We had to be daring.

"Well?" Asser demanded, thinking that my hesitation denoted uncertainty.

And still I hesitated because I did not think it could be done.

Yet I could not think what else we could do.

Everyone in that hall was watching me, some with unconcealed dislike, others with desperate hope. "Lord Uhtred?" Æthelflæd prompted me gently.

So I told them.

Nothing was simple. Æthelred argued that Haesten's ambition was to capture Gleawecestre. "He'll use it as a base to attack Wessex," he argued, and reminded Bishop Asser how, many years before, Guthrum had used Gleawecestre as the place to assemble the Danish army that had come closest to conquering Wessex. Asser agreed with the argument, probably because he wanted the thegns to reject my plan. In the end it was Æthelflæd who cut the argument short. "I go with Uhtred," she said, "and those who wish can come with us."

Æthelred would not accompany me. He had always disliked me, but now that dislike was pure hatred because I had rescued Æthelflaed from his spite. He wanted to defeat the Danes, but even more he wanted Alfred dead, Æthelflæd put aside, and his chair turned into a real throne. "I shall assemble the army in Gleawecestre," he declared, "and thwart any attack on Wessex. That is my decision." He looked at the men on the benches. "I expect you all to join me. I demand that you join me. We muster in four days!"

Æthelflæd gave me a quizzical glance. "Lundene," I mouthed to her.

"I go to Lundene," she said, "and those of you who wish to see a Mercia free of the heathens will join me there. In four days."

If I had been Æthelred I would have scotched Æthelflæd's defiance there and then. He had armed men in the hall while none of us wore a weapon, and a single command could have left me dead on the floor's rushes. But he lacked the courage. He knew I had men outside the hall and perhaps he feared their vengeance. He quivered when I approached his chair, then looked up at me with nervous and sullen eyes. "Æthelflæd remains your wife," I told him quietly, "but if she dies mysteriously, or if she sickens, or if I hear rumors of a spell cast against her, then I shall find you, cousin, and I shall suck the eyeballs out of your skull and spit them down your throat so you choke to death." I smiled. "Send your men to Lundene and keep your country."

He did not send men to Lundene, nor did most of the Mercian lords. They were frightened of my idea and they looked to Æthelred for patronage. He was the gold-giver in Mercia, while Æthelflæd was almost as poor as I was. So most of Mercia's warriors went to Gleawecestre and Æthelred kept them there, waiting for an attack from Haesten that never came.

Haesten was plundering all across Mercia. In the next few days, as I waited at Lundene and listened to the reports brought by fugitives, I saw how the Danes were moving with lightning speed. They were capturing anything of value, whether it was an iron spit, a harness, or a child, and all that plunder was sent back to Beamfleot where Haesten had his stronghold above the Temes shore. He was amassing a treasure there, a treasure that could be sold in Frankia. His success brought more Danes to his side, men from across the sea who saw Mercia's impending fall and wanted to share in the land that would be divided when the conquest was done. Haesten captured some towns, those that had not yet been turned into burhs, and the silver from their churches, convents, and monasteries flowed back to Beamfleot. Alfred did send men to Gleawecestre, but only a few, because rumors were now rife of a great Northumbrian fleet sailing southward. It was all chaos.

And I was helpless because, after four days, I led only eighty-three men. They were my own shrunken crew and those few Mercians who had come in response to Æthelflæd's summons. Beornoth was one, though most of the men who had sided with me at Lecelad had stayed with Æthelred. "More would have come, lord," Beornoth told me, "but they're frightened of the ealdorman's displeasure."

"What would he do to them?"

"Take their homes, lord. How do they live, except on his generosity?"

"Yet you came," I said.

"You gave me my life, lord," he said.

My old house was now occupied by the garrison's new commander, a dour West Saxon called Weohstan who had fought at Fearnhamme. When I had reached Lundene, arriving unexpectedly on a rainswept night, Bishop Erkenwald had ordered Weohstan to arrest me, but Weohstan had doggedly ignored the order. Instead he came to see me in the Mercian royal palace that occupied the old Roman governor's mansion. "Are you here to fight the Danes, lord?" he asked me.

"He is," Æthelflæd answered for me.

"Then I'm not sure I have enough men to arrest you," Weohstan said.

"How many do you have?"

"Three hundred," he said with a smile.

"Not nearly enough," I assured him.

I told him what I planned and he looked skeptical. "I'll help you if I can," he promised, but there was doubt in his voice. He had lost almost all his teeth so his speech was a hissing slur. He was over thirty years old, bald as an egg, ruddy faced, short in stature, but broad in the shoulders. He had skill with weapons and a hard manner that made him an effective leader, but Weohstan was also cautious. I would have trusted him to defend a wall forever, but he was not a man to lead a bold attack. "You can help me now," I told him that first day, and asked to borrow a ship.

He frowned as he considered the request, then decided he was not risking too much in granting it. "Bring it back, lord," he said.

Bishop Erkenwald tried to stop me taking the ship downriver. He met me at the wharf beside my old house. Weohstan had tactfully found business elsewhere and though Erkenwald had brought his personal guard, those three men were no match for my crew. The bishop confronted me. "I govern Lundene," he said, which was true, "and you must leave."

"I am leaving." I gestured at the waiting ship.

"Not in one of our ships!"

"Then stop me," I said.

"Bishop," Æthelflæd was with me and intervened.

"It is not a woman's place to speak of men's business!" Erkenwald turned on her.

Æthelflæd bridled. "I am . . ."

"Your place, lady, is with your husband!"

I took Erkenwald by the shoulders and steered him onto the terrace where Gisela and I had spent so many quiet evenings. Erkenwald, much smaller than me, tried to resist my arm, but he stayed still when I released him. The water foamed through the gaps in the old Roman bridge, forcing me to raise my voice. "What do you know of Æthelred and Æthelflæd?" I asked.

"It is not for man to interfere in the sacrament of marriage," he said dismissively.

"You're not a fool, bishop," I said.

He glared up at me with his dark eyes. "The blessed apostle Paul," he said, "instructs wives to submit to their husbands. You would have me preach the opposite?"

"I would have you be sensible," I said. "The Danes want to eradicate your religion. They see Wessex weakened by Alfred's sickness. They would destroy Saxon power in Mercia, then move against Wessex. If they have their way, bishop, then within a few weeks some spear-Dane will be skewering your belly and you'll be a martyr. Æthelflæd wants to stop that and I'm here to help her."

To his credit Erkenwald did not accuse me of treachery. Instead he bristled. "Her husband also wishes to stop the Danes," he said firmly.

"Her husband also wants to separate Mercia from Wessex," I said. He did not say anything to that because he knew it was true. "So who do you trust to protect you from martyrdom?" I asked. "Æthelred or me?"

"God will protect me," he said stubbornly.

"I shall only be here a few days," I said, "and you can help me or hinder me. If you fight me, bishop, you make it more likely that the Danes will win."

He looked across at Æthelflæd and a tremor showed on his thin face. He was smelling sin in our apparent alliance, but he was also thinking of the vision I had given him, a vision of a mail-coated Dane thrusting a blade into his belly. "Bring the ship back," he said grudgingly, echoing Weohstan, then abruptly turned and walked away.

The ship was the *Haligast* that had once been the vessel that carried Alfred up and down the Temes, but it seemed his sickness had caused him to abandon such voyages and so the small *Haligast* had been brought through the treacherous gap between the bridge piers and was now used as a scouting vessel. Her master was Ralla, an old friend. "She's light-built," he said of the *Haligast*, "and she's quick."

"Faster than *Seolferwulf*?" I asked. He had known my ship well.

"Nowhere close, lord," he said, "but she runs well on the wind, and if the Danes get too close we can use shallower water."

"When I was here," I said in a mild voice, "the Danes would run from us."

"Things change," Ralla said gloomily.

"Are the pagans attacking ships?" Æthelflæd asked.

"We haven't seen a trading ship in two weeks," Ralla said, "so they must be."

Æthelflæd had insisted on coming with me. I did not want her company because I have never thought women should be exposed to unnecessary danger, but I had learned not to argue with Alfred's daughter. She wanted to be a part of the campaign against the Danes and I could not dissuade her, and so she stood with Ralla, Finan, and me on the steering platform as Ralla's experienced crew took the *Haligast* downriver.

How many times had I made this voyage? I watched the glistening mudbanks slide past and it was all so familiar as we turned the river's extravagant bends. We went with the tide, so our thirty oarsmen needed only make small tugs on their looms to keep the ship headed downriver. Swans beat from our path, while overhead the sky was busy with birds flying south. The marshy banks slowly receded as the river widened and imperceptibly turned into a sea reach, and then we headed slightly northward to let the *Haligast* drift along the East Anglian shore.

Again it was all so familiar. I gazed at the drab low land that was called East Sexe. It was edged with wetlands that slowly rose to plowed fields, then, abruptly, there was the great wooded hill that I knew so well. The crown of the hill had been cleared of trees so that it was a dome of grass where the huge fort dominated the Temes. Beamfleot. Æthelflæd had been imprisoned in that fort and she gazed at it wordlessly, though she reached for my hand and held onto it as she remembered those days when she was supposedly a hostage, but had fallen in love, only to lose the man to his brother's sword.

Beneath the fort the ground fell steeply to a village, also called Beamfleot, that lay beside the muddy creek of Hothlege. The Hothlege separated Beamfleot from Caninga, a reed-thick island that could be flooded when the tide was high and when the wind blew hard from the east. I could see that the Hothlege was thick with boats, most of them hauled onto the beach beneath the great hill where they were protected by new forts that had been made at the creek's eastern end. The two forts were a pair of beached and dismasted ships, one on either bank, their seaward planking built up to make high walls. I guessed a chain still ran across the Hothlege to stop enemy vessels entering the narrow channel.

"Closer," I growled to Ralla.

"You want to run aground?"

"I want to get closer."

I would have steered the *Haligast* myself except my bee-stung hand was still swollen and the skin taut. I let go of Æthelflæd's hand to scratch the itch. "It won't get better if you keep scratching it," she said, taking my hand back.

Finan had shinned up the *Haligast*'s mast where, with his keen eyesight, he was counting Danish ships. "How many?" I called impatiently.

"Hundreds," he shouted back and then, a moment later, gave a proper estimate. "About two hundred!" It was impossible to make an accurate count for the masts were thick as saplings, and some boats were dismasted and hidden by other hulls.

"Mary save us," Æthelflæd said softly and made the sign of the cross.

"Nine thousand men?" Ralla suggested dourly.

"Not as many as that," I said. Many of the boats belonged to the survivors of Harald's army and those crews had been half slaughtered at Fearnhamme, yet even so I reckoned Haesten had twice as many men as we had estimated at Gleawecestre. Maybe as many as five thousand, and most of them were even now rampaging through Mercia, but enough remained at Beamfleot to form a garrison that watched us from their high wall. The sun's reflection winked from spear-blades, but as I shaded my eyes and gazed at that formidable rampart on its steep hill it seemed to me that the fort was in disrepair. "Finan!" I shouted after a while, "are there gaps in that wall?"

He waited before answering. "They've built a new fort, lord! Down on the shore!"

I could not see the new fort from the *Haligast*'s deck, but I trusted Finan, whose eyes were better than mine. He scrambled down the mast after a few moments and explained that Haesten appeared to have abandoned the fort on the hill. "He has watchmen up there, lord, but his main force is down on the creek. There's a big bastard of a wall there."

"Why abandon the high ground?" Æthelflæd asked.

"It was too far from the ships," I said. Haesten knew that better than anyone, for he had fought here before and his men had managed to burn Sigefrid's ships before the Norseman could bring men down the hill to stop him. Now Haesten had blocked the creek beneath the hill, guarding its seaward end with the beached ships and the landward entrance with a new and formidable fortress. Between those strongholds were his ships. It meant we could probably take the old fort without much trouble, but holding the high ground would not help us because the new stronghold was out of arrow range.

"I couldn't see very well," Finan said, "but it looked to me as if the new fort is on an island."

"He's making it difficult," I said mildly.

"Can it be done?" Æthelflæd asked, sounding dubious.

"It has to be done," I said.

"We have no men!"

"Yet," I said stubbornly.

Because my plan was to capture that stronghold. It was crammed with Haesten's prisoners, all the women and children taken as slaves, and it was in Beamfleot's new fort that his plunder was being stored. I suspected Haesten's family was also there, indeed the families of every Dane ravaging Mercia were probably in that place. Their ships were there too, protected by the fort. If we could take the fort we could impoverish Haesten, capture dozens of hostages, and destroy a Danish fleet. If we could capture Beamfleot we would win a victory that would dismay the Danes and cheer every Saxon heart. The victory might not win the war, but it would weaken Haesten immeasurably and many of his followers, losing faith, would abandon him, for what kind of a leader was a man who could not protect his men's families? Æthelred believed Mercia's salvation was best secured by waiting for Haesten to attack Gleawecestre, but I believed we had to attack Haesten where he least expected an assault. We had to strike at his base, destroy his fleet, and take back his plunder.

"How many men do you have?" Ralla asked.

"Eighty-three at the last count."

He laughed. "And how many do you need to capture Beamfleot?"

"Two thousand."

"And you don't believe in miracles?" Ralla asked.

Æthelflæd squeezed my hand. "The men will come," she said, though she sounded far from convinced.

"Maybe," I said. I was staring at the ships in their sheltered creek and thought, in its way, that Beamfleot was as impregnable as Bebbanburg. "And if they don't come?" I said softly.

"What will you do?" Æthelflæd asked.

"Take you north," I said, "take my children north, and fight till I have the silver to raise an army that can capture Bebbanburg."

She turned her face up to mine. "No," she said. "I am Mercian now, Uhtred."

"Mercian and Christian," I said sourly.

"Yes," she said, "Mercian and Christian. And what are you, Lord Uhtred?"

I looked to where reflected sunlight winked from the spearpoints of the watchmen on Beamfleot's high hill. "A fool," I said bitterly, "a fool."

"My fool," she said, and stood on tiptoe to kiss my cheek.

"Row!" Ralla bellowed, "row!" He shoved the steering oar hard over so that the *Haligast* turned southward and then west. Two large enemy ships were nosing out of the creek, sliding past the new ship-fortresses, their oar-banks catching the sun as they dipped and rose.

We fled upriver.

And, like the fool I was, I dreamed of capturing Beamfleot.

FOUR

Next day Ealdorman Ælfwold came to Lundene. His lands lay in the northern parts of Saxon Mercia, which made them the most vulnerable to Danish attacks, and he had only kept his estates by the expense of hiring warriors, by bribing the Danes, and by fighting. He was old, a widower, and tired of the struggle. "As soon as the harvest is gathered," he said, "the Danes come. Rats and Danes, they arrive together."

He brought nearly three hundred men, most of whom were well armed and properly trained. "They might as well die with you as rot at Gleawecestre," he remarked. He was homeless because his hall had been burned by one of Haesten's bands. "I abandoned it," he admitted. "I'm used to fighting off a couple of hundred of the bastards, but not thousands." He had sent his household servants, his daughters, and grandchildren to Wessex in the hope they would be safe there. "Are the northern jarls truly planning an attack on Alfred?" he asked me.

"Yes."

"God help us," he said.

Folk were moving into the old city. Lundene is really two cities, the Roman one built on the high ground and, to the west, beyond the River Fleot, the new Saxon city. The first was a place of high stone walls and the faded glory of marble pillars, while the other was a malodorous swamp of thatch and wattle, but folk preferred the swamp because they swore the crumbling Roman buildings were haunted by ghosts. Now, fearing Haesten's men more than any specter, they were crossing the Fleot and finding themselves shelter in the older houses. The city stank. The Roman sewers had caved in, the cesspits were not large enough, and the streets became fouled. Cattle were penned in the old Roman arena and pigs roamed the streets. Weohstan's garrison manned the walls, which were high and stout. Most of the battlements were Roman-built, but where time had decayed the stonework there were thick oak palisades.

Finan was leading horsemen north and east every day and brought back news of Danes returning eastward. "They're taking plunder to Beamfleot," he said, "plunder and slaves."

"Are they staying in Beamfleot?"

He shook his head. "They go back to Mercia." He was angry because we did not have enough men for him to attack the Danish horsemen. He could only watch.

Ralla, scouting downriver in the *Haligast*, saw more Danes arriving from across the sea. Rumors had spread that both Wessex and Mercia were in disarray and the crews were hurrying to share the plunder. Haesten, meanwhile, tore destruction across Mercia's farmlands while Æthelred waited at Gleawecestre for an attack that never came. Then, the day after Ælfwold brought his housecarls to Lundene, came the news I had been expecting. The Northumbrian fleet had landed in Defnascir and had made a camp above the Uisc, which meant Alfred's West Saxon army marched to protect Exanceaster.

The Saxons seemed doomed. A week after my foray downriver I sat in the palace hall and watched the fire-cast shadows flicker on the high ceiling. I could hear monks chanting from Erkenwald's cavernous church, which lay next to the Mercian palace. If I had climbed to the roof I would have seen the glow of fires far to the north and west. Mercia was burning.

That was the night Ælfwold abandoned hope. "We can't just wait here, lord," he told me at the evening meal, "the city has enough men to defend it, and my three hundred are needed elsewhere."

I ate that evening with my usual companions; Æthelflæd, Finan, Ælfwold, Father Pyrlig, and Beornoth. "If I had another three hundred," I said, and despised myself for saying it. Even if fate brought

269

me another three hundred warriors I would still not have nearly enough men to capture Beamfleot. Æthelred had won. We had challenged him, we had lost.

"If you were me, lord," Ælfwold, a shrewd man, asked quietly, "what would you do?"

I gave him an honest answer. "Rejoin Æthelred," I said, "and persuade him to attack the Danes."

He crumbled a piece of bread, finding a chip of millstone that he rubbed between his fingers. He was not aware of what he did. He was thinking of the Danes, of the battle he knew must be fought, of the battle he feared would be lost. He shook his head. "Tomorrow," he said quietly, "I take my men west." He looked up at me. "I'm sorry."

"You have no choice," I said.

I felt like a man who had lost almost everything playing at dice and then, like a fool, had risked all that remained on one last throw. I had failed. What had I thought? That men would come to me because of reputation? Instead they had stayed with their gold-givers. Æthelred did not want me to succeed and so he had opened his chests of silver and offered wealth to men if they joined his army. I needed a thousand men and I could not find them, and without them I could do nothing. I thought bitterly of Iseult's prophecy made so many years before, that Alfred would give me power, that I would lead a shining horde and have a woman of gold.

That night, in the upper room of the palace where I had a straw mattress, I gazed at the dull glow of distant fires beyond the horizon and I wished I had stayed in Northumbria. I had been drifting, I thought, ever since Gisela's death. I thought Æthelflæd's summons had given my life a new purpose, but now I could see no future. I stood at the window, a great stone arch that framed the sky, and I could hear singing from the taverns, the shouts of men arguing, a woman's laughter, and I thought that Alfred had taken away the power he had given me and the promised shining horde was a half-crew of men who were beginning to doubt my ability to lead them anywhere.

"So what will you do?" Æthelflæd asked from behind me.

I had not heard her come. Her bare feet made no sound on the stone floor. "I don't know," I admitted.

She came and stood beside me. She touched my hand where it rested on the sill, tracing the ball of my thumb with a gentle finger. "The swelling has gone," she said.

"The itch too," I said.

"See?" she asked, amusement in her voice, "the sting was no omen."

"It was," I said, "but I've yet to discover what it means."

She left her hand on mine, her touch light as a feather. "Father Pyrlig says I have a choice."

"Which is?"

"To go back to Æthelred or find a nunnery in Wessex."

I nodded. Monks still chanted in the church, their droning punctuated by laughter and singing from the taverns. Folk were seeking oblivion in ale or else they were praying. They all knew what the fires of the burning sky meant, that the end was coming. "Did you turn my eldest son into a Christian?" I asked.

"No," Æthelflæd said, "he found it for himself."

"I'll take him north," I said, "and beat the nonsense out of him." Æthelflæd said nothing to that, just pressed her hand on mine. "A nunnery?" I asked bleakly.

"I'm married," she said, "and the church tells me that if I am not with my God-given husband then I must be seen to be virtuous." I was still gazing at the fire-smeared horizon where the flames lit the underside of clouds. Above Lundene the sky was clear so that moonlight cast sharp shadows from the edges of the Roman roof tiles. Æthelflæd leaned her head on my shoulder. "What are you thinking?"

"That unless we defeat the Danes there'll be no convents left."

"Then what will I do?" she asked lightly.

I smiled. "Father Beocca liked to talk of the wheel of fortune," I said, and wondered why I had spoken of him as if he lay in the past. Did I see the end coming? Would those distant fires creep ever closer till they burned Lundene and seared the last Saxon from Britain?

"At Fearnhamme," I said, "I was your father's warlord. Now I'm a fugitive with not enough men to fill a ship's benches."

"My father calls you his miracle worker," Æthelflæd said. "True," she said when I laughed, "that's what he calls you."

"I could work him a miracle," I said bitterly, "if he gave me men." I thought again of Iseult's prophecy, how Alfred would give me power and my woman would be golden, and that was when I turned at last from the distant fires and looked down at Æthelflæd's golden hair and took her into my arms.

And next day Ælfwold would leave Lundene and I would be left powerless.

Three horsemen came first. They arrived in the dawn, galloping across the Fleot's filthy valley and up to the city gates. I heard the horn calling from the ramparts and I threw on clothes, pulled on boots, kissed Æthelflæd, and ran down the stairs to the palace's hall just as the door was thrown open and the three mailed men strode in, their feet splintering the already splintered tiles. Their leader was tall, grim and bearded. He stopped two paces from me. "You must have some ale in this shit-stinking city," he said. I was staring with disbelief. "I need breakfast," he demanded, and then could not help himself. He laughed. It was Steapa, and with him were two younger men, both warriors. I shouted for the servants to bring food and ale, still hardly believing that Steapa had come. "I'm bringing you twelve hundred men," he said briskly.

For a moment I could hardly speak. "Twelve hundred?" I echoed feebly.

"Alfred's best," Steapa said, "and the Ætheling is coming too."

"Edward?" I was too astonished to make any sensible response.

"Edward and twelve hundred of Alfred's best men. We rode ahead of them," he explained, then turned and bowed as Æthelflæd, swathed in a great cloak, entered the hall. "Your father sends his greetings, lady," he said.

"And he sends your brother," I said, "with twelve hundred men."

"God be praised," Æthelflæd said.

The hall filled as the news spread. My children were there, and Bishop Erkenwald and Ælfwold and Father Pyrlig, then Finan and Weohstan. "The Ætheling Edward will lead the forces," Steapa said, "but he is to accept Lord Uhtred's guidance."

Bishop Erkenwald looked astonished. He was glancing from Æthelflæd to me and I could tell he was scenting sin with the eagerness of a terrier smelling a fox's earth. "The king sent you?" he asked Steapa.

"Yes, lord."

"But what of the Danes in Defnascir?"

"They're just scratching . . ." Steapa said, then reddened because he had almost said something that he thought would offend the bishop, let alone a king's daughter.

"Scratching their arses?" I finished for him.

"They're doing nothing, my lady," Steapa muttered. He was the son of slaves and, for all his eminence as the commander of Alfred's bodyguard, he was awed by Æthelflæd's presence. "But the king wants his men back soon, lord," Steapa said, looking at me, "just in case the Northumbrian Danes do wake up."

"So finish your breakfast," I said, "then ride back to Edward. Tell him he's not to enter the city." I did not want the West Saxon army inside Lundene with its tempting taverns and whores. "He's to march north around the city," I ordered, "and keep marching east."

Steapa frowned. "He's expecting to find supplies here."

I looked at Bishop Erkenwald. "You'll send food and ale to the army. Weohstan's garrison will provide escorts."

The bishop, offended by my peremptory tone, hesitated, then nodded. He knew I spoke now with Alfred's authority. "Where do I send the supplies?" he asked.

"You remember Thunresleam?" I asked Steapa.

"The old hall on the hill, lord?"

"Edward's to meet me there. You too." I looked back to the bishop. "Send the supplies there."

"To Thunresleam?" Bishop Erkenwald asked suspiciously, smelling still more sin because the name reeked of paganism.

"Thor's Grove," I confirmed. "It's close to Beamfleot." The bishop made the sign of the cross, but he dared not protest. "You and one hundred of your men are coming with me," I told Weohstan.

"My orders are to defend Lundene," Weohstan said uncertainly.

"If we're at Beamfleot," I said, "there'll be no Danes threatening Lundene. We march in two hours."

It took nearer four hours, but with Ælfwold's Mercians, Weohstan's West Saxons, and my own men we numbered over four hundred mounted warriors who clattered through the city's eastern gate. I left my children in the care of Æthelflæd's servants. Æthelflæd insisted on riding with us. I argued against that, telling her she should not risk her life, but she refused to stay in Lundene. "Didn't you take an oath to serve me?" she asked.

"More fool me, yes."

"Then I give the orders," she said, smiling.

"Yes, my duck," I said, and earned a thump on the arm. At the beginning of their marriage Æthelred had always called Æthelflæd "my duck," an endearment that annoyed her. So now she rode beneath my banner of the wolf's head, Weohstan flew the West Saxon dragon, while Ælfwold's Mercians displayed a long flag showing the Christian cross. "I want my own banner," Æthelflæd told me.

"Then make one," I said.

"It will show geese," she said.

"Geese! Not ducks?"

She made a face at me. "Geese are Saint Werburgh's symbol," she explained. "There was a huge flock of geese ravaging a cornfield and she prayed and God sent the geese away. It was a miracle!"

"The abbess at Lecelad did that?"

"No, no! The abbess was named after Saint Werburgh. The saint died a long time ago. Maybe I'll show her on my banner. I know she protects me! I prayed to her last night and see what she did?" She gestured at the men following us. "My prayers were answered!"

I wondered if she had prayed before or after she had come to my room, but decided that was a question best left unasked.

We rode just north of the drab marshes that edged the Temes.

This was East Anglian territory, but there were no great estates close to Lundene. There had once been beamed halls and busy villages, but the frequent raids and counter-raids had left the halls in ashes and the villages in terror. The Danish King Eohric of East Anglia was supposedly a Christian and had signed a peace treaty with Alfred, agreeing that his Danes would stay away from both Mercia and Wessex, but the two kings might as well have signed an agreement to stop men drinking ale. The Danes were forever crossing the frontier and the Saxons retaliated, and so we rode past impoverished settlements. The people saw us coming and fled to the marshes or else to the woods on the few small hills. We ignored them.

Beamfleot lay at the southern end of the great line of hills which barred our path. Most of the hills were heavily wooded, though above the village, where the slopes were highest and steepest, we could see the old fort which had been made on the grassy dome above the river. We swerved northward, climbing a steep track which led to Thunresleam, and we rode cautiously because the Danes would have seen us coming and they could easily have sent a force to attack us as we rode uphill through the thick trees. I expected that attack. I had sent Æthelflæd and her two maidservants to the center of our column and had ordered every man to ride with his shield looped onto his arms and weapons ready. I listened for the sound of birds fleeing through the leaves, for the clink of harness, for the thud of a hoof on leaf mold, for the sudden shout that would announce a charge of Viking horsemen from the hill above, but the only birds clattering through the leaves were the pigeons we ourselves scared away. The defenders of Beamfleot had evidently yielded the hill to us, and not one Dane tried to stop us.

"That's crazy," Finan said as we reached the crest. "They could have killed a score of us."

"They're confident," I said. "They must know the walls of their fort will stop us."

"Or else they don't know their business," Finan said.

"When did you last meet a Dane who didn't know how to fight?"

We sent men to scout the surrounding trees as we approached

the old hall at Thunresleam, but still no enemy appeared. We had been to this hall years before, back when we had negotiated with the Norsemen, Sigefrid and Erik, and afterward we had fought a bitter battle in the creek beneath the fort. Those events seemed so distant now and both Sigefrid and Erik were dead. Haesten had survived that long ago fight, and now I had come to oppose him again, though none of us knew whether Haesten himself had returned to Beamfleot. Rumor said he was still ravaging Mercia, which implied he was confident that Beamfleot's garrison could protect itself.

The oak-beamed hall at Thunresleam would be at the center of my camp. It had once been a magnificent building, but it had been abandoned many years before and the pillars were rotting and the thatch was black, damp and sagging. The great beams were thick with bird droppings while the floor was a mass of weeds. Just outside the hall was a stone pillar about the height of a man. There was a hole through the stone that was filled with pebbles and scraps of cloth, the votive offerings left by the local folk who had fled our arrival. Their village was a mile eastward and I knew it had a church, but the Christians of Thunresleam understood that their high place and old hall were sacred to Thor and so they still came and sent prayers to that older god. Mankind can never be too safe. I might not like the Christian god, but I do not deny his existence and, at hard moments in my life, I have sent prayers to him as well as to my own gods.

"Shall we make a palisade?" Weohstan asked me.

"No."

He stared at me. "No?"

"Clear out as many trees as you can," I ordered him, "but no palisade."

"But . . ."

"No palisade!"

I was taking a risk, but if I made a palisade I would give my men a place of safety and I knew how reluctant men were to abandon such security. I had often noticed how a bull, brought for entertainment to some feast, will adopt a patch of land as its refuge and defend itself from the attacking dogs with a terrible ferocity so long as it stays in its chosen refuge, but goad the bull out and it loses confidence and the dogs sense the vulnerability and attack with a renewed savagery. I did not want my men to feel safe. I wanted them nervous and alert. I wanted them to know that safety lay not in a fort of their own making, but in capturing the enemy's fort. And I wanted that capture to be quick.

I ordered Ælfwold's men to cut trees to the west, clearing the woods back to the hill's edge and beyond so we could see far across the country toward Lundene. If the Danes brought men back from Mercia I wanted to see them. I put Osferth in charge of our sentries. Their job was to make a screen between us and Beamfleot to warn of any sally by the Danes. Those sentries were in the woods, hidden from the old high fort, and if the Danes came I expected to fight them among the trees. Osferth's men would slow them until my whole force could be brought against the attackers, and I ordered that every man was to sleep wearing his mail coat and with his weapons close by.

I asked Ælfwold to protect our northern and western flanks. His men would watch for the approach of our supplies and guard against reinforcements coming from Haesten's men who still smeared the far horizon with smoke. Then, those orders given, I took fifty men to explore the country about our encampment that rang with the sound of axes biting into trees. Finan, Pyrlig, and Osferth accompanied me, as did Æthelflæd who ignored all my advice to stay out of danger.

We went first to the village of Thunresleam. It was a straggle of thick-thatched cottages built about the scorched and collapsed ruin of a church. The villagers had fled when we climbed the hill, but a few braver souls now appeared from the woods beyond their small fields where the first shoots of wheat, barley, and rye greened the furrows. They were Saxons and the first to approach us were led by a burly peasant with matted brown hair, one eye, and work-blackened hands. He looked up at Ælfwold's banner that showed the Christian cross. I had borrowed the banner to make it clear we were not Danes, and the cross evidently reassured the one-eyed man who knelt to us and beckoned for his companions to kneel. "I am Father Heahberht," he said.

He told me he was priest to the village and to two other settlements farther east. "You don't look like a priest," I said.

"If I did, lord, I'd be dead," he said, "the witch in the fort kills priests."

I glanced southward, though from here the old fort on the hill was not visible. "The witch?"

"She is called Skade, lord."

"I know Skade."

"She burned our church, lord."

"And she took the girls, lord," a woman said tearfully, "even the young ones. She took my daughter and she was only ten years old, lord."

"Why did she do . . ." Æthelflæd began the question, then abruptly stopped as she realized the answer was obvious.

"Have they abandoned the old fort?" I asked. "The one on the hill?"

"No, lord," Father Heahberht answered, "they use it to keep watch. And we have to take food there, lord."

"How many men there?"

"About fifty, lord. They keep the horses there, too."

I did not doubt that the priest told the truth, but the Danes had seen us coming and I reckoned the old fort would have been reinforced by now. "How many men are in the new fort?" I asked.

"They won't let us near the new fort, lord," Father Heahberht said, "but I've watched it from the hill at Hæthlegh, lord, and I could not count all the men inside." He looked up at me nervously. His dead eye was milky white and ulcerated. He was shivering with fear, not because he thought we were an enemy like the Danes, but because we were lords. He forced himself to speak as calmly as he could. "They number in their hundreds, lord. Three thousand men rode west, lord, but they left all their wives and children in Beamfleot."

"You counted the ones who left?"

"I tried, lord."

"Their wives and children are here?" Æthelflæd asked.

"They live on the beached boats, lady," Heahberht said.

The priest was an observant man and I rewarded him with a sil-ver coin. "So who commands in the new fort?" I asked him. "Haesten himself?"

Father Heahberht shook his head. "Skade does, lord."

"Skade! She's in command?"

"We're told so, lord."

"Haesten hasn't returned?" I asked.

"No, lord," Heahberht said, "not that we've heard." He told us how Haesten had started building his new fort as soon as his fleet ar-rived from Cent. "They made us cut oak and elm for them, lord."

"I need to see this new fort," I said and I gave Heahberht another coin before kicking my horse between two of the cottages and onto a field of growing barley. I was thinking of Skade, of her cruelties, of her desperate lust to be a ruler. She could order men by the pure strength of her will, but did she have the skills to deploy them in battle? Yet Haesten was no fool, he would not have left her in com-mand if he doubted her ability, and I did not doubt that he had also left her sufficient troops and competent advisers. I kicked the horse again, riding south now into the trees. My men followed. I rode recklessly, careless that the Danes might have men in the woods, though we saw none. I sensed that Skade's garrison was content to stay behind its walls, confident in their ability to resist any attack.

We reached the edge of that high ground where the land dropped steeply to the web of creeks and inlets that threaded the marsh. Beyond that was the wide Temes, its southern shore just visible in the distant haze. Four ships idled in the middle of that great spread of light-reflecting water. They were Danes patrolling for prey and watching for any Saxon warships coming downstream from Lundene.

And to my right I could see Caninga and its creek, and the great fleet of boats beached on Caninga's shore. The new fort was just visible around the shoulder of the high hill where the old fort stood. What had Father Heahberht said? That only about fifty men guarded the old ramparts. I could see spear-tips glinting by the north-facing gate and there looked to be far more than fifty, and the wall they defended was in good condition. I knew that the southern wall, overlooking the creek, had decayed, but the landward defenses had been kept in good repair. "Skade saw us coming," I said, "and reinforced the old fort."

"She's got enough spears there," Finan agreed.

"So we have to capture two forts," I said.

"Why not let this one rot?" Finan asked, gesturing at the old fort.

"Because I don't want those bastards behind our backs when we attack the new fort," I said, "so we have to kill them first."

Finan said nothing. No one spoke. The war we had been fighting all our lives had forced rulers to build forts because forts won wars. Alfred protected Wessex with burhs that were nothing but large, well-manned forts. Æthelred of Mercia was building burhs. Haesten, so far as we knew, had not yet dared attack any burh for he knew that his men would die in the ditches and under the high walls. He wanted to weaken Mercia and starve the burh's defenders before he dared attack those ramparts. The two forts at Beamfleot were not burhs, but their defenses were just as formidable. There were walls, ditches with stakes, and doubtless, down on the creek, a moat. And behind the walls were men who knew how to kill, spear-Danes and sword-Danes, and they waited for us not in one fortress, but two.

"We have to take both forts?" Æthelflæd asked timidly, breaking the silence.

"The first will be easy," I said.

"Easy, lord?" Finan asked with a crooked grin.

"And quick," I said, sounding a good deal more confident than I felt. The old fort was formidable, and it was large, but I doubted the Danes had committed enough men to defend every yard of its ramparts. Once the Ætheling Edward's troops reached me I reckoned I would have enough troops to assail the old fort in several places at once, and those assaults would thin out the defenders until one of our attacks broke through. It was not much of a plan, but it would work, though I feared it would be expensive in men. Yet I had small choice. I had to do the impossible. I had to take two forts and, if truth be told, I had no idea how to take the second newer fort by the water. I just knew it had to be done.

We rode back to our camp.

Everything became confused next morning. It was as though the Danes woke up to the threat we posed and decided to do what they should have done the previous day.

They knew we were camped around Thunresleam's old hall. I had placed a large number of sentries in the woods south of the hall, but doubtless some clever Dane had avoided them to spy on the newly cleared space about the hall, and Skade, or whoever advised her, decided an attack at dawn would kill many of us and discourage the rest. Which was a clever enough idea, except that it was obvious, and to prepare for it I had roused every man in the heart of the starlit night. I ordered the sentries back from the trees, made sure we were all awake, then we saddled horses, pulled on mail, and left. The campfires still smoldered, suggesting we were sleeping. Our departure made enough noise to disturb the dead in Thunresleam's small graveyard, but the Danes were presumably making their own noise and had no idea we had decamped.

"We can't do this every morning," Ælfwold grumbled.

"If they're going to attack us," I said, "it will be this morning. By tomorrow we'll be in their high fort."

"By tomorrow?" He sounded surprised.

"If Edward comes today," I said. I planned to assault the old fortress as soon as I possibly could. I just needed enough men to make eight or nine simultaneous attacks.

We rode to the village and we waited there. We were four hundred men ready for battle. I knew it was possible the Danes had detected our move, and so I insisted we stayed in our saddles. The newly woken villagers brought us sour ale and Father Heahberht nervously offered me a cup of mead. It was surprisingly good, and I told him to give some to Æthelflæd and her two maidservants, the

281

only women with our force. "If the Danes attack," I told her, "you'll be staying here with a bodyguard." She looked at me dubiously, but for once did not argue.

It was still dark. The only sounds were the clink of bridles and the thump of restless hooves. Sometimes a man spoke, but most just slumped asleep in their saddles. Smoke drifted from holes in the hovel roofs, an owl called forlorn from the woods, and I felt a chill bleakness descend on my spirit. I could not rouse myself from that bleakness. I touched Thor's hammer and sent a prayer to the gods to send me a sign, but all I heard was the owl's mournful cry repeated. How could I take two forts? I feared the gods had forsaken me, and that by coming south from Northumbria I had forfeited their favor. What had I told Alfred? That we were here to amuse our gods, but how could those gods be amused by my betrayals? I thought of Ragnar's disappointment and that memory gored my soul. I remembered Brida's scorn and knew it was deserved. I felt worthless that morning as the sky's edge lightened behind me to a streak of gray, I felt as though my future held nothing, and the feeling was so strong that I was close to despair. I twisted in the saddle, looking for Pyrlig. The Welsh priest was one of the few men I trusted with my soul, and I wanted his counsel, but before I could summon him a man called out a warning. "There's a horseman coming, lord!"

I had left Finan and a handful of men as our only sentries. They were posted at the edge of the fields, halfway between the village and the old hall and Finan had sent one man to warn me that the Danes were moving. "They're in the woods, lord," the man told me, "by our camp."

"How many?"

"We can't tell, lord, but it sounds like a horde."

Which could mean two hundred or two thousand, and prudence suggested I should wait till Finan could estimate the enemy more accurately, but I was in that bleak mood, feeling doomed and desperate for a sign from the gods, and so I turned to Æthelflæd. "You wait here with your bodyguard," I said, and did not wait for an answer, but just drew Serpent-Breath, taking comfort from the sound of the long steel scraping through the scabbard's throat. "The Danes are at our camp!" I shouted, "and we're going to kill them!" I spurred my horse, the same stallion I had taken from Aldhelm. It was a good horse, properly schooled, but I was still unfamiliar with him.

Ælfwold spurred to catch me. "How many are there?" he asked.

"Enough!" I called to him. I was feeling reckless, careless and I knew it was foolish. But I reckoned the Danes would attack the encampment and almost immediately realize we had anticipated them, and then they would be wary. I wanted them unaware and so I kicked the stallion into a trot. My whole force, over three hundred men, was streaming along the track behind me. The day's first shadows were being cast into the furrows and birds were flying up from the woods ahead.

I turned in my saddle to see spears and swords, axes and shields. Saxon warriors, gray-mailed in a gray dawn, grim-faced beneath helmets, and I felt the battle anger rising. I wanted to kill. I was in that bleak mood, assailed by the certainty that I had to throw myself on the mercy of the gods. If they wanted me to live, if the spinners were willing to weave my thread back into the golden weft, then I would live through this morning. Omens and signs, we live by them, and so I rode to discover the will of the gods. It was foolish.

Horsemen appeared on our left, startling me, but it was only Finan and his seven remaining men who galloped to join us. "There might be three hundred of them," he shouted, "or maybe four hundred!"

I just nodded and kicked the horse again. The track to the old hall was wide enough for four or five men to ride abreast. Finan probably expected me to halt our horsemen short of the space we had cleared about the old hall and line the men in the trees, but the carelessness was on me.

Light flared ahead. The daylight was still gray, night shrouding the western horizon, but the sudden new light was red and bright. Fire. The Danes, I guessed, had lit the hall's thatch, so now let it light their deaths. I could see the edge of the trees, see the fallen trunks we had felled the day before, see the dull glow of dying campfires and the dark shapes of men and horses and the glimmer of reflected fire from helmets, mail, and weapons, and I kicked the stallion again and roared a challenge. "Kill them!"

We came in a ragged order, bursting from the trees with swords and spears, with hatred and fury, and almost as soon as I entered the clearing I realized we were outnumbered. The Danes had come in force, at least four hundred, and most were still mounted, but they were scattered throughout the encampment and few realized we were approaching until our horses and blades appeared in the dawn. The largest body of the enemy was at the clearing's western edge, staring across the dark land toward the faint glow of light betraying the fires of Lundene. Maybe they suspected we had given up any hope of capturing the forts and, under the cover of night, had slunk back toward the distant city. Instead we were coming from the east with the growing light behind us, and they turned as they heard the first screams and shouts.

We were lit red by the growing fire of the old hall's burning thatch. Red fire was flashing from the horses' bared teeth, from our mail, from our blades, and I was still shouting as I swung my sword at the first man. He was on foot and holding a broad-bladed spear that he tried to level at my horse, but Serpent-Breath caught him on the side of the head and I lifted the sword and lunged it at another man, not bothering to see what damage I did, just spurring on to provoke more fear. We had surprised them, and for a moment we were the lords of slaughter as we spread from the track and cut down dismounted men who searched for plunder around the dying campfires. I saw Osferth hammer a man's head with the flat of an ax blade, knocking off the man's helmet and hurling him back into one of the fires. The man must have been in the habit of cleaning his hands after eating by running them through his hair because the grease caught the flames and flared sudden and bright. He screamed and writhed, head like a beacon as he staggered to his feet, then a rush of horsemen overrode him. A hoof threw up a spew of sparks and riderless horses fled in panic.

Finan was with me. Finan and Cerdic and Sihtric, and together we rode for the large group of mounted warriors who had been staring west across the night-shadowed land. I was still shouting as I charged into them, sword swinging at a yellow-bearded man who deflected the blow with his raised shield, then he was struck by a spear below the shield, the blade ripping through mail and into his belly. I felt something strike my shield, but could not look to my left because a gap-toothed man was trying to lunge his sword through my stallion's neck. I knocked his blade down with Serpent-Breath and cut at his arm, but his mail stopped the blow. We were deep among the enemy now, unable to ride farther, but more of my men were coming to help. I lunged at the gap-toothed man, but he was quick and his shield intercepted the sword, then his horse stumbled. Sihtric slashed with an ax and I had a glimpse of splitting metal and sudden blood.

I was trying to keep my horse moving. There were dismounted Danes among the riders, and a slash across my stallion's legs could bring me down and a man was never so vulnerable as when he topples from a saddle. A spear slid from my right, sliding across my belly to lodge in the underside of my shield and I just back-swung Serpent-Breath into a bearded face. I felt her shatter teeth and ripped her back to saw her edge deeper. A horse screamed. Ælfwold's men were deep in the fight now and our charge had split the Danes. Some had retreated down the hill, but most had gone either north or south along the crest and now they reformed and came at us from both directions, bellowing their own war cries. The sun had risen, dazzling and blinding, the hall was an inferno and the air a whirl of sparks in the new brightness.

Chaos. For a moment we had held the advantage of surprise, but the Danes recovered quickly and closed on us. The hill's edge was a confusion of trampling horses, shouting men, and the raw sound of steel on steel. I had turned northward and was trying to drive those Danes off the hill, but they were just as determined to slaughter us. I parried a sword blow, watching the man's gritted teeth as he tried to cut my head off. The clash of swords jarred up my arm, but I had stopped his swing and I punched him in the face with Serpent-Breath's hilt. He swung again, striking my helmet, filling my head with noise as I punched a second time. I was too close to him to use the sword's edge, and he hit my sword arm hard with the rim of his shield. "Turd," he grunted at me. His helmet was decorated with twists of wool dyed yellow. He wore arm rings over his mail, denoting a man who had won treasure in battle. There was fury in his fire-reflecting eyes. He wanted my death so badly. I wore the silver-decorated helmet, had more arm rings than he did and he knew I was a warrior of renown. Perhaps he knew who I was, and he wanted to boast that he had killed Uhtred of Bebbanburg and I saw him grit his teeth again as he tried to slice the sword at my face and then the grimace turned into surprise, and his eyes widened and the red went from them as he made a gurgling sound. He shook his head, desperate to keep hold of his faltering sword as the ax blade cut his spine. Sihtric had swung the ax and the man made a mewing noise and fell from the saddle, and just then my horse screamed and staggered sideways and I saw a dismounted Dane thrusting a spear up into the stallion's belly. Finan drove the man over with his horse as I kicked my feet out of the stirrups.

The stallion collapsed, twisting and kicking, still screaming, and my right leg was trapped beneath him. Another horse stepped a hair's breadth from my face. I covered my body with the shield and tried to drag myself free. A blade crashed into the shield. A horse stepped on Serpent-Breath and I almost lost the blade. My world was a thunder of hooves, screams, and confusion. I tried to pull free again then something, blade or hoof, struck the back of my helmet and the confused world turned black. I was dazed, and in the darkness I heard someone making pathetic moaning noises. It was me. A man was trying to drag my helmet off and, when he realized I was alive he put a knife at my mouth and I remember thinking of Gisela and desperately checking that Serpent-Breath's hilt was in my hand, and it was not, and I screamed, knowing I was denied the joys of Valhalla, and then my vision turned red. There was warmth on my face and red before my eyes, and I recovered my senses to realize that the man who would have killed me was dying himself and his blood was pouring onto my face, then Cerdic heaved the dying man away and pulled me from beneath the dead horse. "Here!" Sihtric thrust Serpent-Breath into my hand. Both he and Cerdic were dismounted. A Dane shouted victory and lunged with a thick-hafted spear from his saddle and Cerdic deflected the thrust with a blade-scored shield. I stabbed the horseman's thigh with Serpent-Breath, but the blow had no force and his spear sliced at me, thumping hard into my shield. The Danes were scenting triumph and they pressed forward and we felt their blows chopping on the linden wood. "Kill their horses," I shouted, though it came out as a croak, and some of Weohstan's men arrived on our right and drove their horses at the Danes and I saw a Saxon twist in his saddle, his spear hand hanging from his bloody arm by a scrap of bone or tendon.

"Jesus! Jesus!" a man shouted and it was Father Pyrlig who joined us. The Welsh priest was on foot, belly stretching his mail, a spear like a small tree trunk in his hands. He carried no shield and so used the spear two-handed, driving the blade at the enemy's horses to keep them at a distance.

"Thank you," I said to Cerdic and Sihtric.

"We should go back, lord," Cerdic said.

"Where's Finan?"

"Back!" Cerdic shouted, and he unceremoniously grabbed my left shoulder and pulled me away from the Danes.

Finan was fighting behind us, hammering an ax at the Danes on the southern part of the crest where he was supported by most of my men and by Ælfwold's Mercians. "I need a horse," I snarled.

"This is a muddle," Pyrlig said, and I almost laughed because his tone and his words were so mild. It was more than a muddle, it was a disaster. I had led my men onto the hill's edge and the Danes had recovered from the attack and now they surrounded us. There were Danes to the east, to the north and to the south, and they were trying to drive us over the crest and pursue us down the steep slope where our bodies would be a smear of blood beneath the rising sun. At least a hundred of my Saxons were dismounted now and we formed a circle inside a desperate shield wall. Too many were dead, some killed by their own side for, in the maelstrom, it was hard to know friend from foe. Many Saxons had a cross on their shield, but not all. There were plenty of Danish corpses too, but their living outnumbered us. They had my small shield wall surrounded, while their horsemen were harrying the still mounted Saxons back into the woods.

Ælfwold had lost his stallion and the Mercian forced his way to my side. "You bastard," he said, "you treacherous bastard." He must have thought I had deliberately led his men into a trap, but it was only my stupid carelessness, not treachery, that had led to this disaster. Ælfwold raised his shield as the Danes came and the blows hammered down. I thrust Serpent-Breath into a horse's chest, twisted and thrust again, and Pyrlig half hoisted a man from the saddle with a tremendous lunge of his heavy spear. But Ælfwold was down, his helmet ripped open, his blood and brains spilling onto his face, but he retained enough consciousness to look at me reproachfully before he started to quiver and spasm and I had to look away to ram the sword at another Dane whose horse tripped on a corpse, and then the enemy pulled back from our shield wall to ready themselves for another attack.

"Jesu, Jesu," Ælfwold said, and then the breath stuttered in his throat and he said no more. Our shield wall was shrunken, our shields splintered and bloodied. The Danes mocked us, snarled at us, and promised us agonizing deaths. Men moved closer together and I should have encouraged them, but I did not know what to say because this was my fault, my recklessness. I had attacked without first discovering the enemy's strength. My death, I thought, would be just, but I would go to the afterlife knowing I had taken too many good men with me.

So the only course was to die well, and I pushed past Sihtric's shield and went toward the enemy. A man accepted the challenge and rode at me. I could not see his face because the rising sun was behind him, blinding me, but I slashed Serpent-Breath across his stallion's mouth and thrust my shield up to take his sword's blow. The horse reared, I thrust at its belly and missed as another man swung an ax from my left, and I stepped away and my foot slid in a slippery tangle of guts spilled from a corpse eviscerated by an ax. I went onto one knee, but again my men came to rescue me. The stallion thumped down and I stood, lunging at the rider, sword striking him somewhere, but I was sun-dazzled and could not see where. To my right a stallion, a spear impaled in its chest, was coughing blood. I was shouting, though I do not remember what I shouted, and from my left came a new charge of horsemen. The newcomers were screaming war cries.

Die well. Die well. What else can a man do? His enemies must say of him that he died like a man. I lunged again, driving the horse away and a sword smacked into the top of my shield, splitting the iron rim and driving a splinter of wood into my eye. I rammed the blade again and felt Serpent-Breath scrape on bone as she tore the rider's thigh. He hacked down. I blinked the splinter away as his sword cracked on my helmet, glanced off and thumped my shoulder. The mail stopped the blow that had been suddenly weakened because Father Pyrlig had speared the rider in his side. The Welshman dragged me back toward the shield wall. "God be thanked!" he was saying over and over.

The newcomers were Saxons. They rode under the banner of Wessex's dragon, and at their head was Steapa, and he was worth ten other men, and they had come from the north and were slicing into the Danes.

"A horse!" I shouted, and someone brought me a stallion. Pyrlig held the nervous beast as I mounted. I pushed my boots into the unfamiliar stirrups and shouted at my dismounted men to find themselves horses. There were too many dead beasts, but enough riderless stallions still lived white-eyed amidst the slaughter.

A huge crash announced the collapse of the burning hall's roof. The flaming beams fell one by one, each spewing a new thrust of sparks into the smoke-darkened sky. I spurred to the ancient votive stone, leaned from the saddle, and touched the stone's top as I said a prayer to Thor. A spear had lodged itself through the hole in the pillar and I sheathed Serpent-Breath and took the long-hafted weapon. The blade was bloodied. The spearman, a Dane, lay dead beside the stone. A horse had stepped on his face, mangling it and leaving an eyeball dangling over his helmet's edge. I gripped the ash shaft and spurred the horse toward the remnants of the fight. Steapa and his men had utterly surprised the Danes who were turning to flee back to the safety of the fort, and Steapa was following. I tried to catch him, but he vanished among the trees. All the Saxons were in pursuit now, the thick woods filled with horses and fugitives. Finan somehow discovered me and rode alongside, ducking beneath branches. A wounded and dismounted Dane flinched from us, then fell to his knees, but we ignored him.

"Sweet Jesus," Finan shouted to me, "but I thought we were doomed!"

"Me too!"

"How did you know Steapa's men were coming?" he asked, then spurred after a fleeing Dane who kicked his horse frantically.

"I didn't!" I shouted, though Finan was too intent on his prey to hear me. I caught up and aimed the spear at the small of the Dane's back. Leaf mold flew up into my face from the hooves of the enemy's horse, then I lunged and Finan sliced back with his sword and the Dane dropped from the saddle as we galloped past.

"Ælfwold's dead!" Finan called.

"I saw it! He thought I betrayed him!"

"He kept his brains in his arse then. Where have the bastards gone?"

The Danes were riding for the fort and our pursuit had taken us slightly eastward. I remember the green sunlight bright in the leaves, remember thumping past a badger's earth, remember the sound of all those hooves in the greenwood, the relief of living after what seemed certain death, and then we were at the edge of the trees.

And still there was chaos.

In front of us was a great stretch of grass where sheep and goats normally grazed. The land sloped down to a saddle, then rose more steeply to the gate of the old fort high on its domed hill. The Danes were galloping for the fort, eager to gain the protection of its ditch and ramparts, but Steapa's men were among the fugitives, slashing and hacking from their saddles.

"Come on!" Finan shouted at me, and kicked back with his spurs.

He saw the opportunity before I did. My immediate thought was to stop him and to stop Steapa's undisciplined charge, but then the recklessness took hold again. I shouted some wordless challenge and spurred after Finan.

I had lost all sense of time. I could not tell how long that fight on the hill's edge had taken, but the sun was risen now and its light shimmered off the Temes and lit the high grass saddle a glowing green. The stream of horsemen stretched from the woods to the fort. My laboring horse was breathing hard, sweat white on its flanks, but I kicked it on as we converged on that turf-churning horde of pursuers and pursued. And what Finan had understood before me was that the Danes might close the gate too late. He understood that they might be in such panic that they did not even think to close the gate. So long as their own men pounded across the ditch's causeway and beneath the wooden arch they would leave the gate open, but Steapa's men were so mixed with the Danes that some might get through, and if enough of us could get inside that wall then we could take the fort.

Later, much later, when the poets told of that day's fight, they said Steapa and I attacked Thunresleam's old hall together, and that we drove the Danes in panic and that we assaulted the fort while the enemy was still reeling from that defeat. They got the story wrong, of course, but then, they were poets, not warriors. The truth was that Steapa rescued me from certain defeat, and neither of us assaulted the fort because we did not need to. The first of Steapa's men were allowed through the gate and it was only when they were inside that the Danes realized the enemy had entered with their own men. Another desperate fight started. Steapa ordered his men to dismount and they made a shield wall at the gate, a wall that faced both into the fort and out toward the sunlit slope, and the Danes trapped outside could not break that shield wall and fled instead. They spurred down the steep westward-facing slope, riding desperately toward the new fort. And we simply dismounted and walked through the gate to join Steapa's spreading shield wall inside the old fort.

I saw Skade then. I never discovered whether she had led the horsemen to Thunresleam's burning hall, but she commanded the men in the old fort and she was screaming at them to attack us.

But we were now in overwhelming numbers. There were at least four hundred Saxons in Steapa's wall, and more kept arriving on horseback. The proud banner of Wessex flew above us, the embroidered dragon spattered with blood, and Skade screamed at us. She was on horseback, in mail, bareheaded, her long black hair lifting in the wind as she brandished a sword. She kicked her horse toward the shield wall, but had enough sense to check as the round shields lifted in unison and the long spears reached toward her.

Weohstan came with more horsemen, and he led them about the right flank of Steapa's wall and ordered a charge. Steapa shouted at the wall to advance and we marched up the slight slope toward the great halls that crowned the hill. Weohstan's men swept ahead of us and the Danes, understanding their fate, fled.

And so we took the old fort. The enemy fled downhill, a man dragging Skade's horse by its bridle. She sat twisted in her saddle, staring at us. We did not follow. We were weary, bloodied, bruised, wounded, and amazed. Besides, there was a shield wall of Danes guarding the bridge which led to the new fort. Not all the fugitives were going to that bridge, some were swimming their horses across the deep narrow creek to reach Caninga.

The dragon was flown from the old fort's walls and, next to it, Ælfwold's cross. The flags announced a victory, but that victory would mean nothing unless we could capture the new fort, which, for the first time, I saw clearly.

And cursed.

FIVE

Æthelflæd joined me on the rampart. She said nothing at first, but, careless of who watched, just put her arms round me. I could feel her body trembling. My battered shield was still looped on my left arm and it covered her when I drew her close. "I thought you were dead," she said after a while.

"Who told you that?"

"No one," she said. "I was watching."

"Watching? Where?"

"From the edge of the encampment," she said calmly.

"Are you mad?" I asked angrily, and pushed her away so I could look down at her. "You wanted the Danes to capture you?"

"There's blood all over your face," she said, touching my cheek with a finger. "It's dried. Was it bad?"

"Yes, but that will be far worse." I nodded down at the new fort.

The fort was built at the foot of the hill, where the steep grassy drop leveled into a gentler slope that ended as a low ridge snaking into the marsh beside the creek. It was near low tide and I could see the intricate mudbanks where the creek melded into marsh, and I saw how Haesten had built his new fort on that last tongue of firmer ground, but then had dug a broad moat to protect the eastern wall from a frontal assault. He had made the fort into an island, three times as long as it was wide. The southern rampart stretched along the creek and was protected by the deep-water channel, the western and northern walls looked over wide flooded inlets and endless tide-haunted marshes, while the short eastern palisade, which held the

293

main gate and was facing us, was protected by its newly dug moat. A wooden bridge crossed the moat, but now that the last fugitives were safely across, men were dismantling it and carrying the roadway's wide planks back into the fort. Some of the men were working in the water, which, at the center of the moat, only came to their waists. So the moat could be crossed at low tide, though that was small consolation because the difference between high and low tide here was at least twice the height of a well-grown man, which meant that when the moat was fordable the farther bank would be a steep slope of glutinous and slick mud.

The interior of the fort was crammed with buildings, some roofed with planks and others with sailcloth, but no thatch, meaning Haesten was guarding against the possibility of fire-arrows setting his stronghold alight. I guessed many of the beams and posts to make the houses had been taken from the village which had been dismantled and burned, its ruins lying to the east of the new fort where the hill's lower slope was widest. There were scores of Danes inside the long fort, but even more were evidently living aboard their ships. Over two hundred of the high-prowed war vessels were beached high on the creek's farther bank. Most had been dismasted and some had awnings stretched across their crutch-supported masts. Washed clothes were drying on the awnings, while in the hulls' shadows children played in the mud or else gaped up at us. I also counted twenty-three moored ships, all of them with their masts in place and with sails furled on their yards. Every one of those moored ships had men aboard, suggesting they could be made ready for sea at a moment's notice. I had been thinking of bringing vessels downstream from Lundene, but the evident preparedness of the moored ships suggested that any small fleet we deployed would quickly be overwhelmed.

Steapa shambled toward us. His face, so fearsome because of the taut skin and feral eyes, looked suddenly nervous as he knelt to Æthelflæd and pulled off his helmet, leaving his hair tangled. "My lady," he said, blinking.

"Get up, Steapa," she said.

This was a man who would take on a dozen Danes and whose

sword was feared in three kingdoms, but he was in awe of Æthelflæd. She was royalty and he was a slave's son. "The Lady Æthelflæd," I said imperiously, "wants you to go down the hill, cross the moat, beat down the gates, and bring the Danes out."

For a moment he believed me. He looked alarmed, then he frowned at me, but did not know what to say.

"Thank you, Steapa," Æthelflæd said warmly, saving Steapa from his confusion. "You won a magnificent victory! I shall make sure my father knows of your triumph."

He brightened at that, but still stammered. "We were lucky, my lady."

"We always seem to be lucky when you fight. How is Hedda?"

"She's well, lady!" He beamed at her, astonished she should condescend to ask such a question. I could never remember the name of Steapa's wife, a tiny creature, but Æthelflæd knew, and even knew the name of his son.

"Is my brother near?" Æthelflæd asked.

"He was with us in the fight," Steapa said, "so he must be close, my lady."

"I shall find him," she announced.

"Not without a bodyguard," I growled. I suspected some fugitive Danes were still in the woods.

"The Lord Uhtred thinks I'm a baby who needs protecting," Æthelflæd told Steapa.

"He knows best, lady," Steapa said loyally.

Æthelflæd's horse was brought and I cupped my hands to let her mount. I ordered Weohstan and his horsemen to escort her as she rode back toward the smoke of the burning old hall, then I gave Steapa a thump on his back. It was like punching an oak tree. "Thank you," I said.

"For what?"

"For keeping me alive."

"You seemed to be doing well enough," he muttered.

"I was just dying slowly," I said, "till you came along."

He grunted and turned to stare down at the fort. "That be a bastard," he said. "How do we take it?"

"I wish I knew."

"Has to be done though," he said, almost as a question.

"And quickly," I stressed. It had to be quick because we had our hand on the enemy's throat, but he still had both arms free. Those arms were the savage troops harrying Mercia who had left their families and ships in Beamfleot, and many of those men valued their ships more than their families. The Danes were opportunists. They attacked where they sensed weakness, but as soon as the fighting became too hard they boarded their ships and sailed away to find feebler prey. If I destroyed this huge fleet then the crews would be stranded in Britain and, if Wessex survived, they could be hunted down and slaughtered. Haesten might be confident that Beamfleot's new fort was impregnable, but his followers would soon be pressing him to raise our siege. In short, once the Danes ravaging Mercia knew we were a real threat and were present in real numbers, they would want to return to protect their ships and families. "Very quickly," I added.

"So we have to cross that ditch," Steapa said, nodding down at the moat, "and put ladders against the wall." He made it sound simple.

"That's my idea too," I said.

"Jesus," he muttered and made the sign of the cross.

Horns sounded to the north and I turned to stare across the saddle of land where the scattered corpses of men and horses still lay and where still more horsemen were appearing from the far woods. One rider was carrying a vast dragon banner, which told me the Ætheling Edward had arrived.

Alfred's son paused outside the fort, sitting on his horse in the sunlight while servants and packhorses hurried through the gate and up to the larger of the two halls. Both halls were in disrepair. Finan, who had searched them both, joined us on the rampart and said that the halls had been used as stables. "It'll be like living in a cesspit," he said.

Edward still waited beyond the gate with Æthelflæd beside him. "Why isn't he coming into the fort?" I asked.

"He has to have a throne," Finan said, and laughed at the expression on my face. "It's true! They've brought him a rug, a throne, and god knows what else. An altar too."

"He will be the next king," Steapa said loyally.

"Unless I manage to kill the bastard while we're crossing that wall," I said, pointing to the Danish fort. Steapa looked shocked, then cheered up when I asked him how Alfred was faring.

"He's as good as ever!" Steapa said. "We thought he was dying! He's much better now. He can ride again, even walk!"

"I heard he'd died."

"He nearly did. They gave him the last rites, but he recovered. He's gone to Exanceaster."

"What's happening down there?"

Steapa shrugged. "Danes made a camp and are sitting inside it."

"They want Alfred to pay them to leave," I suggested. I thought of Ragnar, and imagined his unhappiness because Brida would undoubtedly be urging him to assault Exanceaster, but that burh was a hard one to attack. It lay on a hill, the approaches were steep, and Alfred's trained army was protecting its stout ramparts, which was why, at least by the time Steapa left, the Danes had made no attempt to attack it. "Haesten was clever," I said.

"Clever?" Steapa asked.

"He persuaded the Northumbrians to attack by saying he'd distract Alfred's army," I explained, "and then he warned Alfred of the Northumbrian attack to make sure he didn't have to fight the West Saxons."

"He has to fight us," Steapa growled.

"Because Alfred is just as clever," I said. Alfred knew Haesten was the greater threat. If Haesten could be defeated then the Northumbrians would lose heart and, in all likelihood, sail away. Ragnar's Northumbrians had to be held at bay, which is why so much of the West Saxon army was in Defnascir, but Alfred had sent his son and twelve hundred of his best men to Beamfleot. He wanted me to weaken Haesten, but he wanted much more than that.

He wanted the Ætheling Edward's reputation to be burnished by the victory. Alfred had not needed to sent the Ætheling. Steapa and his men were indispensable to me, while Edward was a liability, but

Alfred knew his own death could not be too distant and he wanted to be certain that his son succeeded him, and for that he needed to give Edward a warrior's renown. Which is why he had asked me to give Edward my oath and I reflected bitterly that my refusal had not prevented Alfred from manipulating me so that I was here, fighting for the Christians and fighting for Edward.

The Ætheling at last entered the fort, his arrival announced by horn blasts. Men knelt as he rode to the hall and I watched him acknowledge the homage with graceful waves of his right hand. He looked young and slight, and I remembered Ragnar asking if I wanted to be King of Wessex and I could not resist a sudden, bitter laugh. Finan glanced at me curiously. "He'll want us in the hall," Steapa said.

The big hall stank. The servants had shoveled the horse dung to one side, and raked out most of the stale floor-rushes, but the hall still reeked like a latrine and buzzed with fat flies. I had feasted here once, back when the hall was lit by fire and loud with laughter and the memory made me wonder if all the great high-beamed feasting halls were doomed to decay.

There was no dais, so Edward's chair was set on a great rug and next to him was a stool on which Æthelflæd sat. Behind the brother and sister was a dark group of priests. I knew none of them, but they evidently knew me because four of the six churchmen made the sign of the cross when I approached the makeshift throne.

Steapa knelt to the Ætheling, Finan bowed, and I nodded my head. Edward evidently expected more obeisance from me and waited, but when it was plain that I had offered him all I was prepared to give he forced a smile. "You did well," he said in his high voice. There was neither warmth nor conviction in the compliment.

I slapped Steapa's back. "Steapa did well, lord."

"He is a loyal warrior and a good Christian," Edward said, implying that I was neither.

"He's also a big ugly brute," I said, "and he makes Danes shit themselves with fear."

Edward and the priests all bridled at that. Edward was steeling himself to reprove me when Æthelflæd's laughter cut across the hall. Edward looked annoyed at the sound, but composed himself. "I am sorry that the Lord Ælfwold died," he said.

"I share your sorrow, lord."

"My father," he said, "has sent me to capture this nest of heathen pirates." He spoke in the same way that he sat; stiffly. He was horribly conscious of his youth and of his fragile authority, but, like his father, he had intelligent eyes. He was lost in this hall, though. He was frightened of my blood-spattered face, and frightened of most of the older warriors who had been killing Danes when he was still sucking on his wet nurse's tits. "The question," he said, "is how."

"Steapa already has the answer," I said.

Edward looked relieved and Steapa looked alarmed. "Speak, Steapa," Edward said.

Steapa looked at me in fright so I answered for him. "We have to cross the moat and climb the wall," I said, "and we can only do that at low tide, and the Danes know it. They also know we have to do it quickly."

There was silence. I had stated the obvious and that clearly disappointed Edward, but what did he expect? That I would have some sorcerous scheme born from pagan wiles? Or did he believe angels would fly from the Christian heaven and attack the Danes inside the fort? There were only two ways to capture Beamfleot. One was to starve the Danes, and we did not have the time to do that, and the other was to storm the walls. Sometimes, in war, simple is the only answer. It is also likely to be a blood-soaked answer, and all the men in the hall knew it. Some looked at me reproachfully, imagining the horror of trying to scale a high palisade manned by murderous Danes. "So," I went on confidently, "we need to be busy. Weohstan," I turned to him, "your men will patrol the marshes to stop messengers leaving the fort. Beornoth, take Lord Ælfwold's men and threaten the ship-forts at the creek's end. You, lord," I looked at Edward, "your men must start making ladders, and you," I pointed at the six priests, "what are you good for?"

Edward just stared at me in horror and the priests looked offended. "They can pray, Lord Uhtred?" Æthelflæd suggested sweetly.

"Then pray hard," I told them.

There was silence again. Men expected a council of war, and Edward, who was notionally in charge, would have liked the pretense that he was making the decisions, but we did not have time to argue. "Ladders," Edward finally said in a puzzled voice.

"We climb them," I said savagely, "and we need at least forty."

Edward blinked. I could see he was debating whether to slap me down, but then he must have decided that victory at Beamfleot was preferable to making an enemy. He even managed a smile. "They will be made," he said graciously.

"So all we have to do," I said, "is get them across the moat, then use them to climb the wall." Edward's smile faded.

Because even he knew men would die. Too many men.

But there was no other way.

The first problem was crossing the moat, to which end I rode north the next day. I was worried that Haesten would lead his men back to relieve the siege and we sent strong scouting parties west and north to watch for the coming of that army. In the end it never did come. Haesten, it seemed, was confident of Beamfleot's strength and of the courage of its garrison, so instead of trying to destroy us he sent his raiding parties ever farther into Mercia, attacking unwalled towns and villages that had thought themselves safe because they were close to the West Saxon border. The skies over Mercia were palled with smoke.

I rode to Thunresleam and found the priest, Heahberht. I told him what I wanted, and Osferth, who was leading the eighteen men who accompanied me, gave the priest a spare horse. "I'll fall off, lord," Heahberht said nervously, staring with his one eye at the tall stallion.

"You'll be safe," I said. "Just cling on. That horse will look after you."

I had taken Osferth and his men because we were riding north into East Anglia and that was Danish territory. I did not expect trouble. Any Dane who wished to fight the Saxons would already have ridden with Haesten, so those who had remained on their land probably wanted no part of the war, yet even so it was prudent to ride in force. We were just about to go north from the village when Osferth warned me that more horsemen were approaching, and I turned to see them coming from the woods that screened Beamfleot.

My first thought was that Haesten's army must have been seen far to the west and these horsemen rode to warn me, but then one rider raised a dragon banner and I saw it was the flag of the Ætheling Edward. Edward himself was with them, accompanied by a score of warriors and a priest. "I haven't seen much East Anglian territory," he explained his presence awkwardly, "and wish to accompany you."

"You're welcome, lord," I said in a voice that made it amply clear he was not.

"This is Father Coenwulf," Edward introduced the priest who gave me a reluctant nod. He was a pale-skinned man, some ten years or so older than Edward. "Father Coenwulf was my tutor," Edward said with an affectionate tone, "and is now my confessor and friend."

"What did you teach him?" I asked Coenwulf, who made no answer, but just stared at me with indignant and very blue eyes.

"Philosophy," Edward said, "and the writings of the church fathers."

"I learned just one useful lesson as a child," I told him. "Beware the blow that comes under the shield. This is Father Heahberht," I gestured at the one-eyed priest, "and this is the Ætheling Edward," I said to the village priest who almost fell from his horse in terror of meeting such an exalted prince.

Father Heahberht was our guide. I had asked him where there might be ships, and he had said that he had seen two trading ships being hauled from a river to the north less than a week before. "They aren't far away, lord," he had told me. He said the ships belonged to a Danish trader and had been beached for repairs. "But they may not be seaworthy, lord," he added nervously.

"It doesn't matter," I said, "just take us there."

It was a warm, sun-kissed day. We rode through good farmland that Father Heahberht said belonged to a man called Thorstein who had ridden with Haesten into Mercia. Thorstein had done well for himself. His land was well watered, had fine woodlands and healthy orchards. "Where's his hall?" I asked Heahberht.

"We're going there, lord."

"Is this Thorstein a Christian?" Edward wanted to know.

"He says so, lord," Heahberht stammered, blushing. He obviously wanted to say more, but fear meant he could not find the words and he just gazed slack-jawed at the Ætheling. Edward waved the priest ahead of us, but the poor man had no idea how to quicken his horse so Osferth leaned over to take his bridle. They trotted ahead with Heahberht gripping the saddle's pommel for dear life.

Edward grimaced. "A country priest," he said dismissively.

"They do more harm than good," Coenwulf said. "One of our duties, lord, will be to educate the country clergy."

"He wears the short tunic!" Edward observed knowingly. The Pope himself had ordered priests to wear full-length robes, a command Alfred had enthusiastically endorsed.

"Father Heahberht," I said, "is a clever man, and a good one. But he's frightened of you."

"Of me!" Edward asked, "why?"

"Because he's a peasant," I said, "but a peasant who learned to read. Can you even imagine how hard it was for him to become a priest? And all his life he's been pissed on by thegns. So of course he's scared of you. And he wears a short robe because he can't afford a long one, and because he lives in mud and shit, and short robes don't get as filthy as long ones. So how would you feel if you were a peasant who meets a man who might one day be King of Wessex?"

Edward said nothing, but Father Coenwulf pounced. "Might?" he demanded indignantly.

"Might indeed," I said airily. I was goading them, reminding Edward that he had a cousin, Æthelwold, who had more right to the throne than Edward himself, though Æthelwold, Alfred's nephew, was a poor excuse of a man.

My words silenced Edward for a while, but Father Coenwulf was made of sterner stuff. "I was surprised, lord," he broke the silence, "to discover the Lady Æthelflæd here."

"Surprised?" I asked, "why? She's an adventurous lady."

"Her place," Father Coenwulf said, "is with her husband. My lord the Ætheling will agree with me, is that not so, lord?"

I glanced at Edward and saw him redden. "She should not be here," he forced himself to say and I almost laughed aloud. I realized now why he had ridden with us. He was not much interested in seeing a few miles of East Anglia, instead he had come to carry out his father's instructions, and those instructions were to persuade Æthelflæd to her duty. "Why tell me?" I asked the pair.

"You have influence over the lady," Father Coenwulf said grimly.

We had crossed a watershed and were riding down a long and gentle slope. The path was edged with coppiced willows and there were glimpses of water far ahead, silver sheens bright beneath the pale sky. "So," I ignored Coenwulf and looked at Edward, "your father sent you to reprove your sister?"

"It is a Christian duty to remind her of her responsibilities," he answered very stiffly.

"I hear he is recovered from his illness," I said.

"For which God be praised," Coenwulf put in.

"Amen," Edward said.

But Alfred could not live long. He was already an old man, well past forty years, and now he was looking to the future. He was doing what he always did, arranging things, tidying things, trying to impose order on a kingdom beset by enemies. He believed his baleful god would punish Wessex if it were not a godly kingdom, and so he was trying to force Æthelflæd back to her husband, or else, I guessed, to a nunnery. There could be no visible sin in Alfred's family, and that thought inspired me. I looked at Edward again. "Do you know Osferth?" I asked cheerfully. He blushed at that and Father Coenwulf glared as if warning me to take that subject no further.

"You haven't met?" I asked Edward in pretended innocence, then called to Osferth. "Wait for us!"

Father Coenwulf tried to turn Edward's horse away, but I caught hold of the bridle and forced the Ætheling to catch up with his half-brother. "Tell me," I said to Osferth, "how you would make the Mercians fight."

Osferth frowned at the question, wondering just what lay behind it. He glanced at Edward, but did not acknowledge his half-brother, though the resemblance between them was startling. They both had Alfred's long face, hollow cheeks, and thin lips. Osferth's face was harder, but he had lived harder too. His father, ashamed of his own bastard, had tried to make Osferth a priest, but Osferth had turned himself into a warrior, a trade to which he brought his father's intelligence. "The Mercians can fight as well as anyone," Osferth said cautiously. He knew I was playing some game and was trying to detect it and so, unseen by either Edward or Coenwulf who both rode on my left, I cupped a hand to indicate a breast and Osferth, despite having inherited his father's almost complete lack of humor, had to resist an amused smile. "They need leadership," he said confidently.

"Then we thank God for the Lord Æthelred," Father Coenwulf said, refusing to look directly at Osferth.

"The Lord Æthelred," I said savagely, "couldn't lead a wet whore to a dry bed."

"But the Lady Æthelflæd is much loved in Mercia," Osferth said, now playing his part to perfection. "We saw that at Fearnhamme. It was the Lady Æthelflæd who inspired the Mercians."

"You'll need the Mercians," I told Edward. "If you become king," I went on, stressing the "if" to keep him unbalanced, "the Mercians will protect your northern frontier. And the Mercians don't love Wessex. They may fight for you, but they don't love you. They were a proud country once, and they don't like being told what to do by Wessex. But they do love one West Saxon. And you'd shut her up in a convent?"

"She is a married . . ." Father Coenwulf began.

"Oh, shut your mouth," I snapped at him. "Your king used his daughter to bring me south, and here I am, and I'll stay here so long as Æthelflæd asks. But don't think I'm here for you, or for your god, or for your king. If you have plans for Æthelflæd then you had better count me as a part of them."

Edward was too embarrassed to meet my eyes. Father Coenwulf was angry, but dared not speak, while Osferth grinned at me. Father Heahberht had listened to the conversation with a shocked expression, but now found his timid voice. "The hall is that way, lords," he said, pointing, and we turned down a track rutted by cart wheels and I saw a reed-thatched roof showing between some heavy-leaved elm trees. I kicked ahead of Edward, to see that Thorstein's home was built on a low ridge above the river. There was a village beyond the hall, its small houses straggling along the bank where dozens of fires smoked. "They dry herring here?" I asked the priest.

"And they make salt, lord."

"Is there a palisade?"

"Yes, lord."

The palisade was unmanned and the gates lay open. Thorstein had taken his warriors with Haesten, leaving only a handful of older men to protect his family and lands, and those men knew better than to put up a fight they must lose. Instead a steward welcomed us with a bowl of water. Thorstein's gray-haired wife watched from the hall door, but when I turned to her she stepped back into the shadows and the door slammed shut.

The palisade enclosed the hall, three barns, a cattle shed, and a pair of elm-timbered slipways where the two ships had been hauled high above the tideline. They were trading ships, their fat bellies patched pale where carpenters were nailing new oak strakes. "Your master is a shipbuilder?" I asked the steward.

"They've always built ships here, lord," he said humbly, meaning that Thorstein had stolen the shipyard from a Saxon.

I turned on Osferth. "Make sure the women aren't molested," I ordered, "and find a wagon and draft horses." I looked back to the steward. "We need ale and food."

"Yes, lord."

There was a long low building beside the slipways and I went to it. Sparrows quarreled beneath the thatch. Once inside I had to let my eyes adjust to the gloom, but then I saw what I was seeking. Masts and spars and sails. I ordered my men to carry all the spars and sails out to the wagon, then walked to the shed's open end to watch the river swirl past. The tide was falling, exposing long steep slicks of mud.

"Why spars and sails?" Edward asked from behind me. He was alone. "The steward brought mead," he said awkwardly. He was frightened of me, but he was making a great effort to be friendly.

"Tell me," I said, "what happened when you tried to capture Torneie."

"Torneie?" Edward sounded confused.

"You attacked Harald on his island," I said, "and you failed. I want to know why." I had heard the story from Offa, the dog-man who carried his news between the kingdoms, but I had not asked anyone who was there. All I knew was that the assault on Harald's fugitives had ended in defeat and with a great loss of men.

He frowned. "It was . . ." He stopped, shaking his head, perhaps remembering the men floundering through the mud to Harald's palisade. "We never got close," he said bitterly.

"Why not?"

He frowned. "There were stakes in the river. The mud was thick."

"You think Beamfleot will be any easier?" I demanded, and saw the answer on his face. "So who led the attack on Torneie?" I asked.

"Æthelred and I," he said.

"You led?" I asked pointedly. "You were in front?"

He stared at me, bit his lower lip, then looked embarrassed. "No."

"Your father made certain you were protected?" I asked, and he nodded. "What about Lord Æthelred?" I went on, "did he lead?"

"He's a brave man," Edward said defiantly.

"You haven't answered me."

"He went with his men," Edward said evasively, "but thank God he escaped the rout."

"So why should you be King of Wessex?" I asked him brutally.

"I," he said, then ran out of words and just looked at me with a pained expression. He had come into the shed trying to be friendly and I was raking him over.

"Because your father's the king?" I suggested. "In the past we've chosen the best man to be king, not the one who happened to come from between the legs of a king's wife." He frowned, offended and uncertain, voiceless. "Tell me why I shouldn't make Osferth king," I said harshly. "He's Alfred's eldest son."

"If there is no rule to the succession," he said carefully, "then the death of a king will lead to chaos."

"Rules," I sneered, "how you love rules. So because Osferth's mother was a servant he can't be king?"

"No," Edward found the courage to answer, "he can't."

"Luckily for you," I said, "he doesn't want to be king. At least I don't think he does. But you do?" I waited and eventually he responded with an almost imperceptible nod. "And you have the advantage," I went on, "of having been born between a pair of royal legs, but you still need to prove you deserve the kingship." He stared at me, saying nothing. "You want to be king," I went on, "so you must show you deserve it. You lead. You do what you didn't do at Torneie, what my cousin didn't do either. You go first into the attack. You can't expect men to die for you unless they see you're willing to die for them."

He nodded to that. "Beamfleot?" he asked, unable to disguise his fear at the prospect of that assault.

"You want to be king?" I asked. "Then you lead the assault. Now come with me, and I'll show you how."

I took him outside and led him to the top of the river bank. The tide was almost out, leaving a slippery slope of gleaming mud at least twelve feet high. "How," I asked him, "do we get up a slope like that?"

He did not answer, but just frowned as though considering the problem and then, to his utter astonishment, I shoved him hard over the edge. He cried aloud as he lost his footing, then he slipped and floundered on his royal arse all the way down to the water where at last he managed to stand unsteadily. He was mud-smeared and indignant. Father Coenwulf evidently thought I was trying to drown the Ætheling, for he rushed to my side where he stared down at the prince. "Draw your sword," I told Edward, "and climb that bank."

He drew his sword and took some tentative steps, but the slick mud defeated him so that he slithered back every time. "Try harder," I snarled. "Try really hard! There are Danes at the top of the bank and you have to kill them. So climb!"

"What are you doing?" Coenwulf demanded of me.

"Making a king," I told him quietly, then looked back to Edward. "Climb, you bastard! Get up here!"

He could not do it, cumbered as he was with heavy mail and with his long sword. He tried to crawl up the bank, but still he slid back. "That's what it's going to be like," I told him, "climbing out of the moat at Beamfleot!"

He stared up at me, filthy and wet. "Do we make bridges?" he suggested.

"How do we make a bridge with a hundred farting Danes throwing spears at us?" I demanded. "Now come on! Climb!" He tried again, and again he failed. Then, as his men and mine watched from the top of the bank, Edward gritted his teeth and hurled himself at the greasy mud for one last determined attempt, and this time he managed to stay on the slope. He used his sword as a stick, inching higher and the men cheered. He kept slipping back, but his determination was obvious, and every small step was applauded. The heir to Alfred's throne was plastered with mud and his precious dignity was gone, but he was suddenly enjoying himself. He was grinning. He kicked his boots into the mud, hauled on the sword, and at last managed to scramble over the bank's edge. He stood, smiling at the cheers, and even Father Coenwulf was beaming with pride. "We have to climb the moat's bank to reach the fort," I told him, "and it will be just as steep and slippery as this slope. We're never going to make it. The Danes will be raining arrows and spears. The bed of the moat will be thick with blood and bodies. We're all going to die there."

"The sails," Edward said, understanding.

"Yes," I said, "the sails." I ordered Osferth to unfold one of the three sails we were stealing. It took six men to unwrap the great sheet of stiff, salt-caked cloth. Mice scampered out of the folds, but once it was spread I had men drape the sail down the mudbank. The sail itself offered no footholds because sailcloth is fragile, but ropes are sewn into it and thus every sail is a crisscross of reinforcing ropes, and those latticed lines would be our ladders. I took Edward's elbow and he and I walked down the sail to the water's edge. "Now," I said, "try again. Full speed. Race me!"

He won. He ran at the bank and his boots caught on the sail ropes and he reached the top without using his hands once. He grinned with triumph as I came behind, then he had a sudden idea. "All of you!" he called to his bodyguard. "Down to the river and climb back up!"

They were suddenly enjoying themselves. All the men, mine as well as Edward's, wanted to try the network of sail ropes. There were too many men, and eventually the sail slid down the bank, which is why I was taking the spars. I would thread the lattice of ropes onto the spars, then lash the spars into place so that the makeshift rope ladder would be stiffened by the spruce frame and, I hoped, stay in place. On that day we just pegged the sail to the bank and ran races, which Edward, to his evident delight, won repeatedly. He even found the courage to talk briefly with Osferth, though they discussed nothing more important than the weather, which the half-brothers evidently found agreeable. After a while I ordered the men to stop scrambling up the sail, which had to be laboriously refolded, but I had proved it would work as a means of climbing out of the fort's moat. That would just leave the wall to cross, and those of us who did not die in the moat would almost certainly die on the ledge of land beneath the wall.

The steward brought me a small horn cup of mead. I took it and for some reason, as my hand closed on the cup, the bee sting, which I had thought long vanished, began to itch again. The swelling was entirely gone, but for a moment the itching was back and I stared at my hand. I did not move, I just stared, and Osferth became worried. "What is it, lord?"

"Get me Father Heahberht," I said and, when the priest arrived, I asked him who made the mead.

"He's a strange man, lord," Heahberht said.

"I don't care if he's got a tail and tits, just take me to him."

The sails and spars were loaded on the wagon and escorted back to the old fort, but I took a half-dozen men and rode with Heahberht to a village he called Hocheleia. It looked a peaceful and half-forgotten place, just a straggle of cottages surrounded by big willow trees. There was a small church, marked by a wooden cross nailed to the eave. "Skade didn't burn this church?" I asked Father Heahberht.

"Thorstein protected these folk, lord," Heahberht told me.

"But he didn't protect Thunresleam?"

"These are Thorstein's people, lord. They belong to him. They work his land."

"So who's the Lord of Thunresleam?"

"Whoever is in the fort," he said bitterly. "This way, lord." He led me past a duck pond and into a thicket of bushes where a small cottage, thatched so deep that it looked more like a pile of straw than a dwelling, stood in the trees' shadows. "The man is called Brun, lord."

"Brun?"

"Just Brun. Some say he's mad, lord."

Brun crawled from his cottage. He had to crawl to get beneath the thatch's edge. He half stood, saw my mail coat and golden arm rings, and fell back to his knees and scrabbled with dirt-crusted hands in the earth. He mumbled something I did not hear. A woman then emerged from beneath the thatch and knelt beside Brun and the two of them made whimpering noises as they bobbed their heads. Their hair was long, matted and tangled. Father Heahberht told them what we wanted and Brun grunted something, then abruptly stood. He was a tiny man, no taller than the dwarves that are said to live underground. His hair was so thick that I could not see his eyes. He pulled his woman to her feet, and she was no taller than him and certainly no prettier, then the pair of them gabbled at Heahberht, but their speech was so garbled that I could hardly understand a word. "He says we must go to the back of the house," Heahberht said.

"You can understand them?"

"Well enough, lord."

I left my escort in the lane, tied our two horses to a hornbeam, then followed the diminutive couple through thick weeds to where, half hidden by grass, was what I sought. Rows of hives. Bees were busy in the warm air, but they ignored us, going to and from the cone-shaped hives that appeared to be fashioned from baked mud. Brun, a sudden fondness in his voice, was stroking one hive. "He says the bees talk to him, lord," Heahberht told me, "and he talks back."

Bees crawled up Brun's bare arms and he muttered to them. "What do they tell him?" I asked.

"What happens in the world, lord. And he tells them he's sorry."

"For the world's happenings?"

"Because to get the honey for the mead, lord, he must break the hives open, and then the bees die. He buries them, he says, and says prayers over their graves."

Brun was crooning at his bees, singing like a mother to her infants. "I've only seen straw hives," I said. "Maybe straw hives don't need to be broken? Maybe the bees can live?"

Brun must have understood what I said for he turned angrily and spoke fast. "He doesn't approve of skeps, lord," Heahberht translated, speaking of the woven straw hives. "He makes his hives the old-fashioned way, out of plaited hazel twigs and cow dung. He says the honey is sweeter."

"Tell him what I want," I said, "and tell him I'll pay well."

And so the bargain was struck and I rode back to the old fort on the hill and thought there was a chance. Just a chance. Because the bees had spoken.

That night, and the following two nights, I sent men down the long hill to the new fort. I led them the first two nights, leaving the old fort after dark. Men carried the sails, which had been cut into two, then each half sewn to a pair of spars so that we had six wide rope ladders. When we attacked in earnest we would have to go into the creek, unfurl the six wide ladders, and lay them against the farther bank, then men would have to climb the latticed ropes carrying real ladders that must be laid against the wall.

But for three nights we just feigned attacks. We went close to the moat, we shouted and our archers, of whom we had just over a hundred, shot arrows at the Danes. They, in turn, shot arrows back and hurled spears that thumped into the mud. They also threw fire-brands to light the night and, when they saw we were not attempting to cross the moat, I heard men shouting orders to stop throwing the spears.

I learned the walls were well manned. Haesten had left a large garrison, so many that some Danes were not needed in the fort at all, but instead guarded the ships drawn up on Caninga's shore.

I did not go down the hill on the third night. I let Steapa lead that feint while I watched from the high fort's walls. Just after dark my men brought a wagon from Hocheleia and in it were eight hives. Brun had told us that the best time to seal a hive was at dusk, and that evening he had closed up the entrances with plugs of mud mixed with cow dung that now slowly hardened. I put my ear next to one hive and heard a strange humming vibration.

"The bees will live till tomorrow night?" Edward asked me.

"They don't have to," I said, "because we're attacking in tomorrow's dawn."

"Tomorrow!" he said, unable to hide his surprise, which pleased me. By making feint attacks during the early darkness I wanted to persuade the Danes that we would be launching our real attack shortly after dusk. Instead I would go at them at daybreak next morning, but I hoped that Skade and her men were already convinced, like Edward, that I planned an attack at nightfall.

"Tomorrow morning," I said, "and we leave tonight, in the dark."

"Tonight?" Edward asked, still astonished.

"Tonight."

He made the sign of the cross. Æthelflæd who, with Steapa, was the only other person I had told of my plans, came to stand beside me and put her hand through my arm. Edward seemed to shiver at the sight of our affection, then forced a smile. "Pray for me, sister," he said.

"I always have," she replied.

She looked at him steadily and he met her gaze for an instant, then looked at me. He started to speak, but nervousness made the first word an incoherent croak. He tried again. "You would not give me your oath, Lord Uhtred," he said.

"No, lord."

"But my sister has it?"

Æthelflæd's arm tightened on mine. "She has my sworn loyalty, lord," I said.

"Then I have no need of your oath," Edward said with a smile.

That was generous of him and I bowed in acknowledgment. "You don't need my oath, lord," I said, "but your men need your encouragement tonight. Speak to them. Inspire them."

There would be little sleep that night. It took men time to prepare for battle. It was a time of fear, a time when the imagination makes the enemy seem ever more fearsome. Some men, a few, fled the fort and sought shelter in the woods, but they were very few. The rest sharpened swords and axes. I would not let men feed the fires, because I did not want the Danes to see anything different about this night, and so most weapons were honed in the dark. Men pulled on boots, mail, and helmets. They made poor jokes. Some just sat with bowed heads, but they listened when Edward spoke to them. He went from group to group and I remembered how uninspiring his father's first speech had been before the great victory at Ethandun. Edward was not much better, but he had an earnestness that was convincing, and men murmured approval when he promised that he would be the first man in the attack.

"You must keep him alive," Father Coenwulf told me sternly.

"Isn't that the responsibility of your god?" I asked.

"His father will never forgive you if Edward dies."

313

"He has another son," I said flippantly.

"Edward is a good man," Coenwulf said angrily, "and he'll make a good king."

I agreed with that. I had not thought so before, but I had begun to like Edward. He had a willingness about him, and I did not doubt he would prove brave. He feared, of course, like all men fear, but he had kept those fears behind the fence of his teeth. He was determined to prove himself an heir, and that meant going to the place of death. He had not balked at that idea, and for that I respected him. "He'll make a good king," I told Coenwulf, "if he proves himself. And you know he must prove himself."

The priest paused, then nodded. "But look after him," he pleaded.

"I've told Steapa to look after him," I told Coenwulf, "and I can't do better than that."

Father Pyrlig, dressed in his rusted mail, a sword at his waist and with an ax and a shield slung from his shoulders, came from the dark. "My men are ready," he said. I had given him thirty men whose job was to carry the hives down the dark hill and across the moat.

I looked eastward. There was no sign of any new light there, but I sensed the short night was coming to its close. I touched Thor's hammer. "Time to go," I said.

Steapa's men were making a racket at the hill's foot, a noise to distract the Danes as hundreds of men now left the fort and, in the clouded darkness, went down the steep slope. In front were Edward's men carrying the ladders. I saw the torches flaring at the moat's edge and the flicker of arrow feathers whipping up toward the ramparts. The air smelled of salt and shellfish. I thought of Æthelflæd's farewell kiss, of her sudden and impetuous embrace, and the fears surged in me. It sounded simple. Cross a moat, place the ladders on the small muddy ledge between moat and wall, climb the ladders. Die.

There was no order to our advance. Men found their own way down the hill and their leaders called softly to assemble them where the charred ruins of the village offered some small concealment. We were close enough to hear the Danes jeering as Steapa's men withdrew. The torches that had been thrown to illuminate the ditch smoldered low. Now, I hoped, the Danes would stand down. Men would go to their beds and to their women, while we waited in the dark where we touched our weapons and our amulets and listened to the ripple of water as the tide drained from the wide marshes. Weohstan was out in the tussocked swamps and I had ordered him to display his men to the fort's west in hope that some defenders would be drawn that way. I had two hundred other men to the east, ready to attack the beached ships at the creek's farther end. Those men were commanded by Finan. I did not like losing Finan as my shield-neighbor, but I needed a warrior to seal the Danish escape, and there was no man so fierce in battle, nor so clearheaded, as the Irishman.

But neither Weohstan nor Finan could show themselves till dawn. Nothing could happen till dawn. There was a slight drizzle coming cold on a west wind. Priests were praying. Osferth's men, carrying the furled sails, crouched among tall nettles at the edge of the village, just a hundred paces from the moat's nearer bank. I waited with Osferth, a yard or so in front of Edward who spoke not a word, but just clutched the golden cross that hung at his neck. Steapa had found us and waited with the Ætheling. My helmet was cold on my ears and neck, and my mail coat felt clammy.

I heard Danes speaking. They had sent men to collect the spears after each of our feint attacks, and I supposed that was what they were now doing in the small light of the dying torches. Then I saw them, just shadows in shadows, and I knew the dawn was almost upon us as the gray light of death spread behind us like a stain on the world's rim. I turned to Edward. "Now, lord," I said to him.

He stood, a young man at battle's edge. For a heartbeat he could not find his voice, then he drew his long sword. "For God and for Wessex," he shouted, "come with me!"

And so the fight for Beamfleot began.

SIX

For a moment everything is as you imagined it, then it changes, and the details stand out so stark. Details of irrelevant things. Perhaps it is the knowledge that these small things may be the last you will ever see in this life that makes them so memorable. I recall a star flickering like a guttering candle between the clouds to the west, the clatter of arrows in the wooden quiver of a running archer, the shine of wolf-light on the Temes to the south, the pale feathers of all the arrows lodged ragged in the fort's wooden wall, and the loose links of Steapa's mail jangling and dangling from the hem of his coat as he ran to Edward's right. I remember a black and white dog running with us, a frayed rope knotted about his neck. It seemed to me we ran in silence, but it could not have been silent. Eight hundred men were running toward the fort as the sun touched the earth's rim with silver.

"Archers!" Beornoth shouted, "archers! To me!"

A few Danes were still collecting spears. One watched us in disbelief, his arms clutching a bundle of ash shafts, then he panicked, dropped the weapons, and ran. A horn sounded from the ramparts.

We had divided our men into troops, and each one had a purpose and a leader. Beornoth commanded the archers who assembled on our left, immediately in front of the bridge pilings that stood gaunt in the moat. Those archers were to harass the Danes on the ramparts, to pour arrows at them, to force them to duck as they tried to repel us with spears, axes, and swords. Osferth commanded the fifty

316

men whose job was to place the sailcloth ladders in the moat, and behind him came Egwin, a veteran West Saxon, whose one hundred men would carry the climbing ladders to the wall. The rest of the troops were to make the assault. As soon as the ladder carriers were across the moat the attacking troops were to follow, climb the ladders and trust in whatever god they had prayed to through the night. I had ordered the men into troops, and Alfred, who loved lists and order, would have approved, but I knew how soon such careful plans collapsed under the shock of reality.

The horn was challenging the dawn and the fort's defenders were appearing on the ramparts. The men who had been collecting spears climbed the moat's far side with the help of a rope lashed to a piling by the fort's entrance, but one of them had the sense to slash through the rope before running into the fort. The great gates closed behind him. Our archers were shooting, but I knew their arrows would do small damage against mail coats and steel helmets. Yet it would force the Danes to use shields. It would cumber them, and then I saw Osferth's men vanish into the moat and I bellowed at the following troops to wait. "Stop and wait!" The last thing I needed was a mass of men trapped in the moat's bed, churning about under a hail of spears and impeding Osferth's men. Better to let those men do their job and Egwin's after them.

The bottom of the moat had sharpened stakes hidden beneath the low water, but Osferth's men found them easy enough to haul from the soft mud. The latticed sails were unrolled on the opposite bank and their spars were anchored by spears that were thrust deep into the mud. A bucket of burning charcoal was thrown from the ramparts. I saw the bright fire fall then die in the wet muck below. The fire hurt no one and I suspected a Dane had panicked and emptied the pail too early. The dog was barking at the moat's edge. "Ladders!" Osferth bellowed, and Egwin's men charged forward as Osferth's warriors hurled spears up at the high wall. I watched approvingly as the ladder carriers scaled the steep moat bank, then shouted for the assault troops to follow me to the newly placed ladders.

Except it was not like that. I try to tell folk what a battle is like, and the telling comes out halting and lame. After a battle, when the fear has subsided, we exchange stories and out of all those tales we make a pattern of the fight, but in battle it is all confusion. Yes, we did cross the moat, and the rope netting of the spread sails worked, at least for a while, and the ladders reached the Danish wall, but I have left out so much. The welter of men thrashing in the ebbing tide, the fall of heavy spears, blood dark in dark water, screams, the sense of not knowing what happened, of desperation, of hearing the solid thumps of blades hurled from the parapet, the smaller sounds of arrows striking home, the shouts of men who did not know what was happening, men who feared death, men who bellowed at other men to bring ladders or to haul a spar back up the muddy bank. And then there was the mud as thick as hoof glue and just as sticky. Slick and slippery mud, men covered in mud and streaked with blood and dying in mud and always the Danes shrieking insults from the sky. The screams of men dying. Men calling for help, crying for their mothers, weeping on their way to the grave.

In the end it is the small things that win a battle. You can throw thousands of men against a wall, and most will fail, or they will cower beyond the ditch, or crouch in the water, and it is the few, the brave and the desperate, who fight through their fear. I watched a man carry a ladder and slam it against the wall and climb with a drawn sword, and a Dane poised his heavy spear and waited. I shouted a warning, but then the spear was driven straight down and the blade cut through the helmet and the man shook on the ladder and fell backward, blood sudden in the dawn and a second man thrust him out of the way, screamed defiance as he climbed and slashed a long-hafted ax at the spearman. At that moment, as the sun flooded the new day, it was all chaos. I had done my best to order the attack, but the troops were now mixed together. Some were standing up to their waists in the moat's water, and all were helpless because we could not get the ladders to stay against the wall. The Danes, though they were dazzled by the new sun, were knocking the ladders aside with their heavy war axes. Some ladders, their rungs made from green wood, broke, yet still brave men tried to climb the high palisade. One of the sailcloth ladders slid back and

I watched men drag it back into place as the spears fell about them. More fire was thrown from the ramparts, the flare of it lighting helmets and blades, but men extinguished the embers by rolling in mud. Spears thudded into shields.

I picked up a fallen ladder and threw it against the wall and climbed, but a man cannot climb a ladder holding sword and shield, so my shield was slung on my back and I had to snatch at the rungs one by one with my left hand while holding Serpent-Breath in my right and a Dane caught hold of her blade with a gloved hand and tried to pull her from my grasp, and I ripped her backward and lost my balance and fell onto a corpse, and then Edward began to climb the same ladder. He wore a helmet circled with gold and surmounted by a plume of swan's feathers that made him a target and I could see the Danes waiting to snatch him over the rampart so they could take his fine armor, but then Steapa knocked the ladder sideways so that the Ætheling fell into the mud.

"Dear God," I heard Edward say in a mild voice, as though he had spilled some milk or ale, and that made me laugh. The handle of a thrown ax banged on my helmet. I turned, picked up the weapon, and slung it at the faces above me, but it went wide. Father Coenwulf helped Edward to his feet. "You shouldn't be here," I snarled at the priest, but he ignored me. He was a brave man for he wore no armor and carried no weapons. Steapa covered Edward with his huge shield as the spears hurtled down. Somehow Father Coenwulf survived the blades. He held a crucifix toward the jeering Danes and shouted a curse at them.

"Bring ladders here!" a voice bellowed. "Bring them here!" It was Father Pyrlig. "Ladders!" he shouted again, then he took a hive from one of his men and turned to the wall. "Have some honey!" he roared at the Danes and tossed the hive upward.

The wall was around ten feet high and it took strength to throw that sealed hive up over the parapet. The Danes cannot have known what the hive was, perhaps they mistook it for a boulder, though they surely knew no man could throw a boulder that far. I saw a sword slash at the hive, then it disappeared over the parapet. "Another!" Pyrlig shouted.

The first hive must have landed on the fighting platform. And it must have broken.

The hives were sealed. Brun had waited till the cool of the evening, when all the bees had returned home, and then he had closed off the entrances with mud and dung. Now the first hive's shell, which was nothing but dried cow dung braced with hazel twigs, split like an eggshell.

And the bees came out.

Pyrlig threw a second hive and another man hurled a third. One failed to cross the parapet and fell back to the mud where, miraculously, it did not shatter. Two others were floating in the moat. I never did discover what happened to the rest of the hives, but the first two were sufficient.

Bees began to do our work. Thousands and thousands of angry, confused bees spread among the Danish defenders and I heard sudden shouts of startled pain. Men were being stung on their faces and hands, and the small distraction was all we needed. Pyrlig was bellowing at men to get the ladders set. Edward placed a ladder himself and tried to climb it, but Steapa thrust him aside and went first. I climbed another.

I cannot tell you how the fort at Beamfleot was taken, because I can recall nothing but the chaos. Chaos and bee stings. I do know that Steapa reached the top of the ladder and cleared a space by swinging a war ax so wildly that the blade very nearly slashed through my wolf-crested helmet, and then he was over the parapet and using the ax with murderous efficiency. Edward followed. Bees flickered all around him.

"Shout at your men," I told him, "tell them to join you!"

He looked wild-eyed at me, then he understood. "For Wessex!" he shouted from the wall.

"For Mercia!" I bellowed, and now men were joining us fast. I did not feel the bee stings, though later I discovered I had been stung at least a dozen times, but we had been expecting to be stung, while the Danes were taken by surprise. They recovered fast enough. I heard a woman's voice screaming at them to kill us, and I knew

Skade was close by. A group came along the platform and I faced them with shield and sword, took an ax strike on the shield and gouged Serpent-Breath into the man's knee, and Cerdic was with me, and Steapa came to my left and we were screaming like demons as we forced our way along the wall's wooden platform. A spear struck my helmet, knocking it askew. The sun was still showing beneath the clouds, casting a long-shadowed, dazzling brilliance, and its light flashed from sword-blade and ax-edge and spear-point, and I was shoving the shield into the Danes, stabbing Serpent-Breath past its edge, and Steapa was howling and using his massive strength to thrust the defenders aside, and everywhere, everywhere, were bees. A Dane tried to kill me with an ax blow that I took on my shield and I remember his open mouth, yellow stumps of teeth and bees crawling on his tongue. Edward, just behind me, killed that Dane with a sword thrust into his mouth so that the bees were washed out by the gush of blood. Someone had fetched the dragon banner of Wessex and was waving it from the captured parapet, and men were cheering as they crossed the moat and climbed the remaining ladders.

I had turned left at the wall's top and was fighting my way along the narrow platform, and Steapa had understood why, and he did most to clear the defenders in front of us so we could reach the larger platform that stood above the gate. And there we made our shield wall, and there we fought against the Danes as Pyrlig and his men used their axes on the big gate.

I must have shouted at the Danes, though what I cannot tell now. The usual insults. And the Danes fought back with a wild ferocity, but now we had our best warriors on the wall and more were coming all the time, so many that some jumped down into the fort and the fighting began there. One man kicked the shattered remains of a hive down into the fort and more bees swarmed out, but I was above the gate, protected now by the corpses of Danes who had tried to evict us. They still came. Their best weapons were heavy spears that they lunged over the corpse-barrier, but our shields were stout. "We need to get down to the gate!" I shouted at Steapa.

Osferth heard me. It had been Osferth who leaped from the gate's top when we had defended Lundene, and now he leaped again. There were other Saxons inside the fort, but they were horribly outnumbered and were dying fast. Osferth did not care. He jumped to the ground just inside the gate. He sprawled for a moment, then was on his feet and shouting. "Alfred! Alfred! Alfred!"

I thought it was a strange war cry, especially from a man who resented his natural father as much as Osferth, but it worked. Other West Saxons leaped to join Osferth who was fending off two Danes with his shield and hacking his sword at two others.

"Alfred!" Another man took up the shout, then Edward gave a great scream and leaped off the rampart to join his half-brother. "Alfred!"

"Protect the Ætheling," I shouted.

Steapa, who regarded his first duty as keeping Edward alive, jumped down. I stayed on the rampart with Cerdic because we had to stop the Danes from recapturing the stretch of wall where our ladders were set. My shield was battered with spears. The linden wood was splintering, but the corpses at our feet were an obstacle and more than one Dane stumbled on the bodies to add his own to the pile. Still they came. A man started clearing the bodies away, tipping them down inside the fort, and I lunged Serpent-Breath into his armpit. Another Dane thrust a spear at me. I took the thrust on my shield and sliced Serpent-Breath back at the grimacing face framed by a bright steel helmet, but the man twisted aside. I saw him glance down and knew he was thinking of leaping down to attack my men below and I stepped onto a corpse and stabbed Serpent-Breath under his shield, twisting her as she tore into the flesh of his upper thigh, and he slammed his shield at me, then Cerdic was beside me and his ax chopped into the spearman's shoulder. My shield was heavy with the weight of two spears that were lodged in the wood. I tried to shake them off, then ducked as a huge Dane, bellowing curses, charged me with an ax that he swung at my helmet. He crashed bodily into my shield, helpfully dislodging the spears, and Sihtric split the man's helmet with an ax. I remember seeing blood drip from the rim of my shield, then I hurled the dying man off. The man was shaking as he died. I rammed Serpent-Breath over his body and the blade jarred on a Danish shield. Below me I heard the swelling shouts. "Alfred!" they bellowed, then "Edward! Edward!"

Steapa was worth any three men and he was killing with his huge strength and his uncanny sword-craft, but he had help now. More and more men leaped down to make a shield wall just inside the closed gate. Osferth and Edward were shield-neighbors. Father Coenwulf, who was determined to stay close to the Ætheling, had leaped down and he now turned and lifted the gate's locking bar. For a moment he could not push the gate open because Pyrlig's axmen were still chopping at its huge timbers, then they heard Coenwulf's shouts that they should stop. And so the gates opened and, under the rising sun, and beneath the smoke and amidst the swarming bees, we took death to Beamfleot.

The Danes had been surprised by our attack. They had thought Steapa's men were withdrawing in the dawn, and instead we had assaulted them, but the surprise had not lessened their resolve, nor had it given us any great advantage. They had recovered fast, they had defended the wall stoutly, and if we had not sent the bees to join the fight they would surely have repulsed us. But a man being stung by a swarm of enraged bees cannot fight properly, and so we had been given that small chance to reach the parapet, and now we had opened the gate and Saxons were scrambling across the moat and charging into the fort, and the Danes, sensing disaster, broke.

I have seen it so often. A man will fight like a hero, he will make widows and orphans, he will give the poets a challenge to find new words to describe his achievements, and then, quite suddenly, the spirit fails. Defiance becomes terror. Danes who, a moment before, would have been dreadful foemen, became desperate seekers for safety. They fled.

There were only two places they could go. Some, the less fortunate, retreated along the fort to the buildings which filled its western end, while most jostled through a gate in the long southern wall which led to a wooden quay built on the creek's bank. Even at low tide the creek was too deep for a man to cross on foot and there was no bridge; instead a ship was tethered athwart the channel and the Danes were scrambling over its rowing benches to reach Caninga's shore where a mass of men who had played no part in the fort's defense waited. I sent Steapa to clear those men away and he led Alfred's housecarls across the makeshift bridge, but the Danes were in no mood to face him. They fled.

A few Danes, very few, leaped from the southern and western ramparts to wade the ditches, but Weohstan's horsemen were in the marsh and they gave short and brutal ends to those fugitives. Many more Danes stayed inside the fort, retreating to its farther end behind a ragged shield wall that broke apart under a flail of Saxon blades. Women and children screamed. Dogs howled. Most of the women and children were on Caninga, and they were already demanding that their men take to their ships. A Dane's ultimate safety is his ship. When all goes wrong a man puts back to sea and lets the Fates take him to another opportunity. But most of the Danish ships were beached because there were simply too many vessels to moor in the narrow channel. The men on Caninga ran from Steapa's attack. Some waded into the creek to board the floating ships, but it was then that Finan struck. He had waited until the men guarding the channel's eastern end were distracted by the evident disaster unfolding to the west, and then he had led his West Saxons, all of them from Alfred's own household troops, across the mudflats. "The fools had only raised the ship's flank on the seaward side," he told me later, "so we attacked the other. It was easy."

I doubted that. He lost eighteen men to their graves and another thirty were gravely wounded, but he took the ship. He could not cross the creek, nor block the channel, but he was where I wanted him to be. And we were in the fort.

Howling Saxons were taking revenge for the smoke above Mercia. They were massacring the Danes. Men trying to protect their families shouted that they surrendered and instead were chopped down by ax and sword. Most of the women and children ran to the big hall, and it was there that the vast plunder sent back by Haesten's men was collected.

I had sailed to Frisia to find a treasure hall and instead I found it in Beamfleot. I found leather sacks bulging with coins, crucifixes of silver, pyxes of gold, heaps of iron, ingots of bronze, piles of pelts, I found a hoard. The hall was dark. A few shafts of sunlight came through the small windows of the eastern gable that was hung with the horns of a bull, but otherwise the only light came from the fire burning in the central hearth and around which the treasure had been heaped. It was on display. It told the Danes of Beamfleot that Haesten, their lord, would be a gift-giver. The men who had given Haesten their allegiance would become rich, and they only had to come into this hall to see the proof. They could stare at that shining hoard and see new ships and new lands. It was the hoard of Mercia, only instead of being guarded by a dragon, it was protected by Skade.

And she was angrier than any dragon. I think at that moment she was possessed by the furies who had given her a madness that was terrible. She was standing on the treasure heap, her black hair unhelmeted and tangled to wild strands. She was screaming challenges. A black cloak hung from her shoulders, beneath which she wore a mail coat, and over which she had draped as many gold chains as she had been able to scoop from the plunder. Behind her, on the high dais where a great table stood, was a huddle of women and children. I saw Haesten's wife there, and his two sons, but they were as scared of Skade as they were of us.

Skade's shrieking howls had stopped my men. They were half filling the hall, but her fury had cowed them. They had killed a score of Danes, hacking them down onto the rush-covered floor, which was soaked with fresh blood, but now they just gazed at the woman who cursed them. I pushed through them, Serpent-Breath red in my hand, and Skade saw me and pointed her own sword-blade toward me. "The traitor," she spat, "the oath-breaker!"

I bowed to her. "Queen of a marsh," I sneered.

"You promised!" she screamed at me, then her eyes widened in surprise, a surprise that was instantly overtaken by fury. "Is that her?" she demanded.

Æthelflæd had come to the hall. She had no business there. I had told her to watch and wait at the old high fort, but as soon as she saw our men crossing the ramparts she had insisted on coming down the hill. Now the men parted for her, and for the four Mercian warriors who had been deputed to guard her. She wore a pale blue dress, very simple, its skirt wet from crossing the creek. Over it she had a linen cloak and around her neck was a silver crucifix, yet she looked like a queen. She wore no gold, and her dress and cloak were mud-smeared, yet she glowed, and Skade looked from Æthelflæd to me and screamed like a dying vixen. Then, lithe and sudden, she leaped from the treasure heap and, her mouth a rictus of hate, lunged with the sword at Æthelflæd.

I simply stepped in front of her. Her sword slid from the iron rim of my battered shield and I thrust the iron boss hard forward. The heavy shield crashed into Skade with such force that she let go of the sword and cried aloud as she was thrown back onto the treasures. She lay there, tears now at her eyes, but with the fury of madness still in her voice. "I curse you," she said, pointing at me, "I curse your children, your woman, your life, your grave, the air you breathe, the food you eat, the dreams you have, the ground you tread."

"As you cursed me?" a voice said, and out of the shadows at the hall's edge there crawled a thing that had once been a man.

It was Harald. Harald who had led the first assault on Wessex, who had promised Skade the queen's crown of Wessex, who had been wounded so gravely at Fearnhamme and who had found refuge among the thorns. There he had inspired a defense so stout that Alfred had eventually paid him to leave, and he had come here, seeking Haesten's protection. He was a broken man, crippled. He had watched his woman go to Haesten's bed and he had a hate in him that was every bit as great as Skade's.

"You cursed me," he told her, "because I did not give you a throne." He lurched toward her, his legs helpless, dragging himself along by his strong arms. His yellow hair that had been so thick was straggling now, hanging like string about his pain-lined face. "Let me make you a queen," he said to Skade, and he took a golden torque from the treasure pile. It was a beautiful thing, three strands of gold twisted together and capped with two bear heads that had eyes of emerald. "Be a queen, my love," he told her. His beard had grown to his waist. His cheeks were sunken, his eyes dark, and his legs twisted. He wore a simple tunic and leggings beneath a rough woolen cloak. Harald Bloodhair, who had once led five thousand men, who had burned Wessex and struck fear into Alfred, pulled himself across the rushes and held the torque toward Skade, who looked at him and just moaned.

She did not take the offered crown and so he lifted the gold and placed it on her hair and it sat there, askew, and she began to cry. Harald dragged himself still closer. "My love," he said in a strangely affectionate voice.

Æthelflæd had come to my side. I do not think she was aware of it, but she had taken my shield arm and clung to me. She said nothing.

"My precious one," Harald said softly, and he stroked her hair. "I loved you," he said.

"I loved you," Skade said, and she put her arms around Harald and they clung to each other in the fire's light and a man beside me started forward with an ax. I stopped him. I had seen Harald's right hand move. He was stroking Skade's hair with his left hand, now he fumbled beneath his cloak with his right.

"My love," he said, and he crooned those two words again and again, then his right hand moved fast, and a man who has lost the use of his legs develops great strength in his arms, and he drove the blade of the knife through the links of Skade's coat, and I saw her first stiffen, then her eyes widened, her mouth opened, and Harald kissed her open mouth as he ripped the blade upward, ever upward, dragging the mail coat with the steel that tore through her guts and up to her chest, and still she embraced him as her blood spilled across his withered lap. Then at last she gave a great cry and her grip loosened and her eyes faded and she fell backward.

"Finish what you began," Harald growled without looking at me. He reached for Skade's fallen sword, wanting it to be the key to reaching Valhalla, but I remembered how he had murdered the woman at Æscengum. I remembered how her child had cried and so

I kicked the sword away and he looked up at me, surprised, and my face was the last thing he ever saw in this world.

We took thirty of their ships and the rest we burned. Three escaped, sliding past Finan's men as they hurled spears they had discovered stacked in the bilge of the grounded boat that was one of the two forts guarding the entrance. The Danish garrison of the other boat, the one beached on Caninga, released the big chain that blocked the entrance and so the three boats escaped to sea, but the fourth had no such luck. It was almost past Finan when a well thrown spear thumped into the steersman's chest and he slumped over, the steering oar slewed hard in the water and the ship ran her bows into the bank. The next ship rammed her and she began to take on water through sprung strakes as the incoming tide floated her back up the creek.

It took all day to hunt the survivors down through the tangle of marsh, reeds, and inlets of Caninga. We captured hundreds of women and children, and men picked those they wanted as slaves. That was how I met Sigunn, a girl I discovered shivering in a ditch. She was fair, pale and slight, just sixteen, a widow because her husband was dead in the captured fort, and she cringed when I stepped through the reeds. "No," she said over and over, "no, no, no." I held out my hand and, after a while, because fate had left her no choice, she took it and I gave her into Sihtric's care. "Look after her," I told him in Danish, a language he spoke well, "and make sure she's not hurt."

We burned the forts. I wanted to hold onto them, to use them as an outlying fortress to protect Lundene, but Edward was emphatic that our fight at Beamfleot was simply a raid into East Anglian territory, and that to hold the forts would break the treaty his father had made with East Anglia's king. It did not matter that half East Anglia's Danes were raiding with Haesten, Edward was determined that his father's treaty should be honored, and so we pulled down the great walls, piled the timbers in the halls, and set fire to them, but first we took away all the treasure and loaded it onto four of the captured ships.

Next day the fires still burned. It was three days before I could step among the embers to find a skull. I think it was Skade's, though I cannot be certain. I rammed a Danish spear butt-first into the fire-hardened earth, then rammed the skull over the broken blade. The scorched bone face stared sightless toward the creek where the skeletons of almost two hundred ships still smoked. "It's a warning," I told Father Heahberht. "If another Dane comes here, let them see their fate." I gave Father Heahberht a large bag of silver. "If you ever need help," I told him, "come to me." Out by the moat, where the fires had not reached, but where so many West Saxons and Mercians had died, the mud was still littered with dead bees. "Tell Brun," I said, "that you said a prayer for his bees."

We left next morning. Edward rode west, taking his troops with him, though first he had said farewell, and I thought his face had taken on a sterner, harder look. "Will you stay in Mercia?" he asked me.

"Your father wants that, lord," I said.

"Yes, he does," he said. "So will you?"

"You know the answer, lord," I said.

He looked at me in silence, then there was the slightest smile. "I think," he said slowly, "that Wessex will need Mercia."

"And Mercia needs Æthelflæd," I said.

"Yes," he said simply.

Father Coenwulf lingered a moment longer. He leaned down from his saddle and offered me a hand. He said nothing, just shook my hand then spurred after his lord.

I sailed with the captured ships to Lundene. The sea behind me was silvered pink beneath the skeins of smoke that still drifted from Beamfleot. My own crew, helped by a score of clumsy Mercians, rowed the ship that held Haesten's wife, his two sons, and forty other hostages. Finan guarded them, though none showed defiance.

Æthelflaed stood with me at the steering oar. She gazed behind to where the smoke shimmered and I knew she was remembering the last time she had sailed from Beamfleot. There had been smoke then too, and dead men, and such sorrow. She had lost her lover and saw only the bleak dark ahead.

Now she looked at me and, as her brother had done, she smiled. This time she was happy.

The long oars dipped, the river banks closed on us, and in the west the smoke of Lundene veiled the sky.

As I took Æthelflæd home.

HISTORICAL NOTE

In the middle of the nineteenth century a railway line was made from London's Fenchurch Street to Southend and, when excavating at what is now South Benfleet (Beamfleot), the navvies discovered the charred remnants of burned ships among which were scattered human skeletons. Those remains were over nine hundred years old, and they were what was left of Haesten's army and fleet.

I grew up in nearby Thundersley (Thunresleam) where, in Saint Peter's churchyard, was a standing stone pierced by a hole, which local lore claimed was the devil's stone. If you walked three times around it, counterclockwise, and whispered into the hole it was said that the devil could hear you and would grant your wishes. It never worked for me, though not for lack of trying. The stone, of course, long predated the coming of Christianity to Britain and, indeed, the arrival of the Saxons who first brought the worship of Thor and so gave the village its name.

Just to the west of our house was a precipitous slope that falls to the plain leading to London. The escarpment is called Bread and Cheese Hill and I was told the name came from Saxon times and meant "broad and sharp," being a description of the weapons used on the hill in a long ago battle between Vikings and Saxons. Maybe. Yet, strangely, I never learned how important Benfleet was to the long story of England's making.

In the last decade of the ninth century, Alfred's Wessex was again under determined assault from the Danes. There were three attacks. An unknown leader (whom I have called Harald) led one fleet to

333

Kent, as did Haesten. Meanwhile the Northumbrian Danes were to mount a shipborne assault on Wessex's south coast.

The two Danish forces in Kent had both been raiding in what is now France and had accepted lavish bribes to leave those lands and assault Wessex instead. Haesten then took more bribes to withdraw from Wessex, and even allowed his wife and two sons to be baptized as Christians. Meanwhile the larger force of Danes advanced westward from Kent, eventually to be defeated at Farnham in Surrey (Fearnhamme). That battle was one of the greatest victories of the Saxons over the Danes. It shattered the large Danish army, forcing the survivors to carry their wounded leader northward to find refuge on Torneie (Thorney Island) a site that has now disappeared under the development surrounding Heathrow Airport. The fugitives were besieged there, but the siege failed and the Saxons again used silver to get rid of them. Many of the survivors went to Benfleet (then part of the kingdom of East Anglia) where Haesten had made a fortress.

Haesten, despite his protestations of friendship, now went on the offensive by attacking Mercia. Alfred, who protected Mercia, was distracted by the assault of the Northumbrian Danes, but he sent his son Edward to attack Haesten's base at Benfleet. That assault was wholly successful and the Saxons were able to burn and capture Haesten's vast fleet, as well as recapture much of Haesten's plunder and take countless hostages, including Haesten's family. It was a magnificent victory, though it by no means ended the war.

Mercia, that ancient kingdom that filled the heart of England, was without a king in this period, and Alfred, I am certain, wished to keep it that way. He had adopted the title "King of the Angelcynn," which described an ambition rather than a reality. Other Saxon kings had claimed to rule the "English," but none had ever succeeded in uniting the English-speaking kingdoms, but Alfred dreamed of it. He would not achieve it, but he did lay the foundations on which his son Edward, his daughter Æthelflæd, and Edward's son, Æthelstan, succeeded.

The device that saved the Saxons from defeat was the burh, those fortified towns which were the response of rulers all across Christendom to the threat of the Vikings. Viking soldiers, for all their fearsome reputation, were not equipped for sieges, and by fortifying large towns in which folk and their livestock could take shelter, the Christian rulers constantly thwarted Viking ambitions. The Danes could roam across much of Wessex and Mercia, but their enemies were safe in the burhs that were defended by the fyrd, a citizen army. Eventually, as at Fearnhamme, the professional army would face the Danes and, by the end of the ninth century, the Saxons had learned to fight every bit as well as the northmen.

The northmen are usually called Vikings and some historians suggest that, far from being the feared predators of myth, they were peace-loving folk who mostly lived amicably with their Saxon neighbors. This ignores much contemporary evidence, let alone the skeletons that are doubtless still buried beneath the railway at Benfleet. Alfred organized Wessex for war and built hugely expensive defenses and he would have done none of that if the Vikings were as peaceably inclined as some revisionists want us to believe. The first Vikings were raiders, looking for slaves and silver, but soon they wanted land as well and so settled in the north and east of England where they added to England's place names and to the English language. It is true that those settlers eventually assimilated into the Saxon population, but other northmen still lusted after the land to their south and west, and so the wars continued. It was not till William the Conqueror came to England that the long struggle between Scandinavians and Saxons ended, and William, of course, was a Norman; the word denoting "northmen" because the rulers of Normandy were Vikings who had settled on that peninsula. The Norman Conquest was really the last triumph of the northmen, but it came too late to destroy Alfred's dream, which was the creation of a unified state called England.

I have been (and will be) mightily unfair to Æthelred. There is not a scrap of evidence to suggest that Alfred's son-in-law was as small-minded and ineffective as I make him out to be, and I recommend, as a corrective, Ian W. Walker's superb book *Mercia and the Making of England* (Sutton Publishing, Stroud, 2000). As for Æthelred's wife, Alfred's daughter Æthelflæd, she has been strangely forgotten in our history, even at a time when feminist historians have labored to bring women out from the shadows of patriarchal history. Æthelflæd is a heroine, a woman who was to lead armies against the Danes and do much to push the growing frontiers of England wider and deeper.

Farnham and Benfleet were two body blows against Danish ambitions to destroy Saxon England, yet the struggle of the Angelcynn is far from over. Haesten is still rampaging through the southern midlands, while Danes rule in both East Anglia and Northumbria, so Uhtred, now firmly allied to Æthelflæd, will campaign again.